THE WICKED LADY

ELENA COLLINS

Boldwood

First published in Great Britain in 2024 by Boldwood Books Ltd.

Copyright © Elena Collins, 2024

Cover Design by Alice Moore Design

Cover Photography: Shutterstock and Alamy

The moral right of Elena Collins to be identified as the author of this work has been asserted in accordance with the Copyright, Designs and Patents Act 1988.

Every effort has been made to obtain the necessary permissions with reference to copyright material, both illustrative and quoted. We apologise for any omissions in this respect and will be pleased to make the appropriate acknowledgements in any future edition.

A CIP catalogue record for this book is available from the British Library.

Paperback ISBN 978-1-80280-036-4

Large Print ISBN 978-1-80280-037-1

Hardback ISBN 978-1-80280-035-7

Ebook ISBN 978-1-80280-038-8

Kindle ISBN 978-1-80280-039-5

Audio CD ISBN 978-1-80280-030-2

MP3 CD ISBN 978-1-80280-031-9

Digital audio download ISBN 978-1-80280-033-3

Boldwood Books Ltd
23 Bowerdean Street
London SW6 3TN
www.boldwoodbooks.com

Near the cell, there is a well
Near the well, there is a tree
And under the tree the treasure be

— WELL-KNOWN HERTFORDSHIRE RHYME

To Liam and Maddie.

THEN AND NOW...

Many years ago, at the time of day between dusk and nightfall, the grey sky becomes murky and light plays tricks with the eyes. It is hard to discern the shape on the horizon: it could be a tree, a shadow, or a waiting figure on horseback. The moon is already rising, thin as paper. The last light of the pale sun has almost drained. Nomansland Common is a stretch of grassland and scrub, a crowded cluster of trees, shaded woodlands cloaked in eerie silence. A crow caws, a wood pigeon lifts itself into the air on noisy wings, then the stillness stretches again.

Something stirs in the distance, the single flap of a coat, the snort of a horse. A woman is watching for her moment. She feels the dull thud of her own heart quicken beneath her jacket. This might be her last time. But she has no choice: desperation is a cruel friend. She takes a deep breath and leans forward in preparation.

Rolling wheels rumble from afar, the dull clattering of hooves echoes, before the rocking coach and four horses thunder down the old road.

The passengers hear her before they see her: the rhythmic approach of her horse, her wild scream, a rising cloud of dust in the dirt track road as she hurtles towards them, her pistol raised.

* * *

Now, it is the time of day between day and evening. Nomansland Common is still, except for unsettled dust that swirls from the side of the road. A young man walks his dog through the woods across the tufted grassland, allowing the Labrador to rush ahead, to frolic and play. The man is deep in thought, his mind crowded with troubles that clash together like moving rocks. He does not notice the shadow by the trees, the single flap of material, the watchful eyes of a woman who waits in the gloom.

She sees him pass, her head to one side. He is new to her. She recognises something in him; he is alone, wounded, his heart is heavy. She knows how that feels. She follows him for a while at a distance, unseen.

The dog stops running abruptly: he senses something. He bares his teeth, lies flat against the earth and whines. The man pauses, listening. For a second, he hears the hollow whisper of a voice carried on the wind. The dimming light confuses his eyes. He stares around, but there is no one there, just himself and his dog waiting in the gloom as the wind rearranges his hair like the touch of a woman.

1

THE PRESENT – PECKHAM, LONDON

'I'm sorry, Charlie.'

Charlie Wolfe continued to stare through the window of the first-floor flat. The hot July haze hung in the air; the clouds filtered sunshine. On the pavement below, a woman in a headscarf pushed a baby in a stroller, as she did every evening around six, on her way to the Kudu Grill. A man parked a white van and clambered out, rushing to open the back door, tugging out a box of tools. Two fashionable women hurried past swinging handbags, talking together. The world continued as normal. But Charlie's life had changed forever. He was single now. Luna was leaving.

Charlie stared into the glass at his reflection, a young man, leanly muscular, handsome at twenty-nine, with dark curly hair and soulful brown eyes. She stood behind him, his Luna no more, light brown hair spilling over tanned shoulders, her face filled with apologies.

She said it again.

'I'm really sorry.'

He didn't turn. 'You don't have to go.'

'I do...' He watched her take a breath. 'You know I do.'

'You could turn it down. You could stay here.'

'I can't do that...'

'Cornwall might be miles away from London, but I could still visit at weekends...'

'Charlie, no. We both need fresh starts.'

'But why?' He turned round and grasped her hand. She didn't tug it away, but it was as cold as a fish in his palm. 'We love each other.'

'We do. We did,' Luna said with as much patience and regret as she could muster. 'We've had three happy years here. Mostly happy. I still love you, but not in that way. We're going in different directions.'

'Why are we?' Charlie knew why. He heard the whine in his voice. 'I'll go wherever you go...'

He looked over her shoulder. Alan was asleep on the couch, a tangle of black paws; his tail still wagged. He was probably dreaming of gnawing bones and chasing cats. He wasn't sad like Charlie was.

Luna's eyes were full of kindness. 'I have to go by myself. This job is just what I need. I've had my fill of tiny roles that don't suit me, being an understudy, in chorus lines, working in coffee shops to help pay the rent.'

'You loved that job as a bingo caller...' Charlie grinned at the memory, happy again just for a moment. Then he sighed. 'Luna, we've had such good times together. Precious moments... Don't say you're leaving forever. When your run in Cornwall is done – come home.'

'I can't promise that.' Luna shook her head, her hair shining like silk. He longed to reach out and touch it. 'You need to move on too.'

'You might get a better offer?' Charlie sounded deflated, resigned. 'Now you're assistant choreographer for *Kiss me, Kate*, you think there'll be a handsome dancer who'll sweep you off your feet? The bloke playing Petrarch?'

'Petruchio,' Luna said sadly. 'No, I don't want that. I want you to find out who you are, and I want to do the same. Things have been awful for you, working at Blanche Harris...'

'I'm leaving at the end of term – it was always a temporary contract,' Charlie insisted.

'This is an opportunity then... take time, do something you love.'

'I could come with you,' Charlie said hopefully. 'I don't want to be a music teacher. I want to do something else.'

Luna squeezed his hand; Charlie wasn't sure if it was affection or frustration. 'You have to find a new path, just as I'm doing. This is everything I wanted, choreographing a big musical. You know how hard I worked for it. This is the break I dreamed of...'

'But.' Charlie's voice was like scraping metal in his throat. 'I don't want to be here without you.'

'Get someone in to help pay for the rent. Do some supply work in different schools...' Luna seemed to deliberately misunderstand him. 'Or do something completely different. Travel. See the world.'

'That was our dream, to travel together, to discover new places – it won't be the same without my Luna...' Charlie felt his eyes fill and his vision blur. 'Please – don't go.'

'I have to...' Luna kissed him, a brush of lips. 'I've got a ticket. My bags are packed...'

'What am I going to do?' Tears were warm on his cheeks. 'Please, Luna...'

Luna's face was damp: she was crying too. 'Your job made you so miserable. You changed – you weren't the Charlie I met – you were someone else, someone stuck in a place he didn't want to be. You have to seize this moment – make it *your* time.' Luna's blue eyes were wild with determination. 'Find Charlie Wolfe again. He's not a music teacher who plays the saxophone for ten minutes a day and marks bag loads of books every night until gone eleven – he's not the grumpy man who lies on a couch and grumbles about the price of rent in London. He's a special man, full of warmth and love and creativity and fun. He's in there somewhere, waiting to blossom and grow and fulfil his potential. Find him again, Charlie.'

Charlie knew she was right.

He gave a weak nod. 'Then can I ring you? Is there a chance we might...?'

Luna wiped her eyes, turning abruptly to pick up the two bags that stood by the door. 'Who knows?' She took a breath. 'Let's not think about that. Let's just say goodbye and wish each other everything we dreamed of.' Her voice tailed off and Charlie assumed that she didn't hold out much hope.

He watched as she disappeared through the door, hearing it click behind her, a final clunk. Then she was gone.

Charlie stood at the window and watched Luna below as she tugged her cases towards the kerb. The last of the sunshine made her hair gleam. He saw a taxi stop, its engine thrumming. She piled her cases inside and she didn't look up or wave as the taxi pulled away.

Charlie turned back to the couch, where Alan was snoring, his front paws crossed. The Labrador opened one round eye, half interested.

'She's gone, Alan,' Charlie muttered, feeling a constriction in his throat. 'Luna's gone...'

He threw himself on his knees and wrapped his arms around the black dog, sobbing into the warm fur. Alan licked his face once. He understood. But Charlie knew he had some serious thinking to do now, some important decisions to make.

* * *

'I'm sorry, Charlie.'

Charlie was getting used to apologies. It was Friday, the last day of term at Blanche Harris Academy, and his last day as a music teacher there. He was in the staffroom clutching a paper cup of cheap red wine, talking to Rhydian Craddock, the balding, humourless deputy head.

Charlie said, 'Oh, I don't mind leaving, not really. I mean, I'm looking at it as an opportunity.' His words sounded hollow.

Rhydian wasn't listening. 'We're very grateful to you for filling the gap. Had Sara not been coming back from maternity leave in September, I'm sure we'd have kept you on.'

A loud shriek came from the corner. Lydia, the head teacher, thirty-something in a bold print summer dress, was laughing at a joke with the English department as she filled paper cups with Prosecco. She wouldn't miss Charlie either. He wondered if she'd find the time to pop over and say goodbye. Probably not – he'd be off in a moment. He'd only come to show his face briefly.

Rhydian was still talking and Charlie said, 'Pardon?'

'I was asking what you were planning to do next. Teaching, or...' Rhydian paused, as if there was no alternative.

'I might sell my body...' Charlie offered his cheekiest grin. He'd always found Rhydian sombre and dismissive; at least he didn't have to walk on eggshells any more.

'To medical science?' Rhydian looked confused.

'To women,' Charlie said, but Rhydian didn't smile.

'Oh well, I suppose, if it pays the rent,' the deputy head muttered without understanding, before wandering away to talk to Angela, the head of languages.

Charlie stared into his beaker of vinegar-sour red wine. He didn't want it. He was ready to cycle back to his flat, then he'd take Alan for a walk, buy something for tea.

The flat. That was a problem. He couldn't afford to stay, not now. Even though it was tiny, one bedroom – two, if he put a bed settee in the living room – it was too expensive and he didn't really want a flatmate anyway. He needed to think outside the box. He could buy a van and go travelling. He had the money that his mother had given him when she'd sold her garden centre business and retired last year. He'd thought of it as wedding money for him and Luna. Now it was just money.

His mother had divided the sum equally between herself, him and Sonny, his brother who was working in Spain, and warned them both not to squander it, although she had done little else but travel and enjoy herself for the past year. He might use a little of it to get him through the summer, or find part-time work to make ends meet, but he had to come up with something sensible soon. His options were limited, that was the trouble.

'What to do, what to do?' he said to himself as he grabbed his shoulder bag and his saxophone, racing out of the staffroom and down the stairs of Blanche Harris Academy, without a backward glance. There was no one he'd miss. He rushed out through the school gates into the fresh air to collect his bicycle and almost cheered.

He paused, staring at the backdrop of flats and houses, asking himself how he felt, and decided that a weight had been lifted. Luna had been right – his beautiful, talented, impetuous Luna whom he loved and missed more than he could say. He'd been lost in the bottomless hole of a temporary teaching job, of high rents and repetition and a lack of direction in life. She'd told him to find himself.

He took a deep breath of London air and it felt good to be free. But somewhere else was calling him, a new place, a promising bright future.

The only problem was that he had no idea where it was.

2

1648 – HUNTINGDONSHIRE

'I'm sorry, Katherine, but I am the bearer of tidings. Things cannot remain as they are. You are of an age now.'

Lady Alice Bedell, devoted wife of Sir Capel Bedell of Hamerton, waited for the girl to look up from her book, but her head remained down as she read, her dark ringlets brushing the pages.

Alice attempted to raise her voice, but it was weak and reedy. 'Katherine – I am speaking. You will listen.'

'Oh, I am sorry...' Katherine Ferrers looked up languidly, her wide eyes innocent. 'I was reading, Aunt Alice. I love the Metaphysical poets...'

'Such unconventional verse is not for a girl of your years.' Alice pressed pale lips together. 'I would suggest the Bible is more appropriate.'

'I have read it all, Aunt. My grandfather and my parents were good Protestants and I was well taught.' Katherine returned to the book. 'And they would have enjoyed the poetry of John Donne – just listen to how ardently he expresses his love for God in these few lines...' Katherine began to read in a clear voice.

> 'Batter my heart, three-person'd God; for you
> As yet but knocke, breathe, shine, and seeke to mend;
> That I may rise, and stand, o'erthrow me, and bend

Your force, to breake, blowe, burne, and make me new.'

'Hardly suitable verse for a young girl.' Alice shuddered, as if the words were too passionate for a child. 'Now put the book down and sit up straight. I have things I must impart.'

'Oh, do tell.' Katherine clapped her hands. 'I look forward to good news. Sometimes, I am weary here by myself. You have told me it is too cold to go riding on Carbonel, although I would gladly go. I long to spend time with him in the stables. And if the snow comes, as you say it will, I wish to ride him through the village, even though the wind is cold. It is exciting to be outside...'

'Katherine.' Alice took a breath, clearly losing patience. 'You were sent here to live with me by your relatives, Richard and Anne Fanshawe, in the hope that you might lose your wild ways. But you will not be tamed. Richard Fanshawe is an important man, and devoted to the Royalist cause. His wife is dutiful. You would do well to learn from her obedience.'

'But I am not like Anne. She is humble and demure. Her husband is an important man. He was Secretary of War to the Prince of Wales, and she stays at home in a big empty house and does little else but wait for him.' Katherine was perplexed. 'I thought I was brought here because I am an orphan and heir to a fortune. I heard my stepfather say before he went to prison for fighting at the Battle of Marston Moor that it would be good for everyone if I lived with my aunt in Huntingdonshire, and here I have been since...'

Alice frowned. 'But you are ready for better uses now. Your stepfather has plans for you.'

'Oh?' Katherine's eyes danced. 'Tell me I can go back to Hertfordshire, to our old manor house. I loved being at The Cell. I would remember my father there, may God rest his soul, who died when I was six, and my brother, who died soon after. When I was a child, our home was filled with laughter.'

'Do you remember your mother, Katherine?'

'I do. I loved her dearly. She married my stepfather, Simon Fanshawe, and we lived in Oxford for a while and we visited King Charles. But poor

Mother found life difficult with my stepfather because he is so severe, and she laughed less and less, then she died.'

'You are very like her, I believe,' Alice said. 'You have her wilful manner.'

Katherine's expression was suddenly sad. 'She told me I must speak up for myself. She said that I have a mind and a heart and I should use them both to be strong, no matter what Sir Simon tells me I must do. He asked me to call him Father, but I will not. I do not like him. My father was Knighton Ferrers, and my grandfather Sir George Ferrers, and they were good men who loved God and cared for the people who worked for them. My stepfather does not love me. He finds me headstrong and intolerable. I heard him say so...'

'Enough.' Alice seemed to remember she had something else to say. 'It is your stepfather's wish that I talk to you. Katherine, you are almost fourteen years old...'

'My birthday is in May, so I will be fourteen in five months.'

'Do you know a young man called Thomas Fanshawe?'

'I do.' Katherine's eyes flashed. 'I met him twice in London. He is two years older than I and he is considerably ill-favoured and arrogant. I know he is my stepfather's nephew, but I like him not at all.'

'Ah...' Alice coughed, a dry, muffled sound. 'I am here to tell you, Katherine, that you and Thomas will be married here in Hamerton, in April...'

'Why must I?' Katherine was astonished.

'Your stepfather has arranged it all.'

'Then please tell him, Aunt, to *un*arrange it. I have no wish to marry anyone at all and, certainly, I have no wish to marry Thomas Fanshawe. He is conceited, his chin is weak—'

'Enough.'

'But I am not yet fourteen. I have no need of a husband.'

'But Thomas has need of a wife,' Alice said sadly.

Katherine knew immediately. 'You mean he is penniless and he requires one with a fortune – *my* fortune, because I am sole heir to my grandfather's estates.' She stood up, suddenly angry. 'You must tell my stepfather that I will have none of his nephew. I do not wish to marry.'

'You are a young woman and Sir Simon is your stepfather,' Alice said. 'You must do as you are told.'

'Why must I?'

'Because that is God's way.'

'It is not – it cannot be so,' Katherine said crossly. 'God gave me a voice to use and now I am using it to say no.'

'Katherine, in April, young Thomas Fanshawe will make you his wife and you will live in the mansion house in Hertfordshire.'

'What will I do there?'

'You will make your husband happy. You will love and obey him.' Alice's cheeks reddened. 'That is what we women must do...'

'I will neither love nor obey Thomas Fanshawe,' Katherine retorted. 'It is impossible.'

'It is decided. You will do his bidding. You will bear his children.'

'Bear? What does that mean?' Katherine had no idea. 'And will they not be my children?'

'I fear you have much to learn before your marriage, and it falls to me to instruct you,' Alice said kindly. 'Although I have no idea how to ease your burden.'

'Then do not ease it. Let us forget about him completely. Perhaps then it may not happen.' Katherine rushed to the window. 'Look, Aunt, the skies are a brilliant white, as if they are filled with heaviness, and the horizon is the colour of pale roses. Will it not snow?'

Alice came to stand behind Katherine, placing a hand on her shoulder. 'I fear it may.'

'Then let us not talk of marriage. Let us think of the snow that will fall soon, the fat twirling flakes that fill the air as if the angels are plucking a goose in the heavens. I long to go out and visit Carbonel and ride him in the blizzard.'

Alice took a breath. 'A young lady who is about to marry should spend less time riding a stallion and more time in sober contemplation.'

'But I love to ride,' Katherine said excitedly. She turned to her aunt and kissed her cheek. 'We will talk of this at supper time. For now, I care nothing for Thomas Fanshawe and his sour face.'

'Katherine...' Alice called, but the girl had rushed to the door in a flurry of frothing fabric and dancing ringlets, and was gone.

Alice sank into the chair, shaking her head, and picked up the poetry book, opening it at the page Katherine had been reading. She read aloud:

> *'And in this flea our two bloods mingled be;*
> *Thou know'st that this cannot be said*
> *A sin, nor shame, nor loss of maidenhead.'*

Alice closed the book quickly. The erotic words were too much for her to bear. She fanned herself with her hand and wondered what would become of wild, untamable Katherine. Perhaps marriage would change her for the better, Alice thought. But she feared it would not. In her experience, it seldom changed any woman's life for the better.

* * *

Katherine tugged on a hat, a warm jacket, leather boots, and rushed to the stables. She inhaled the sweet scent of hay and leaned her face against the long nose of her black stallion: she was used to sharing her deepest secrets with the horse.

She murmured, 'I will have none of Thomas Fanshawe, Carbonel. They cannot make me marry him. And if they do, I will not bend to his demands. The idea is insufferable.' She placed a kiss against the horse's cheek. 'I know who I am. I am Kate Ferrers, and I will never be Mistress Fanshawe, not even if they call me that. Come, you and I will ride through the falling flakes.'

She heard a light footstep behind her and turned to see the stable boy, standing at a respectful distance, his eyes lowered.

'Can I be of service, miss?'

'I was about to saddle Carbonel – I am going out for a ride, George.'

'In this cold weather, miss? Begging pardon, but it's snowing...'

'Even better,' Katherine said.

'Then I'll get him ready.' George touched his cap and hurried over to where the saddles were kept. He came back hauling a saddle, which he heaved on the horse, attaching it with deft fingers.

Katherine patted Carbonel encouragingly and climbed onto the horse. She placed her right leg over the pommel of the saddle, easing herself and her skirts into a balanced side-saddle position.

George stood back. 'Don't you go getting cold, miss.'

'I won't.' Katherine was about to urge the stallion forwards when she hesitated. 'George – how old are you?'

'Sixteen, miss.'

'Sixteen?' She stared at him. He was the same age as the man she was going to marry. George was still a child – he was small, elfin inside his jacket and breeches. His gaunt face looked strained, his lips thin, his cheekbones hollow. 'And are you married?'

'No, miss...' George offered a twisted smile. 'I live with my ma and she has seven other mouths to feed. I can't afford to be married.'

'Nor can Thomas Fanshawe,' Katherine said cynically.

'Begging your pardon, miss?' George asked.

Carbonel was eager to go; Katherine tugged the reins skillfully to hold him still. 'When you do get married, George – what sort of woman will she be?'

'I never thought about it...' His face closed for a moment. 'One day I might be able to get a wife, and she'd be a God-fearing woman who works hard, who can look after me and the kiddies, who can cook and make ends meet...' He pushed a hand beneath his damp nose. 'It might be nice if she looked all right, had a few teeth...'

'And would you love her?' Katherine asked.

'Love?' George shook his head. 'No, miss. My ma and my dad never had time for love – they had too many mouths to feed. Then my dad got took last winter with the typhus and so did my baby brother. We all have to help out, especially me, working here whenever I can. No, I don't reckon any of us has got time for no love.'

'I see.' Katherine took a deep breath. 'Well, I won't be gone more than an hour, George – and when I'm back, I can put Carbonel away myself if you wish...'

'Oh, no, miss – that's my job. If you took it away from me, what'd I do?'

'Then we'll see to his needs quickly and you can take yourself home to your mother. I hope she has something tasty roasting in the pot and a good fire.'

'I do that – collect the firewood. With a bit of luck, Ma will have some pottage going, and a scrag end of mutton would make it even better.'

Katherine looked at him again; he was undersized, his hands rough and his nails blackened. She reminded herself to organise for a pheasant to be sent round, or a rabbit. Perhaps Aunt Alice's cook might have a pastry or two. It would fill the children's bellies. It troubled her that George's life was so hard.

She gave him her sweetest smile. 'Thank you, George.'

'What for?'

'For the care you give to Carbonel.'

The stable boy looked perplexed.

Katherine dug her heels in lightly and Carbonel turned, springing forwards, trotting from the shadows of the stables into the bright light. It had already started to snow, flakes swirling, hanging momentarily on the air before tumbling to the ground. Carbonel began to trot towards the hills.

'Faster,' Katherine whispered and Carbonel broke into a canter. He turned towards a field and blustered forward into the blizzard. Katherine whooped loudly, exhilarated by the speed, her eyes blinded, filled with wet snow. She yelled again in excitement and a sudden realisation that she was galloping into the unknown; that was how her life would be now, hurtling forward with no idea where she was going or what would befall her. But she had her wits, she had her courage; she was headstrong. Come what may, she would never be Thomas Fanshawe's placid little wife. He might take her inheritance, her family home, but he couldn't take her spirit from her. What would be would be – she might not be able to change it. But she'd never submit to it.

She wasn't afraid.

3

THE PRESENT

The crisp white invitation in Charlie's hand was crumpled at the edges. He stared at the gold lettering, inviting Charlie Wolfe and Luna O'Rourke to attend the wedding of Ben Barron and Rachael Klein. He stood alone in a dark corner of a plush banqueting suite in Battersea, watching the bride and groom take their first dance, swaying together to 'Baby I'm Yours' by the Arctic Monkeys.

Charlie shoved the invitation back in his smart jacket pocket and took another swig of his pint. He gazed around. Luna should have been here, hanging onto his arm in a pretty spangly dress, whispering in his ear about wanting to dance with him as soon as the chance came. He felt the low pain beneath his heart that made it hard to breathe. He'd assumed they'd come to Ben's wedding together – they'd been friends since their time at Goldsmiths, where they'd both studied music. Ben had only known Rachael for a year. They'd had a whirlwind romance, an engagement after six months, a wedding after twelve. Ben had known she was the one after two days. Charlie felt sad again.

He swigged the last of his pint and felt the alcohol blur his vision. In an instant, he wondered why he hadn't asked Luna to marry him. He had no idea if she'd have said yes – it had never been anything they'd discussed.

Sadly, he realised, they'd been people who lived in the moment, both spontaneous, making no plans for anything further than a week away.

He dragged himself to the bar and ordered another pint, his fifth. He felt sweaty beneath the shirt and tie and the smart jacket. He gulped thirstily. His throat was dry.

Someone was standing at his elbow. He turned groggily to see a young woman who was probably his age. Her hair was silky like Luna's, smooth and straightened, but that's where the comparison ended. She was taller, with dark hair and dark brows. She shrieked over the music, 'I'll have a gin and tonic if you're buying.'

Charlie didn't care either way – he leaned over to the barman, who was a hopeful-looking boy of some twenty years, and ordered her a drink. When it came, she reached for the balloon glass, took a huge gulp and then patted his arm.

'I don't know you,' she yelled, as if it was his fault.

Charlie stared into his pint, half empty already. 'I'm Charlie.' That was all she needed to know.

'I'm Juliet. Rachael's cousin. Are you here on your own?' Juliet asked, placing her glass heavily on the counter.

Charlie grunted. It was too difficult to say it.

'Do you live in London?'

He moved his head slightly. He didn't want to encourage her. It wasn't her fault; he wasn't in the mood for company, especially that of a woman he'd just met who was on a drinking mission.

She assumed he'd answered and said, 'I live in Lewisham. My three flatmates and I all work in the same hospital – Queen Elizabeth. What do you do?'

Charlie met her eyes. He was trying not to be rude. 'Not much. I've just given up my job.'

'What did you used to do?'

'Music teacher...' Charlie was feeling sluggish.

'You're a musician?' Juliet looked pleased. 'What instrument do you play?'

'Saxophone,' Charlie replied automatically and Juliet burst out laughing. He had no idea why she found it funny. He added, 'I play the guitar too... and drums...'

'Are you in a band?' Juliet asked. 'I love live music.'

Charlie watched her drain the gin from her glass. She blinked, one eyelid closing more than the other. He asked, 'Have you had much to drink?'

'Champagne – a few of these – not nearly enough. Oh...' Her eyes opened with delight as she listened to a few bars of music booming from speakers. 'It's "Prince Charming" – Adam and the Ants. The dandy high-wayman. Let's dance.'

'I don't...' Charlie protested. He used to dance with Luna, his arms around her, his cheek against hers. Or she'd dance – he'd seen her many times, so beautiful, delicate, strong. When they'd first met, she'd been out of work, but she was a wonderful dancer. She'd been a gazelle in *The Lion King*, a chorus girl in a hip-hop musical. And she was an incredible choreo-grapher, so imaginative. He wondered fleetingly how she was getting on in Cornwall with her new job. She hadn't messaged him. She probably wouldn't.

Somehow, he found himself on the dance floor opposite Juliet, heaving this way and that. People were dancing all around him, dad dancers, slow dancers, energetic cavorters. He was hardly moving, but Juliet was enjoying the music; she knew all the words, eyes closed, waving her arms. She fell forward against Charlie and he held her up. She staggered a little, so he helped her over to a table where there were empty chairs.

A man who was tucking into cake leaned forward, his elbows on the linen cloth. He caught Charlie's eyes and laughed. 'Your girlfriend's had one too many...'

'She's not my...' Charlie began, but it was pointless.

Juliet sat down with a bump and lurched forward, her face on her arms, dark hair spilling over the white cloth, mixing with crumbs.

He muttered, 'I'll get you some water.'

Charlie waited for several minutes at the bar to buy two sparkling waters, one for Juliet, the other for himself. He took both glasses to the table where he had left Juliet, but her seat was empty. He looked around. She was on the dance floor bopping with a man in a dark suit. They were both bawling out the lyrics of 'Ballroom Blitz' by The Sweet. Charlie watched, feeling sad. He could have easily been there with Juliet, dancing for all he was worth, trying to forget his loneliness. But what was the point?

He drank both glasses of water in quick succession and felt his mind clear. Ben and Rachael were busy, talking to guests; he wouldn't trouble them now by telling them he was going home. He'd send a text tomorrow, with thanks for the invitation and good wishes. He turned without another thought and headed towards the exit sign.

Outside, in the cold air, London city life bustling around him in darkness, he hailed a taxi and told the driver his address. He bundled himself inside and closed his eyes.

* * *

It was almost midnight. Alan was grunting, asleep on the couch, his paws crossed, his beady nostrils whistling. Charlie was sitting on the floor, empty cans of beer littered around him, piles of half-eaten takeaway. He hadn't cleaned up since Luna had left almost two weeks ago. The flat was a mess. His life was a mess. Alan opened a doleful eye in Charlie's direction. Charlie almost laughed at Alan's insight. But the dog was right. Charlie had no job, the rent was due; he was letting things slip.

He reached for his phone and searched for Luna's number, wondering where she would be. The evening performance of *Kiss me, Kate* would have finished; she might be talking to the cast, going through a few moves with the chorus line. Or she might be in the bar, winding down. He pictured her, slim in jeans and a sloppy jumper, talking to a man who'd be taller than him, who'd have a job, prospects. Charlie put a fist to his head to propel the image away. Alan was staring at him roundly.

'What?' Charlie asked, but he knew. If the dog could speak – and Alan was the closest to a speaking pet Charlie would ever meet – he would tell his owner to stop feeling sorry for himself and look at his options. 'Right, Al...' Charlie counted on his fingers. He had savings from his mother. He had qualifications, experience. No, he wouldn't return to teaching – the last school had not been easy; it had dented his confidence. He could do session work, or give music lessons. It would bring in some money, not much. He scratched his head. He could work for Uncle Bill again.

Bill Sutton lived nearly thirty miles away, in St Albans. It might be possible for Charlie to give him a hand with his building business: Charlie had worked for Uncle Bill since he was sixteen and as a student, during holidays. He was 'handy', those were Bill's words. But if he had a car, it would take ages to drive to St Albans through London, and going by train would mean a lengthy commute each day. Uncle Bill was all right though – his mother's brother, he was positive, cheery and he liked a pint and a catch-up. Charlie could always ask. It would cost nothing.

His phone was still in his hand. His fingers flew over the touchscreen.

> Any jobs going, Uncle Bill? I'm at a loose end – I've got a hungry dog to feed... Fancy a drink sometime?

Charlie stared at his phone for a few minutes and suddenly felt tired. It would take all the energy he had to clean his teeth and tug off the suit and tie. He'd leave it on the bedroom floor. It was time to crash out. Tomorrow was another day – he'd deal with it all then.

* * *

Charlie woke to slobbering kisses over his face, his cheeks, his eyes. He thought briefly of Luna, then he was aware that Alan was lying on his chest, all doggy breath and hot rasping tongue. It was past breakfast time, and the Labrador had no intention of letting Charlie forget it.

Charlie reached out a hand to pat the silky fur. 'All right, Al. Just give me a minute...'

He staggered into the living room in boxers and stared around, bleary eyed, dismayed. The place was a mess. He hadn't played his sax in days. He'd let things go. But enough was enough: it was time for a change.

He filled Alan's bowl full of kibble, vegetables and rice, poured himself a pint of water and picked up an empty bin bag. As he stuffed it full of twisted cans and smelly plastic food trays, he gave himself a quiet telling-off. Charlie had no intention of being part of the big plastic pollution problem in the country's waste systems and the world's seas. His passion for the environment was always something he'd shared with Luna, persuading her to use compostable and recyclable materials. Luna was filling his thoughts again – he needed to get a grip in more ways than one.

Charlie ruffled Alan's velvet ears. 'Eat up. I'll have a quick shower and clean up in here, then we'll go for a walk in the park, shall we?'

Alan wagged his tail; his face was busy with his food.

* * *

Two hours later, the flat was pristine. Alan, on his lead, and Charlie were walking through the triangular open space of Peckham Rye Park, enjoying the bright August sunshine as they strolled past sweet-scented wildflower meadows. Charlie was dressed too warmly, frowning furiously in the summer heat; the excessive intake of alcohol at Ben's wedding had left him feeling a little jaded, but he was determined to look on the bright side.

Alan bounded at his heels as Charlie muttered to the dog, explaining his feelings as if to an agony aunt.

'She won't come back, Al – and I don't blame her. I was stuck in a rut. It got worse after the Christmas concert at Blanche Harris. It was the worst concert I've ever done. "Gaudete" was totally depressing – and it means "rejoice" in Latin!' He pulled a face. 'I knew the GCSE students were going downhill. I was going downhill too. All I ever did was complain.'

Alan woofed: he couldn't disagree.

'Luna was right. I need to find who I really am. She's in Cornwall, following her dream. And I expect after that she'll go back to Dublin, to her family. Our paths won't cross again...' Charlie sighed. Alan was looking at him, a pink tongue hanging like a sock. 'I have to man up. We'll have to move out of the flat, I suppose.'

Alan bounded forward, chasing something in the grass, making Charlie rush after him. The meadow was vibrant, all cornflowers, poppies, white flowers, foliage.

Charlie paused, ruffling his hair. 'What do you think, Al? Where should we go?'

Alan's eyes shone with the absolute trust that he would make the right decision.

'I could buy a van with some of Mum's money and we could go to see Sonny. Spain might be nice in the winter; I could pick up some work. I could teach English, or even do some music tuition. As long as we have food, dog food, my sax and each other...'

Alan woofed in agreement. Charlie felt his phone vibrate in his jeans pocket. He tugged it out.

'Hello – Uncle Bill. Oh, it's great to hear from you. You've what?' He listened for a moment, full of interest. 'Where is it? Outside St Alban's? But... do you think it's a good buy?' He listened again and murmured, 'Double? Really? And we'd do it together? Well, I'd be up for that, if you're sure...' Charlie stood still, ignoring Alan, who pawed his jeans. 'Yes, a project like that is just what I'm looking for. What? Oh, no, no – living in squalor and chaos for several months wouldn't be a problem at all.' He laughed to himself, thinking of the mess he'd just cleaned in the flat. 'No, I'm sure. I'm used to it. Yes... when?' Alan was still staring soulfully. Charlie patted his head with gentle fingers. 'That's great, Uncle Bill.' He pushed back his sunglasses and rubbed his eyes. 'Right, well, I'll meet you tomorrow. Not at all. Alan and I will look forward to it.'

Alan looked up expectantly as Charlie ended the call.

Charlie grinned. 'That was Uncle Bill. He's got a project on the other side of St Albans and he wants us to take a look at it. It's a bit of a dive right now, but he reckons it's a good investment. We can do the place up and double the price. An old cottage close to the woods on the edge of common land, quite big. It's empty and Uncle Bill thinks that he can get it cheaply. We'll renovate it, me and Uncle Bill, and you can help us...'

Alan barked with delight.

'I agree, Alan. It will help me get my life on track. Physical work all day – I'll get fit again and I'll be able to leave my troubles behind. What do you think?'

Alan sat on the ground, cocked his head to one side and lifted a paw.

Charlie sighed. 'You're right – one step at a time. Let's go and get a cup of coffee, shall we? And I've got doggie treats in my pocket. You know, I have a funny feeling, Al – a new start in St Albans might be just what we need...'

4

1648 – HERTFORDSHIRE

Katherine looked every bit the joyful English bride as she stood in her room, except for the frown on her face. Her dark hair had been swept up, making her features all the more delicate and youthful. No expense had been spared with her pale blue dress, the lustrous satin bodice embroidered with roses, peas and beans, forget-me-nots, tulips, irises, carnations and bellflowers, the skirt finished with a detailed scalloped edge. She disliked the low neckline, insisting on her mother's cluster of pearl necklaces at her throat.

The truth was that she disliked everything: the dress, the husband-to-be, the whole idea of marriage.

Lady Alice hovered uncomfortably as she supervised the bustling silent maid, to whom Katherine had declared she would rather be out riding on her horse than standing in the cold in the most uncomfortable dress she had ever worn.

Alice made a low sound, her face troubled. 'I fear it is time we were at the church, Katherine. You must meet your groom and it is unwise to keep him waiting.'

'He may wait forever for all I care – he will be no husband of mine,' Katherine said simply. 'I have no wish to marry him.'

'You have said this often, but it will not change anything, Katherine. We should go downstairs.' Alice glanced at the maid, who scuttled away, the door closing silently behind her. 'My dear, it is not good to speak of these things in front of servants.'

'I don't care who hears me – I'd say it to Thomas Fanshawe himself, with his weak chin and his scornful expression,' Katherine flared.

'You have much to learn...' Alice began.

'*From him?* The boy who will be my husband so that he can take my father's fortune? Not I...' Katherine retorted.

'We women must learn to bear the yoke...'

'Why must we, Aunt?' The skin between Katherine's brows puckered. 'What has he done to deserve such a gift from my family? I like him not at all and he likes me just as little. Neither of us wishes to marry.'

'Your father has chosen.'

'My *stepfather*.'

'Katherine,' Alice said kindly. 'You must be wise. A woman does not choose the man she is to wed. Many women do not like the man chosen for them. In fact, I—'

'*You*, Aunt? You are Lady Bedell, wife of Sir Capel Bedell of Hamerton. You want for nothing.'

'And my husband is often absent,' Alice explained patiently. 'I am mistress of this house. So must you be, when you return to the manor house in Hertfordshire. Two servants – a man and a woman – wait there already to take care of whatever you wish. And I imagine young Thomas Fanshawe will not be with you for long.'

'Oh? Where will he go?' Katherine's tone was defiant. 'I hope he will go there soon.'

'He is like all the Fanshawe men – he will contribute heavily to the Royalist cause.' Alice looked forlorn. 'He may be absent more often than he is at home.'

'I still do not wish to marry him, Aunt. But if I can be mistress of my own manor house and do as I wish there...'

'Oh, I think it most likely...'

'Then I will eat sugared almonds for breakfast and ride my horse all day – I may take Carbonel to Hertfordshire with me, mayn't I, Aunt?'

'He shall be our gift to you.'

Katherine smoothed her dress, placing a finger against the cluster of pearls. 'Then I'll greet this horrible marriage with a lighter heart.' She thrust her chin in the air. 'Come, let us go to church. And afterwards, when we ride to Hertfordshire and I take my place in my parents' home, I will tell this buffoon of a husband exactly what I think of him and he can just go away and leave me to myself.'

Alice looked away, wondering what would come of this feisty young woman, hovering on the brink of a future she would not wish on anyone.

* * *

Half an hour later, Katherine found herself standing next to Thomas Fanshawe at the altar of All Saints Church. She observed him discreetly from the corner of her eye; he was wearing a smart doublet with large lace collars, breeches and leather boots with deep cuffs. He was only sixteen, barely a hair on his chin. His face was soft as a suet pudding and his eyes were exceptionally cold.

He looked at her, his lips curved in a smile, but she did not feel empathy or warmth. It was the haughty expression of a young man who was confident that he was coming into a fortune. She heard his thin voice recite in a sing-song from *The Book of Common Prayer*, '...to love and to cherish, till death us do part, according to God's holy law, and this is my solemn vow.'

It would be her turn next; she had been instructed what to say, to keep her eyes low, to show humility. But she was confused as she considered the words *love* and *cherish*. She had no idea how to love and cherish this cold-eyed child who stood next to her.

It was her turn to pledge her vows. Katherine felt her legs tremble beneath the satin gown, stumbling over the word 'obey'. It couldn't be possible, could it, that Thomas would tell her what she would do and she would submit to his wishes? She mumbled, 'Till death us do part, according to God's holy law. In the presence of God, I make this vow.'

Katherine caught her breath. How could she promise to love this young man in front of God? She didn't love Thomas Fanshawe – she would never love him. How could she be asked to live in the same house as this strange, distant boy for the rest of her days?

For a moment, she felt herself weaken and lose hope. Then Aunt Alice's words came back to her; she would be like every other woman in her family: her husband would often be absent, and she would be able to live as she wished. That was indeed a blessing from God.

She gave Thomas a bold stare, as if challenging him to disagree with her. He was looking down at his leather boots. He held out his hand and she placed hers neatly on top as they turned to walk down the aisle.

As Katherine strolled past the congregation, she heard her cousin Anne, an elegant young woman wearing a gown of rich satin, talking to her Aunt Alice. Her voice was low. 'Indeed, despite her fortune, she will certainly become poor Kate now...' Katherine strained her ears, pausing to listen as Anne declared, 'A wife should come to a marriage with nothing but her good name, but Kate's fortune will be at her husband's disposal.' She drew herself tall. 'I myself was very like Kate at her age, wild, spirited. But my family was ruined in the civil war, having lent large sums of money to the king, and our home was plundered.'

'Marrying Sir Richard gave you a comfortable life...' Alice agreed.

'It did. But Thomas's union with Kate is a mercenary one,' Anne said sadly. 'I feel so sorry for her – she's no more than a child, and she has no idea what lies ahead. But she needs to learn to be modest and decorous, as every wife should be...'

Katherine took a breath, avoiding the eyes of everyone in the church. In an instant, she promised herself that she'd never be like Anne, who simply gave birth to more babies and ran the household for an ambitious husband. She kept her nose in the air and swept towards the open door, one step ahead of the bridegroom, murmuring, 'I am my father's daughter – I am Kate Ferrers. I will never call myself Fanshawe. And as for you, Thomas, don't you ever expect me to honour and obey you, because I will not.'

And with that, she smiled bravely and stepped out into the April sunshine, a beautiful blushing bride.

* * *

The carriage ride back to Hertfordshire was long, almost sixty miles, and it was hard-going and bumpy over dusty dirt tracks. Katherine sat opposite her cousin Anne, nine years older than her and sophisticated in a silk gown, who had offered to stay for a few days to mentor her. Thomas was staring awkwardly through the window. Katherine refused to meet his glinting eyes, doing her best to ignore him completely and engage Anne in conversation.

'The first thing I will do when I'm back in the manor in Markyate is to go for a ride on Carbonel. I know he will be weary after the journey tonight, but tomorrow he will be fresh again. It is springtime, cousin, and I will ride him on the common through all the long summer evenings.'

'You may find you have much to do to fill your time now you are married,' Anne said with a knowing look. 'You must keep house for your husband, organise the servants, decide on his meals.'

'He can do that for himself,' Katherine replied, ignoring Thomas, who gaped at the passing countryside through the carriage windows, his expression bored.

'It is what a wife is expected to do,' Anne explained.

'Am I expected to eat his food for him too?' Katherine sniffed. 'I shall ask for the best treats for myself – sugared almonds and sweet fruits.'

'You have two very competent servants.' Anne smiled. 'My husband has hired John and Beatrice Simmonds to assist you. They are good people and will advise you well.'

'And what will they do?'

'Beatrice will cook and wash, and serve you each day. John will organise whatever you need, empty chamber pots and brush floors. He will assist Thomas in anything he wishes. And there will be a groom for the stables...' Anne took a breath. 'For you will have several horses.'

'She will have no more than one for herself. Of course, I'll keep the carriage horses, and my stallion,' Thomas said flatly, still staring through the window. 'My father will sell the rest.'

'But a horse needs a companion – Carbonel will be lonely,' Katherine said quickly.

Thomas ignored her. 'My father has instructed that one of my new properties will be put up for sale, since the Fanshawe family assets have been cut. The money will go some way to—'

'Your new properties?' Katherine sat up straight. 'What properties do you own?'

Thomas examined his fingers. 'As your husband, I now control your monies, properties, assets...'

Anne coughed gently, a reminder. 'Everything belongs to Thomas now.'

'Do I belong to Thomas too?' Katherine said angrily.

Anne almost nodded. 'You must concern yourself with wifely duties. Then, when the children come, you will be a mother...'

'Where will they come from, these children?' Katherine looked from Anne to Thomas, her expression confused. 'From *him*? How will that happen?' She took a breath. 'Will he buy them with my considerable fortune?'

Thomas's ears were burning red. He blinked and looked away.

'Children will arrive in time. It is the natural way. I myself have already borne two babies and lost two more...' Anne said sadly. 'But I will have many, God willing, to please my husband.'

Thomas wriggled uncomfortably. 'I will remain at my manor house in Hertfordshire for just a few days. Then I will make arrangements to travel to Ireland. My father has suggested I sell the manor at Flamstead.'

'My father's manor?' Katherine gasped. 'But you can't...'

'Apparently it will fetch a good sum. Our family has need of the money.' Thomas yawned, as if it was not Katherine's business.

'And what of me?' Katherine demanded. 'What will I do while you run off with my father's money and play the loyal soldier to the king?'

'You must stay home... and see to things there, like a patient wife. That's what my father said would happen.' Thomas seemed bored. 'Of course, he will sell some of the farmlands around it, so that I may serve the king as I intend.'

'You may do nothing of the sort,' Katherine said crossly. 'I forbid it.'

Anne took Katherine's hand and squeezed it lightly. 'Things are changing, Kate. You must change with them. But I will keep an eye on you.' She leaned forward confidentially. 'You can come up to The Strand and meet me there when Thomas is away. We will have such fun in London. There will be parties, and interesting people to meet.'

'My father has arranged an allowance for you – enough to pay servants and to run the house modestly.' Thomas stretched his tired legs. 'But it might be good for you to visit London from time to time. I would not prevent it.'

Katherine whirled towards him. 'And if you did, I would not listen to you. I will do as I wish.'

'I think you will discover that to be increasingly difficult,' Thomas muttered.

Anne pressed Katherine's hand again. 'Patience, cousin Kate. Many women find themselves as you do now – at the brink of a new marriage, unsure of what it may bring. But let me assure you...' She lowered her voice. 'There are ways and means to make sure that everyone is kept happy. You have a new husband, your old home in Hertfordshire, your horse, and I will be close by, in London. Believe me, things may be a lot better than you think. It is simply for you to reach out and take the gifts that life will surely bring.'

Katherine turned to look at Thomas. He was not pleasant, attractive or friendly. She did not like anything about him. At that moment, she had no idea what gifts Anne was referring to.

5

THE PRESENT

On Friday morning, Charlie and Alan took the tube from Peckham Rye to St Pancras, then the train to St Albans. It was the hottest day of the year, so Charlie packed light snacks for Alan, a bowl and some water.

They arrived at the station just before lunch and found Uncle Bill waiting, a wide grin on his face.

'Charlie... my boy.' Bill embraced him in a bear hug. He was a short man, lean and sinewy but well-muscled, with a thick crew-cut of grey hair. He had a scar across the bridge of his nose – a run-in with a screwdriver, he'd always said. He knelt down. 'Alan – nice to see you too, boy.' Bill ruffled the top of the Labrador's head. 'Right – so. We'll drive to the village – Wheathampstead – and get some lunch, shall we? Then we'll take a look at the cottage.'

'Great.' Charlie was hungry – he'd fed Alan breakfast and made do with a packet of peanuts on the tube. He followed Bill to the car park. 'How's Auntie Marcia?'

Bill put on his martyr face and groaned. 'She's spending all my money as ever. Her latest thing is false nails. They look like talons dipped in blood. I asked her how she can cook Sunday lunch with those things and she threatened to scratch my eyes out.' He laughed. 'Only joking. She's good – wonderful, in fact.'

Charlie smiled at the image: Auntie Marcia was fifteen years younger than Bill – that would make her around forty-five – and originally from Honduras. They'd been happily married for seven years after Bill's split from Auntie Carole, who'd left him for a plumber who just happened to be the best man at their wedding. Auntie Carole had been quiet and placid, but Auntie Marcia was fierce in all things: her spicy cooking, her fiery temper, her welcoming hugs. She and Bill seemed very happy together, Charlie thought – their constant affectionate bickering was a game they both enjoyed. He thought about Luna again and felt sad. They had never argued. But she'd left him just the same.

Bill clapped a hand on Charlie's shoulder as if he'd read his thoughts. 'Come on – let's go to The Sycamore Tree. I looked the place up on Google. They do great grub.'

They had reached the white van with the words Bill the Builder on the outside and a cartoon of a smiling muscly man in a yellow hard hat. Bill opened the back door and Alan leaped into the boot behind a dog-guard. Charlie crawled into the front, moving newspapers and empty cartons and Coke cans out of the way. It reminded him of his flat before the big tidy-up.

'Ah, so, yeah – I meant to say...' Bill scratched his head. 'I was sorry to hear that Luna left. She was a nice girl. I thought you and she were, you know, keepers.'

'She was nice. She is,' Charlie said, glad that Bill had brought it out into the open so they could move on. He forced a grin. 'Hey, but I'm looking forward to seeing this cottage. It's a new start for me, Uncle Bill – just what I need.'

'That's what I thought – new life, new direction,' Bill agreed. 'We'll check the place over and if it's any good, we'll make an offer and set to, fixing it up. I reckon we can get started in a few weeks.'

'That would give me time to give notice on the flat, pack my stuff...' Charlie paused as Bill swung the van around a corner so quickly it almost felt as if the wheels had left the ground. 'And I'll have transport – I can bring my bike with me from London.'

'Ah, no – forget the bike. I can sort something else out – you can drive, can't you?' Bill muttered cryptically as he swerved to avoid a man on a mobility scooter. 'Pub's just up here. I fancy chips. Marcia's got me on a diet. No carbs. It's all stuff I don't like – fish with no batter, small portions of chicken.'

Alan woofed in agreement from the boot of the van, then they were in The Sycamore Tree car park, Bill reversing too quickly, far too close to a shiny Mercedes.

Charlie clambered out of the narrow gap into the sweltering sunlight and blinked. 'I can smell food.' His stomach was growling.

They sat in the bar, which was crowded with several men drinking pints in overalls, as if they had finished work for the day. Bill ordered cod and chips twice and bought Charlie a pint of Neck Oil, a half for himself. A young woman brought two plates, her curly red hair tied back, freckles spattered on her nose, and Bill said, 'Cod and chips and the sun shining outside. You can't beat proper deep-fried food.'

The woman smiled and bustled away.

Bill grunted, 'If the food's as tasty as the waitresses we'll be all right,' and proceeded to dig in. 'Mmm. Good bit of grub. Can't beat chips and good ale for a Friday lunch. Don't let Marcia know.'

Charlie shook his head. He had barely noticed the waitress; he wasn't sure Uncle Bill should be making offhand personal comments, and he had no intention of telling his auntie that Bill had strayed from her dietary regime. The food tasted good enough, the chips crispy, the batter light, and he'd always been a sucker for mushy peas. Alan was tucked beneath his seat, lapping thirstily from a bowl. Charlie took a mouthful of his pint and reminded himself that he had a house to view that afternoon. He oughtn't to drink too much.

Bill wiped his lips on the napkin. 'So, this house – number one Constable's Cottages, Ferrers Lane... it's one of three in a row, the biggest one at the end.' He sat up straight, ready to talk business. 'Number two and three look in good condition for their age – they were built in the seventeenth century, all lime plaster and cobb walls. They all have a garden at the back, but number one has been owned by the same couple for forty-five years apparently and it's in need of renovation. I think it needs gutting – new beams, new floorboards, new lintels, windows, the lot.'

'Where would I stay?' Charlie was momentarily alarmed. 'I have Alan to think of.'

'We could do one room up and you could doss down there, while we rebuild the rest of the house. Or...' Bill rubbed his hands together. 'I could get an old caravan for the back garden.'

Charlie closed his eyes for a second, realising how much his life was about to change; it would be a real project, a lot of work. 'Uncle Bill – do you think I'm up to it? I mean – I haven't done any building for a few years now.'

'Remember that big place we worked on when you were a student in London? It was up at Lemsford.' Bill guffawed. 'We gutted the whole living room only to find that the room upstairs had rotten floorboards. They just came to dust in our hands. We hauled them all out, replaced them with new ones. That was a big job.'

'It was.' Charlie remembered; it had been during the summer holidays. He'd been staying at home, hopeful, crazy about music, playing in bands. He'd spent the entire eight weeks worrying that he'd damage his fingers and wouldn't be able to play his sax properly when the new term began. 'We made some money that summer. It helped me out a lot...'

Bill's eyes shone. 'You used to turn up in the mornings with a huge sandwich box full of crisps and biscuits, and I'd have stolen most of them by lunchtime.' He paused, thinking. 'I'd just split up with Carole, and I was on my own – I was useless at cooking and I never had any food in. Your dad had just left your mum. It was hard for her, you know, Charlie. What were you then, nineteen? Sonny must have been twenty-two. Do you know, I haven't seen Sonny in ages...'

'Sonny's always loved travelling – he's not a homebird, like me. I think he was in Australia when Mum and Dad broke up.' Charlie pushed his plate away. He wasn't hungry now.

Bill reached out for the remaining chips, pushing them into his mouth with greasy fingers.

'I never thought your dad was good enough for our Jayne, truth be known, Charlie. She's always been a free spirit, a bit of a hippie. Like Sonny.' Bill's face filled with regret. 'My dad – your grandad – used to say that to me. He'd say, "I don't trust that Kevin – it'll never last..."'

'Maybe our family has a curse...' Charlie stared at his hands. 'Mum and

Dad split up, Sonny's relationships never amount to much, now Luna's left me...'

'Oh, Jayne's all right now. Retired, with the travelling bug... her motto is still that girls just wanna have fun.'

'I don't see much of Mum nowadays.' Charlie tugged himself up straight and forced a smile. 'But that's just the way of the world, Uncle Bill. I'm looking forward to new challenges. Me and Alan...' He could feel the Labrador's tail wagging against his ankle. He put down his hand and touched the damp nose. 'We'll be great. So – shall we go and have a look at this cottage?'

'No rush...' Bill grinned. 'I see they've got sticky toffee pudding on the menu. I need to make hay while the sun shines – or, more to the point, while Marcia's not here to nag me.' He looked around. 'Now where's that pretty red-haired waitress...?'

* * *

An hour later, Bill and Charlie stood outside Constable's Cottages, Alan on a lead, while a woman in a white blouse and navy skirt flourished a set of keys. She clearly recognised Bill from the first viewing.

'How nice to see you again, Mr Sutton. And this must be your son?'

'Nephew. Charlie Wolfe,' Bill said, and Charlie stuck out a hand for the woman to shake.

'Lara Wade, of Thomas, Wade and Scott.' She squeezed Charlie's hand. Beneath her heavy make-up, she looked quite young. She offered him a professional smile. 'So – shall we go in?'

'So, the thing is...' Bill was already in the doorway. 'Charlie and I are looking for a place to renovate. We're builders...' He winked at Charlie. 'Businessmen, after a project.'

'Oh, I think you'll find this place is the perfect doer-upper.' Lara pushed the door open. It creaked softly, a perpetual ache. 'I imagine you'll put it back on the market and sell it for a huge profit.'

'That's the plan,' Bill said, striding into the hall.

Lara followed him, clipboard in hand.

Charlie felt Alan pull back on his lead for a moment. The smell of damp, dust and something sharp and mouldy filled his nostrils. He looked down and saw the dog's trusting eyes. 'Come on, boy – let's see what you think – it might be home for a while...'

Lara turned on a light as she passed a switch, and a swinging bulb illuminated the dim walls. Charlie followed her into an empty room. He noticed low-hanging cobwebs in the corners and above the windows, silver trails of dusty gossamer, trapped flies, leggy spiders. The wallpaper was pale and blotched, the wooden window frames rotten. An old stone fireplace was crumbling, the hearth soot-blackened, the remains of burned wood and pale ash piled in the grate. Charlie couldn't help himself. 'When did the last people live here? The nineteen-fifties?'

'The house has been empty for two years,' Lara said swiftly. 'It was owned by an elderly couple. The gentleman became widowed and he died in his nineties.'

'Who owns it now?' Charlie asked.

'There's a daughter – she lives in Scotland. We're acting on her behalf.' Lara indicated a door to another room. 'This could be a dining room.'

She hurried though to a smaller room. The wallpaper was pale, peeling. Charlie sniffed. He could smell damp.

Lara smiled as if the potential was clear to see. 'Shall we go through to the kitchen?'

Charlie followed his uncle and Lara, Alan dragging on the lead, into the coldest room he'd ever entered. There was no indication of the warm summer's day outside: the air was ice.

The kitchen was bare, apart from a cracked Belfast sink and several cupboards, the doors hanging off. An old greasy boiler that might once have been cream-coloured squatted in the corner, near a chimney breast. Dirty checked curtains hung in tatters.

Charlie spoke quietly. 'Someone actually lived here?'

'Let's go upstairs,' Lara suggested, treading carefully on wooden steps that groaned at each footfall.

They passed an antiquated bathroom, a huge space with a tiny window, weak floorboards, a cistern with a chain that stood like a tall ghost, a cracked bath with rusty taps.

Another door creaked, and they were inside a dark bedroom. This time, the light switch failed to work. Lara looked up at the ceiling. 'Oh, there's no bulb in here. But this is the master bedroom. As you can see, it's huge – it has the potential to be a wonderful room.'

Charlie looked at an ancient brass bed, the stained covers, the abandoned shoes on the floor stuffed with straw, and felt an overwhelming sadness.

Lara moved to the window, tugging back ragged curtains. 'There is a beautiful view of the woodlands and the common from here.'

Charlie and Alan joined her. Bill was busy knocking on hollow walls with his fist, his boots treading rhythmically on squeaking floorboards.

Lara pointed towards the woods, full of oak and silver birch, and beyond, a long stretch of grassland. Sunshine glimmered through branches. 'Nomansland Common.' Lara smiled. 'Isn't this just the perfect view to wake up to each morning? And great for dog walkers...' She beamed at Alan, then at Charlie. 'Once this place has been done up, you just might not want to sell it. It's perfectly positioned for the countryside, a sweet village, and Wheathampstead is close to St Albans and convenient for London. Hertfordshire has everything. I'm sure you can see the place has bags of potential.'

'The floorboards will need replacing.' Bill was bringing in his many years of experience, making judgements, working out costs. 'The whole place needs serious upgrading. I want to have a look at the roof, check everything is structurally sound.'

It was certainly a big project. Charlie tried to imagine what the cottage would look like once it had been renovated. White walls, bigger windows letting in much more light, a smart and functional kitchen. It could be a beautiful home.

'Take a look around – see for yourselves.' Lara smiled.

Charlie wandered onto the landing, Alan hesitating by his side, watching silently as he peered into the other bedrooms. He imagined a bright music room for his saxophone and guitars, an office stuffed with shelves of books. He and Luna would have made it into a fabulous home. They could have turned the smallest room into a cheery nursery...

He took a step back. This cottage was nothing more than a project, a way of making his savings work for him, of bridging the gap in time from when he'd been a useless teacher and an unwanted lover to a future when he could see where he wanted to go.

Charlie told himself to stop the self-pity. Life had offered him an opportunity, and he was big and strong enough to step up. It was time he counted his blessings.

But as he looked up at the ceiling, the overhanging cobwebs and dangling spiders, and felt the chill wind that blew against his skin through the gaps in the window frames, he shivered. Number one Constable's Cottages felt desolate and empty. He couldn't imagine it ever being any different.

6

1659 – HERTFORDSHIRE

Kate Fanshawe was standing at the window of The Cell, her manor house in Markyate, Hertfordshire, staring out onto the lawn, where a beam of April sunshine made an emerald path on the damp grass. Despite the brightness outside, the beautifully furnished living room felt cold. Kate realised with a jolt that she had been married for eleven years. It seemed like a lifetime ago that she had stood next to Thomas Fanshawe in the church at Hamerton and muttered shaky vows, hardly believing the words she spoke before God.

She swallowed a lump in her throat: Carbonel had died two months ago and he had been her constant companion through the years of being alone. Now a new horse was waiting for her in the stables, an ebony mare that Kate had named Shadow. She ought to go out and ride her; it would lift her spirits. After all, her marriage to Thomas was a sham: he seldom spoke to her and she avoided his company. The only blessing to have come from their union was that he was mostly absent and they hardly ever saw each other.

Cousin Anne, who had birthed several more babies, some surviving, others dying before or after birth, was constantly asking her if there might be a child on the way. Apparently, the Fanshawe family was desperate for an heir. But Kate would be twenty-five next month. She was realistic about her empty marriage: it left her lonely, but she was strong, her own mistress, and as independent as she could be on her limited allowance.

A muffled sound at her elbow brought her from her thoughts and she turned to see John Simmonds standing quietly, his head bowed. He was in his late thirties, thin of hair and face, a serious man, unlike his chirpy wife Beatrice, who was in the kitchen preparing dinner. John was waiting for permission to speak.

Kate spoke kindly. 'Is everything well, John?'

'Word has been received from your husband who is travelling from Ireland, mistress.'

Kate almost smiled. John was loyal and avuncular – he seldom mentioned Thomas by name, as if he disapproved of his absence. She wondered what news was coming next. 'He's not on his way home, surely?'

'It appears that there is some stirring of rebellion in the north counties – rumour has it that your husband is involved with an English landowner and politician from Cheshire by the name of Booth, a conspiracy to return King Charles to the throne.'

Kate brightened. 'So Thomas will not be coming home yet?'

'No, but I am sent to tell you that he has given orders that the property at Bayford is to be sold.'

'To pay for his efforts to restore the king?' Kate said. 'But recently he had the house and land at Ponsbourne sold to Stephen Twee of Watford. Twee paid just five thousand pounds for it and I saw not a penny. Thomas gives me an allowance, but it is becoming less and less. Sometimes I wonder how we shall manage.'

'Others in the village fare much worse. It falls to me to tell you of it.' John coughed politely. 'The master has sold off some of the farmlands around Markyate. It has made many of the tenants homeless. He is not a popular man among local people, although some agree with his actions because they are loyal to the king.'

'Do not mention the Sequestration Act of 1643 – that is all Thomas can speak of when he is here.' Kate covered her ears. 'Some of our estates have been placed in the hands of local commissioners. The income from Ware Park goes straight to Parliament.' Her face was distraught. 'But my heart aches most for those poor people whose means of earning a living has been taken from them. Can you ask Bea if she will cook some extra food and take it round to the Hargreves, the Woollcotts and the Salters?'

'Of course.' John inclined his head. 'And there is the tenant farmer from Ayers End. I do not know his name. Your husband intends to raise the rent on his land. He owes money, I fear, and the master has ordered him to pay or to get out.'

'Then I will call on him and tell him not to worry about it until he has enough money to pay,' Kate said. 'Thomas is not here. What can he do about it?'

'Indeed.' John suppressed a smile. 'Allow me to tell you that Beatrice is cooking a leg of mutton for dinner. The smells from the kitchen promise a hearty meal.'

Kate raised her chin. 'Please would you divide it and take it to the Woollcotts and the Salters. They have ten children between the two families and, last time I called round to their cottages, all they had to eat was cabbage soup with barley. Feed the leg of mutton to them. I will have the piece of fish that was left over from supper last night, and a glass of Thomas's wine.' She noticed John's surprised expression. 'I will not go hungry – we are not destitute yet. And ask Bea to make some cake – you know I have a sweet tooth – and take half of it for yourselves.'

John inclined his head. 'You are kind, mistress.'

'I wish I could do more...' Kate turned back to the window. The sunlight illuminated each blade of grass. The weather was beautiful – spring was a season of hope. It was always cold inside the manor house, but the blue skies lifted her spirits. 'John, please will you ask Peter to saddle my mare? I need to be outdoors, to feel the breeze in my face, to breathe again...'

* * *

The light in the stables was dim, but it felt good to mount Shadow. Kate arranged herself in her usual side-saddle position, the sweet scent of hay in her nostrils. The other stables were empty; when she was younger, there had been seven or eight horses at The Cell. Kate wondered if she could buy a companion for Shadow. In truth, she had no idea about her own finances nowadays – she didn't know what she could afford.

She smoothed her skirts as Peter, eighteen years old and blushing, adjusted the footrest. Kate watched him kindly. 'How is your mother now, Peter?'

'She does well.' Peter was clearly putting a brave face on it. 'It was hard losing little Eliza. But it is one less mouth to feed.' He stared at his busy fingers, embarrassed.

'Your mother has five little Salters...'

'She does. Since my dad died, it's down to me to bring in the money. And my brother Edwin and my sister Maggie work on the farm now, which helps.'

'How old is your sister?'

'Fourteen, mistress.'

'I was married at almost fourteen...' Kate was thoughtful. 'Peter, looking after Shadow is a great responsibility. I may decide to pay you a little more...'

Peter bent his head respectfully and mumbled thanks. His brow knitted in confusion. 'Thank you, mistress...'

'No, I should thank you, Peter. I wish you and your family...' Kate almost smiled. 'I wish you a pleasant supper tonight.'

'Mistress,' Peter repeated, even more perplexed.

Kate urged Shadow onwards into the daylight, trotting across the courtyard, smiling at the thought of the Salters sitting around their table eating their share of a leg of mutton. She was enjoying the warmth of the spring sun on her skin, imagining the family's delight. She'd never been a great eater of meat anyway – she preferred sweets.

The ride to Nomansland Common was a great pleasure, and when she reached the woods, Kate called to Shadow to go faster and the mare responded with a sudden gallop. Kate held the reins skilfully, charging on the soft ground, twigs crunching beneath hooves, towards the open horizon, breathing hard, enjoying the exhilaration of being at one with the horse. She imagined how it might feel to ride as men do, astride a horse's back. Of course, it would be difficult in long, heavy skirts and it was frowned upon: side-saddle protected a woman's virginity. It was considered vulgar for any woman to ride astride.

Kate leaned forward, galloping downhill. She'd been a wife for eleven years, but Thomas had never visited her bed once, and she was happy that way. As the horse thundered beneath her, she wondered what it might be like to love a man. She thought of her mother, cousin Anne, Aunt Alice. Each of those women was unhappy in marriage. Men were strange, privileged people, she thought, whatever their class: they possessed everything and expected women to bend to their whims and wishes. No, she was better off as she was, independent, able to do as she wished, although it smarted that Thomas was spending her money, and there was nothing she could do. The young groom, Peter Salter, the poor families in the village, the tenant farmers – their plight worried her. Then something John had said came back to her and she tugged Shadow's reins, turning abruptly back towards the dirt road.

'There's someone I want to visit before we go back,' she murmured. 'A tenant farmer who lives not far from here. Did John tell me his name...?'

Kate rode Shadow onwards along the dusty road, twisting right after a mile along a narrow track towards Ayers End Lane, at the end of which was an old farmhouse. She passed a field where a few sheep grazed. There were more fields that would be used for growing crops – wheat, barley, rye and oats. She surveyed the land with a practised eye: the farm looked well-kept; the farmer ought to be making a fair living. Wheat was most valued to make good bread. Barley was roasted to make malt for ale. And the sheep would fetch a good price at market for their wool, milk, meat and lambs. Yet John had said this farmer was struggling. She imagined a tired wife, several thin, ragged children, a poor man with a bent back working long hours at the plough.

Kate dismounted hurriedly at Ayers End Farm, stroked Shadow's nose and paused in front of the house. The front door was open. She called, 'Is anyone home? Is there a mistress of the house?'

There was no reply, so Kate stepped inside. The cottage was gloomy, the dirt floor dusty and uneven. She blinked in the darkness and found herself in a small room, a fire in the corner, a pot bubbling over the flames.

The smell from the steam was savoury: vegetables, perhaps a piece of bacon.

She wondered if an old woman lived there, the farmer's mother perhaps, so she shouted, 'Good morrow, Mother. Are you upstairs?' She stood at the bottom of rickety wooden steps and listened, gazing up to the bedroom nestling in the attic roof. There was no sound, except for the light scurrying of a rat.

She moved closer to the fire. A plate with a pricker and a spoon lay near the hearth, containing a half-eaten morsel of bread, a piece of cheese. Nearby was a jug of ale. Kate picked it up. It had been warmed for drinking: someone had paused for lunch and left in a hurry.

Kate was puzzled. Why had the house been suddenly abandoned? She headed through the back room, a pantry where vegetables were stored next to a sack of grain. She tugged open the back door and drew a sharp breath.

A man stood outside, his arms folded, his face in shadow. His voice was low as distant thunder. 'What the hell are you doing here?'

Kate composed her face into a haughty expression. 'I am Mistress Kate...'

'I know who you are. You're Katherine Fanshawe – wife of Thomas, from The Cell in Markyate. I suppose he's sent you because he's too much of a lily-livered poltroon to come himself and tell me I'm evicted. Is that it?'

Kate was surprised. The man's tone was rough and disrespectful. She had never been spoken to that way in her life. She took a deep breath to steady herself. The words spilled from her mouth. 'Good man, I simply came here to tell you that my husband's decision to raise the rents on Ayers End Farm...'

The man took a step towards her and suddenly she saw him properly and she couldn't speak. He was about her age; his eyes glowed like burning coal; his dark hair tumbled in waves over his eyes and he reminded her of a painting she had once seen of Vulcan, the Roman blacksmith god of fire and volcanoes. Everything about him was dark and commanding: his flashing eyes, heavy brows, sunken cheekbones. She couldn't help noticing his soft lips and his gleaming teeth. What a smile he would have. But now he was furious, and she wondered if she was in danger.

She took a step back and examined him again. The man wore dark breeches, but his shirt was open and his skin glistened with sweat. He had clearly been working hard. He was breathing heavily. She wanted to reach out a hand, to touch his leanly muscled arm, ask him what was troubling him. Instead, she said, 'I wonder, might we discuss...?'

'I haven't time to talk to you now,' he muttered. 'There is a mare about to foal in the barn and she is labouring hard.'

Kate's eyes widened. 'A mare? I can help. I know how to assist.'

'You?' The farmer stared at her with contempt. He clearly considered her too frail or too rich to help.

'Yes, I have witnessed the birth of a foal many times.' Something expanded in Kate's chest – indignation at his reaction, or concern for the mare, she wasn't sure which – but she was already moving forward, urging him towards the barn. 'Lead on. There is no time to waste.'

7

THE PRESENT

It was a damp late September afternoon as Charlie moved his things into number one Constable's Cottages on Ferrers Lane. He was surprised by how quickly Uncle Bill's offer had been accepted and the sale completed. They had agreed their share: Charlie would put in seventy-five per cent of the purchase price and Bill the other twenty-five per cent, and Bill would buy all the materials. He estimated that the work would take nine months and, when the house was resold, they'd both make a tidy profit. Meanwhile, Charlie would help Bill with other building jobs that came up in the St Albans area, which would give him a small income. To that end, he now drove an old white van with the words Bill the Builder and Nephew on the side, courtesy of his uncle, who'd declared that all advertising was good.

Charlie parked the old van outside the cottage on the narrow drive and threw the back doors open, revealing his life packed in just a few boxes. Methodically, he started to take his belongings inside. Alan was at his heels as he carried his saxophone, guitars, cases and several cardboard boxes into the large living room, a hollowed space. He wheeled his bicycle as far as the doorway and stared despondently at the front garden, a tangle of weeds and overgrown brambles.

Charlie placed his hands on his hips. 'Well, that little lot didn't take long...' He watched as Alan wagged his tail and said, 'Here we are – home sweet home. Shall we go inside and christen the place with a sandwich and something fizzy? I think I have a bottle of sparkling water...'

Alan woofed and Charlie closed the door behind them, leaving the rain drizzling outside. The breeze in the hall chilled his skin, and he felt the hairs on his arms prickle. He led the way into the living room and looked around, making a soft sound of resignation.

'No heating. Just the remains of an old fireplace. We'll need to get some logs in for the winter, Al, or we'll freeze.'

The room was bare, the walls damp, old paper peeling forlornly. Lumpy anaglypta from the nineteen seventies.

Charlie looked around, trying to muster as much positivity as he could. 'It's a big room. We could put the TV on the wall over there, and we could get a huge comfy three-piece suite...' He paused, imagining himself and Alan sprawled on a large sofa together, watching TV, eating popcorn. It could happen – the room could be made to be warm and homely. Alan's basket could be placed in the corner near a radiator belting out heat, next to a bowl of appetising doggy treats. He could put some pictures on the wall, maybe some of his guitar heroes, Hendrix, Jimmy Page, David Gilmour, Charlie Parker playing the sax. Some Banksy posters – 'Girl With Balloon', 'Pulp Fiction'. He liked the idea of a poster that reminded him to DO MORE OF WHAT MAKES YOU HAPPY.

But the cottage was a doer-upper, not his own place. Charlie took a deep breath: a home of his own was a long way off. For now, he'd forget about making the cottage too comfy. It was just a project, that was all. It seemed to him that everything in his life right now was temporary. Except for his dog.

He followed an excited Alan through the empty kitchen, making a mental note to try to light the old boiler tomorrow. He doubted it would work: it was rusty, grimy, but he'd clean it and see if he could get it going. He had an air fryer, a toaster and a kettle, so he'd survive – he'd be able to make basic meals using that lot, and at least he had running water, electricity.

He grabbed a suitcase, feeling a surge of optimism. 'Let's go upstairs and see our room, Alan.' He grinned. 'We'll be living in luxury, you and me.'

The stairs creaked beneath his feet, the dull groan of ancient wood. He stood on the landing and glanced into the gloomy bathroom. 'We have an immersion heater and soon we'll put a shower in here, Alan, and one of those modern free-standing baths. The room's a good size so I think it'll fit. Let's see if Uncle Bill agrees. We'll make it so nice – scented candles, a plant or two...' Charlie was at it again, putting down roots. He heard his voice echo from the beams and looked up. The landing ceiling was patched with damp. A naked light bulb hung down.

He wandered into the bedroom, Alan a reluctant shadow behind him. The room was completely empty now, the old bed gone, along with all traces of the former occupant, except for a sharp musty smell. There was a single mattress on the floor that Bill had brought round a few days ago, a pillow and a brand-new duvet decorated with Bob the Builder images. Typical Uncle Bill. Charlie couldn't help smiling. He threw himself down on the smooth cover and placed his hands behind his head. Alan leaped on top of him, resting his chin on Charlie's belly.

'Home...' Charlie murmured, looking up at the ceiling. Flaps of plaster hung precariously. He chewed his lip in thought – he couldn't underestimate the toughness of this renovation, the long hours, the late nights. He was in for a cold hard winter. 'Character building.' Charlie forced a grin as he ruffled Alan's fur. 'How about a bit of food, Alan? You can have kibble in your favourite bowl, and I'll make myself that sandwich – some soft multi-seeded bread, mature cheddar, a bit of pickle and cheese and onion crisps...' He sat up in one movement. 'Come on, Al... this is the single life.'

* * *

They ate sitting on an old rug on the kitchen floor, Charlie swigging water from a bottle. He didn't see any point in investing in much furniture, although he was beginning to recognise the need for some decent lighting. It was almost six o'clock, still bright outside, but inside, the rooms were gloomy and there was a stubborn chill in the air.

Tomorrow was Sunday and Uncle Bill and Auntie Marcia were coming round early to help settle him in. They were going to take him out for lunch, and then on Monday morning the work on the cottage would begin properly.

His phone pinged and Charlie's heart leaped as it always did. Of course, it was never a text from Luna, but he always hoped. He stared at a WhatsApp group message of some of his uni friends – Ben and Rachael were sharing photos from their recent honeymoon in Umbria and Tuscany. The photos were gorgeously vivid, all blue skies and terracotta villages, lush green fields, high mountains merging with low-hanging clouds. Rachael posed in shorts and T-shirt in front of the vast waters of Lake Trasimeno and Ben stood proudly next to the misty spray of Marmore Falls.

Charlie closed his eyes and imagined himself there with Luna, sharing a glass of Chianti and nibbling *crostini Toscani*, enjoying *panzanella*, *bistecca alla Fiorentina*, *fagioli con salsiccia*. The words sounded delicious, they oozed romance and sunshine and so much happiness.

He shivered and his fingers moved on the phone, typing in *Kiss Me, Kate*, *The Minack Theatre* and *Hall For Cornwall*. He knew he shouldn't, but he hoped it wouldn't hurt, just this once.

But it did. Photographs of the cast filled the screen, stills of the performance, glossy snaps of The Minack in all its wild rocky glory at the edge of the ocean. Then there she was, assistant choreographer Luna O'Rourke, her shining hair, her blue eyes and tender smile. For a moment, she was in his arms again, murmuring sweet words. Then it was too much to bear.

Charlie was on his feet, tugging on his jacket, calling to Alan over his shoulder. 'I'll get your lead, Al. We're going outside. Time for a walk.'

Alan was at his heels instantly. Charlie grabbed the bunch of keys on the steel ring that represented his life now and everything he owned – the van, the cottage and his few belongings within – and headed hurriedly for the front door.

Nomansland Common was accessible across the road, stretching for miles. Charlie gazed up at the dishwater sky, a line of pale cloud in the distance. It was still light; it mightn't rain again for a while. He hurried forward to keep warm. 'Come on, mate – I bet all the dog walkers are out now for their evening stroll. You never know – you might meet a gorgeous Labradoodle...'

The thought of a doggie romance made him smile as he set off at a pace through the woodlands, Alan trotting at his side. A stiff breeze blew in and Charlie turned up his jacket collar, reminding himself that he'd need to invest in a heavy winter coat and wellingtons. He'd never have worn such clothes in London, but things had changed in such a short time. He was a builder, a homeowner. The thought made his heart lift. The change of location, of lifestyle would keep him sane.

The common was deserted, and the light was draining away. Charlie increased his speed along a muddy path flanked by trees and undergrowth. He enjoyed the rhythm of his steps, the way his feet squelched slightly in the mud and how Alan plodded happily next to him. They loved Peckham Rye Park, the busyness of crowds, the diversity and the modern landscaping. But Nomansland Common was a vast empty space that made Charlie feel somehow liberated and alone – a feeling that was appealing.

In the distance, something rustled, the shifting of brittle leaves, a crow flapping its wings. There was no one to be seen, but Charlie had the distinct feeling that he was being watched. He glanced towards a cluster of trees on the top of the hill. It would be easy for someone to observe him from there. Suddenly, Charlie was aware that the comparative safety of London was far away; the bustling crowds were no more. Here, he was isolated.

He found himself blinking nervously towards the rustling trees. Someone was there, he felt it, waiting, watching him and his dog walk on the lonely common. He was helpless – worse, he was edgy.

Alan picked up on his mood and eyed him anxiously. Charlie bent down and found a small stick – it was a perfect bone shape. He hurled it and yelled, 'Fetch, boy!' Alan hurtled happily after the stick, picked it up in his soft mouth and came bounding back. Charlie rubbed the dog's head affectionately. 'Well done, Al.' He looked up at the sky through narrowed eyes. 'It's clouding over – it might rain soon. Shall we head back home?'

Alan woofed and Charlie felt safe again. He had a good companion in Alan. He would be fine.

He turned back towards Constable's Cottages, his hands deep in his pockets, the wind blowing through his hair. He imagined how chilly the common would be in late autumn and early winter. But he'd have a good stove in the hearth by then, a power shower, maybe even central heating. The cottages were in sight. He increased his pace.

The curtains were closed in number three Constable's Cottages, but a woman stood unseen, watching the young man with his collar turned up, the black Labrador trotting at his side. She saw him approach from the woodlands, opening the gate to number one, hurrying down the path. She paused for a moment, thinking, then she immersed her hands in a bucket of elderberries and hot water, the dark liquid swirling between her fingers.

8

1659

Kate knelt next to the pale mare who was lying on her side in the gloomy barn, specks of dust dancing on the air. She had never felt so uncomfortable. Her fine woollen petticoat was too warm. Her kirtle with a stiffened bodice to give her a good shape in the fashionable way was completely the wrong garment for helping a foal into the world. She quickly undid the spiral lacing at the front and watched the farmer as he readied himself to help the foal.

The mare began to strain, the amniotic sac visible, then the foal's front feet appeared, one ahead of the other, soles down. As the small nose emerged, then the head, Kate helped the farmer to ease the foal gently from the mare. She had never been so aware of the old sumptuary laws of the land, that clothes should dictate social class. Here was she, in a beautiful red and black gown now splashed with blood, and the man next to her was in dirty breeches, his pale shirt loose. He appeared not to notice as he muttered instructions to her as if she was any ordinary farmer's assistant. 'Look to the mare, can you? That's good – the foal's almost out now. Steady, Beleza, steady girl.'

Kate glanced at the farmer as he stroked Beleza's back, leaving his hand against her spine, his voice was warm with encouragement. She had never seen anyone behave so kindly towards a mare during birthing – her previous experience was that every attention was given to the foal's safe arrival, but the mare was invariably ignored.

Kate moved to the horse's head and patted her neck, feeling the steamy warmth rise from her flesh. She murmured, 'Nearly done, Beleza. Your foal is here, and we will be with you for what follows, then you may rest.'

The farmer gave a muted cry and the foal was lying in the straw, warm and round-eyed.

Kate noticed Beleza raise her head, curious, accepting her newborn, and she felt tears spring to her eyes. She wondered how it might feel to bring a child into the world, to hold him or her in her arms. Until now, she had never considered it, despite having seen many foals born, but for some reason, her throat was constricted by a sadness. She had been denied so many things that other women took for granted.

'It is good,' the farmer murmured. 'Beleza, you have done well.'

'She has,' Kate agreed, wiping her face on her lacy sleeve.

'And you have done well too.' The farmer stood up. 'It was easier having an assistant.'

'Does your wife not assist you?' Kate stood up too.

'I have no wife.' The farmer glanced at the foal, changing the subject. 'It is a male. What shall we call him?'

'I've no idea...' Kate began.

'You choose.'

Kate looked at the man, his glowing eyes with gold flecks, his flexing broad shoulders. 'Vulcan...'

'A good name.' The farmer held out a grimy hand. 'I'm Raife Chetwyn.' He grinned and Kate knew she'd been right: he had the most charmingly beautiful smile.

'Kate Ferrers,' Kate began. 'Fanshawe...' She looked down at her now-grubby dress, the soiled sleeves, the loose bodice, and began to tug the lacing tight again. Her hands were dirty.

Raife Chetwyn seemed oblivious of his open shirt and his grubby breeches as he bent to inspect the foal and to pat Beleza's pale neck. Kate found it difficult to look away.

'Thirsty work, birthing.' He straightened and offered the disarming smile again. 'Could I get you something? A cup of ale?'

Kate noticed he didn't call her 'mistress'; his eyes met hers and there was a defiance there, a boldness she'd never seen before. She'd never met a man who might offer her a simple cup of warm ale in a humble farm cottage. How could she refuse?

She glanced around the stables. 'Do you have other horses?'

'Three more, two stallions and another mare.' He glanced back at Beleza. 'You must have many horses at Markyate.'

'Just my mare, Shadow.' Kate bit her lip. 'Thomas has sold the rest...'

Raife appeared not to hear. 'The new foal will be useful here.'

'But the farm does not thrive?' Kate asked.

'I do what I can. Come, let's go inside.' Raife jerked his head towards the door. 'We can talk while we eat.'

'Will Vulcan be well now?' Kate enjoyed the sound of the foal's name; it felt good to have been asked to choose it, and she had chosen well.

'He will,' Raife said. 'The cord did not break during delivery, but it will usually break when the mare or foal gets up.'

Back inside the cottage, Raife washed his hands in warm water from the blackened pot over the fire and Kate copied him. They sat by the fire's ruddy glow.

Kate held a cup of warm ale while Raife cut good bread into chunks, placing cheese on two plates. He handed one to her. 'Here.'

'Thank you.'

'I was glad of your work today.'

'I helped but a little...' Kate gulped the warm ale. She was thirsty.

'I was concerned about the birth. It can be difficult for one person if something goes amiss – once, years ago, when a mare was with foal, I found it was covered with red membranes as it emerged and I had to tear the sack open quickly or the foal would have died.'

'Why?' Kate was intrigued by his depth of knowledge and expertise.

'The foal could not breathe by itself.' Raife looked at his large hands and Kate glanced at them too – rough, capable hands.

She asked, 'Do you run the farm alone?'

Raife nodded as he chewed.

'And who makes the bread? Who cooks?'

'I do. Who else would do it?'

'Have you always been alone?' Kate noticed how his eyes shone in the firelight; they were softer now, thoughtful.

'Not always.' Raife turned to look at her. 'I hear you live alone, in the big manor, The Cell, up at Markyate.'

Kate felt anger flame. 'Who says that?'

'Everyone knows it.' Raife gave a short laugh. 'Your husband spends all your money, gives it away to the king.'

'I care nothing for his company.' Kate tossed her head. 'I have my horse, my servants. I live well.'

'But it must be lonely in such a big house.'

'It must be lonely in a small one too,' Kate retorted.

Their eyes met and held. He said, 'It is.'

Kate was silent. She looked around the wooden table, the hearth with its blackened pot, the crooked stairs leading to the gloomy room in the attic and she felt tears fill her eyes. How nice might it be to live here in this simple house with such a man. She imagined the company, the conversation. In the daytime, he would work on the farm; they would tend to the animals together. As the light faded outside, they would sit in a darkened room with just the firelight and the glow of a tallow candle illuminating their faces. She imagined his arms around her, pulling her against his chest...

Kate stood up. 'I must go.'

'You have not finished your food.'

'I am sufficed – thank you – I am expected back at The Cell...'

Raife stood too. 'You never told me why you came here.' He frowned, remembering. 'I believe your husband intends to raise the rent...'

'No,' Kate said quickly. 'I came to say that I will not allow him to. He does not understand how hard it is for farmers to make a living and I intend to tell him that he will receive no more extra money from his tenants.'

'You will do that?' Raife asked.

'I will. And I will find ways to help some of the families who are struggling. At The Cell, my allowance from Thomas is modest, but I am most fortunate compared to the families in the village. I will not allow them to starve.'

'You would do much.' Raife's eyes full of admiration. 'I thank you.'

'You have no need to thank me...' Kate walked towards the door. She had felt equal to this man when they were in the stables delivering a foal. Now she felt like the rich wife of a landowner, a bountiful lady bestowing charity. It piqued her that a gulf had come between her and the handsome man in dusty breeches who stood holding out a rough hand for her to shake. She took it.

'It was a pleasure meeting you,' Raife said with a nod of his head.

'I was the more fortunate,' Kate said quickly and hurried outside to where Shadow was waiting patiently on the dirt track.

Raife followed her as if to help her to mount, but she swung herself onto the horse's back, her right leg over the pommel of the saddle. She saw the farmer's gaze move to her shapely ankle and calf, then back to her face. He said nothing as she rode away.

Kate's mind raced as Shadow galloped back to the manor. She thought of the farmer. Raife Chetwyn led a hard and solitary life. She compared the simplicity of Ayers End Farm to the luxury and comfort of the manor, his plate of bread and cheese to the sumptuous meals that Beatrice cooked. How easy was her life in comparison, yet she had felt a yearning to stay with him.

The image of Thomas filled her thoughts, the way his eyes always avoided hers. She recalled his weak chin, his disinterested conversation. He was her husband, but they felt no affection for each other. His slim fingers had never touched hers; his thin lips had never kissed her mouth, and the idea of it repulsed her. She recalled the farmer's strong hands, rough and skilful as he'd helped Vulcan into the world. She imagined his mouth against hers, warm, passionate kisses.

Something had changed within her since she'd met Raife Chetwyn. Kate felt different: her skin tingled, her pulse raced. As she'd sat opposite him and shared a cup of ale, she'd become aware of his disturbing presence that had both unsettled and thrilled her. Yet she trusted him; something instinctive in her turned to him. She'd always been composed and calm, but now she felt skittish, impulsive. She was filled to the brim with a happiness she'd never known, an aching sense of longing. It was both wonderful and terrifying. And she didn't understand it.

She surged forward on Shadow's back, increasing speed, and tried to put Raife Chetwyn from her mind. He was a farmer, an ordinary man, not of her class. He was her husband's tenant – a man to whom she had made a promise she could not keep. She'd had no right to say what she did and now she regretted it. Quickly, she told herself it didn't matter. Thomas would put up the rent as he wished. The farmer would realise she'd spoken impulsively. He'd think her foolish – he'd know she had no power to keep her word. Besides, she wouldn't see him again. She would put their meeting from her mind, and all the hectic, conflicting, powerful emotions that went with it.

The Cell was in sight, and the small cottages of Markyate village. Kate would ask John if he'd taken the mutton to the Salters and the Woollcotts. She'd concentrate on looking after those people in the community who were less fortunate. They needed her and she was desperate to help them. That would go some way to appeasing her conscience, her embarrassment for the hollow promise to Raife Chetwyn she'd never be able to keep.

She rode furiously into the courtyard of The Cell and clambered down from the horse. Peter was there to meet her, to take Shadow's reins and lead her to the stables.

Kate stood shivering, her mind crowded with thoughts. She'd visit the Hargreve family first thing tomorrow. She imagined their delight at the linen-covered basket filled with a cake, extra loaves of bread, a bit of bacon. In her imagination, she knocked on the door of their little cottage, but it was not Mother Hargreve whom Kate saw standing in the doorway smiling with delight. It was Raife Chetwyn in dusty breeches.

Kate exhaled slowly to calm herself. What had passed between her and Raife Chetwyn that afternoon had confused her. And now she had no idea what to do.

9

THE PRESENT

Charlie woke up on Monday morning and for a moment he couldn't remember where he was. Then he noticed the crisp new Bob the Builder duvet cover and felt the hard mattress beneath him. It occurred to him that he was home, but as he stared around at unpacked boxes, bare floorboards and the thin strip of sunlight streaming through the grimy window, he felt a surge of apprehension. He told himself that it was natural to feel uneasy – he'd invested all the money that his mother had given him on a project that might not be successful. Not that his mum minded – she'd sent him a 'welcome to your new home' text yesterday and announced that she was off to see Sonny in Spain.

He heard a sound downstairs and assumed it was Alan mooching around, his tail wagging against something. But it was louder, a thumping against a door. Charlie grabbed his phone and realised it was after eight o'clock – he'd slept in. He tugged on a T-shirt, boxers and jeans and hurried downstairs.

Alan was sitting in front of the door listening to someone knocking outside. A familiar voice yelled, 'Get up, lazybones, we've got an old cottage to renovate.'

Charlie opened the creaking door and blinked in the bright sunlight.

Uncle Bill was grinning, holding out a small square container. 'I bought you some breakfast.' He presented Charlie with something that was still warm and smelled of fried eggs.

Charlie lifted the kitchen paper and saw a white bread roll. The egg inside was well cooked with crispy edges and drowned in ketchup. He smiled enthusiastically. 'Thanks, Uncle Bill.'

'And look who else I've met,' Bill declared. He stood to one side, to reveal a woman leaning over the hedge that separated number one from the middle cottage. 'This is Marilyn from number two. We've just been chatting while I've been waiting for you to move your lazy bones out of bed.'

'Hello...' Marilyn, middle-aged, smiling in crisp jeans, waved pink-tipped fingers. 'I was going to come and introduce myself yesterday, but I saw you go out together in the morning and I didn't see you come back.'

'My wife and I took Charlie out for Sunday lunch.' Bill made a sound somewhere between a belly laugh and a groan. 'There's a great pub in St Albans. The Wheatsheaf. They do huge roasts there. Do you know it?'

'I don't go into St Albans much,' Marilyn said sadly. 'I'm on my own. Divorced. My mother lives in Redbourn. I visit her a few times a week. She's eighty-five.'

Charlie looked at his neighbour in her white blouse, with her short neat grey hair, her slight frame, and wondered if she'd complain when he practised his music. She looked pleasant enough.

'I'll bring you a cake round later,' Marilyn promised. 'Do you like carrot cake? I usually do a bit of baking at the beginning of the week. Of course, when old Mac was here, I'd see him from time to time, but he wasn't fond of visitors.'

'Mac?' Charlie asked.

'Gerald MacAllister, the previous owner. He was a widower. The estate agent said he lived until a ripe old age, remember?' Bill said.

'He did,' Marilyn agreed. 'I didn't have much to do with him really – he kept himself to himself until he died two years ago. The old place was just left empty then. I didn't think anyone would ever buy it.' She brightened. 'It'll be nice to have a new neighbour. And you're builders, you say?' She looked hopefully at Bill.

'We are. Charlie's a musician too. Very talented.'

'Oh, that's nice. Do come and have a chat when you have a minute though,' Marilyn said. 'I've got a loose tile on the roof – the water comes in on my landing sometimes... I have to put a bucket out when it rains.'

'Of course – I'd be glad to help,' Bill said affably. 'We're making a start on this place today. We'll gut it entirely, replace everything from top to bottom...' He checked to make sure that Marilyn was impressed. 'Come on, Char – I've got a flask of coffee and a sandwich for myself. We need to get organised – a quick planning meeting, then we'll get down to it. And...' He indicated Alan, who was sitting patiently, hopeful with a front paw raised. 'I'd say this young man hasn't had his breakfast yet either. He looks hungry.'

Alan woofed in agreement.

* * *

It was almost nine o'clock by the time they'd finished breakfast. Bill had wanted to talk about how Marcia had given him a hard time yesterday about cholesterol. She was annoyed that Bill had eaten extra roast potatoes at lunch, and in the evening, he'd sat in front of the television munching sausage rolls. 'I said to her – I'm a builder, Marce...' He pulled an exaggeratedly shocked face. 'I said – what do I do all day? Hump stuff up ladders, mix cement, stick bricks in holes. It keeps me fit. And look at me – there's not an ounce of fat...'

Charlie nodded. He had to admit that Bill didn't look at all overweight. He was muscled and compact, very fit for sixty. He took another swig of coffee from his flask. 'Auntie Marcia's just concerned about you. She cares...'

'She does, bless her,' Bill said fondly. 'Mind – she's got a good catch here. Look at me. In my prime. Well-honed and well heeled. What woman wouldn't...?' He laughed. 'You got a young lady in mind, Charlie? After – you know, your Luna...?'

'I'm taking time off – for good behaviour,' Charlie joked. It was easier to make light of how he felt. 'And I've got this place – a project to throw myself into. I was thinking, as well – I might put a few feelers out, see if anyone wants a music tutor? I could keep my hand in, guitar lessons, saxophone – you know, local kids, evenings...'

'Great idea. Now...' Bill rubbed his hands together. 'This place. What do you think? We'll start upstairs, I thought...'

'Won't we do up the kitchen first?' Charlie was disappointed.

'Ah, you don't have an old builder's experience.' Bill grinned. 'We start upstairs. What would be the point in making downstairs nice, then traipsing all the concrete and rubble through the place when we do the bedrooms?'

'I see – I just thought I'd have a kitchen first, maybe a nice living room with a TV.'

'Now don't you start putting down roots, Charlie. This place is a project. Strictly business. You can't get attached...'

'I know but—'

'Well, look – Marcia has an old portable TV we used to keep for the spare bedroom – you can have that,' Bill grunted. 'As long as you've got water and electricity, you can always have a wash down in a bucket.' He saw Charlie's appalled expression. 'It's not as if you've got anyone to smell nice for, although I know you young lads like to smell like a lady's boudoir... Let's give that bathroom the once-over, rip a few floorboards out, have a look at the ceiling. We'll make it nice, then we'll make a start on your bedroom.' Bill offered a cheeky expression. 'A single lad needs a tidy pad, just in case...'

Charlie struggled into his overalls. 'I went for a walk on Saturday evening, Uncle Bill, I forgot to say. It's lovely out in the woods.'

'The cottage is perfectly positioned, what with Markyate down the road, the village, the common. That's what first attracted me to it. And you only have two neighbours. Marilyn seems a bit of all right.'

Charlie had no idea what he meant. 'Have you seen the other neighbour, the one in number three?'

'No, I haven't, but the place looks well-kept. There are solar panels on the roof. I had a quick butcher's when I went past. I reckon they've got a rainwater harvesting system too – it collects all the rainfall via a drainpipe.'

'Oh?' Charlie was impressed. 'Could we have one of those here?'

'Small steps, sunshine.' Bill beamed. 'This is a doer-up-and-seller.

Once this place is done, maybe you'll find a permanent pad somewhere else and we'll give it some thought. I'm a great believer in solar panels. I wish Marcia and I had got them earlier. Still.' He indicated the stairs. 'Onwards and upwards. My ladder's in the van with all my stuff – we can't hang around here talking all day.'

* * *

That evening, Charlie lay on the mattress with Alan, listening to jazz on the radio. His saxophone was next to him; he'd been playing along, practising riffs and phrases.

Charlie took a sip from a bottle of water and nibbled a bit of the carrot cake Marilyn had brought round that evening. She'd kept him talking for ages, saying how nice she thought his uncle Bill was and when might he take a look at her loose tiles?

He rolled over on his back. It was not yet nine o'clock, but he was tired and his limbs ached. What he'd give for a nice hot bath! They'd made a lot of progress today, but he'd chipped so much plaster from the walls that he had to wash his hair twice in a bucket of warm water to get it clean.

Charlie closed his eyes and decided that in a few days' time he'd visit the pub and meet the local residents. Perhaps they had quizzes or music nights. He'd ask if they used musicians, if he could get a gig. Certainly, he ought to integrate into the community. He'd find the village post office, advertise himself as a music teacher. He needed to be sociable, get his mojo back. Then, when the cottage had upstairs rooms, he'd invite some of his friends from London to stay.

His eyelids had started to become heavy and his mind drifted to the previous occupant. He wondered if the old man had died in the very bedroom he was sleeping in. He told himself not to worry; it was a cold shell of a house that had been empty for two years. Old houses carried a residual sense of loneliness. He would breathe life into the place, give it a new lease...

Then he was asleep, deeply. Too deep to dream.

* * *

He woke with a start and sat upright. The radio was whining, so he turned it off. Alan was already wide awake. Charlie could see his shadow in the darkness. The dog was alert, listening for a sound he'd heard once already. For a moment, Charlie wondered if there was a burglar downstairs. Then he heard it again, a hollow, empty echo of a distant hoof.

He moved swiftly in the dimness of the room towards the window, his phone in his hand. He noticed the time was 2.46 before he flicked on the torch and pointed it outside. The garden was full of shadows that could have been dancing witches. He was letting his imagination run wild; the bushes and weeds waved in the breeze. He stared over to the woodland, which was a dark mass. Alan leaned against him as if seeking warmth and comfort.

Charlie strained his ears. He had heard a sound clearly, as if someone was not far from the house. The wind made the thin panes rattle, a shivering of glass.

There it was again. The rhythmic sound of hoof beats in the distance, coming from the trees, heading towards the road. He pressed his nose to the grimy pane and tried to make sense of the direction. Then he saw what might have been a mounted rider. Charlie looked at a slight figure who leaned forward, moving purposefully. He saw the single flap of a coat, heard a soft snort.

The horse hovered, approached, then seemed to rear up outside the gate. The figure reined the beast in, looking up towards the window. Charlie thought that the rider noticed him and for a moment he couldn't look away. It was too dark to see clearly, but a shiver shook him like lightning.

The rider waited a few more seconds, part of the darkness, then, in an instant, the shape was gone.

Charlie stood frozen, wondering what he had just seen.

10

1659

Kate stood in her chamber, thinking. Cousin Anne's invitation to a party at The Strand had come at the perfect time. It was just what she needed, several days in London where she could connect with old friends and meet new people, talk lightly about things that didn't really matter. She was sure that by immersing herself in superficial chatter she would forget Raife Chetwyn. She would have the chance to breathe again, to remind herself who she was.

But every time her thoughts returned to him, her heart thumped, and she didn't feel in control of her own emotions. She recalled his muscled arms, sweat gleaming as he had helped the mare with the new foal. Something in her heart expanded, but at the same time it shook her with fear: she couldn't harness the powerful new feelings.

Kate concentrated on helping Beatrice to pack her best dresses. She'd need to wear something fetching, and take a warm cloak against the cold London air. Then there were her pearls, her best evening dresses.

Beatrice was happily chattering, oblivious of the storm of emotions that raged in Kate's heart. 'You should have seen Goodwife Salter's face, how delighted she was. The piece of mutton I gave her was almost as big as her youngest boy. And when John showed them the cake I'd made, the children's eyes nearly popped out. I mean, it was only a honey cake, but it had plenty of good butter in. Hopefully, it will fatten the poor Salter kids up. They look thin as church mice.'

Beatrice stood up from the trunk she was packing and smiled. She was in her mid-thirties now. Still childless, she treated Kate like a daughter. She was red-cheeked, reminding Kate of a rosy apple. She was John's opposite, lively to his languid, shorter and rounder to his lean and tall, but they were the kindest couple. Kate would always be grateful to them. They had welcomed her back to The Cell eleven years ago as a new bride. And Beatrice knew better than anyone how indifferently Thomas treated Kate and had always been sympathetic to her plight, offering a smile that showed that she understood.

'So, mistress – what about jewellery?' Beatrice said cheerfully. 'You'll need something special to wear in London. You have the pearls. What about your mother's bracelet, the gold and topaz one? And the lovely sapphire brooch?'

'My husband has sold them.' Kate smiled to cover the sadness she felt. 'But there is the ruby cabochon ring my father gave to my mother, and she gave to me. I will wear that. It reminds me of her...'

'You've made a good choice,' Beatrice said. 'And the master cannot sell it if you're wearing it...'

'I'm sure he'd sell me too if he could get a good price, Bea.' Kate shuddered at her poor attempt at a joke. 'But when you talk about the Salters, the Hargreve family and the Woollcotts, I almost feel ashamed to wear jewels. Those poor people cannot eat precious stones. I know that they are starving. But Thomas continues to demand more rent.'

'My John says it's because of the Sequestration Act – that Parliament demands it...'

'It is because of Thomas himself, Bea. He is a selfish man.'

'Ah, mistress, I know how unfortunate you have been. But at least he is often absent, and you are left to do as you please.'

'I would rather have been a farmer's wife, living simply with a man I could love...' Kate felt the blood rise in her cheeks.

'Perhaps such a hard life would not suit a woman like you...' Beatrice gave her a look and Kate wondered if she had betrayed her feelings somehow.

'A woman like me? Do you mean that I am weak and that I must do as I am bid?'

'No, you have always been spirited, wild at heart...'

'Then perhaps I should follow those whims even more?' Kate paused, thinking. 'I shall do more for the poor people of the village. It is not right that their children starve and that they work for low wages, and that Thomas puts up their rents.'

'Or you should distance yourself from such matters,' Beatrice said knowingly. 'Although you are a gracious woman, mistress, and your heart is bountiful and kind, it is not your place to question the decisions of your husband.'

'I care little for his decisions.' Kate tossed her ringlets. 'While I am in London, I will think more on how I may be of service to the villagers. John says Thomas is away in the north country. I hope he will not return for months. Maybe by then I can have done something significant for the poor families.'

'I know you well, mistress, and I must warn you to be cautious.' Beatrice met Kate's eyes, her own flashing a warning. 'I do not know why, but something about your expression – you have a new recklessness about you.'

'Not I.' Kate laughed. 'I go to London to join my cousin Anne and to talk to matronly women about dresses and dancing and playing games.'

'I am sorry to speak so frankly. I think only of your safety.' Beatrice placed a kindly hand on Kate's arm.

'I thank you for it,' Kate said. 'Now I will see you Sunday next. And I will tell you all about Anne's children and what all the ladies in London are wearing this season...'

Beatrice pressed Kate's hand. 'Go with God, mistress – I pray he will protect you.'

'Oh, I'm sure he will,' Kate said as she shrugged on her cape.

* * *

An hour later, Kate sat in a rattling carriage pulled by four strong horses as it shuddered along the dirt track approaching Nomansland Common. She gazed through the window. It was a pleasant spring evening, the air warm, but it would be dark by the time she reached London. The journey would take six hours; the coach smelled foul and the wooden benches were hard, her feet set on muddy straw.

She pushed her head through the open window, breathing in the sweet scent of the wild flowers and damp grass. In the distance, she noticed farmlands, ploughed fields, and her thoughts drifted to Raife Chetwyn. Her body responded with a familiar thudding of her heart, but she pushed the image of him away. She would have a splendid time in London. It would be fun to visit the capital: the strange stench of fish markets and the raucous racket of playhouses excited her. She'd be invited to fashionable houses belonging to wealthy merchants and she and Anne would visit shops selling expensive wares, although she knew Thomas would disapprove. But London was a wonderful place; she looked forward to meeting acquaintances she hadn't seen in a long time, enjoying intelligent conversation with fascinating writers and poets. It was good to spend time with sparkling people, especially since she knew that they enjoyed her company and showed no interest in her husband whatsoever.

Kate allowed herself a moment's recollection: the last party she had attended had been at Christmastime. She had spent an hour talking to Samuel Pepys, a witty man who told her an amusing story. He'd suffered for a while from a constant pain in his side and blood in his urine. His mother and his brother John were also troubled with the same complaint, so he had bravely undergone a terrifying operation in a bedroom at the home of his cousin, Jane Turner. Samuel had made Kate laugh; the procedure had been such a blinding success and the pain had stopped miraculously. So from that day, he resolved to hold a celebration to his bladder and drink Gascon wine on each anniversary of the operation.

Kate enjoyed London, travelling everywhere by boat because the streets were narrow and crowded, the entire city smelling of horse dung. But there were two things she disliked. One, she'd watched a bear baiting once, and it had upset her, seeing the poor beast led to a pit, chained to a stake by its leg. Spectators had cheered wildly and placed bets as a pack of bulldogs was unleashed into the arena to torment the poor bear. She had left early and wondered at the nature of men who could enjoy the suffering of other creatures.

Another time, when she had been at London Bridge and at Bridge Gate, she'd seen the rotting heads of men beheaded for treason. It had made her shudder: the price of betrayal was a dreadful death. And London had its dark side; there were many poor and ragged people living in squalor; there were rats and diseases...

Kate tugged herself from her thoughts, glad that she lived in Markyate. Residing at The Strand all the time would not suit her. She loved the common too much, riding her horse among the shadowy trees.

She heard a shout outside, felt the coach slow down and wondered what the problem was.

The coach driver gave a sharp cry and the horses came to a stop outside a small house with barns and stables. Kate looked out and saw a man she recognised as Lambert Wilmott, the parish constable. He had visited The Cell often to speak to Thomas about business and Kate always felt uncomfortable in his presence. He seldom spoke to her directly, but his gaze was appraising and disrespectful. He was a man with a large stomach, which made him sway as he walked, and currently he was rolling towards the coach.

He leaned in and Kate could smell his rancid breath as he spoke. 'Good morrow and well met, Mistress Fanshawe. I hope your husband is well.'

'I believe him to be so,' Kate said politely, wishing to say as little as possible.

'The driver tells me you are travelling to London.'

'It is true,' Kate replied.

'And you have paid for the use of this coach?'

'I have – the sum of twenty shillings...'

'Is your journey for business – or for pleasure?' Lambert licked his lips.

'I go to see my cousin Anne at her home on The Strand.' Kate met his eyes, noticing the gleam of interest.

'And when you will return?'

'On Sunday next.'

'I must warn you, mistress, to exercise caution during the journey...' He glanced at her neckline. 'Those are expensive pearls you wear.'

Her hand flew to the cluster of necklaces at the throat. 'My father gave these to my mother...'

'And there are many people on the roads – thieves, vagabonds – who would take them from you. I am vexed to warn you that there are villains about who might endanger your fair life.'

'Who?' Kate frowned.

'Why recently, a most notorious pickpocket and highwaywoman, Moll Frith. She was dubbed "Cutpurse" and was said to be foul-mouthed, incredibly ugly, and to dress like a man and smoke tobacco.'

'What happened to her?'

'She fell down and died of dropsy.'

'So, Moll Frith will not trouble me tonight, Master Wilmott.' Kate raised an eyebrow.

'There are increasing numbers of robbers who regularly watch the coach routes.' He reached a claw out and grabbed her wrist. 'What would you do if such a man forced the coach to stop and tried to take your pearls?'

'Do you think I would faint away, Constable?' Kate was amused. 'Do you think I need an officer to protect me?'

His eyes went to her throat again. 'I believe that to be my duty, Mistress Fanshawe.'

'But you're here, talking to me. You would not be there when this robber stopped the coach,' Kate said simply. 'So if he tried to attack me, I would shoot him with the pistol I keep in my stocking.'

Constable Wilmott studied her ankle, shocked, and Kate suppressed a laugh.

'Do you have a pistol there, Mistress Fanshawe?' His eyes were wide.

'If I did, I would not tell you.' Kate smiled. 'It would be my secret alone...'

His expression was ridiculous; she had no such pistol, but it amused her to think that Wilmott believed it possible.

She leaned out of the carriage. 'Please drive on. I wish to be in London before it is too dark. A solitary woman such as I might tremble at the thought of who might lurk on Nomansland Common.'

She heard the driver crack his whip and the horses bolted forward. Lambert Wilmott's face was twisted in anger as she rolled away, leaving the constable's cottage far behind. Kate shook her head, thinking the parish constable a foolish man. But something prevented her from laughing; he knew her husband, he liked to talk: he could be a dangerous enemy. Men like him were best avoided.

11

THE PRESENT

Charlie slept badly, his mind filled with tattered dreams and the echo of hooves. He woke early, staring at the cracks in the ceiling, listening to Alan snoring at the other end of the bed. He padded towards the window and looked out. It was just light, the sky still purpled and bruised from the sunrise, a mist low on the damp ground. But there was no one there...

'Come on, mate – let's make the most of the day...' Charlie dressed himself quickly as the Labrador lifted his head quizzically. 'We're off for a stroll in the beautiful Hertfordshire countryside.'

It was refreshing to be outside at dawn, with Alan on his lead, heading into the crowded woodlands that led to the common. On the open ground, he let the dog loose to run. Charlie was looking for hoofprints in the damp earth. What he saw last night from his bedroom window had looked like a horse and rider, although the shape had seemed to dissolve in the air. Hoof prints would prove someone had been there, that the sound of a passing horse had been real.

The alternative was unthinkable.

He followed the path he believed the rider would have taken, inspecting the ground for indentations as Alan trotted ahead. Charlie called to him, 'Don't go too far, Alan – wait for me.'

He hurried through the trees towards the scrubland beyond. It was a mellow autumn morning, the horizon obscured by the damp low-lying haze. But there were no prints of horse's hooves on the path, no evidence of a horse galloping through the woodlands at all.

'Hello...' A light voice came from a young woman coming towards him in a bright duffel coat, a woollen hat covering some of her red hair. She was around his age, and he was surprised to see that she had bare legs above her wellington boots, despite the damp air. A fluffy white dog walked calmly at her side.

'Hello.' Charlie turned to the dog. 'That's an interesting breed – is he a husky?'

'No...' The woman smiled. 'She's a Samoyed – she's called Bianca.'

Charlie didn't know what else to say, so he called, 'Alan, come and meet Bianca.'

Alan bounded over and sat down, staring up at Charlie.

The woman paused. 'Alan. That's a great name.' She grinned. 'Bianca used to belong to my auntie, but she found her a bit hard-going when her hip started to give her pain, so I took her on a year ago. Bianca, I mean – not my auntie. I'm so glad I did.'

'I adopted Alan when he was a year old,' Charlie said. 'I've had him for two years. He's great company. He chews my shoes occasionally, but he's well behaved.'

Alan woofed in agreement, offered a smug expression, then he rushed off to play in a heap of leaves.

The woman reached down to pat her dog. 'I often walk Bianca out here before breakfast while I'm in PJs – I suppose now the winter's coming I ought to dress more warmly. But the weather's so mild. Sadly, we'll see more warm autumns – it's a signal of climate change.'

'Right...' Charlie glanced at Alan, who was snuffling at the bark of a tree.

'He shouldn't chew oak bark – it's toxic to dogs,' the woman said and Charlie called, 'Alan.'

Alan looked up and bounced back, to sit at his heel.

'He's very obedient,' the woman remarked, looking down at Bianca, who hadn't moved. She was pristine, her pink tongue hanging out.

'He is...' Charlie wasn't sure what to say – he was keen to resume his walk.

The woman said, 'You're from number one?'

It took him a moment to work out that she was referring to Constable's Cottages. He nodded. 'Yes, I'm doing the place up.'

'I know – I live in number three.'

'The one with the solar panels.'

'Yes.' The woman offered an engaging smile.

Charlie examined her face. She had freckles; her skin was almost translucent.

She held out a hand. 'I'm Edie Berry.'

'Charlie Wolfe.' Charlie shook her hand briefly. So this was his other neighbour.

'Are you a builder?' She seemed to want to talk.

'Among other things,' Charlie said cryptically.

'Oh, me too, I'm a Jill of all trades,' Edie said chirpily. 'Well, I have several projects on the go. I hardly have time to do them all, but it keeps me out of trouble.'

Charlie nodded as if he understood, and peered over her shoulder. The sun was coming up, bright autumn rays that blinded his eyes.

'Were you foraging?' Edie asked.

'Pardon?'

She laughed lightly, as if he had made a joke. 'When I came along the path, you were staring at the ground. I wondered if you were foraging – or if you'd lost something.'

'No...' Charlie frowned. 'You don't own a horse, do you?'

'I wish,' Edie said. 'I love riding. But no.'

'Only, I thought I heard one last night.'

'Did you? What time?' A small knot appeared between Edie's eyes. Charlie noticed they were hazel and the word sunburst came into his mind. Then Luna's gaze came back to him, blue eyes, round, full of kindness, but so determined on the day she left him.

He remembered Edie had asked him a question. 'Early morning? Two-ish?'

'Oh...' Edie seemed to register his words. 'Well, let me know if you see her again.'

'Her?'

'Mmm.' Edie looked uncomfortable as she reached down to ruffle the Samoyed's white fur. 'Come on, Bianca – it's breakfast time.' She took a few steps along the path, then she called over her shoulder, 'Nice to meet you, Charlie. Come round sometime. I have some homemade wine I need to crack open...'

Charlie watched her go, the bright coat, leopard-print wellingtons, bare legs. He'd met both neighbours now: Edie, and Marilyn from number two. One had made him a carrot cake and the other was offering him wine. Cakes and wine – that wasn't a bad proposition from neighbours.

* * *

Charlie stopped work for an early lunch with Uncle Bill. They were sitting close together on a hop up work platform in the kitchen, shoulders touching. Charlie accepted a flask of hot tea and said, 'Oh – I nearly forgot – I met our other neighbour this morning.'

'Did you?' Bill attacked an egg sandwich. 'The one with the solar panels and the rain harvesting system?'

'Yes, she's called Edie... something.' Charlie had forgotten her surname.

'Edie? Older woman, was she?'

'No, she was my age.'

'Oh.' Bill chuckled. 'Single? Did you ask her? You ought to get round there – chat her up a bit.'

'She's not really my type,' Charlie said flatly. 'She had a fluffy dog, a Samoyed...'

'A Sammy Head? They bark a lot, don't they?' Bill had finished his sandwich and was reaching into his bag. 'Noisy sods.'

'I've haven't heard a dog barking since I moved in. Bianca, she's called.' Charlie smiled – he remembered the dog's name.

'What was she like?' Bill wanted to know.

'The dog or Edie?'

'Edie, you numpty...'

'She was friendly enough. She was walking the dog still wearing pyjamas. She had leopard-print wellies on.'

'You'd better stay clear – she sounds a bit eccentric.' Bill grinned. 'I sneaked a chocolate bar into my packed lunch somewhere – Marcia would be furious if she knew – ah, here it is.' He flourished a huge bar of milk chocolate. 'Want some?'

'No thanks.'

'We're making good progress on the bathroom. You know, Char...' Bill pushed three squares of chocolate into his mouth. 'The rate we're going, we could have the bath and shower in and have started on the bedroom by the end of October.' He stood up, stretching his arms, then he clutched his stomach. 'Ooh, that hurt more than it should.'

Charlie was alarmed. 'Are you all right, Uncle Bill?'

'Indigestion. I had it bad last night. I overdid the mac and cheese Marcia made. I had two massive helpings.'

Charlie felt a surge of envy. 'I love macaroni cheese.'

'I'll get Marce to make you some and you can heat it up here.' Bill rubbed his stomach. 'I had an ache in my back – that's indigestion, isn't it? It went right up to my arms, and my neck, even my jaw hurt. I told Marce her cooking was just too tempting. Of course she told me off. Any excuse.'

'Perhaps you should take it easy, Uncle Bill?'

'Rubbish – hard work and exercise keep me fit and young...' Bill laughed. 'I'm as fit as a butcher's dog.' He indicated Alan, who was stretched on a rug, snoozing. 'Look at him. It's a dog's life. Come on, Charlie – back to work for us. No peace for the wicked.'

* * *

An hour later, Charlie and Bill were nailing floorboards in the bathroom. Charlie scrutinised the newly plastered walls and ceiling, the double-glazed window, and felt a surge of pride. 'This is going to look so good.'

'The mutt's nuts,' Bill agreed without looking up. 'You need to nail the new floorboards at a ninety-degree angle to the original boards for the most stable fit... We'll get the skirting and trim done next. Tonight, you could give the boards a sand down and have a think about varnishing them.'

'I have plenty of time.' Charlie stood up, stretching the muscles in his legs. He looked through the window. 'Those trees in the woodlands are oak and silver birch. Alan and I had a great walk this morning. It's lovely out on the common, just me and him...'

'I bet.' Bill was occupied with nails. 'Nice spot, this. I knew you'd like it. I was talking to a friend of mine in St Albans – he lives off Watling Close, and he reckons we'll be able to sell this place for over double what we paid for it.'

Charlie was hardly listening. 'I saw something funny early this morning...'

'A woman in pyjamas and leopard-print wellies...' Bill grunted, a nail in his mouth as he hammered in another.

'It was about half two this morning. I woke up and heard something just outside, in the woods. It looked like a figure on horseback.'

'Oh?' Bill looked up. 'That's a funny time to be out riding...'

'It was strange...'

'You were probably dreaming, Charlie,' Bill grunted.

'It didn't feel like a dream.' Charlie frowned as he remembered something Edie said to him earlier: *Let me know if you see her again.* Charlie clutched his hammer in his fist, thinking that it was an odd comment. It sounded as if Edie had seen her before. *Her?* What sort of woman rode a horse down from the common through dark woodlands during the night? The horsewoman had paused; she had looked up at him, Charlie was sure of it. He shivered again.

'Are you all right, Charlie?' Bill grunted from where he huddled on his knees on the floorboards, his hammer raised. He gave another short snort. 'You're staring out the window, all funny – just as if you'd seen a ghost.'

* * *

Hours later, Charlie sat at a small table nursing a pint of Neck Oil in The Sycamore Tree, with Alan sprawled on the carpeted floor at his heels. Tuesday nights were quiet in the pub: a family of seven, two adults and five children, all wearing lumberjack shirts, was finishing a meal in the restaurant. There were balloons tied to chairs with the number fourteen on, so it was clearly a birthday celebration.

It was ten o'clock. Charlie had worked late and he felt he deserved a pint. He and Uncle Bill were almost ready to put the bath and the shower in. It would feel lovely to have a hot bath, to be properly clean. Warm water in a bucket wasn't anything like a luxurious soak in a steaming bath to ease aching muscles. He wondered if he could pop round to Edie's house and ask to use the shower – Edie Berry, that was her name. He should have remembered – Berry suited her, she seemed to know a lot about nature – she'd warned Charlie about letting Alan snuffle toxic plants and moss from the bark of an oak. He gave a small laugh: she had made a comment about climate change, so she was probably an ardent activist, an eco-warrior. Charlie imagined she showered in cold rainwater (so maybe borrowing her shower was a non-starter). Perhaps her house was simple and rustic, mandalas on the walls, dreamcatchers at the windows, the air scented with joss sticks. He wondered if she believed in ghosts – she had referred to the horse's rider as 'she'.

Another thought occurred to him – perhaps he should ask her to lend him a dreamcatcher – the sight of the rider in the darkness outside his home had rattled him more than he liked to admit.

He swallowed the last dregs of his pint. He was being silly and felt a sting of guilt. He had no right to prejudge her.

Charlie pushed a fist beneath his chair and Alan licked his fingers. 'You and I need to find some company, Al...' Alan stood up, ready to go home. 'Perhaps I should have invited Edie for a drink – and Marilyn too. I need to get a life.'

Alan woofed once and followed Charlie obediently to the pub door.

Charlie called over his shoulder, 'Thanks. Goodnight...'

'Take it steady, mate,' the barman called after him. He was a middle-aged man, wearing a crisp white shirt, his light hair thinning on top. Charlie should have introduced himself, explained that he'd bought number one and made an effort to be friendly. He'd come back later in the week and try again.

It was completely dark outside, apart from the lights on the pub wall and in the car park. There were no headlights, no traffic as Charlie and Alan crossed the road and walked down gloomy Ferrers Lane. The trees were dense on one side and the common was open grassland on the other. Alan trotted next to him as Charlie increased his pace, passing the entrance that led to the cricket club on the right, the car park to the open common on the left. For some reason, he was keen to be home as soon as possible. The air was cold and stung his face, but there was something else that made him quicken his step.

He pulled his phone from his pocket and switched on the torch as he and Alan turned right onto the narrow path flanked by whispering trees, leading to Constable's Cottages. The meagre beam was just enough to see the road ahead, but Charlie knew the way now. If he kept to the left, he'd avoid a deep pothole. Then, another left turn at the edge of the woodland would bring him just moments from home.

His skin was prickling beneath his jacket and T-shirt, a cold that seemed to soak into the bone. He glanced down to where Alan was loping obediently at his heels and felt a pang of gratitude that he had a constant companion. Then he stopped for a moment, listening.

Alan was immobile too, his ears up. Charlie waited. There was the crackle of rustling leaves, as if someone was close by, watching him. He was being silly; the night wind lifted foliage, made the air cold. It was nothing more.

Charlie set off again quickly. A bird fluttered high in the branches of a tree and it made his heart jolt. He realised he was holding his breath; his pulse was leaping. Just for the relief of hearing his own voice, he said, 'We're nearly home, Al.'

He heard it behind him, a horse breathing through its nose. He froze. Something passed by him at speed, a fast movement of air as if an invisible rider whistled past, brushing his arm. He felt the touch of fingers against his neck, cold as icicles.

He pointed the torch down towards the dog. Alan was cowering, baring his teeth, his eyes shining in the darkness. Charlie felt the breath in his chest shudder. He took off at a run, his dog at his heels, his feet slapping on tarmac. He couldn't get home fast enough.

12

1659

Kate didn't want to go home yet. She was having too much fun in London. She was attending a glittering party at a merchant's house, not far from The Strand, where she was staying with Anne. The ballroom was magnificently decorated, music playing from lutes, a harpsichord, much singing and dancing. An ornate table was weighted with too many dishes of meat, eggs, oysters and cows' tongues on silver plates. A gold voiding dish was already half full of chewed bones.

Anne's husband, Richard, and some of the other men were playing Iryshe and Treygobe, throwing dice. Occasionally, a roar of triumph would be heard from the far corner when someone had won, then a groan of disappointment from the other players. In a corridor, several very young women were chattering gaily together, singing and dancing to 'London Bridge is Broken Down', whispering closely about the other ladies' fine costumes and the handsome men dancing alongside them in the hall.

Kate was sipping spiced wine, talking to her cousin, gazing longingly at the sweets on the table. There were dishes of honey and marzipan, her favourites; edible sculptures called subtleties, of animals, castles, trees and people. Anne wore a beautiful dress made from silver taffeta embroidered in gold with fur trimming and an elegant cap of velvet. Kate's own robe was modest, but she held her head confidently, dressed in an embellished blue gown and embroidered headdress, rows of pearls at her throat, knowing that admiring glances came her way. Anne was aware of it too.

'It is a shame Thomas cannot take his place by your side. There are others here tonight who wish they had a pretty wife such as you.'

Kate smiled. 'I'd rather be here with you, cousin. This townhouse is truly beautiful. And the owner is a gracious man – I have heard Thomas speak of him as a Parliamentarian.'

'He is a Member of Parliament, but he and Richard knew each other as schoolboys.' Anne groaned at the mention of politics. 'His wife is a most pleasant woman.'

'I remember when my father was alive, we had such magnificent parties at The Cell.' Kate closed her eyes. 'Everything was so grand there once – the banqueting hall, the library full of so many books...'

'The Cell is still a beautiful home,' Anne said. 'Was it not once a Benedictine priory?'

'It was, in the twelfth century until around a hundred years ago. But a home is made by the people who fill it and I am often alone.'

'If only you had children...' Anne misunderstood, placing a hand kindly on Kate's. 'I have borne thirteen thus far, but only my four daughters survive. I long for a son. My little ones bring me more joy than I imagined possible. I named Katherine after you.'

'Thomas and I do not share a bedroom...' Kate said simply. It was unwise to say too much to Anne, who would be sure to pass on everything to her husband. She knew the Fanshawes expected her to provide an heir for Thomas. 'Thomas is often away, so in his absence, I have taken myself off to sleep in the chamber I slept in when I was six years old, with the secret passage that leads to the kitchen. I used to make use of it as a small child – I'd often creep from my room at night down to the kitchen to steal sweet treats that our cook used to leave out.'

'It is a shame The Cell is not as it once was,' Anne agreed. 'I visited Markyate as a child and I thought it the most wonderful place.' She surveyed the grand hall with its high arches, watching the musicians and the sedate dancers, their chins tilted high. 'You should sell it and move here to London. We could have such fun.'

'Oh, I could not – it is all that remains of my father's memory,' Kate said quickly. 'But this house is most beautiful, a perfect place for a party.'

'It may look perfect, but the servants work hard to keep it so. Here they burn asafoetida in the roof often, and the cellars, so that the rats will go elsewhere.' Anne looked sad. 'Rats are everywhere in London, and they bring disease. I believe they will be the undoing of the people here. And oh, the fleas. My children's heads are always full of them, despite Mary's ministrations.'

Kate remembered. 'Bea fills a dripping pan with Venice turpentine mixed with a little honey, then puts the trap in the bed in the morning between the sheets. By evening, she finds fleas sticking in the turpentine, as thick as wasps in a honey pot.'

'I will have to tell this to Mary, and she can do the same.' Anne shuddered. 'Meanwhile, let us not think of these things.' She lifted her goblet to her lips. 'Oh, my cup is quite empty. I must ask for it to be filled.'

'And I can see someone I know.' Kate smiled at the man who was striding purposefully towards her, a goblet of wine held high, as Anne shuffled away. She held out her hand. 'Master Pepys, it is so good to meet you again.'

'Mistress Fanshawe.' Samuel Pepys kissed her hand gallantly. 'I note you still attend parties alone.'

'It is by far the superior way to attend parties,' Kate quipped.

'So where is your good-for-nothing scoundrel of a husband this time?' Samuel asked. Kate enjoyed his company; he was her age, flamboyant, wearing a fashionable long wig and a silk scarf, a man who cared everything about his appearance but who pretended not to give a jot.

'Thomas is fighting in the north for the king, I believe,' Kate said by way of explanation.

'Does he know you are here? Would he not be furious?'

'I doubt he knows – or that he cares.' Kate raised an eyebrow.

'Thomas Fanshawe is a rascally fellow, without a penny in his purse,' Samuel said, inspecting the lace cuffs of his jacket. 'The way he lives off your inheritance is an outrage and a disgrace. Everyone thinks so... The scallywag will spend every penny you have,' Samuel retorted. 'Then what will you do, my dear?'

'I will live off my wits,' Kate said. 'And how is your wife?'

'Elisabeth does not enjoy these gatherings,' Samuel replied. 'She's a descendant of French Huguenots, so she's decidedly phlegmatic. Whereas I am sanguine – I revel in a good banquet and dancing and dressing in my best.'

'We both married too young,' Kate said sadly. 'Were you not two and twenty, and your poor wife fourteen years old?'

'As is the fashion, but I enjoy myself still – I live the high life in London, and you hide away in Hertfordshire and grow increasingly poor.' He took her hand. 'Perhaps you should move here – it would be certainly less dreary if you came to more parties.'

'Anne tells me constantly that I should. Have you always lived in London, Samuel?'

'Oh no – I spent my childhood in the countryside. I was the fifth of eleven children, but quickly the oldest survivor. My mother sent me to live with a nurse, Goody Lawrence at Kingsland, but I didn't like it there. London is in my veins – they are dark with Thames river water.' Samuel gave a laugh and pointed at a severe-looking man. 'Oh look – there's Master Andrew Marvell. Have you met him? He has a wonderful mind – he writes the most incredible lyric poems, Latin poems, and political and satirical pamphlets. You wouldn't believe it to look at him that he'd be capable of writing such lines...'

'What lines?'

'Oh, the most wonderful poem about seduction...' Samuel coughed lightly and began to quote.

> *Let us roll all our strength and all*
> *Our sweetness up into one ball,*
> *And tear our pleasures with rough strife*
> *Through the iron gates of life.'*

Kate held her breath. 'He speaks of love – of not holding back from it, making the most of the brief time we have to live.' She felt her pulse quicken. 'Oh, how true that is.'

'He might be better to spend less time on writing and more time on lovemaking – see how unhappy he looks,' Samuel commented. 'Although I agree with his sentiments exactly. I myself am a little too fond of fondling the breasts of my maid Mary Mercer while she dresses me each morning.'

Kate chose to ignore his comment – she had heard rumours of Samuel's many affairs. 'I have never spoken to Master Marvell.' She watched the poet, who was some fifteen years older than her, busy in conversation.

'Perhaps it's best not to meet him tonight. He's a Yorkshireman and a Parliamentarian, a wonderful satirist and poet, but he's inclined to bad humour. I myself sway between King and Parliament, depending on whom I am speaking to. Tonight, however, due to the allegiance of our wonderful hosts, I am for Cromwell... the Royalists' army is more focused on looting than battle tactics. The sack at this house is exceptional, the meats are delicious. Have you tried the cows' tongues?'

'I have not. Samuel, do my husband's loyalties to the King anger you? I know nothing would possess him to come to a gathering such as this and he would disapprove of my being here.'

'I care not for the man, Kate, but I am a good friend of his wife's.' Samuel pointed to an older man who was engrossed in a serious conversation with several others. 'Over there is John Milton. Do you know him?'

'We have met, a year ago, when I was visiting Anne,' Kate said. 'I found him a brilliant man, but I fear he found me tedious.'

'Not at all. He has recently been widowed and a man has need of a good wife. He lost two wives, both due to complications after their lying in. I fear it has made him a little phlegmatic and cold, but I expect he will marry again and that will cure him of his sourness.'

Kate wondered if Samuel was joking. She leaned towards him. 'You seem to know everyone here.'

'Almost.'

She put her mouth close to his ear. 'Then pray, introduce me to a good jeweller who pays well...'

'Why, my dear Kate – what do you wish to buy?'

'Not to buy, but to sell...' Kate touched the cluster of pearls at her throat. 'Your talk of husbands and penury has given me an idea. I know of people living on Fanshawe farmlands who have more need of these little stones than I do.'

* * *

The following morning, Kate made an excuse to Anne that she was going shopping for spices for Beatrice and took a coach to a grand house in Bread Street Hill. She was shown into an ornate drawing room by a lean manservant with a stoop, where she waited for ten minutes for Master Joshua Garvey to arrive. He wore a tight doublet, padded trunk hose and stockings, and shook her hand with plump fingers as he met her eyes hopefully.

'Master Pepys tells me you are his friend.' He placed a stubby finger over his mouth. 'And I believe these beautiful pearls belong to you, mistress, and that you wish to sell them before your husband does. But not a word of it will pass my lips.'

'Thank you,' Kate said politely. She glanced around the room: elegant portraits framed in gold hung on the wall, bowls of gold and silver on a low table. The jeweller was clearly a rich man, and shrewd. 'I want the best price, though – or I will take my business elsewhere.' She took the pearls from beneath her dark velvet cape and held them out, allowing the light to gleam on the surface. She felt a moment's sadness – they had always been favourites. But they were expensive, they would fetch a good price.

'What lustre...' Joshua Garvey held his breath. 'These pearls have been in your family for a while?'

'Indeed, but either I will sell them now or my husband will sell them later. And I have need of money for an... investment I wish to make.' Kate flourished the pearls. 'Name your price.'

Garvey held out his hand and Kate reluctantly placed them in his moist palm. He inspected them carefully, turning them over once, once again. 'They are lovely...'

'And they have significance.' Kate held her breath. 'Pearls are used as talismans to provide protection during battle...'

'Your husband is away fighting, Mistress Fanshawe?'

'It matters not in the sale of these pearls, Master Garvey...'

He leaned towards her and whispered a number in her ear, followed by the word *guineas*.

Kate whisked the pearls from his hand and drew them beneath her cape, turning quickly, making for the door. 'I fear I am wasting my time here, sir...'

'But it is a fair price.'

'I was led to believe you were an honest jeweller – not a common cutpurse.'

'Mistress...' Garvey called out desperately. Kate was halfway through the doorway. 'Mistress, I will give you half as much again.'

Kate whirled back. 'Double your sum.'

'You are asking too much...'

'I know what the pearls are worth.' Kate's eyes flashed with indignation. 'I will show myself out, *sirrah!*'

Garvey winced at the derogatory word. 'But Mistress Fanshawe...'

'You have insulted me, and I will take my pearls elsewhere.' She was ready to leave.

Garvey panted, 'Double... I will pay double...'

'My price has since risen, due to your tardiness – it is now double and twenty guineas more.' Kate held up the pearls. 'My farmers deserve the highest price.'

Garvey lowered his head and held out his hand to shake. 'You drive a hard bargain, mistress.'

'The pearls are worth every penny, you know it.'

'I will not make a great deal of profit when I sell them on...'

'It matters little to me.' Kate took his hand. 'You will give me double – and twenty guineas more – or the price will rise yet again.'

'As you wish.' Garvey reached eager fingers for the pearls.

'Money first, then I will hand you my necklace,' Kate said firmly.

She heard him mutter the word 'shrew' beneath his breath, then he gave a small bow, a pretence of politeness.

'Thanking you, mistress. And come to me again when you have more jewels to sell. But' – Garvey recoiled like a snake – 'I feel sorry for your poor husband. Today you have taken more money from Joshua Garvey than any man ever could. Beshrew me if you are not some kind of highway robber in the making...'

'Be careful what you say, Master Garvey.' Kate raised an eyebrow. 'Did not our great William Shakespeare say "We know what we are but know not what we may be..."'

13

THE PRESENT

Charlie stood in the bathroom, his hands on his hips, and grinned. 'It's amazing, Uncle Bill.'

'I said we'd do it.' Bill agreed. 'Five o'clock, and the room's finished, by the first Friday in October too – bang on schedule. We'll begin on your bedroom on Monday.'

'I'll make a start on getting the plaster off the walls first thing tomorrow. Tonight, I'm having a shower.'

'All work and no play?' A momentary look of concern crossed Bill's face. 'Come for dinner with me and Marce. She's cooking *pupusas*, a stack of them, full of oozy cheese...'

'Sounds tempting, but I want to put all my time into doing up the house.'

'You haven't stopped working, every day, weekends...' Bill folded his arms stubbornly. 'I'm worried about you. A young lad of your age should be down the pub, out with friends, girls...'

'We all meet on WhatsApp,' Charlie protested, but he knew Bill was right. 'OK, I'll take a break next weekend. We'll go out for Sunday lunch – my treat.'

'What do you do here on your own?'

'I'm not on my own – I have my best mate.' Charlie glanced at Alan, who was snoozing in his basket. 'We lie on the mattress and read or listen to music, or I play the sax. Sometimes we just sit at the window and look out at the common...' He lapsed into thought: he hadn't heard or felt the strange horse and rider since the night he and Alan had walked back from The Sycamore Tree in the dark. 'Uncle Bill – do you believe in ghosts?'

Bill laughed. 'The only spirit I believe in is one at the bottom of a glass. I just bought some of that Scotch they advertise on TV, the one with the unpronounceable name. It's very good stuff, mind. You should come over one evening and we could have a session...' He noticed Charlie's expression. 'You're not saying this house is haunted?'

'Oh, no – the place is just crying out to be given some TLC. It's the woodlands outside, the common. It can be a bit creepy at night-time...'

'Can it?' Bill's eyes widened. 'I'll be driving home in the darkness before long – I don't want to hear any bumps and bangs.'

On cue, a thumping came from the front door.

Bill leaped with fright. 'Now who the hell's that?'

'I'll go.' Charlie winked, hurrying downstairs.

Marilyn from number two stood outside, smiling, holding out a plate with a Victoria sponge on it. 'Hello, Charlie.'

'Hi – that cake looks tempting.'

'Oh, it's for your Uncle Bill. I'm sure he'll give you a slice...' Marilyn glanced over his shoulder. 'Is he in? I wanted to say thank you. He fixed the loose tile on my roof quick as you like, and he wouldn't take a penny for it. And when he came down from the ladder, he was all hot and bothered...'

'He's not a fan of heights,' Charlie explained. 'That's not great when you're a builder. But he manages.'

'How?' Marilyn was impressed.

'He doesn't look down,' Charlie said.

'Is he still here? His van's parked next to yours...'

'Yes, we were just packing up...' Charlie heard Bill clattering downstairs and moved out of the way to let him through.

Bill offered Marilyn a smile. 'That looks nice. Did you make it for Charlie?'

'For you,' Marilyn insisted. 'To say thanks for fixing the tile.'

'It looks good. My wife will kill me, eating cake.' Bill took the plate gratefully. 'But I love a bit of sponge.'

'I'd make cake for you every week if you were my other half,' Marilyn said, smoothing her hair. 'Your wife is from Honduras, you say?'

'Yes, she's a great cook. You'll have to meet her.'

'Bring her round for a cuppa,' Marilyn suggested. 'And you can take a look at my window frames, if you would. They are getting a bit rotten – I'm not sure if I need replacement windows. I don't suppose you put windows in, do you?'

Charlie took in her hopeful expression. 'Uncle Bill can do anything – he's the best builder in St Albans.'

'Oh, I'm sure,' Marilyn cooed.

'We were just talking about ghosts,' Bill said with blustering confidence. 'Charlie reckons it's a bit creepy around here...'

'I've lived here for fifteen years and I've never been troubled by any ghosts. I don't believe in them, to tell the truth.' Marilyn's face was an expression of disbelief. 'There are those who think they have seen something a bit odd down Ferrers Lane, but I don't have a vivid imagination. Down to earth, that's me.'

Charlie was ready to ask about the rumours concerning Ferrers Lane, but Bill said, 'Well, it's Friday night and there will be a hot meal waiting for me on the table. You sure you won't come, Charlie?'

'He needs to get out more,' Marilyn agreed. 'I can hear him most nights playing his music.'

Charlie grinned an apology. 'I have a date with my new power shower tonight. Tomorrow I'm starting on my bedroom.'

'Oh? What will you do to that?' Marilyn asked.

'I thought a big four-poster bed, scarlet walls for passion, quadrophonic speakers blaring out Barry White – it'd be a nice little love nest,' Bill teased.

'Or all black and white with Playboy bunny wallpaper?' Marilyn suggested.

Charlie had no idea if she was being serious, so he said quickly, 'White walls, clean lines, lots of space for my musical instruments...'

'There's no girlfriend then?' Marilyn observed.

'No one at the moment,' Charlie said.

'He had one, but she went off to Cornwall to follow her career,' Bill explained.

'Oh, what a shame,' Marilyn said. 'Can't you google yourself a new girl-friend? Everyone gets them off the internet now. Not that I'd do internet dating – I like to meet people in the flesh...' She glanced at Bill.

Charlie decided not to take the conversation any further. He offered his chirpiest grin. 'You get off home, Uncle Bill, and have some downtime. I need to take Alan for a walk.'

'On the common, through those shady woods? Ooooh.' Bill gave an exaggerated shiver. 'You'd better watch out for the ghost.'

Charlie shuddered involuntarily. 'I will. I mean, there's probably no ghost there. Imagination, that's all. We'll just take a walk and then we'll get some food. I'm air frying sweet potato jackets with tahini and I might have a beer...'

'You youngsters know how to live,' Bill said with a wink. He glanced down – Alan had woken up and lumbered downstairs. He was now leaning against Charlie's legs, looking up hopefully. 'Someone's ready for his walkies.'

'He's such a well-behaved dog,' Marilyn said. 'I never hear him barking.'

'He'd be useless as a guard dog,' Bill joked. 'Right, I'll see you bright and early on Monday, Char.'

'I'll have the walls started, the old plaster off,' Charlie promised, but Bill was whistling, on his way towards the van and Marilyn was disap-pearing inside number two. Charlie bent down and hugged Alan. 'Peace and quiet, eh, mate? Just me and you. What about a nice walk.' He placed a kiss on the dog's nose. 'And no more visitations, right? We don't believe in ghostly horsewomen, do we, Al?'

* * *

Twenty minutes later, Charlie was under the shower, hot water bouncing off his skin, steam misting up the cubicle. His eyes were closed and he was in heaven. The temperature was turned up just a little too much, the water almost excruciatingly hot, and Charlie loved the way it enveloped him, making him feel clean and warmed through. He began to sing at the top of his voice. For some reason, he was bawling out Bon Jovi's 'Livin' on a Prayer', hitting the high notes with extra gusto. Why not? He had a power shower – the world was his oyster.

He heard something – a creak, a step on the landing, a voice. He stopped singing mid-note; the only sound was the persistent rainfall of the shower. If there was an intruder, why wasn't Alan barking?

Charlie pressed the button and the shower was silent.

There was another sound just outside the door. He could hear a light movement. A quiet voice said, 'Hello, Alan – you remember me? Good boy.'

'Who's there?' Charlie could hear the tension in his voice.

Someone was standing in the doorway, looking at him. Through the shower screen, he could see a small frame, loose curls of red hair, a black jacket. The figure jerked back out of sight again. Her voice came from the landing. 'I'm so sorry – the front door was open. I did knock.'

'Hang on.' Charlie's hands went to his thighs, then he yelled, 'Give me a moment...'

He clambered out of the shower, reaching for towels, one around his waist, another on his head, patting away moisture with a third. Quickly, he pulled on a T-shirt, boxers, jeans. Water streamed from his hair down his face. He hadn't rinsed it properly – it was sticky and thick with conditioner.

'Hello...?' he called out, trying to sound blasé. Towel in hand, he rubbed his hair vigorously as Edie Berry came into the bathroom looking sheepish.

'Charlie – oh, I'm so sorry...'

'I didn't realise I'd left the door open.'

'You had. I knocked – and when I couldn't get an answer, I came in... I heard running water. I wondered if there was a leak... so I just came up, then I heard you singing. I'm sorry, really... that was stupid of me...' Edie glanced around the bathroom nervously. 'It's looking good.' She was even more awkward now. 'I mean, the decorating...' She blushed with embarrassment and Charlie felt no better.

He offered a grin as compensation.

'I enjoyed your rendition just now of "Livin' on a Prayer"... you've got a good voice,' Edie mumbled by way of an apology, then she said, 'Sorry – I shouldn't have come up.'

'So, Edie, what can I do for you? I mean...' His skin was still damp, his face was wet, and he had soap in his eyes. 'Did you come here for something in particular...?' Alan scurried into the bathroom, leaping excitedly. Charlie murmured, 'Calm down, mate – it's only Edie...' He wondered if he sounded dismissive.

'I wanted to invite you for supper tomorrow.' Edie looked away, deliberately avoiding Charlie's eyes. 'If you're not doing anything?'

'No...'

'Then come round and have something to eat with me... as neighbours...'

'Right...'

'I mean – I haven't welcomed you here yet... to Constable's Cottages.'

Charlie took a breath. 'No, yes, that would be great, thanks.'

Edie was studying his damp T-shirt, then she looked away again. 'Is there anything you don't eat? I mean, foods I should avoid? Allergies?'

Charlie tried to think of something to say. 'I'm not a great fan of cucumber...'

'I won't use cucumber then. Are you OK with mushrooms?'

'Real ones?' Charlie replied without thinking. 'I mean... proper mushrooms from a shop?' He was digging a hole. 'As opposed to foraging on the common?' He was making things worse.

'I get them from the supermarket.' Edie laughed.

Charlie looked relieved. 'That's good.'

'I'll make a risotto,' Edie said. 'And I've got some homemade elderberry wine. Is that all right?'

'It sounds lovely.' Charlie was almost looking forward to an evening with Edie. It would be nice to have home-cooked food, a glass of wine, maybe sit by an open fire in a house that was completely renovated. As opposed to an unheated derelict shell and an air fryer.

'Oh – and can you bring Alan?' Edie added. 'Bianca would love to see him.'

'Is she OK with other dogs?'

'She's an angel,' Edie said. 'Right, I'd better go. I've got a shift to cover in The Sycamore Tree tonight.'

'Ah...' Charlie put a fist to his head – he remembered where he'd first seen Edie, in the pub, the day Uncle Bill had treated him to cod and chips when they'd first viewed the house. She'd brought their meal. 'Do you work there?' Charlie shook his head, feeling foolish – of course she worked there – she'd just said so. 'I mean – is that your job? Full time?'

'No – I just do a few shifts to make a bit of pocket money,' Edie said.

Charlie wasn't sure if she was joking. In truth, he hadn't got the measure of her yet. It might be a strange dinner, sharing risotto and home-made wine with someone he hardly knew. But he was grateful – the company would be welcome; he'd let himself become solitary. 'Thanks for the invitation...'

'You're welcome – I'm looking forward to it. So – I'll see you... around seven?' Edie said, and with that she disappeared downstairs, calling, 'I'll close the door behind me.'

Charlie stood in damp clothes and wondered if he ought to get back in the shower and wash his hair properly. Two scalding-hot, delicious showers, one after the other, might be just what he needed. Alan cocked his head to one side quizzically, and Charlie laughed out loud. 'What are you staring at, Alan? You'd better have a wash too. Tomorrow night, you have a hot date with a Samoyed...'

14

1659

The carriage and four horses clattered through the gated entrance to The Cell on Sunday afternoon. Kate peered through the window and felt her spirits soar. She adored The Cell; her home was the backdrop to her happiest memories: walking with her parents in the grounds as a child, listening to their stories beside the lake, by the leaping fountain. She loved everything about the place: the grass was a gleaming emerald in the last of the sunlight, and the building had a sturdiness and a familiarity to it that tugged at her heartstrings. She felt safe, protected, she belonged there.

As the carriage pulled up outside the main entrance where John was waiting, Kate clambered out, looking every bit the fashionable London lady. She examined her soft gloves as the driver dealt with her luggage before heaving himself back in his seat, lifting his whip as the horses trotted away.

Kate was in a merry mood. 'It's so good to be home, John. Where is Bea? Is she cooking dinner? I've brought her some wonderful spices from Baynard's Castle – cloves, pepper and cinnamon, and a red powder called paprika. And I have brought some Gascon wine, which I know you will enjoy.'

'Thank you, mistress.' John inclined his head. 'I trust you had a successful journey, and that your time in London was profitable.'

'Oh, it was...' Kate thought of the silk purse full of guineas that she carried. She was already imagining what she would do with the money, how she might help the Salters, the Hargreves and the Woollcotts. And, at the back of her mind, she imagined riding Shadow to Ayers End Farm to enquire how Vulcan was progressing, and to tell Raife Chetwyn that he need not pay rent on the farm for the rest of the year. She imagined the light in his eyes as she told him the good news.

John's voice dragged her from her thoughts. '...So I had him put in the stables, mistress. You can imagine my surprise. I was not expecting a caller yesterday afternoon...'

'Pardon, John...?' Kate gave him her full attention.

'While you were away, you had a visitor. Yesterday, a gentleman called to see you. He expected you to be at home, I believe. He brought you a horse. I had Peter take the beast to the stables. A stallion, his name is Midnight. Peter thinks he is a very fine specimen. The gentleman who brought him...'

'What gentleman?'

'A Master Chaplin, if I heard his name aright,' John said. 'He spoke quietly, but I believe he was called Chaplin. Ralph Chaplin.'

Kate caught her breath. He was referring to Raife Chetwyn. She trembled at the thought that he had called round to see her, that he had brought her a gift, a horse. Her thoughts moved quickly: perhaps it might be better if John did not know his name.

'Did Master... Chaplin say why he called? It was very kind of him to send a horse for me. I have wanted a companion to Shadow for a long time. How much...' Kate took another quick breath. 'How much do I owe him?'

'It appears you owe him nothing.' John's face was composed, as if Kate's acquaintances were none of his concern. 'Master Chaplin said the horse was a gift. He said you did him a kindness. He said you would understand.'

'Oh...' Kate had no idea what to say. 'Well, I am glad of it. I owe Master Chaplin my thanks, at least.' She glanced over to the stables. 'I long to see the stallion. Perhaps I might ride Midnight before we eat? It would be very pleasant to—'

John coughed. 'I think it may be wise to wait until tomorrow morning, mistress...' His eyes moved to the open door behind him.

'Why would I wait?' Kate said. 'Is there another matter I need to deal with in the house?' She was suddenly anxious. 'Is Bea well?'

'Oh, she enjoys good health, thank you. No, mistress, something pressing needs your attention...' John lowered his voice. 'He has come home.'

'Who has?' Kate's eyes widened.

'Master Thomas...'

'He is home? To stay?' Kate was momentarily stunned. 'I thought he was in the north counties...'

'He arrived this morning. His visit is fleeting, I believe,' John said sombrely. 'He wishes to speak with you. I told him you were away in London. He was not aware of your absence, but he intends to stay tonight and leave tomorrow. There is an uprising in Cheshire and he will return there to fight for the king.'

Kate felt suddenly exhausted. 'I will speak to him. Where is he now?'

'In the library, mistress.'

'I shall go to my room first. I am weary after my journey and I wish to bathe. I would like some of the Castile soap that makes me smell so sweet. Thomas may wait downstairs while I change my clothes. Please would you ask Bea to come up to my chamber?'

'Mistress, I will.'

'John...' Kate offered him a troubled expression. 'Why do I always feel downcast when Thomas comes home?'

John made a muffled sound. 'Perhaps it is because he invariably asks you for money, mistress.'

Kate thought of the guineas in her purse. She had sold her jewellery to help local people. The money was never intended for Thomas to help the king. A frown formed a knot between her eyes. 'Well, this time, John, I will tell him no.' She swept up the steps into the house. 'I have funded the Royalist army for long enough. It's about time I told him that there are other priorities.'

* * *

An hour later, Kate strode into the library wearing a fresh linen shift, an elaborate crimson kirtle and gown, a pretty cap. It was important to be well-dressed and coiffed, to show Thomas that she needed nothing from him. She had told Beatrice this as she dressed; she was mistress of The Cell whether Thomas was home or not, and she was determined that he would know it.

He stood up as she came in; she noticed he had been leafing through two books. She glanced at the titles: *The Anatomy of Melancholy* by Robert Burton; *Microcosmographie* by John Earle. The books interested her as little as her husband did.

She held out a hand in greeting. 'It is pleasant to see you, Thomas. You look well.'

Kate thought about her words. In truth, it wasn't pleasant to see him, and he didn't look particularly well; his clothes were crumpled, as if he cared little for his appearance. He had gained weight; his chin was rounded and soft.

She believed he seemed uncomfortable about something – he had bad news. He couldn't meet her eyes.

'I'm not staying, Katherine.'

She feigned disappointment. 'You will stay for supper, surely? Beatrice has cooked lamb...'

'I will have supper in the dining room with some wine. I will retire to my room afterwards. I leave tomorrow.'

'For Ireland?' Kate pretended not to know how he spent his time.

'For Cheshire. George Booth leads our advancing armies, and I intend to join him. This time, our uprising will be successful and we will restore Charles the Second as the rightful king of England...'

Kate was half listening. 'So why have you come here? Why did you not stay in Cheshire?'

'I need money.' Thomas took a step forward. 'The king needs money.'

'You mean the king needs *my* money...' Kate made her expression firm. 'You have sold my father's properties in Flamstead and Fullerton, and the land at Bayford, Ponsbourne and Agnells. But you will not sell any more of the farmland. The farmers do their best to make their lands profitable and pay high rents – I have seen much work at Ayers End Farm – and I will not see good people made homeless.'

Thomas sneered. 'You have no say about what I do, Katherine. Anyway, the money from small farms is not enough. The king needs much more.'

'What more do I have that you can sell, Thomas?' Kate met his eyes. 'You have in these last eleven years taken my inheritance and profited from my father's lands...'

'I will sell this place.'

'This place?' It took Kate a moment to understand his words. 'The Cell? My home?'

'It belongs to me. The Cell will fetch a good sum. It will go a long way to help the king recover from the treacherous—'

'You speak of treachery?' Kate was astonished. 'And yet you will sell my home? No, Thomas.'

'I have already decided it. I will find a buyer...'

'And what of me? Where will I live?'

'You can stay at The Strand with your cousin.'

'In London? With Anne and her children?' Kate inhaled. 'But I live here.'

'You will live here for a few months more. Then you will move to London.'

'I don't want to live in London, Thomas.'

'It matters not. I have decided it,' Thomas said simply.

'Then you can *undecide* it.' Kate was furious. 'I forbid you to sell my home.'

'There is little to be done.' Thomas smirked. 'The king needs money and your needs are of little importance to me.'

'You will not put me from my home,' Kate asserted.

'What would you do? Do you have other properties I can dispose of in place of The Cell?' Thomas seemed bored with the conversation. 'It is time for me to have supper. I need a good glass of wine. There is no more to discuss.' He stretched languorously and made to leave.

As he passed Kate, she grabbed his arm.

He offered a supercilious look. 'You are not important in this matter,

Katherine. You will do as I bid. In several months' time, you will move to
London.'

Kate spoke before she knew it. 'I will give you money.'

'What money?' Thomas looked as if he might laugh. 'You would buy
The Cell from me?'

'I will give you money for the king. In exchange, you will not sell my
home.'

'You would do that? How, may I ask?' Thomas looked barely interested.

'I will find a way,' Kate said determinedly.

'Then we will talk more when you do...' Thomas said smugly as he
moved towards the door. 'Now, if you'll excuse me.'

Kate heard the door click and her first wish was that her husband
would choke on the roast leg of lamb he would eat for supper. But she
stood for a moment, resolute, thinking. She had sold her pearls. There
were just a few remaining jewels she could sell, special pieces that had
belonged to her mother. It might keep Thomas happy for a while. But the
money would not last long. She would have to find another way to keep
him from selling her beloved home.

She pressed her fist to her mouth, thinking hard. She was a woman, a
wife. She had no father she could turn to, no relatives. If she had been a
man, it would have been easier – she could make decisions about what
happened to her.

Frustration took her for a moment, hot tears in her eyes. 'That man will
not decide what befalls me. I will not allow it.'

Her small fists were clenched, as if she would hit him. The injustice
made her blood boil. Why should Thomas have power to determine what
became of her? It was not fair. But she would not cry; she would not yield.

Then, out of desperation, out of complete hopelessness, it came to her.
There was a way. It made no sense – it was reckless, daring, bound to fail.
But it was a chance and suddenly Kate's pulse was racing with the idea that
she could do something to decide her own fate.

Yes, there was one way – only one.

Kate would not go down for supper. She had some thinking to do, some
organising. Tomorrow, before Thomas left, she would chatter gaily, smile;

she would be in a merry mood, and he would suspect nothing. But tonight, she'd stay in her room. She had plans to make.

15

THE PRESENT

Charlie was out of practice. That was the only reason he was behaving so indecisively. It had taken him almost half an hour to make up his mind about what T-shirt to wear. He had an old Greenpeace T-shirt with a Roy Lichtenstein blonde woman on the front, her speech bubble proclaiming 'Not in my Backyard', while a disposal truck deposited noxious waste. Luna had bought it for him two years ago. Under the circumstances, it wouldn't be a good choice to wear for dinner with Edie.

Perhaps he should wear a smart shirt with black jeans? He had a candy-striped one that was clean, all pink and green, worn once. His mother had bought it for him and he thought it made him look like a stick of rock.

It occurred to him that he had precious few clothes he'd chosen and bought for himself. He tried on a plain white Henley top and decided it would show up the risotto he was bound to spill down the front.

He'd never normally take this amount of time over what to wear. What was happening to him? Usually, he'd just throw on anything clean and be confident that it fitted him well and he looked good in it. It didn't even matter what he wore tonight – it was just a neighbourly supper. He wasn't attracted to Edie, nor was she attracted to him.

He paused to think about that one. She had seen him in the shower.

She hadn't looked away. For some reason, the idea of a woman finding him attractive made him feel sad. He was in no position to do anything about a relationship. He might never be...

He found a black cotton T-shirt and teamed it with black jeans. He'd look like a jazz musician, but it didn't matter. It was ten past seven – he was late. But at least it wasn't far to go, and Alan was ready, watching him keenly from his basket.

Charlie wondered if he smelled of the damp in the cottage. He sprayed some eau de toilette on his wrists, an Yves Saint Laurent that Luna had loved. She'd said it made him smell masculine, whatever that meant. All roads led back to Luna.

When he arrived at number three, Alan at his heels, Edie opened the door in a short floral dress and bare feet. Her red curls had been clipped up, but tendrils were falling over her face. Charlie assumed it was because she'd been cooking. She might have been wearing eyeliner, Charlie wasn't sure.

She smiled, a little nervous. 'Charlie – come in, come in. Welcome. Alan too. I hope he hasn't eaten – I've made him dinner.'

Charlie was surprised. 'Mushroom risotto?'

'No, mushrooms are toxic for dogs...' Edie ushered him inside. 'I've made him some roast sweet potatoes, carrots, peas, pumpkin and brown rice. He'll love it. Bianca does.'

'Right.' Charlie followed Edie into the spacious farmhouse kitchen and stopped to take in the layout: glowing lights, wooden cabinets, a stainless-steel sink, a small round table. 'This is nice.'

'I designed it – all the wood is reclaimed, and I got the Aga to cook on and heat the water. The floor is cork – did you know that the bark of the cork oak regrows after being cut and can be harvested every nine years?'

Charlie was impressed. 'Did you do all this by yourself?'

'I got someone to help me put it in.'

'It must have been expensive...' Charlie wished he hadn't mentioned money. 'I mean, renovating costs a lot. I know that.'

Edie shrugged as if she didn't mind explaining. 'I came out of a relationship with a house to sell. We split the money and it gave me the chance to create the sort of home I wanted. Oh, here she is...'

Bianca strolled in, noticing Alan, who sat quietly at Charlie's feet. She walked up to him, sniffed him for three seconds and moved away.

Edie was delighted. 'They are friends.'

'That didn't take long,' Charlie said awkwardly, wishing he felt so calm after such a short introduction. He remembered the bottle of wine he was holding. 'I brought this – I know you've got your own homemade but...'

Edie took it and placed it on the worktop. 'Chilean Merlot. Great.'

Charlie wasn't sure if she really meant that – her placid facial expression might have meant it would be thrown straight down the sink after he left, and for a moment he was tempted to take it back.

Edie indicated the table. 'Shall we eat?'

She ladled rice into bowls as Charlie made himself comfortable. She placed two bowls down on the floor for Alan and Bianca, and the two dogs were immediately snuffling noisily. Edie sat down.

Charlie ate a mouthful of his risotto. It was very tasty. 'This is good. Are you a vegan?'

'Flexitarian. There's butter in this dish. I eat plant-based a lot, but tonight's a night off.'

'I eat anything and everything,' Charlie admitted.

'Except cucumber,' Edie remembered and laughed to break the tension. She poured a burgundy-coloured wine into two tumblers. 'I make my own wine. Elderberry and blackberry in the autumn and elderflower in the spring.'

Charlie took a gulp. 'Lovely.'

'No chemicals,' Edie explained. 'So, hopefully, less chance of a hangover.'

'Oh.' Charlie wasn't sure what to say. 'So we can drink the whole bottle.'

'More if you like – I have a cellar full.'

They were quiet for a while, then Charlie said, 'Do you like living here?' just as Edie said, 'How are you settling in?'

They both laughed nervously.

'It's a bit quiet,' Charlie admitted. 'Most of my friends are still in London. I was born in Luton, but I went to Goldsmiths in New Cross and stayed in London afterwards.'

'Why live here then?' Edie asked simply.

'The chance came up to work with Uncle Bill.' He tried again. 'My teaching job came to an end.'

'Oh, it must be so hard, teaching...' Edie was full of sympathy. 'I'm training to be a lawyer. My degree is in criminology. I decided to do a GDL, that's a top-up graduate law degree. I'm doing distance learning over two years out of Birbeck. I've nearly finished the course – two more units...' Edie noticed his empty bowl. 'Can you eat a bit more?'

Charlie rubbed his stomach. 'Just a small shovel full. It's good.'

'You're going to make number one look wonderful. Then what? Will you sell it?' Edie said as she ladled more rice into his bowl.

'Yes. Then I'll travel the world, just me and Alan and my sax.' Charlie gazed affectionately at the black Labrador, who'd finished eating and had curled up on Bianca's cushion. Bianca had taken herself off to another room.

'You're not sure where you'll go yet?' Edie asked.

'Not really.' Charlie shook his head. 'Sometimes I just think I'll buy a camper van and a ticket for a boat and see where we end up.'

'I get that.' Edie offered a kind smile. 'I've had times when it felt like the best thing was to up sticks and start again...'

Charlie was playing with his food. Suddenly he didn't feel hungry. He said, 'You seem to have life all sorted out.'

'Me?' Edie asked. 'How do you make that out?'

'Lovely home, all beautifully done, and you're studying for a law degree...'

'That's such hard work. And I have to find time for it and to work in the pub and see my friends in Markyate at least once a week or I'll turn into a hermit.'

'What's Markyate like?' Charlie asked. 'It's not far away, is it?'

'It's where I lived before.' Edie had finished eating. 'My mum lives there. A really sweet village. Easy access for London, Oxford, Luton airport...' She began to clear the dishes. 'It's good-sized but friendly. The Swan is a great pub.'

Charlie was about to suggest that they went there one night for a drink – it might be something to pass the time. But instead he said, 'I must check it out...' He thought for a moment. 'It might be a good place to offer music lessons. It would be a way of' – he grinned, remembering Edie's phrase – 'making some pocket money.'

'I'll talk to my friend Priya. Her sister Nila has two kids and she thinks they should learn an instrument. Maybe you can teach them both saxophone...'

'How old are they?'

Edie pulled a face. 'One's eleven, the other's thirteen? I ought to know... Priya's been my friend for years.' She poured more wine into Charlie's glass, despite it being half full. 'I've made key lime pie for dessert.'

'Oh, great.'

'I hope the avocados don't go too brown...'

'Brown avocados in a key lime pie?' Charlie grinned. 'You're really selling it...'

'Shall we help ourselves to a slice and then we can go into the living room. The heating is on...'

'Log fire?' Charlie asked as he watched Edie slice two huge pieces of perfect key lime pie.

'I have a heat pump system with the solar panels,' Edie said.

'You're just completely rocking it here, aren't you?' Charlie was full of admiration. He dug into the dessert and chewed thoughtfully. It tasted creamy, tangy and sweet at the same time. 'You can't taste avocados at all – it just tastes normal.'

'Normal?' Edie burst out laughing. 'I don't hear that word very often. I'm sure my mother thinks I'm a bit wild.'

'Same, but my mum's the one behaving like a teenager at the moment. She's always off somewhere.' Charlie was chewing. 'My brother Sonny's the golden boy.'

'My mum didn't want kids – she doesn't like them,' Edie mumbled. 'But she keeps asking me when I'm going to have them.'

'Ah...' Charlie said. 'At least I don't have that to contend with.'

'Everything in its own time,' Edie said. 'I never rush anything.'

'So – what's Edie short for? Edith?'

'Eden – as in the garden of,' Edie explained. 'And are you Charles or just Charlie?'

'Just plain Charlie.' Charlie grinned. He licked his lips. 'That was lovely.'

'Do you like John Coltrane?' Edie asked lightly.

'Do I?' Charlie raised his eyebrows. 'He's one of my idols.'

'Then I'll put his music on Spotify. You go in the other room – I'll bring you a drink. Tea, coffee?'

'Coffee please.'

'Coming up.'

Charlie wandered out of the kitchen, feeling a little concerned that he hadn't offered to wash up. Alan trotted behind him as he surveyed the living room. It was bright, full of natural fabrics and wood. There were hardwood beams, pendant lights with bamboo and wicker shades, several green plants. Bianca was curled up on a soft cushion. He flopped down on the sofa and Alan settled by his feet just as 'My One and Only Love' began to play through the smart speaker.

Charlie closed his eyes and immediately he saw Luna's smile, her swaying dance. He sat up, blinking, and made his way over to the large curtains, tugging them back. It was hard to see anything outside; at the end of the garden, he could make out the silhouette of Edie's little car. Beyond, the trees were swaying in the night breeze. It felt warm and safe to be inside.

Edie came into the room, offering him a mug of coffee. She murmured, 'I never tire of the view. The woodland is so beautiful. And there's fifty-two acres of open space, perfect for me and Bianca. There are so many incredible trees – silver birch, oak. And I've seen mistle thrushes and jays – even cuckoos.'

'Why is it called Nomansland?' Charlie asked as he took the mug of coffee. 'Is it because no man should venture there?'

'Nothing half as sinister,' Edie said. 'During the fifteenth century, the monasteries of St Albans and Westminster argued over the common – they each wanted it for their own parish. The common acted as the no-man's land between the two warring factions. It took twenty years to sort it.'

'Ah, I thought it might be something ghostly.' Charlie stared out into the trees moving in darkness. 'It does feel eerie at times...'

'You mean Ferrers Lane,' Edie said. 'That's quite spooky. There's a myth about a young woman of noble birth who used to ride on the common five hundred years ago.'

'Really?' Charlie forced a laugh, remembering the sensation of the horse and rider that had rushed past him on the wind.

Edie came to stand closer, staring through the glass. 'I often feel there's someone watching me when I'm out walking with Bianca. Rumour has it that she's still out there, the lone rider. The locals have a name for her – they call her The Wicked Lady... because of what she did.'

16

1659

Kate stood in her chamber, hardly believing what she saw in the mirror. The image looked a little like her, but not much. She saw a slim young man wearing a long velvet coat, a waistcoat, breeches and leather boots. She tied her hair back in a ribbon and offered the glass her most serious expression. She'd need a hat, a kerchief. And one other thing – the thought of carrying it inside her coat made her heart race.

Thomas always kept a flintlock pistol in his chamber, in a drawer. But it now lay on her bed. She had stolen it as soon as he had left the library to sup.

She glanced at the plate of food Beatrice had brought up on a tray. The roast lamb was cold now. She wasn't hungry – she was too nervous to eat. She'd complained of a headache and said she wouldn't come down for supper – Thomas could eat alone.

Kate reached for the glass of claret and drank it thirstily in gulps. Her hands were shaking. She feared she might lose her nerve. She glanced again in the steel mirror, striking a pose, hands on hips. She didn't look at all formidable or terrifying. But she had to go ahead with her plan. She couldn't lose The Cell; she needed to take charge of her life.

The silk gown and kirtle lying on the bed told the story of her past; her waistcoat, breeches and boots were her present. As for the future – she couldn't think of that. She'd heard Constable Lambert Wilmott tell her husband long ago that a highway robber could expect to live only a few years after taking to the road. Kate hoped she'd be lucky and not be caught – she'd pay her husband, live happily in The Cell and help out the poor families of Markyate.

She whisked a low-crowned hat from the bed, one with a broad brim that was turned up on three sides, and pushed it down over her head. It was Thomas's, the latest fashion. He would not miss it – he had others.

Kate took a deep breath. She was ready: she'd do it now. She moved towards the door that led to the secret passage. In moments, she'd be in the kitchen, out through the back door, in the stables. She'd take Midnight. No one would recognise him as her horse.

* * *

The evening light was beginning to dwindle. The young highway robber sat astride the dark horse, watching from the woodlands, a kerchief disguising her features. She had only ever ridden side-saddle before. Kate was breathing heavily. It had been a long ride from Markyate along the dusty lane, although Midnight was strong, sturdy and compliant. Her nerves were on edge; every sound in the bushes made her tremble: leaves rustling, the cry of a bird. The sky was indigo, a red strip on the horizon where the sun was sinking. A coach must surely come by soon, or it would be too dark.

Kate pulled the kerchief up over her nose and recalled that, not long before she was born, a law was passed that imposed the death penalty for being armed and disguised on high roads and open heaths. She knew the parish constable would be on the lookout for robbers on horseback and footpads, who could be violent and worked in gangs. She hoped she didn't meet any of them on the common. Her fist tightened around the flintlock pistol and she wondered if she would use it if the need arose.

She pressed her heels against Midnight's belly and he plodded forward, his hooves crunching against twigs. It felt natural to be riding a horse as a man did; the stallion responded quickly to every movement of her body. From the darkness of the dense trees, she could see the open common, the road and, beyond, the constable's cottage and stables. She imagined Constable Wilmott out there somewhere, watching, his pistol loaded. For a moment, Kate almost turned the horse around. The idea of being a highway robber was reckless, foolish.

She held her breath: there was a sound in the distance, becoming louder. On the wind, she could hear clattering hooves, the rumble of wheels. A coach was approaching – she could hear it distinctly. It was now or never.

She adjusted her neckerchief over her nose again and spurred Midnight forward.

A coach and four horses was passing as fast as it could, on the way to London. Kate tugged Midnight's reins, assessing the situation. There were two drivers. There would be passengers – Kate had no idea how many. What if one of them had a pistol? What if the driver was armed and tried to overpower her? For a second, Kate felt her nerve falter.

Then she was hurtling forward, Midnight's hooves thundering beneath her, bearing down fast on the coach and four that rattled along oblivious. Kate was delighted that Midnight was so responsive and intelligent. Raife had taught him well; he had chosen perfectly. A moment's gratitude flooded through her: she needed to trust her horse completely now. She drove Midnight directly at the coach, assessing the speed, measuring the point at which she'd cut it off.

She lifted her pistol and charged. 'Stop. Stop at once or I'll fire...'

The coach driver tugged the reins and the coach came to a standstill, dust rising like smoke around the wheels. The driver made to move and Kate kept her voice as low as possible.

'Stay exactly where you are or I will shoot.'

The coach driver muttered, 'May the devil rot you, young knave...'

'You have good reason to be alarmed.' Kate cocked her head to one side and saw two nervous faces peering from inside the carriage. 'But I will not harm you if you do as I say. Now, if you please – your passengers should step from the coach, one by one...'

Kate watched, her heart thudding, as an elderly gentleman and his wife emerged shakily from the coach. The woman reached for her husband's hand as if she would faint, and he held it tightly.

'Do not shoot us...' he begged. 'We are merely on our way to London to greet our new grandson...'

'Be silent. Deliver your purse.' Kate's voice was as strong as she could manage, given her shallow breathing. She turned to the woman. 'You, mistress. Bring me his purse, his guineas, and don't delay.'

The woman didn't move. 'I am afeared.'

'I will not harm you,' Kate said gently. 'Bring the money. And I'll have your gold necklace and brooch – and the rings on your fingers, if you please.'

The woman nodded and shuffled forward as her husband handed her his silk purse and watched with glazed eyes. The woman's hands shook as she handed over money and jewels. Kate thrust them into her pocket.

'I thank you, mistress,' Kate said kindly. 'I wish you a speedy journey.' As an afterthought, she murmured, 'May God bless your grandson...'

She turned Midnight and galloped away as quickly as she could, her heart banging beneath her jacket, her breath coming in gulps. Head down, she pressed Midnight onwards, through the woodlands towards the lane, back towards Markyate, to the safety of The Cell.

＊ ＊ ＊

By the time Kate returned home, the sky was ink black but for tiny stars and a hooked yellow moon. She returned Midnight to the stables, patting his damp neck, allowing him to put his head down, to eat and drink.

Making sure no one was about, she sneaked through the kitchen and up to her room. She wished she had a glass of wine to calm her racing pulse. Once in her chamber, Kate threw herself on her bed, still wearing her man's clothes, and counted her money. The old gentleman had been rich; his purse was fat. She had made a pretty penny from one single robbery. And the jewellery was valuable; Kate decided to return to London soon, to visit Joshua Garvey.

She flopped back onto the soft down of her bed, closing her eyes, feeling suddenly guilty that she had deprived grandparents of their money. But it was done. She had committed a highway robbery. The thrill of it made her skin tingle. She felt suddenly powerful, as if she could do anything she wished. She wondered if she would stop a coach again; if a second time might not be foolhardy. She had been lucky tonight but would she be so fortunate?

* * *

The next morning, Kate woke up late and dressed in a crisp linen shift, a velvet gown embellished with ribbons and lace and a pretty linen cap. She went down to breakfast humming a little tune, sitting alone at the long table in the dining room.

Beatrice bustled in, placing a dish of bread with butter and sage in front of her, a goblet of warm ale. 'You are late this morning, but you are in a good humour, mistress.'

'I suppose I am.' Kate smiled. 'Has my husband left for Cheshire yet?'

'Peter is preparing his horse now. He will leave anon...' Beatrice muttered.

'That is well – but I intend to see him before he departs.'

'Oh?' Beatrice raised an eyebrow.

'I must wish him well. He goes to fight for the king,' Kate said cryptically. 'Bea – I am hungry this morning. May I have some more bread? And some cooked fruit? With honey?'

'I have some rhubarb, freshly stewed... the strawberries are not ripe yet.'

'Then rhubarb it is, please.' Kate smiled. 'Thank you, Bea. Then, after breakfast, I wish to ride Shadow.' She reached out a hand and pressed Beatrice's wrist. 'Bea – you know I am truly grateful for all you do for me here, you and John...'

'I know it, mistress.' Beatrice looked a little surprised.

'Can you find some cake and some bread? I wish to take some food to the Salters this morning. Peter's family has no father, and the children often go hungry.'

'Mistress, they will bless you for your kindness.'

'Perhaps I need as many blessings as I can get,' Kate murmured. She heard footsteps outside the door. 'Is that Thomas, on his way?'

'I think he is ready to leave for the north.' Beatrice looked sad. 'He intends to go without wishing you goodbye.'

'Then my breakfast can wait.' Kate picked up her skirts and rushed out, leaving Beatrice puzzled, standing by the table. 'Thomas. Thomas – I need to speak with you...' Kate caught up with her husband at the door. 'Thomas, I might have missed you...'

Thomas frowned. 'We seldom say farewell, Kate. I always believe you care not if I return safely...'

'You go to fight a battle for the king. I know the risks you take... I wanted to wish you well.' Kate took a breath. She was used to being indifferent to Thomas. But things needed to change; there was a bargain to be struck. She needed his compliance: she would not allow him to sell her home.

Thomas looked taken aback. 'You have never shared my passion to fight for the king...'

'It is true, I have not,' Kate said kindly. She gave a small shrug. 'I know the Fanshawe men are loyal, and that you want Charles to be on the throne again...'

'That is why I must sell this place.'

'Do not.' Kate grabbed his arm. 'Thomas, delay, I beg you...'

'We spoke of this yesternight...' Thomas lowered his voice. 'Do you have money for me?'

'I do.' Kate slipped the silk purse into his hand. 'There is plenty here. And plenty more will follow.'

He glanced at the heavy purse and his brows came together in surprise. 'Where did you get this?'

'I sold some things I did not need.' Kate thought it best to gloss over the details. 'And I will send you more.'

'How?'

'I am a woman of means,' Kate quipped as she turned away. 'I wish you Godspeed, Thomas. May your time in Cheshire be fruitful.'

'Thank you, Kate.' Thomas took a deep breath as if he was about to say something important. 'You have not been a dutiful wife and I have treated you harshly in the past, but I'm sure you know my loyalty is first to the king.'

'We have not tried our best to understand each other,' Kate said simply.

'It is true,' Thomas agreed. 'But we are older now. Perhaps we can learn to be civil, at least?'

'We are separate people,' Kate said. 'Our marriage is a convenience. And I am content that it should remain this way. I will find money for you as long as you will allow me to stay here.'

'I will expect no more of you than to be my wife in name. To serve the king is all I desire.'

Kate had the bargain she wanted. 'Then in return I will give you money when I can, you will not sell the manor house and you and I will live as we see fit...'

'So be it,' Thomas said slowly. 'I must go. My horse waits...'

'Then I wish you a safe journey, for who knows when we next will meet.' Kate inclined her head. 'May God protect you, Thomas.'

She whirled away, back to the dining room, and took her seat, reaching for the goblet of warm ale. She took a thirsty gulp.

'And may the Lord protect me too. For I fear I shall have much need of it...'

17

THE PRESENT

It had been a very hard week at work. Flushed with the success of finishing the bathroom on schedule, Charlie had intended to plaster and paint the walls and fix the floor of the main bedroom. But, on Monday, Uncle Bill had phoned to say he'd been asked to do some work in St Albans on a kitchen extension. Apparently, Mrs Callow, a lady who was recently widowed and in her late seventies, had been let down by her original builder and was desperate for help. Bill couldn't say no and it was two weeks' work. Charlie would have to manage by himself. So he had managed as best as he could, tottering on a ladder, plastering and painting bedroom walls, while Alan watched him from his soft bed, paws in the air, a smile on his face.

On Wednesday afternoon Charlie had popped round to see Edie. She had been in the middle of an essay on equity and trusts, whatever that meant. Edie, in round glasses and a serious face, her hair tied back, had told him the work was tough-going and she was desperate for a cuppa. They'd had a quick break, she had mentioned that Nila wanted to meet him, and arranged for a visit, then he had gone straight back to work on the bedroom.

On Saturday, Charlie drove along the A5183 to Markyate, Alan comfortably dozing in the back. He was looking forward to the appointment that afternoon with Nila Sharma, the elder sister of Edie's friend Priya. More to the point, he was excited about meeting her sons Kavish and Joshit, who were interested in learning the saxophone. He had taken the trouble to dress smartly in a jacket and a white shirt in an effort to look professional. In truth, he was dog-tired and would have rather stayed in bed, although his bed was simply a mattress, now on the floor of the second bedroom.

Charlie drove through Markyate, taking in the scenery as the village sparkled in the sunshine. He passed a café that advertised fresh food, a gym. The Swan Inn was on the left. There was a chip shop opposite and Charlie could imagine himself coming out of the pub on a Saturday night and crossing the road to buy chips. That had been a common night out in his student days, but he hadn't done it in ages. He wondered fleetingly how his friends were doing back in London. He'd been invited to a party tonight – Richard, a friend originally from Belfast, was having a house-warming. He liked Richard, so Charlie wondered why he'd said he was busy. It was a mistake to be antisocial. He resolved to accept every invitation to go to London from now on.

In truth, he knew why he'd lied about being otherwise engaged. He didn't want to go on his own, not yet. It didn't feel right.

He drove along the High Street, the satnav telling him to turn left along Cavendish Road and then right onto Grange Close. He paused outside a chalet-style brick house with a gravel drive. This was the place.

Nila answered the door. She was a slim woman wearing a blue jumper and dark trousers, and she shook his hand formally. 'I'm pleased to meet you, Mr Wolfe.'

'Charlie,' he said quickly as he was ushered inside, saxophone case in his hand.

He followed Nila into a light room with huge windows, a soft carpet beneath his feet, and he immediately wondered if he should have removed his trainers. There were posed family pictures all over the wall which was papered in a plain colour.

Two boys sat quietly on the sofa, both with dark hair and serious faces. Nila said, 'Kavish, Joshit, this is Mr Wolfe.'

'Charlie,' Charlie said again.

'He could be your saxophone teacher, if you want to learn.'

Kavish, the elder of the two, must have been around thirteen, as Edie had said. 'I want to play the sax. But Josh doesn't. He has asthma.'

'He's right,' Joshit said unhappily. 'I'll be rubbish.'

'Not necessarily.' Charlie offered his most optimistic expression. 'I've taught loads of kids who have asthma. One of the best ways to manage asthma is to do breathing exercises, and learning a wind instrument can definitely help.'

'Will it cure Josh's asthma?' Kavish wanted to know.

'Can you play a tune on your saxophone now?' Joshit asked.

Charlie turned to Nila. 'Shall I play a bit?'

'If you wish.' Nila sat next to her boys, hands folded, looking interested as Charlie took out his saxophone, wiped a disinfecting cloth over the mouthpiece and handed it to Joshit.

'You try first. Blow in the mouthpiece – just to see how it feels.'

Joshit blew hard and Kavish laughed. 'It sounds like a little cow farting.'

Nila looked embarrassed.

Joshit handed it to Kavish, who took a deep breath and blew harder. Joshit said, 'And that's a big cow farting.'

Charlie wiped the mouthpiece again and began to play the famous solo from 'Baker Street' by Gerry Rafferty. Both boys watched him, mouths open.

When he finished, Joshit said, 'That's so cool...'

Kavish asked, 'Can you teach me to play like that?'

'If you want to learn, you have to practise a lot,' Charlie explained. 'But I can teach you all of the fingerings, basic music theory...' He glanced at Nila. 'They'll have to commit to practising. It's the same with any instrument, sax, guitar, even drums.'

'Would you like a cup of coffee?' Nila asked Charlie. 'We can take an espresso in the kitchen and chat. Boys – can you find a book to read? And definitely no *Clash of Clans* while I'm out of the room.'

Charlie watched both boys tug phones from their pockets as Nila led the way to a pristine stainless-steel kitchen. He sat on a chrome stool and thought about Edie's reclaimed wood kitchen and how he might design his own.

Nila placed an espresso in a glass cup in front of him and asked, 'Is this OK?'

'Great, thanks – I'll have to be quick though. I have Alan in the back of the van. He's my dog – I don't like to leave him for long, even when the weather is cool.' Charlie took a sip. 'So, what do you think about lessons for the boys?'

'Sahil and I both think it's a great idea. He can't be here at the moment – he's at work – he's an anaesthetist at the hospital in Hemel Hempstead. But he wants the boys to learn an instrument.'

'Do they play anything at the moment? Can they read music?'

'Kavish started the piano when he was seven,' Nila said. 'But the teacher didn't really engage him. He's a lively character, and he likes his own way. Joshit is timid – he gives up easily.'

'I like a challenge.' Charlie grinned. 'Do you have a saxophone for them to use at home?'

'No – what should I get?'

'For young students, I'd suggest starting with alto saxes. They can cost around four hundred pounds, although you can pick up second-hand ones reasonably inexpensively. But you probably need to be confident that the boys want to learn before you invest in an instrument each. You could rent one to start with.'

'I'll talk to Sahil tonight.'

'I could come over one evening, give them a trial lesson and see how they get on?'

'Do you think it might be better if they were taught separately?' Nila looked worried. 'Kavish can be a bit dominant.'

'Why don't you talk it over with your husband and then call me? Learning an instrument isn't for everyone but it's a great discipline and a lovely skill to have.' Charlie finished his espresso. 'The boys can play alone for fun or in bands... it's a really nice social door opener...' He paused, remembering. He had been playing his saxophone in a group when he had met Luna. He'd seen her dancing in the crowd and she had noticed him. He recalled the exact moment. It had been a meeting of eyes, minds, souls. He turned his attention back to the coffee dregs in the cup. 'Thanks – that was lovely.'

'I'll talk to Sahil and maybe you can come over in the week.' Nila stood up. 'Priya told me you were new to the area. Do you know Markyate at all?'

'No – I live on the edge of the common, Ferrers Lane, near Wheathampstead.'

'Ferrers Lane. That area's steeped in legend. The boys learned about it in school. She came from Markyate, you know,' Nila said.

'Who did?'

'The Wicked Lady... somebody Ferrers. The highway robber woman. She lived in The Cell, the manor house just round the corner.'

'Did she? Is it open to the public? I'd like to go there and look round.' Charlie was keen to pick up local knowledge.

'No, it's privately owned. You could drive past it, I suppose, and peek over the wall.'

'Is it hard to get to?' Charlie asked.

'No, just follow the road out of Markyate and turn left onto the main road. It's on your right.'

'Right.' Charlie held out his hand. 'Nice to meet you, Nila.'

'You too, Charlie.' Nila shook his hand once. 'I so hope you can teach my boys some music.' She sighed. 'I worry about them – it's all *Minecraft* and mobile phones...'

'I'll do my best – give me a bell,' Charlie said.

Back in the living room, Kavish was on his phone. As soon as Nila came in, he stuffed it under a cushion and sat up straight. Joshit had opened the saxophone case and was cradling the instrument in his arms.

'Oh, that's Charlie's saxophone...' Nila folded her arms. 'I'm so sorry.'

'Not at all.' Charlie was delighted. He noticed Joshit's immediate awkwardness and crouched down next to him. 'It's quite heavy, isn't it?'

Joshit shook his head. 'I like it. It's cool. It's like a machine gun.'

'It's the long neck,' Charlie said, encouraging. 'Just a minute.' He wiped the mouthpiece. 'Go on, see if you can get a sound out of it. Press the keys and see what happens.'

Kavish leaned forward, interested.

'Place your right-hand thumb under the thumb rest,' Charlie said encouragingly. 'Place your top teeth on top of the mouthpiece so that the reed rests on your lower lip – that's right. Now blow.'

Joshit blew. A single note sounded. The boy jerked back. 'My lips feel funny.'

'You get used to it,' Charlie said.

Both boys laughed and Kavish said, 'Can I try?'

Nila looked on, her eyes shining.

* * *

Ten minutes later, after checking on Alan, who opened one eye as if he hadn't noticed anyone was missing, Charlie was in the van and on his way. He followed the main road carefully, busy Saturday traffic all around him, onto the A5183, driving towards Dunstable. He saw the manor house almost immediately – or, he saw a tall wall at least, the vast gardens, trees and grasslands behind it. He pulled into the entrance at the side of the road and looked at red-brick pillars and iron stone gates.

He frowned. 'I bet this isn't original...'

The name of the house caught his eye: The Cell. He assumed the building must have been associated with monks early on, before it became a manor house.

The entrance was tidy: in front of the gates on both sides, the grass was neatly mown and there were flowering bushes. A smooth gravel drive led beyond the gates, turning left and right. He couldn't see the house properly. The grounds of The Cell looked like it might have been imposing once, but there was nothing ghostly about it now, nothing sinister.

He recalled the strange cold presence that had rushed past him on horseback on Ferrers Lane. Could The Wicked Lady have lived in such a house? And was she really a highway robber?

Charlie had to admit, he was intrigued.

'Well, Ms Ferrers,' he muttered to himself. 'I wonder who you really were...'

18

1659

'I wish to see Mistress Fanshawe.'

The commanding nasal voice came from the front entrance. Kate could hear John saying, 'I will see if she's available, sir.'

'Available or not, I will see her.'

Kate was dressed warmly for riding, in a long skirt, a cloak, hat and boots. She had intended to go out – it was a glorious May morning, and the sun was as yellow as dripping honey. She swept towards the entrance, her hand out in greeting, and said, 'Constable Wilmott. What a pleasure to see you.'

He puffed out his chest. 'I wish I could say the same, mistress. But I come on most unpleasant business.'

'Oh?' Kate smiled even as she felt her heart lurch beneath her bodice. She had not expected to see the parish constable, his face clouded and serious, his eyebrows furrowed. 'How may I help?'

He leaned forward. 'I wish to speak with you on a matter of grave importance.'

'Then speak of it quickly.' Kate could smell his rancid breath. 'I am on my way to the stables. I intend to take Shadow out riding.'

'I pray you, don't go near Nomansland Common...'

'And why ever not?' Kate feigned surprise. 'It is most pleasant there. It's an arduous ride, I grant you, but it is good for the health of both myself and Shadow to exercise...'

'It is no longer safe for a woman to be alone on Nomansland. You must not venture...'

'But you live there, Constable Wilmott.' Kate made her expression as uninterested as she could. 'How could I be unsafe with an officer appointed by the justice of the peace?'

'Two nights ago, there was a robbery on the common just before nightfall.'

'A robbery?' Kate raised a gloved hand to her mouth. 'Heaven forbid it.'

'A most heinous one.'

'A gang of footpads, low criminals, I assume? Was anyone hurt?' Kate looked anxious.

'No, but we have a notorious rascal terrorising the common. A high-wayman, mistress – a most bold and audacious young man. He held up a coach and stole a purse full of guineas from a gentleman from Caddington. And he pilfered the man's wife's gold jewellery.'

'Oh, that is dreadful. How will we all be safe?' Kate gasped dramatically.

The constable grunted agreement. 'These highway robbers are common as crows. I intend to catch him, mistress. I have a description from the coach driver.'

'Oh?' Kate felt her breath come in gulps and arranged her face in the pretence of shock. 'Do tell.'

'He is very well-mannered and genteel. He pretends to be a gentleman, but he is a rogue and a ruffian. He is extremely ill-favoured, with light hair, broad shoulders, a black beard, and he is around twenty years of age.'

Kate breathed a sigh of relief and touched her dark curls thankfully. 'Well, I hope I will never meet him.'

The constable's face was purple. 'God's wounds, I hope I do. He will receive a swift acquaintance with my pistol.'

'If you please, sir...' John coughed. 'I think my mistress has heard enough about the young robber – I am concerned for her peace of mind.'

'But she has no husband here to protect her. It is my responsibility to warn women about dangerous highwaymen,' the constable said sullenly.

'It is your responsibility to catch him.' Kate fanned herself with her hand. 'Thank you for the visit, Constable. I will continue with my riding – I expect our young highwayman will be unlikely to appear again.'

'Oh? Why do you say so, mistress?' Wilmott asked.

'No doubt he has heard that you are after him...' Kate met his eyes. 'I am sure he will be too afeared to venture out ever again. Good day.'

She turned on her heel and flounced away, leaving the constable and John watching her go. They did not see her hand over her mouth as she suppressed a laugh.

* * *

In the stables, Kate mounted Shadow, her foot on the pommel, wondering why women were encouraged to ride so when being astride a horse's back was so much easier.

Peter looked at her adoringly. 'My mother said to thank you for the food you sent...' he said gratefully. 'We haven't eaten as well in a long time.'

Kate leaned forward. 'There will be more where that came from. And I've asked John to give you a little extra money today, so that your mother can buy what she needs.'

'Thanking you, mistress.' Peter couldn't hide his surprise. 'Begging your pardon, but has the master come into a fortune?'

'Not at all...' Kate said. 'I have been to London – I sold a few items I didn't need and it just seemed right to share my good luck.'

Peter inclined his head. 'Mistress, I have given the new stallion some attention this morning. Midnight is a good horse. I had to remove a lot of dirt from the hooves and he stood quietly while I soaked them in warm water and brushed them. You must have been riding him quite a distance. Do you think I should take him to the village smithy soon...?'

'As you see fit, Peter. But...' Kate's thoughts raced. 'If you are asked, you must say that Midnight belongs to my husband, not to me...'

'Of course, mistress.'

'Midnight was given to me by a farmer in payment for... rent,' Kate said by way of explanation. 'Of course, like everything in the house, the horse belongs to my husband, but I would hate for tongues to wag...'

'I understand,' Peter said, with a look that implied he would do anything for her.

'Well, it is a beautiful day – the summer is almost upon us, and this time of year, riding out makes me feel alive.' Kate peered into the gloom of the barn to the sunlight that illuminated the courtyard. 'I intend to ride Shadow some distance again today – perhaps you should ask the smithy to shoe both horses.'

'I will,' Peter said humbly.

Kate tugged the reins and Shadow trotted obediently towards the light.

The journey along the dirt track was long, but it was wonderful to be in the open air, grassland and trees on either side. Acres of farmland that had once belonged to Kate's father and grandfather, now sold by Thomas, stretched into the distance.

Kate's thoughts preoccupied her as she rode: perhaps there was a kind of peace between her and Thomas now. Certainly, they'd come to an understanding that they would expect nothing more of each other than to live their own lives, and that would continue as long as she could give him money. He would be away from The Cell for some time, and she thought about how to spend the summer. Not out on the highway alone. Her career as a robber had been short, and it was wisest to stop now. The constable knew about the robbery, and he was not the sort of man to cross. It was not just that he was determined to make an arrest; there was something about the twist of his mouth, the way his eyes narrowed as he looked at her. He was a spiteful man and she did not trust his motives. Indeed, she'd been fortunate to escape capture the first time.

Unconsciously, she found herself riding towards Ayers End Farm; she paused outside the lane that dissected patchwork fields and gazed towards the farm cottage. She wondered how the little foal was progressing. Vulcan. It might be pleasant to call in to say thank you to Raife Chetwyn for the gift of a stallion.

Shadow trotted obediently towards the farmhouse. Kate wondered what Master Chetwyn would say if he knew that her first ride on Midnight had been in the guise of a highway robber.

At the farm cottage, Kate dismounted and knocked on the door. It was ajar and she assumed Raife was in the stables, so she lifted her skirts and hurried towards the large barn. Her heart began to thud and Kate felt strangely uneasy at the idea of seeing him.

Inside the gloomy barn, specks of dust danced on the thin beam of light that filtered in. The scent of straw and the warm aroma of the horses filled her nose. She peered into one of the stables and saw Vulcan standing next to his mother, Beleza, whose head was down, munching hay. Kate felt a glow of pleasure to see mare and foal thriving. But Raife Chetwyn was nowhere to be seen.

Kate scurried outside and glanced towards a field. She watched as Raife led a horse with a plough, three men behind him bending over at their work. Kate knew they were sowing spring crops, barley, oats and beans. She glanced at the other men, shabbily dressed, hunched, faces lined. Her eyes moved to Raife, muscular in breeches and boots, his torso glistening as he worked. She caught her breath; it was difficult to look away. He hadn't noticed her arrival and Kate wondered if she should call to him, if he would come across and talk.

Then an idea came, one that filled her with excitement. She ran back to the cottage, through the door and into the lounge, where a cauldron of water and a pottage of cabbage soup with oats was heating over the fire. She glanced around in the gloom, noticing Raife's jacket, his hat. The room smelled smoky, but it also carried a warm scent of the person who spent each day there. She breathed it in deeply before busying herself in the adjoining room, slicing a loaf of Carter's bread made from rye and wheat, cutting cheese and smoked bacon, and arranging them on a plate. She placed a goblet and a jug of ale on the hearth to warm and stood back to survey her efforts.

Her hands had seldom done any real work. She had never prepared a meal for Thomas – why would she? How nice it felt to be able to make a simple meal and imagine Raife coming in from the fields, finding it already prepared. He would be surprised and delighted. But how would he know that it had been Kate who had made his food with care and tenderness?

She glanced at the rings on her hands and selected the ruby cabochon on her index finger, the one her mother had given to her. Excitedly, she tugged it off and dropped it into the empty goblet she'd placed next to the jug of ale. It would be a gift from her to him in return for the stallion. Kate imagined him finding the ring in his cup, that smile curving his lips – he'd know it was her. She enjoyed the thrill of leaving him a message, of something secret communicated between them that no one else could share. It felt like a bond – it was delicious.

* * *

Kate was deep in thought as she rode Shadow over the common towards Markyate. The sunshine sparkled on every leaf; the grass was soft beneath Shadow's hooves. She recalled Raife, handsome and strong, working in the field, doing honest labour, using his hard, rough hands. Each night he would sit in the warm cottage, eating what he grew, what he farmed, sleeping on a straw mattress beneath the thatch. It was a good life, an honourable one. She thought of the men he employed, scrawny and bent over, working for a few coins. They would have families to feed, children.

Just once more, Kate thought. She could do it just once.

The money she'd make from the rich could be divided between those who needed it and her husband, whom she needed to appease.

She made the decision at once. The young highway robber would ride again. One evening, later this week, as a coach passed on the road to London, she and Midnight would gallop forwards, pistol in hand, and she'd steal what she could. She'd return to The Cell with a purse of guineas, and more jewellery to sell.

It would be all right, just one more time. Then she'd never steal again.

As she cantered along the common, she glanced towards the constable's cottage. Lambert Wilmott would be watching for her. She'd need to be careful.

19

THE PRESENT

Charlie worked hard on his own at the cottage for the next week. Uncle Bill was still busy with the extension in St Albans and Charlie had very little time to think of anything other than plastering walls and ceilings and repairing floorboards. On Thursday evening, he drove to Markyate and spent a pleasant hour with Kavish and Joshit Sharma, who were excited to be learning the saxophone. Kavish was more vocal and enthusiastic, wanting all of Charlie's attention, but Joshit was the patient one, listening to instructions carefully, doing exactly as he was told. Afterwards, Charlie spent another hour with Nila and Sahil, a broad-shouldered man with a ready smile and crinkling eyes, drinking coffee and eating samosas. It was agreed that he'd teach the boys together on Thursdays, for an hour each week, and that Nila would look out for a second-hand saxophone for each of them.

On Friday, Charlie stopped for lunch to find a text message from Edie. She addressed him as 'dear neighbour', said she'd had a horrendous week but her essay was finished, she'd sent it off, and she wanted to celebrate. She was working in The Sycamore Tree at lunchtime and she had a few errands to run afterwards, but she'd meet him in the pub bar at seven for a beer. And the chef did a great pie and chips, if he was interested.

At five to seven, in a warm jacket and scarf, Charlie walked into the

restaurant area of The Sycamore Tree. Alan seemed to know his bearings
very well, bounding straight to the table Charlie had sat at last time,
curling up beneath the chair. Charlie bought a pint of Neck Oil and settled
down. A young waiter, wearing shorts despite the cold weather, his legs
inky with colourful tattoos, brought a menu over. Charlie took in his
slicked-back mullet haircut and said, 'Can I order food when my friend
arrives?'

'Sure...' The waiter smoothed his mullet. 'You live in the cottages up
Ferrers Lane, don't you? The one that's getting done up.'

'I'm doing it myself, pretty much,' Charlie said. It was the truth at the
moment.

'Oh, I couldn't live up there. It's too quiet. I'm from Sandridge.' The
young man looked around the pub. A couple with three children were
eating together in the extension. 'It'll liven up here later. Friday night isn't
quiet for long.'

'Right,' Charlie said, and thought he'd better make conversation. 'I like
living here. I used to live in south London. But it's peaceful here...' As an
afterthought, he said, 'Nice pub.'

'It's a very historic building – dating right back. I think it was built at
the end of the sixteen hundreds.' The waiter brightened. 'We're not
allowed to change the name, The Sycamore Tree. Jerry, who took the place
over last year, wanted to give it a bit of a refresh, serve cocktails, make it a
bit trendy, but he was told he definitely couldn't change the name.'

'Why not?' Charlie asked. 'A sycamore's no big deal.'

'It certainly is here...' the waiter explained. 'Because of the rhyme.'

'What rhyme?' Charlie asked.

'Well...' The waiter posed as if to perform.

'Near the cell, there is a well
Near the well, there is a tree
And under the tree the treasure be...'

'I don't get it,' Charlie said.

'The *tree* – the *sycamore* tree.' The waiter rolled his eyes as if Charlie
was being deliberately obtuse. He turned as a couple came in through the

door, a woman in a leather jacket, a man in a sports top. 'Oh, it's Jen and Ross. They'll have had a hard day. They are always in on a Friday night – they're teachers, up at the Katherine Warington School.' He offered a professional smile. 'I'll be back for your order when your guest comes...'

Charlie took another gulp of beer and glanced down at Alan, who was looking up round-eyed to check all was well. Charlie dangled fingers for him to lick, then he dug in his pocket for his phone. There were messages from his mum and Sonny in Spain. His mother said she was having a wonderful time, loving the glorious sunshine; Sonny said he couldn't wait for her to go back to Luton. There was a WhatsApp invitation from Kofi and Jules, inviting him to join them and some friends in The Copper Tap in Peckham on Sunday to watch a football game. Charlie exhaled – it was always a couple inviting him, a single, to do something he'd have eagerly done two months ago with Luna. How his life had changed.

He read a text from Uncle Bill saying that he was knackered after a long week at work – on two occasions he hadn't finished until seven – but Mrs Callow's extension was done and she wanted him back next year to do some work to a staircase. He'd see Charlie bright-eyed and bushy-tailed on Monday.

Charlie replied to all his texts as cheerily as possible, glancing up from time to time, wondering if Edie had stood him up. He decided it didn't matter. He was halfway through his pint. He thought about buying himself a meal in the pub and eating it alone, if it would make him look sad and unloved, a Billy 'No Mates'.

A pang of regret tugged at his heart. He hadn't intended the life that had chosen him – he'd fallen into it. If only Luna had stayed...

He knew he shouldn't, but his fingers moved to Instagram, typing in her name. Pictures flashed before his eyes: Luna, her hair trailing behind her, dancing on a rock while the sea splashed behind; photos of the cast working with her. Then he noticed a shot that caught his eyes, glued them to the screen: a lean man with dark hair, stylish undercut dreadlocks, a serious serene face. He was clearly a dancer. Luna was in his arms as he lifted her in an arabesque, her skirt spreading like a sail.

Charlie's fingers and thumbs pressed more buttons, typing in 'Luna O'Rourke, Facebook', and there it was, another photo of her with the same man, different dance, different pose. He checked her 'about' information to see if she'd added the words *in a relationship with...* There was nothing. He still felt cheated, bereft. It was hard seeing her in another man's arms.

He heard a chirpy voice and looked up. Edie, in jeans and a duffel coat, hair tumbling, plonked herself opposite him. 'I'm so sorry I'm late.'

'No problem.' Charlie reached for his pint. 'Alan and I were enjoying the ambience. I had a nice chat with the waiter.'

'Shane.' Edie clearly knew him. 'I would have been here sooner, but I popped into Markyate to see a couple of friends and I got held up. Priya says you're doing wonders with her nephews...'

'Joshit and Kavish are great kids.' Charlie yawned. 'I hope I'll be able to keep my energy levels up enough to stay awake.'

'B12 and vitamins C and D,' Edie advised. Charlie had no idea what she was talking about. 'So, Priya and I had an emergency cup of tea with my friend Paige. She's just been dumped. She'd been with Elliott for the last two years – they were going to move in together – and he just dumped her out of thin air. She's devastated...'

'It happens,' Charlie said bitterly.

Shane was hovering by the table. 'Hi Edes – what can I get you to eat?'

'Chestnut and mushroom pie with chips, please – I'm celebrating.'

Shane pulled a face. 'You got the dreaded essay done then?'

'I did.' Edie grinned.

Shane indicated Edie. 'Oh, she's a bright cookie, our Edes. You've got yourself a good catch.'

'We're not together,' Charlie said bluntly and felt an immediate pang of embarrassment as he saw discomfort cross Edie's face.

She recovered quickly. 'Charlie and I are neighbours.'

'Oh yes – Constable's Cottages. What will you have, Charlie?' Shane was easy-going.

'Oh.' Charlie had no idea. 'I'll have the same as Edie...'

'Good choice,' Shane said and rushed away.

'He's your work colleague?' Charlie said, just to make conversation.

'Yes. Shane's lovely,' Edie said. She took a breath. 'So – what are you doing this weekend?'

Charlie wondered if Edie was asking him out. He shrugged. 'I expect I'll be doing some prep work on the house, ready for Monday.'

'I'm going into St Albans tomorrow afternoon with Priya and Paige. You'd be welcome to come with us...'

'Oh, I'm not sure it's for me...'

'There's a wonderful Saturday market, so we're shopping, then we'll stay on for a meal and maybe get a taxi home.' Edie was full of enthusiasm.

'It sounds like a girls' day out...'

'Oh, it wouldn't be – you'd like Priya and Paige. Priya's getting married next year. Her fiancé's lovely. Paige is nice too – she works in the vet's on reception...'

Charlie nodded. He wondered why he didn't feel overjoyed to be asked to go out with Edie and her friends. He decided Edie probably felt sorry for him. Or she thought he was just one of the girls and would blend in easily. He didn't know which of the two scenarios made him feel worse. He thought perhaps he should have stayed at home – he wasn't feeling at all sociable.

Shane arrived with plates of food and Charlie forced a grin and tried his hardest to pull himself together. He didn't want to be a wet blanket.

'The food looks good. And could I get another pint and – Edie – whatever you're having.'

'Oh, a botanical ginger beer, please.' Edie sat up eagerly. 'I didn't realise how ravenously hungry I was. Or how thirsty.'

Charlie dug into his food, telling himself to lighten up. He made a soft sound of enjoyment. 'This pie is great. So tell me all about your essay. It must have felt great to send it off...'

'It was.' Edie waved a hot chip in the air. 'But it's behind me now. How are the renovations going?'

'Good. It's much easier with Uncle Bill though.'

'He'll be back on Monday?'

'Yes,' Charlie said. 'It'll be great to get the main bedroom finished. And I'm aiming for the kitchen to be up and running by Christmas. I might even invite my mum over and cook her Christmas dinner...' He took a breath, reminding himself that it was only a project, not a home.

'That sounds like fun.'

'It would be a fate worse than death...' Charlie gave a twisted smile. 'My mum would hate everything about the house – and my cooking.'

'Then you can invite me instead,' Edie suggested. 'And Bianca.'

'I could. Where's Bianca now?' Charlie asked, pushing a chip furtively beneath the table for Alan to snaffle.

'On my bed asleep.' Edie grinned. 'I hate leaving her though. We'll go for a long walk tomorrow morning.'

'I can keep an eye on her while you're out tomorrow, if you need me to...'

'Oh, thanks, but Bianca will come with me. It'll be a proper girls' day out with her as well...' She met Charlie's eyes. 'But you'd be welcome too.'

'I don't think so...'

'Paige would absolutely love you...'

'Ah,' Charlie said. So that was it – Edie wanted to matchmake Charlie with her newly dumped friend. He gave his brave 'cover all the hurt' grin again. 'Another time – maybe.'

Shane arrived with the drinks and suddenly the pub was filled with families, couples, Friday night revellers. Charlie exhaled slowly and told himself he was just like anyone else there, a man who owned a house down the road, having a friendly meal with a neighbour. That was all there was to it.

* * *

Another pint and a ginger beer later, Charlie and Edie split the bill and stepped outside into the cold air. Alan trotted along happily on his lead, his breath steamy. Edie shivered.

'It'll be Hallowe'en soon,' Charlie muttered as they crossed the road and made for Ferrers Lane. There was little traffic around, a lone car, a shuddering bus.

They walked for a moment in silence, just the crunch of their feet on gravel. Then Edie said out of nowhere, 'Did somebody break your heart, Charlie?'

Charlie said nothing for a while, then he mumbled, 'I don't really talk about it.'

There was more silence, then Edie said, 'I thought so...'

Charlie made a muffled sound that meant the subject was closed.

'So...' Edie took a breath. 'I split up with my boyfriend ages ago. There hasn't really been anyone since then. We sold the house in Markyate and I bought this one here. I didn't want to live in Markyate after Nathan...'

Charlie frowned. 'But I thought it was your home – your friends live there...'

'Mmm, it was.' Edie was thoughtful. 'I just didn't want to see him everywhere I went, with his new girlfriend. In the pub, in the supermarket. It would have been... pretty unbearable.' She forced a laugh. 'Splitting up with him knocked me for six.'

'What happened?' Charlie asked, then he stopped himself. 'I don't mean to pry – don't answer if—'

'No – no, it helps to talk...' Edie exhaled loudly, her breath misting against the cold. 'We were talking about getting engaged. I wasn't sure if I wanted to – I'm not your typical diamond ring sort of girl. But there was plenty of time for that.'

'So what went wrong?'

'It was little things at first, arguments about washing up, silly stuff. Then Nathan would say he was going away for the weekend with the boys – rugby trips, that sort of thing. Of course, he wasn't...'

'He cheated?' Charlie asked.

'It had been going on for months before he finally left. I'd been so stupid – I just ignored all the signs,' Edie said. 'He'd fallen for a woman who was older than him, a divorcée. She was sophisticated, confident, she had a sports car. I felt pretty bad...'

'Why should you feel bad?' Charlie was surprised to feel suddenly protective. 'He didn't deserve you.'

'I won't be hurt again...' Edie gave a shuddering breath. 'I promised myself that.'

They turned the corner and Charlie automatically pulled out his phone, flicking on his torch. He murmured, 'It takes time to heal, I know.'

'It does,' Edie admitted. 'I have trust issues now.' She forced a brave laugh. 'I honestly believe that anyone I become close to will let me down...' Her voice trailed off. 'I'll get over it.'

Charlie wasn't sure what to say. He wanted to tell her about Luna, how she stopped loving him when he still loved her more than anyone in the world. Instead, he said, 'You're right, Edie. We'll get over it. All we need is time.'

'Time...' Edie looked up at him in the dark. 'And good friends.'

'Yep.' Charlie did his best to brighten the moment – they had both become sombre. 'It was great having dinner in the pub with you. We must do it again.'

Edie's eyes shone in the dark. 'I'd like that.'

Charlie felt Alan tug at the lead. 'What is it, Al?'

Alan jerked again, pulling Charlie along. Edie was at his shoulder.

'What is it, mate?' Charlie asked.

Alan stopped dead and turned to the woods, barking loudly.

Charlie gazed into the darkness towards where Alan was looking. 'What can you see?'

'A squirrel, or a badger maybe...?' Edie suggested.

Alan barked once, then he began to whine, a low, eerie sound that came from deep in his throat.

Charlie was concerned. 'Are you OK, Al? Come on – let's get you home. You'll be fine when...' He stopped.

In the gloom, a shape stood next to an overhanging tree, a pale light against dark velvet bark and whispering leaves. He saw her distinctly, the long dress, the low bodice, the cap, the mane of curls. Her eyes met his and he couldn't look away. Something passed between them, a moment of understanding. He shivered and felt Edie clutch his arm.

Charlie whispered, 'The Wicked Lady...'

He held his breath, staring at the figure on horseback. He blinked, his heart thumping, and looked again.

She was gone.

20

Charlie and Edie ran towards number three as fast as they could, Alan nearby on his lead, their heads down as if that would prevent them from seeing the image of the woman.

Edie's hand shook as she tried to push the key into the lock. She dragged Charlie by his arm into the kitchen and stood, breathing hard. 'You saw it?'

Charlie nodded. 'It's not the first time I've seen her.'

'I've felt something eerie before on Ferrers Lane...' Edie closed her eyes, recalling hurrying home on occasions, feeling cold. 'But I've never actually seen her before...'

'I saw her shadow from my window. And I felt her rush past me on the horse...'

Alan barked once. Bianca looked up from her doggy bed, her nose wrinkling, unconcerned.

Edie's hand hovered over the kettle. 'Coffee?'

'Please.'

'Or brandy?'

'Yes, brandy...' Charlie's heart was still thumping. He watched Edie collect two glasses from a cupboard, along with a half-full bottle of amber liquid. She pushed the glasses into his hands, grabbed his jacket sleeve and tugged him into the lounge. They sat together on the sofa, shoulders touching, shivering.

Charlie poured them a glass each before swallowing a mouthful, then another.

'We saw her, Edie. Both of us...'

Edie's eyes were round. 'As clearly as we see each other.'

'Did you see her old-fashioned costume...?'

'And the hat, the hair?' Edie took a swig. 'I can't believe it...'

Charlie's glass was almost empty. He refilled it.

'I've heard a bit about her... Obviously Ferrers Lane is named after her...' Edie closed her eyes, remembering. 'She was called Kathleen, or Katherine... although mostly she's called The Wicked Lady... She must haunt the common.'

'Because she was a highway robber there...' Charlie hadn't realised that he was constantly sipping the sharp brandy. His nerves were shot.

Edie took a deep breath. 'What will we do?'

'Do?'

'Now we know she's outside?'

Charlie was alarmed. 'You don't think she'll come in?'

Edie jumped. 'Can ghosts do that? Follow people into their houses?'

Charlie studied her expression; she was terrified. He needed to restore some calm and he did the only thing he could: make a joke. 'I expect she can't... she wouldn't want to leave her horse – and anyway, she probably can't open doors... or windows.' He grinned. 'Or float through them...'

Edie was even more anxious. 'Charlie, I live by myself – how am I going to sleep?'

'This is the first time you've seen her, isn't it?' Charlie watched as Edie nodded. 'Then she might not come back for years, if ever.' His mind was racing. 'Maybe it's because Halloween's a week away... maybe she'll just hang around for a day or two and then go.'

Edie was unconvinced. 'Do you think so?'

'Definitely.' Charlie made his voice strong, reassuring, although he was improvising wildly.

'I need another drink.' Edie bent down to pick up the bottle, refilled her glass and Charlie's at the same time.

Charlie had already had three pints, and now he was swigging brandy. He told himself the drink was medicinal and took a deep breath.

'Right, Edie – how about...?' He searched for some calming words. 'Let's do some research, find out what happened to her – let's look into her background. Maybe it will explain why she's here...' He felt a coldness go through him, like fingers against his spine. 'I mean, why isn't she haunting The Cell in Markyate? She lived there...'

'Maybe she died in the woods?' Edie's eyes were wide at the thought.

'Or she's just trying to communicate how her life was...' Charlie said, doing his best to be logical. 'You know, as if she wants to explain how it was for her in those days. I sort of felt that when she looked at me.'

'I know what you mean.' Edie asked: 'So, she lived in Markyate – but who with? Was she married? Did she die young or old? Did she have kids?'

'And why was she a robber if she was rich?' Charlie added. 'Was she just looking for a bit of fun, to pass the time when she wasn't meeting other rich people?'

'Maybe she was an independent woman – it would have been a bit unusual in those days for a woman to be a highway robber...' Edie suggested. 'Maybe she fell into being a highway woman by accident?'

'What, like I'm out for a nice ride, oh look – there's a coach and horses, I'll just put a mask on and grab a gun and shout "Stand and Deliver?" for the hell of it...' Charlie was joking, but his skin prickled. He said, 'She's really sad, isn't she, Edie?'

'Did you feel that?'

'I did...' Charlie made a low sound of assent. 'She seems lost, or like she's lost someone precious – like her heart is broken.'

Edie shuddered, a sigh deep in her chest. 'Perhaps that's why we can see her. We're empathic and she sees it in us. We know what it's like to feel sad...' Tears filled her eyes and she drained her glass, as if the brandy would help. 'Charlie. I'm scared...'

He wrapped a protective arm around her and she snuggled closer. 'What are you afraid of?'

'Her...' Edie muttered into his chest. 'Seeing her in my bedroom when I open my eyes at night – hearing her outside, the sound of a horse.'

'You won't... it'll be fine,' Charlie said reassuringly, although the thought had occurred to him too.

Edie was close to him, the warmth of her skin against his. It felt comforting. She smelled of something like nutmeg and the sweetness of it made him sigh without meaning to. He glanced towards Alan, who had settled himself on a rug. Bianca was still in the kitchen, oblivious. He gathered Edie closer, murmuring into her hair, 'Seriously – it'll be all right.'

She didn't move. He thought she looked helpless and he felt suddenly protective. Her hair brushed his face, soft curls.

His lips touched her cheek as he whispered, 'We'll be fine. We'll look out for each other.'

Edie snuffled, wiped her eyes. 'I'm so glad you're my neighbour.'

'Me too,' Charlie said. He inhaled and another sigh shook him.

Suddenly, she was pulling him against her and he was sinking into the softness of her arms. They were kissing.

Charlie closed his eyes and he felt his heart open, as if it had been empty and hollow for so long and he needed to fill it to the brim. His fingers twisted in her hair; she was rose-sweet, lovely. He murmured her name.

'Luna.'

They pulled back at the same time and Charlie said, 'I'm sorry...'

'No, I'm sorry,' Edie said.

They blinked at each other as if in shock, a wide space between them on the sofa now.

Charlie wondered how to explain. 'It's... it's... I like you, Edie. I... made a mistake. The brandy...' He stopped himself abruptly. He was telling her he'd only kissed her because he was drunk. That was unfair, hurtful. And wrong.

'I know.' Edie took a deep breath, as if steeling herself. 'You're not ready for a relationship. And definitely not with me...'

'No, no, I mean...' Charlie was worried about what to say. He'd blurt out the wrong thing – he'd only make things worse. 'I should go. Alan – we should go...'

'You should.' Edie stood up, lifting her chin as if she didn't care.

'I'm sorry,' Charlie said again, on his feet now.

'Not at all.' Edie shook her hair. 'It doesn't matter.'

Charlie wanted to tell her that it did matter. He just felt awful because he might have offended her and he certainly didn't want to do that. But no words would come. He patted Alan. 'We'll get off home now.'

Edie flopped down on the sofa, as if she was drained of energy. She looked as if she'd cry. 'Can you see yourself out please?'

'Of course... right... yes...' Charlie paused at the door, a last attempt to make things right. 'Can we see each other soon?'

Edie nodded. 'If you like.'

'I would...' Charlie gripped the door handle. It was best that he left now. 'Goodnight, Edie...'

He heard her say something flat and emotionless, but it was indiscernible. Then he and Alan were standing at the front door, staring into the darkness. The wind was ice as it touched his face. He stared into the trees, wondering if she was out there. The Wicked Lady.

Then he set off back to number one as fast as he could, his heart heavy as lead.

* * *

Kate sat on horseback on the common, watching, listening for the thunder of wheels and hooves. The light was fading and heavy clouds hung low. It was cold and likely to rain, but she knew the coach would be approaching soon on its way to London; she'd have time to stop it, to steal the passengers' money and be away before nightfall, before the storm came in. Her plan was to canter through the woodlands, pass beyond the river and take the dirt track back to The Cell.

Darkness was half an hour away. The sky was purplish, like a spreading bruise. She inhaled deeply in readiness and could smell the earthy damp of the common, the sharpness of new leaves. Her keen ears became keener, listening for the thrum of wheels, the clop of horses. She gripped the flintlock and promised herself she would never use it.

Just for tonight she was a highway robber. Tomorrow, she'd put the gun back in Thomas's room, wear her best dress, plan to go to London, to sell the jewels. Things would be normal again. Better than normal.

She shivered, a gust from the night breeze tugging at her coat. Beneath her, Midnight snorted gently. Kate knew it was an alarm. Midnight held his head high; he'd detected a threat. She heard the clatter in the distance and she stiffened in readiness.

It came into sight: a coach, four horses, racing along the road to London as fast as the driver could make it. She knew why – she was already notorious.

She adjusted her kerchief over her face, leaned forward and patted Midnight's warm neck. 'This will be the last time. Then we will go home.'

She spurred him on and they were racing towards the coach. With a loud cry, she lifted her pistol and charged, making the driver tug the reins.

The coach came to a halt and she called out, 'Stand – and deliver your purse! Then I will not harm you...'

She watched while three figures – a woman and two men, one considerably younger than the other – clambered shakily from the coach.

One of the men muttered, 'Scoundrel.'

'Be silent,' Kate commanded, her voice low. 'You...' She pointed to the woman with her pistol. 'Mistress, bring me the purses, and your jewels...'

The woman stepped forward hesitantly and Kate said kindly, 'I will not harm you, mistress. I seek only to take your money, not your life.'

The oldest man met her eyes. He was dressed expensively, in a velvet coat, leather boots. 'You will hang on the gallows...'

Kate ignored him, indicating her indignation with a wave of her pistol. With her spare hand, she swept silk purses, a necklace, brooches, rings, into her pockets. Then she inclined her head courteously. 'Please – resume your journey. I wish you Godspeed and a pleasant stay.'

She pointed her pistol while the three passengers clambered back into the coach. She nodded to the driver, who cracked a whip and rode off.

Swiftly, she swung Midnight round and took off for the woodlands, leaning forward, driving him on. It was then that she felt the first drops of rain.

The stallion's hooves thundered on the soft ground beneath the trees, twigs cracking underfoot. Kate and Midnight galloped into the darkness, making for the lane that would lead for Markyate and the long ride home.

She breathed deeply; it had been a good haul, the purses full, the jewellery gold, rubies. She had done well.

The woodlands were almost behind her; beyond was the open land, the lane, the river. She glanced up at the sky; the clouds were low, silver grey; the reddish hue of sunset glimmered on the horizon. The ribbon of the road ahead was visible, curling into the distance. The reins tight in her fist, she hurtled on.

Someone was behind her. She could hear hooves, the sound of someone following her fast. She breathed hard, pushing Midnight forward towards the bridge.

The rider behind her was getting closer. She was sure it was the constable, Lambert Wilmott. Her body tensed, expecting to hear the crack of a pistol, feel a shuddering shock as lead shot hit her in the back.

'On, Midnight, on,' she panted.

The pound of hooves behind her was louder; the man in pursuit was coming closer and closer. Kate drove Midnight on, panting hard from fear and effort. But he was closer still, at her shoulder, leaning out towards her. They had arrived at the river just as his hand took hold of the sleeve of her coat and he tugged it fiercely. She felt herself slipping.

21

THE PRESENT

'What's been eating you all week?' Uncle Bill asked as he tucked into a slice of coffee and walnut cake that Marilyn had brought round earlier. It was eleven-thirty. Bill had his feet up on a box as he sprawled on a hop up work platform in the bedroom, holding a mug of coffee. Alan was lying on his bed, chomping on a chew stick, watching him thoughtfully.

'Oh, nothing...' Charlie shrugged. He knew what was wrong with him. He'd spent the whole weekend working rather than think too hard about how much he might have upset Edie. He offered a grin. 'The bedroom's looking good, Uncle Bill.'

'It is.' Bill glanced round at the smooth walls, the cleanly painted ceiling, the smart floorboards that they were ready to varnish. 'So – spill the beans, Charlie. Why have you got a face like a smacked bum? Fallen out with the girl in number three, have you?'

'What makes you think that?' Charlie asked, wondering why older people knew exactly what the problem was. Everyone except his mother. She wouldn't have noticed.

'Today's Thursday and I haven't seen hide nor hair of her all week, but I've seen you gawping out the window.'

Charlie thought he'd go for shock tactics and change the subject. 'I might have seen a ghost.'

Bill laughed. 'It's Halloween today. I heard a programme about ghosts on the radio when I was driving here this morning – according to a Welsh superstition, on Halloween night, there's a spirit waiting at every cross-roads. Most of them will just let you pass by, but some are up to mischief...'

'Edie and I saw one the other night...'

'When?'

'Last Friday. We had a meal in The Sycamore Tree. On the way back, we saw her in the woods.'

'Her?' Bill didn't move.

'Katherine Ferrers. I looked her up. She was born in 1634. She lived at Markyate. She was a highway woman...'

'I might have heard something about her...' Bill gave a short laugh. 'This is Ferrers Lane, isn't it?'

'Named after her.'

'You sure you and Edie hadn't been on the sauce?'

Charlie remembered the pints of beer, the brandy, and what had happened afterwards. He shook his head to dispel the image. 'We both saw it and we were sure it was her. Edie and I said we'd research her background...'

'That was a week ago,' Bill said. 'Have you been around to see her?'

'She's been busy at work – me too.' Charlie thought it was the easiest answer.

'You ought to get yourself round there.' Bill snorted. 'Take her for another drink. Or at least get yourself out.'

Charlie couldn't help himself. 'I don't know if that's a good idea.'

'I do. Marcia and I were discussing it. You've spent the last two weeks working on this place alone. You need some fun. Why don't you have a few days with your mates in London, just take some time off? I can manage here by myself.'

Charlie was surprised how good the idea sounded. 'I might.'

'Go this afternoon, stay with your friends – do some sofa surfing...'

Charlie brightened. 'Maybe this weekend. I have a lesson with Kavish and Joshit at five...'

'Are you giving music lessons now?' Bill was impressed.

Charlie nodded. 'I'd forgotten how much I enjoyed teaching – the music side of it, not all the time-consuming admin.'

'You didn't enjoy that job at Blanche Harris Academy?'

'No, it wasn't the right place for me. I had tough classes, the workload was horrendous...' Charlie took a breath, remembering how much his confidence had been sapped, how tired he had become poring over endless assessments and grades, how lack of funding meant working against all odds with few instruments and infrequent access to technology.

'Would you go back to it?' Bill asked.

'I might...' Charlie offered an optimistic expression. 'Right school, right time... But I'm enjoying working with you.'

'Then we'd better get back to the grind.' Bill stood up and rubbed his tummy. 'Sausage rolls, egg sandwich, and coffee and walnut cake... not a good combination. Shall we get on with the job in hand?'

Charlie's phone buzzed. 'Oh, I'll get this...' He reached in his pocket. 'It's a WhatsApp message from Kofi and Jules. There's a party tonight at The Copper Tap in Peckham.'

'You should go, Charlie.' Bill was already strapping on his foam knee pads.

'I will.' Charlie gave a laugh. 'It's fancy dress.'

'You could dress up as your ghostly highway woman...' Bill guffawed.

Charlie froze. 'I couldn't do that.' He was surprised how disrespectful the idea felt. 'I'll put a hoodie on and go as the Grim Reaper.' He frowned; even that didn't feel right.

'Stay over – have a few drinks...' Bill suggested. 'Or you could go on the train, then I'll drive down and pick you up and you can stay at mine...'

'It's a long drive, Uncle Bill.'

'An hour and a half. But it's worth it if you enjoy yourself.'

'I can take the van... I'll sleep on someone's couch.'

'Please yourself.'

'Or... hang on.' Charlie looked thoughtful. 'Are you all right by yourself for ten minutes?'

'Right as rain...' Bill watched Charlie hurtling towards the door. 'Where are you off?'

'Apparently there's a shortage of girls at this party, according to Jules – I'm going to find a few...'

Alan leaped from his bed and dropped the remains of the chew onto the floor, scurrying after Charlie, Bill watched them go, shook his head and lifted his paintbrush, an indulgent smile on his face.

Charlie knocked at the door of number three, Alan at his heels, and waited. Briefly, he recalled staggering out of the house, his head down, feeling decidedly ashamed, dazed with alcohol and emotion. He had blundered home, cleaned his teeth and gone straight to bed, feeling both angry with himself and lonely.

He knocked again and Edie appeared wearing glasses and colourful dungarees. Bianca peered round the corner of the door like a guard dog, her face inscrutable. Edie, on the other hand, looked apprehensive.

'Charlie?'

'Are you busy?'

Edie shook her head. 'Well, a bit...' She looked around, as if for help. 'I'm researching UK human trafficking legislation.'

'Why?' Charlie asked, then it occurred to him. 'Oh, for your next essay...'

'Right.' Edie leaned against the door as if barring the way. 'Aren't you working on the house? I saw your uncle's van...'

'I'd like to ask you something...'

'Oh?'

'And say sorry.'

'There's no need.'

Charlie let out a sigh. 'Edie, can I come in?'

'OK.'

She led the way into the kitchen. At the table, a laptop was open, surrounded by books, a notepad, a cup of tea, a sandwich with a bite taken out of it.

Charlie decided he'd throw himself in at the deep end. 'Edie – I wanted to apologise for the other night.'

'You don't have to.'

'We'd been drinking...'

Edie seemed disappointed. 'I know.'

'And we'd seen – what we saw, in the woods... the ghost...'

'We did.'

'I was a bit emotional. I let my feelings get the better of me. I'm sorry. It was nice though. The kiss.'

Edie looked hopeful. 'Oh?'

Charlie squeezed his eyes shut, not sure what to say next. He didn't want to encourage Edie. He didn't want to make her think there was any chance of a relationship – there wasn't. Then he felt a moment of irritation with himself – who did he think he was? Any man would be lucky to spend time with Edie. She was sweet, kind, funny, lovely. He was confused.

He took a breath. 'I'm an idiot.'

'Ah.' Edie clearly didn't know what to say.

Charlie tried again. 'Can we be friends? That's really important to me.'

'Oh...'

'I like you a lot.' Charlie was making a mess of things. He said, 'I wanted to ask. How did your trip to St Albans go the other day? With Paige and Priya?' He was pleased with himself that he'd remembered Edie's friends' names.

'It was great – we had fun.'

'Good.' Charlie grinned. 'So – how would you all like to go to a Halloween party?'

'When?' Edie replied.

'Tonight. Are you doing anything?'

'No. I know Paige asked if we could go somewhere – she said she was fed up that she was staying in...'

'Then come with me. It's in London. We'll have a riot.'

'London? How will we get there?'

'I'll drive you all in the van.'

'But we'll be back really late.'

'Tomorrow's Friday.' Charlie was starting to feel pleased with himself. 'Then it's the weekend. If we roll in at three in the morning, that's fine.'

'Are you sure? I mean, it's a long drive back.'

'I'll run you all home.'

'I'm not working in the pub until lunchtime tomorrow. Paige can stay over with me. I'll ask Priya if she'll come.'

'Great. That would be awesome...' Charlie met her eyes. They were hazel, clear, full of emotion. He found his gaze stuck there for a moment.

Edie paused, then she said, 'I'll text you, shall I?'

'Brilliant.' Charlie turned to go and almost fell over Alan, who had started to move away. 'Oh, I almost forgot – it's fancy dress.'

'What shall I come as?'

'A ghost.' The word stuck in Charlie's mouth and he said, 'Just throw on an old sheet... cut some eye holes... Or...' He took a breath. 'Anything you like...'

'What are you going as?' Edie called after him as he rushed back to work.

'I've no idea... I'll improvise,' he yelled as he hurried back to number one. His heart felt lighter. He was looking forward to the evening.

* * *

At seven o'clock, Charlie and three enthusiastic women in fancy dress sat in his van on their way to London. Charlie was wearing an orange anorak with the hood pulled over his face, teamed with black jeans and brown gloves. No one had a clue who he was supposed to be. He grinned as he drove through St Albans and said, 'I'm Kenny McCormick.'

'Who?' Priya asked. She was dressed as the Corpse Bride, stunning in a bridal gown and veil, impeccable make-up, all wide eyes and pale blue face.

'Kenny from *South Park*,' Charlie explained.

'Why is Kenny spooky?' a voice called from the back seat. It was Paige, who was, according to her own admission, dressed as a sexy bat in a short black dress, boned wings and a fluffy hood.

'You must have heard the phrase "Oh my God, they killed Kenny!"' Edie said, glancing at Charlie. 'So, Kenny must be a ghost...'

'Plus, Kenny died a hundred and twenty-seven times in total – he has the power of immortality – he just wakes up in his bed after having died,' Charlie added.

'I've never watched *South Park*,' Priya said. 'Toby likes it...'

'Where is the fiancé this evening?' Paige asked in a bored voice.

'He's watching football,' Priya replied in an equally bored tone.

'Who needs football?' Charlie smiled, wondering if he'd have been wiser to stay home and listen to the game on his little radio. 'We'll have a brilliant time at the party.'

'Oh, I hope so,' Paige said. 'Edie said all your old friends from uni would be going.'

'It's in a pub in Peckham,' Priya added. 'I bet it's so cool...'

'I haven't been to London in ages.' Edie smoothed the folds of her cape and adjusted her wonky witch's hat. She hadn't gone to the same amount of trouble with her costume that her friends had, but Charlie thought she looked radiant.

'I must go more often,' Charlie said and realised how much his words rang true. He was looking forward to being back in Peckham, meeting his friends, socialising. He'd only drink fruit juice so that he could drive the women home afterwards, but he could imagine the looks on his friends' faces when he strode into The Copper Tap with three gorgeous girls. Besides, it would be nice to get back into the swing of life. Perhaps there might be a chance to play some music with one or two of the others. He missed that too. 'The Copper Tap always has the best nights. I hope you'll enjoy yourselves...'

'I totally intend to,' Paige said. 'I couldn't ever turn down a night out in London.'

'It'll be better than being at home watching Toby watch the football,' Priya agreed.

'And it will be good seeing all the Halloween costumes,' Edie added. 'And dancing. I love dancing. I haven't danced in ages.'

Charlie turned the van onto the motorway. He imagined Edie dancing, dressed as a witch, her cape twirling.

Suddenly it was Luna dancing in her place, the light brown hair twirling over her shoulders. He felt sad and foolish at the same time.

Charlie concentrated on the traffic as it whizzed by, one car passing another, all hurtling to somewhere else, a new destination. It struck him as a metaphor for his own life. He was in the driving seat, holding the wheel, controlling his own speed, navigating into the unknown. It was about time he let Luna go now. It was time to get on with his own life.

Yes, the world was moving forward all the time. He needed to move forward with it. Or he'd be left behind, just like the ghostly woman on horseback...

22

1659

The man caught up with Kate at the river. He grabbed hold of her coat sleeve and tugged it fiercely.

Kate felt herself slip. Her first thought was for Midnight, but she saw the stallion turn towards her, waiting calmly.

She plunged into the cold water, sinking, being lifted in the current, her doublet and breeches heavy and wet. She cried out. The pistol was in her hand. She aimed it levelly at the man who stood over her and said, 'I'll shoot.'

He stepped back.

The water was shallower at the edge, where she lurched for the safety of a rock, heaving herself up on all fours. She tugged herself up, soaked, and he held out a hand. 'Come on – let's get you out of there.'

It was a voice she recognised. Not the constable's, but a friendly voice, husky with warmth. She took his rough hand and immediately remembered shaking it before she'd left Ayers End Farm.

She hauled herself upright. Her hat was askew, her kerchief loose. Her clothes, hair and face were dripping with water. 'Master Chetwyn.'

'Mistress Fanshawe,' Raife replied, his voice gentle.

'Kate...' Kate said quickly. 'My husband's name hardly befits my clothes...'

In the half-light, she thought she saw him smile. He looked at the pistol. 'You will not shoot me?'

'I will not.'

'But here you are on the Markyate Road, dressed as a man...'

Kate pushed wet hair from her eyes. 'You chased me. I thought you were the constable. I almost took a shot at you.'

'And yet I am alive...'

'I am no killer.'

'Then perhaps you will learn to be if you intend to be a highway robber.'

'You mock me.' Kate's lip curled.

'Not I,' Raife said.

'Why did you chase me?'

'I recognised Midnight. I was riding on the common – my livestock roam free there – and I saw you riding away from the coach. I had a suspicion that it was you.'

'How?'

'Such a delicate young man on a horse I used to ride myself?' he said, and Kate thought he was laughing at her. Raife was staring at her clothes. 'Men's habits become you well, but I fear you need to take them off.'

'Pardon?' Kate gave him an icy stare. Beneath the coat, she shivered.

'Come – you are quaking. Ayers End is but a few moments away and Midnight knows the way well. Let's get you to my cottage and I'll find you something to wear, some hot food to warm you up. Besides...' He offered a complicit wink. 'The constable will have heard of the robbery by now and I believe he is keen to capture the gallant young lad who has terrorised the highway on two occasions now.'

Kate stared at him, wondering how much he knew. But he was right. She was so cold that she was visibly shaking and she needed a comforting fire, a cup of ale. She allowed him to help her onto the horse's back, then he leaped onto his own mount and turned, heading up the hill. Kate followed, the pistol limp in her hand, the spoils of her robbery hidden inside her coat. She wondered why she trusted Raife Chetwyn.

* * *

The downstairs room at Ayers End Farm was welcoming and homely. The doublet Raife gave her to wear came to her knees, but it was quilted and cosy. Kate sat in front of the fire on a stool, her hair dripping, a cup of warm ale in her hands. Raife had hung her clothes to dry in the hearth and wrapped a woollen blanket over her knees, tucking her feet in carefully. Her flesh felt numb, her bones brittle to the marrow. She shivered again.

Raife busied himself with two bowls of pottage, rough pieces of rye Carter's bread, placing one carefully on her lap. The firelight reflected an orange blaze in his eyes as he glanced at her. 'How are you feeling, Mistress Kate?'

'I am better, thank you,' Kate muttered gratefully. 'I am glad you caught up with me. It had started to rain and the air was exceedingly icy.'

He was scrutinising her face. Kate wondered what he was thinking. He said simply, 'Eat. You will feel better.'

Kate spooned the stew into her mouth. It was hot, comforting. She said, 'It is delicious. Thank you.'

Raife smiled. 'It is not the fare you are used to, mistress. But it is hearty stew, cabbage, turnips and bacon, beans and herbs, thickened with oats. It will fill your stomach.'

Kate ate each spoonful slowly until she was scraping the bottom of the bowl. She turned to Raife. He was looking at her again, his head to one side, a smile on his lips. 'I am grateful to you, Master Chetwyn. And I thank you for Midnight. He is a good horse.' She glanced at his hand and saw the cabochon ring on his smallest finger.

He followed her eyes. 'You left this for me. I wear it in the evenings after I have finished work to remind me of you.'

The idea of a farmer wearing a lady's ring made her smile. She said, 'I thought you would sell it, that it would fetch a pretty penny...'

'It was a gift,' he said simply. 'I could not sell it.'

Kate lowered her eyes. For some reason, she felt humble. 'You are too kind.'

'Why did you steal from the people in the coach?' Raife asked suddenly.

She looked up, her eyes defiant. 'Those people are rich – they have plenty.'

'You are rich.' A small knot appeared between Raife's eyebrows. 'I do not understand why you need to take their purses.'

'My husband is taxed by Parliament – he gives much money to the king. That leaves us very little. He is in the north right now fighting for Charles.' Kate took a breath. 'He wanted to sell The Cell and I told him that I would not allow it. Since I married him, he has sold off almost all the lands and properties I inherited from my father and my grandfather. He has raised the tenants' rents and made it hard for the poorer people. I own nothing but a few jewels and the clothes I stand in. So I had to do something.'

Raife did not take his eyes from her face. 'I have heard you give money and food to poor families.'

'It is not enough,' Kate said. 'And it is not fair. Besides...' She couldn't help smiling. 'It is not hard to steal from those who are unsuspecting as they drive along the London Road with no idea that I am nearby, waiting...'

'It is dangerous,' Raife said, and she heard the disapproval in his tone.

'I am not afraid of danger,' Kate replied quickly. She took a breath. 'My husband and I do not love each other. Our lives are separate – it has always been that way. All that he wants from me is my money.'

'You are a brave woman,' Raife said, concerned. 'But I think you do not realise the peril you could be in. Constable Wilmott called here a few days ago, asking me if I knew of a young man who spoke in a light, polite voice, and was gallant and courteous as he robbed his victims. I told him I had seen or heard of no such person.' A smile flickered across his mouth and Kate couldn't take her eyes away. 'I know now it was you.'

'It was,' Kate admitted. 'And this was to be my last highway robbery. But now I am not sure. I could do much good with the money I take...'

'It is risky – you are alone and—'

'Do not say "and a woman."' Kate's eyes blazed. 'I have never needed any help from anyone. I was orphaned at six, married at thirteen. I make my own decisions...'

'You are quite incredible...' Raife was looking at her in the way he had before. 'And in the firelight, you are like no one I have ever seen.'

'Am I?' Kate held her breath.

'I heard once of Vesta, the goddess of the hearth fire in the Roman religion. I imagined her a glowing orange, with long hair and gleaming skin, eyes as bright as the dawn. As you are now.' He stood slowly, kneeling next to her stool. With his rough hand, he pushed her hair from her eyes. 'Golden, beautiful.'

Kate felt the familiar thud of her heart. Raife was bathed in firelight too. She recalled the god Vulcan. Her breathing had become shallow.

His voice was just audible. 'You cannot go home now. It is too dark.'

'I shall be missed...' Kate began.

'I will have you back at The Cell by morning,' Raife murmured.

Kate closed her eyes. It would be easy to put Midnight in his stable tomorrow at dawn, to creep into the kitchen and up to her room through the secret passage. 'It is as you say,' she said in a whisper.

'Then stay.' He lifted her in his arms easily and carried her to the stairs that led to the small room beneath the straw roof, climbing steadily. She felt him place her gently on a hard straw mattress, then he was lying at her side, his fingers tracing the skin on her neck, his lips against the vein that pulsed there.

Kate's eyes were still closed. She wouldn't open them. If she was dreaming, she didn't want to wake.

* * *

Charlie was wide awake as he drove home, his three passengers singing at the top of their voices. It was past three. The girls had danced for most of the evening and Charlie and his friends had danced with them. He felt fully alive, as if a new kind of electricity pulsed through him.

At the moment they were all singing Queen's 'Don't Stop Me Now', Charlie and three women who were a little drunk, their heads back as they bawled each line. Edie and Priya had good voices, but Paige's was exceptional, bluesy and filled with melancholy. He wondered if it was so sad because her boyfriend had recently broken off the relationship. Not that she had spoken about him much throughout the evening, or looked particularly sad. She had danced with his friends, then with him, her arms round his neck, her head thrown back. In fact, Charlie had danced with all three girls, then he'd sat in the corner and had a long chat with

Jules, who'd said there was a new jazz club opening up in Southwark soon. Jules was a great bass guitarist; Charlie had played alongside her many times. She reminded him that jazz clubs were always on the lookout for sax players. Charlie had said he'd think about it. He'd like to play in a band again.

Paige launched into Abba's 'Dancing Queen' as they reached St Albans, and on the road to Nomansland Common, she was leading the others in an appropriate rendition of 'Take Me Home, Country Roads' by John Denver. As they approached Ferrers Lane, Charlie couldn't help staring through the windows into the trees, then over towards the open grassland, to see if anything moved in the shadows. What did he expect to see? A woman on horseback moving towards him, her coat flapping in the breeze.

Katherine Ferrers was occupying his thoughts more than she should. Not just her ghost, but the woman she had been, why she'd acted as she did. And what had become of her. She was an enigma.

As he braked outside Constable's Cottages, Paige said, 'It's creepy here.'

'How is it creepy?' Charlie asked.

Edie quickly said, 'It's dark, and it's four o'clock in the morning, and we're all cold. No wonder it's creepy.' She shot Charlie a warning look, as if to say that it was best not to mention the ghost in front of her friends.

Charlie understood – they'd both decided to stay the night with Edie and she didn't want her guests to panic.

'Isn't this a great place to live though,' Priya said. 'It's so remote, like being in your own private world.'

'I love it.' Edie stood in the cold, her arms wrapped round herself. 'Bianca will have missed me...'

'And Alan,' Charlie added.

'Oh, I can't wait to meet Alan,' Paige said.

'What a great name for a dog.' Priya swung her handbag. 'Shall we go in?'

'Are you coming in for a coffee, Charlie?' Paige yelled.

'I won't...' Charlie suddenly felt tired. His limbs ached and he'd be up in four hours – Uncle Bill wanted to attack the upstairs rooms. 'Another time...?'

'Oh, then can we do this again?' Paige jumped up and down to keep warm. The clacking of her heels made Charlie's shoulders stiffen. It sounded like the clop-clop of a horse's hooves.

'That would be nice...' He lifted his car keys. 'Night, Edie... Nice to meet you, Priya, Paige.'

'Aww.' Paige was looking for a hug. 'Until next time, Charlie.'

He rushed through the darkness towards number one, shoving the key in the lock, pushing the door open. He heard Paige's voice, too loud, carrying from the end cottage. 'He's gorgeous, Edie. Do you like him? I mean, if you do... but then, I wouldn't mind...' Her words were covered by Priya's shrieks of laughter, then Edie's muffled whisper.

Once he was inside, Alan leaped up, demanding attention. Charlie ruffled his fur, checked the Labrador's food and water bowls, then dragged himself upstairs towards the spare room.

He cleaned his teeth, tugged off his clothes and flopped onto the mattress in his boxers, covering himself with the duvet. He placed his arms behind his head and sighed. He felt Alan settle down near his feet. He was wide awake.

Charlie's head was filled with sounds and images of the evening: the booming music that made the floors of the upstairs room vibrate, dancing with Paige, her eyes on him all the time, with Priya, with Edie, who smiled and was sweet but seemed less interested in him since the night they kissed.

The kiss. The thought of it moved something primitive in Charlie's stomach. He felt protective, a rush of sympathy: perhaps it was just friendship. Edie was definitely OK. He liked her.

Then, for some reason, another face took her place in his imagination, a strange young woman he'd never met, but in his mind she had delicate features, long dark hair, a coat, breeches, leather boots. He was thinking of Katherine Ferrers, of who she might have been, of why her spirit couldn't rest. Even now she might be outside among the trees, mounted on her horse, watching.

He rolled over, the lady of the highway filling his mind, and still, he couldn't sleep.

23

1659

Kate had never slept so deeply. She opened her eyes and recalled immediately where she was. She was filled with a happiness she had never known. Raife was lying next to her, watching her. She turned shining eyes on him. 'It is good to look at you the moment I wake. I feared last night was a dream.'

'And now?' he asked her, touching her cheek, tracing the curve of her chin, her neck, resting in the dip above her collarbone. He placed a kiss there and she tangled his hair between her fingers.

Kate sighed. 'It is the first day of my life.' She was surprised at her own words. But she was right – she could not look back now she had met him. He filled her thoughts entirely, and she wanted no more than to be with him.

'We are meant to be, you and I,' he murmured against her lips.

'But perhaps I should have behaved as befits a lady. Perhaps I should have been coy, said you nay, pretended to be unsure so that you would persuade me more...'

'Why would you do that?'

'I was a maid...' Kate said. 'And a maid is supposed to lead a gentleman a merry dance before he captures her and makes her his own. Perhaps I was too ready to submit...But I do not care. I cannot regret a moment I have spent in your arms.'

'Playing games may be for others, but not for us.' Raife's expression was full of passion. 'Time is to be seized. It does not wait for the tardy.'

'What do you mean?'

Raife closed his eyes. 'My wife Mary was a religious woman, a Roman Catholic. She was a good woman, steady. She found me impulsive and always in a hurry. She died giving birth to our son – he died too.'

'My family have always been devoutly Protestant.' Kate took his face in her hands. 'I am sorry to hear about what happened to Mary.'

'One moment, I hoped to be a happy father, the next, there was blood soaking her clothes and she slipped away. The child didn't even draw breath...' Raife's eyes opened, filled with tenderness. 'I never thought to love again. Then you came to my door, with your spirited ways and your sweet smile, and I knew you would be mine. We have no time for games and pretences, you and I. We understand that love is to be grasped with both hands. We must use all the time we have left to love.'

Kate shivered. 'Why? What do you think will happen to us?'

'You have a husband. You ride the common in disguise to rob travellers on the highway. I am a poor, struggling farmer.' A grin played around his lips. 'Ours will not be a union like any other. We will always be outsiders, different, in hiding.'

Kate wrapped her arms around him. 'I care for nothing else, only for you.'

'And I for you... my love...' Raife kissed her again and she clung to him as if nothing would prise her away. He held her wrist gently, unclasping her arms from his neck. 'But we must not tarry. I must get you back to The Cell before you are missed.'

'Must I leave you?' Kate had forgotten that she would need to return home.

'This moment reminds me of words I heard once.' Raife kissed her fingers and began to quote lines from a poem she knew well.

> *'Busy old fool, unruly sun,*
> *Why dost thou thus,*

Through windows, and through curtains call on us?
Must to thy motions lovers' seasons run?'

Kate was delighted. 'You know John Donne – "The Sunne Rising". I read his poems as a young girl – my Aunt Alice disapproved. She thought them too erotic, only for the unchaste...'

'The poet tells the sun to go away because he wishes to stay in bed with the woman he loves...' Raife said. 'But your clothes will be dry now. And you must go back.'

'I must,' Kate said, suddenly sad. 'I must pretend to be the wife of Thomas Fanshawe again.'

'We will find a way to be together.' Raife kissed her fingertips. 'Come to me soon. Meanwhile, I must give some thought to your life as a highwayman...' His eyes glowed. 'We will talk of it when we next meet. I cannot have you put your life in danger.'

'You cannot?' Kate pulled back. 'I have never bent to the will of any man. I do not intend now to be told that I may not...'

'I meant no offence, my love.' Raife kissed her. When he tugged away, he said, 'I think only to talk with you when we meet next about how our future might be. Perhaps there is a way we can be together, for all time.'

Kate reached for his hands. 'If only there could be...'

His lips brushed her neck. 'I will make you some food, and then we must ride post-haste to The Cell before someone raises an alarm... I met your good servant John when I brought Midnight. He is ever concerned for you.'

'His hearing is not good...' Kate suppressed a smile. 'He thinks you are called Ralph Chaplin.'

'Then Ralph Chaplin I must be,' Raife said. He took her hand. 'Come, rise. The sun is almost up and we must be gone, until next time.'

* * *

Kate rode back as quickly as she could towards Markyate, Raife at her side on his stallion, Lightning. They were both concerned that someone might notice her disguise and stop them to ask questions. At the gates to The

Cell, Raife kissed Kate swiftly and galloped away. She watched him go, her heart heavy, then she left Midnight in his stall, where Peter would soon find him and care for him. In her men's garments, she crept in the kitchen, glad that Beatrice was not there, and then through the secret passage to her chamber.

She fell on her bed and caught her breath. Her coat was filled with money and jewellery – she'd count it soon and work out how much she had stolen, then she'd divide it between Thomas and the poor families who needed her support. It made her smile to think that in just one night she had stopped a stagecoach, taken the passengers' belongings, fallen in love and spent the whole night with the man she wanted to live out her days with. It had been breathtaking.

Kate knew she would see Raife soon. A plan was forming – she could pretend to go to London, to stay with cousin Anne. She'd go to Ayers End Farm instead and spend the week in his arms, living with him as a husband and wife would live, blissfully happy. That was where her heart was tugging her, even now.

Closing her eyes, sweet moments came back to her: the promises they whispered, how tenderly he had held her, how every second she spent with him was as precious as drops of her own blood.

Kate recalled galloping away from the coach, with Raife in chase, falling in the river, aiming the pistol. What if she had fired in fear? What if it had not been Raife in pursuit – what if it had been the constable and his assistants? Fear clutched her heart. She would need to be careful if she was going to stop another coach. So much more was at stake now. Her life now belonged to someone else – it was not just her own.

She suddenly remembered that she was wearing gentleman's clothes and she leaped up to change into a clean linen shift, a kirtle and gown. She brushed her hair and was just arranging a cap over it when there was a light knock on the door. It opened with a creak and Beatrice was standing humbly. 'Mistress, I beg your pardon, but...' Kate watched as Beatrice's eyes strayed to the bed, to the shirt, coat and breeches. She immediately looked away. 'There is a gentleman to see you...'

'A gentleman?' Kate asked, wondering if Raife had come back, if he couldn't live another second without her.

'Constable Wilmott is in the summer parlour. John asked him to wait there. John told him that you had not yet risen, but he would have none of it. He said he needed to speak to you on a matter of much importance.'

'Oh? What might that be?' Kate felt fear take her by the throat. What if the constable knew she was the gallant highway robber? Or maybe Raife had fallen from Lightning and met with an accident. She forced herself to breathe calmly.

'I do not know, mistress. Only Lambert Wilmott is a persistent man. He will not be told that you were not available. He insisted that he would wait until you arrived.'

'Then I will see him quickly and he can be on his way,' Kate said firmly.

'Very well,' Beatrice said, inclining her head. Kate knew she had seen the man's attire on the bed. Had she seen the jewellery and the silk purses too?

Beatrice's face was still composed as she followed Kate, who swept downstairs, where John was waiting in the vast hall. He offered a polite bow.

'Constable Wilmott has been told that you were busy, mistress. But he is a most stubborn man.'

'I will meet him, John,' Kate said.

Kate saw John and Beatrice exchange looks, and told herself not to make assumptions; they were husband and wife: they often communicated by raising an eyebrow or offering a polite cough.

John led the way. He pushed the parlour door wide, allowing Kate to step inside an elegant room of ceiling beams, intricate wall panelling and high-backed chairs.

Kate held out a hand. 'Lambert...'

Lambert Wilmott took her hand in his own pastry-soft palm. She felt the dampness of his skin. His eyes strayed over her dress, then back to her face. 'Mistress Fanshawe.'

'Would you like tea?' Kate asked politely, her chin high.

'I am not sure that would be appropriate,' the constable said. 'Given the nature of my business.'

'Oh?' Kate's heart knocked beneath her bodice, but her face retained indifference. 'What is amiss?'

'As you know, I am a constable, appointed by the Justice of the Peace to keep the law in the parish. In fact, Master Henry Glanville is an acquaintance of mine, and he allows me to do as I see fit, to—'

'Henry Glanville is a magistrate and a friend of Thomas's. He has dined with us,' Kate said, struggling to keep her voice steady.

'Together, our powers enable us to arrest a man on suspicion of a crime and interrogate him for three days.' Wilmott approached, his small eyes glinting. Kate could smell the bitterness of his breath.

'I am impressed,' Kate said. 'But what has this to do with me?'

'I am here today on a most grave matter...'

'Indeed...' Kate wondered if he was about to arrest her. 'How may I help you?'

'You believe your husband to be away?'

'He is in the north fighting for King Charles,' Kate said. 'His family have always been committed Royalists. My father was too, and his father.'

'He was involved in a rebellion with George Booth, an English landowner and politician. It seems the uprising in the north of England has failed.'

'Oh?' Kate breathed a sigh of relief that she had not been discovered. Another emotion followed, concern for Thomas. 'So where is he now?'

'Master Booth has escaped punishment.'

'Constable, I refer to my husband.'

The constable took his time to answer. 'I believe he has been taken prisoner.'

Kate was alarmed. 'What will become of him?'

'I understand that he will go to the Tower of London where he will be kept for some time.'

'In prison? Poor Thomas...' Kate put a hand to her lips. 'I am truly sorry to hear it.'

'As I am sorry to be the bearer of bad tidings, Mistress Fanshawe.' Lambert Wilmott took a step forward. 'Your husband is placing his loyalties on the wrong side...'

'My husband may do as he wishes,' Kate replied.

'But he would have been wiser to stay at home with his pretty wife and bring an heir into the world.'

Kate's temper flared. 'Do you have a commission from Henry Glanville to negotiate with my private affairs?'

'I simply wished to reassure you that...' The constable narrowed his eyes. 'I will take care of you in his absence.'

'Take care?' Kate took a step back. 'Whatever do you mean?'

'A lonely woman in a large house such as this?' Lambert's tongue flickered again. 'It is my duty to call on you from time to time, to make sure you are not going without anything you may need.' He took a pace forward.

'I need nothing,' Kate retorted. She took a breath. Wilmott was a dangerous man. She needed to prevent the constable following her, finding out about her relationship with Raife. It was best to allow him to think of himself as an ally. Against her natural inclinations, she smiled. 'I thank you, constable. And I know my husband would thank you. If I need assistance, I can call on you.'

'You travel to London often?' Wilmott simpered.

'I do.' Kate intended to travel there in a few days' time. Of course, she would go no further than Ayers End Lane.

'The young ruffian who preys on travellers has struck again.'

'I beg your pardon?'

'The gentleman highwayman who attacks passing coaches...'

'Ah...' Kate took a breath. 'You told me of him. He has broad shoulders, a big beard...'

'He has shaved it off,' Wilmott said, his face so serious that Kate almost laughed. 'The last people he robbed spoke of a polite young man with a light voice, but this time, he had no beard and his shoulders were narrow.'

'Perhaps they were mistaken,' Kate suggested nervously.

'He is barely weaned, so slight he could be mistaken for a woman,' the constable said and Kate shivered. 'But do not disturb yourself, mistress, for I will take care of you. I will soon be made sergeant-at-arms, and I will shoot the snippersnapper on sight.'

Kate shuddered again. The room had suddenly become cold. 'Then pray God the poor young man sees you first...'

'I have sworn to see him on the gibbet.'

Kate took a breath. 'We are fortunate in this parish to have such a vigilant man as you, constable.'

'You grow pale, mistress.' Wilmott grabbed her hand and kissed it. 'Know that I will be here any time you wish it.'

'I am comforted by your words,' Kate said, not knowing how else to respond. 'Now, I have a home to run by myself. I regret that poor Thomas's loyalties have landed him in trouble with the Parliamentarians.'

'It is of his own making. He might have stayed home, paid his taxes and kept his loyalties to himself.' Wilmott seemed keen to continue talking. 'I expect he will be in prison for a long time, mistress.'

'If you'll excuse me, Lambert' – Kate turned – 'I have much to attend to. John will show you out.' She inclined her head one last time. 'I thank you for your concern...'

He opened his mouth, but Kate whirled from the room and hurried up the grand stairs, leaving him gaping.

On the landing, Beatrice was waiting for her. 'Is it true, mistress, that the master has been taken away? The rebellion in the north is over?'

'It is, Bea – and Thomas is in prison, I believe – I may need to go to London soon.' Kate felt a flurry of guilt rise within her. She was sorry for Thomas's predicament, but she had no intention of going to see him. It hurt her to lie to Beatrice, but Kate's intention was to visit another man's arms.

Beatrice gave a light curtsy. 'John and I will remain loyal to you and do our best to care for you in the master's absence.'

'I thank you for that...'

'And to that end...' Beatrice avoided Kate's eyes. 'I think I should tell you that I have washed the clothes you left on the bed. They were much dirtied. The black-soap would not bring out the stains despite the lye in it, but I have used a little ash and urine mixed to make them clean.' Beatrice looked at her feet. 'When they are dried, I will return them to your chamber. Your breakfast awaits in your private dining room. I wish a good morning to you, mistress.'

Kate watched Beatrice rush downstairs, scurrying towards the kitchen, keen to be about her business.

She put a hand to her mouth. Beatrice knew.

24

THE PRESENT

'It's been the week from hell,' Uncle Bill said emphatically, folding his arms. 'I haven't stopped working. I've been flat out here – and Marcia wants the spare room at home painted.' He reached out for a chunk of chocolate cake. 'Thank goodness Marilyn from number two keeps me supplied with cake. I sorted her kitchen shelf out this morning – it's a wonder the pans didn't fall off, it was so wonky.' He took a huge bite. 'Don't tell Marcia I'm eating all this sweet stuff. She's put me on another diet. I think she's trying to kill me.' He indicated the mackerel sandwich in his lunch box. 'Good job I sneaked a cheeky burger from the snack van on the way here.'

'Auntie Marcia wouldn't be too happy...' Charlie grinned as he surveyed their work. 'I think we're almost done. I have a bedroom now. I'll move in properly over the weekend, buy a bed and a second-hand wardrobe.'

'That's a good idea. Now all you need is a nice girlfriend...'

'Oh, Uncle Bill,' Charlie groaned.

'Have you heard from Luna?'

'She's in the past,' Charlie said and meant it.

'So – who are these young ladies you went out with on Tuesday night?' Bill's eyes sparkled with mischief.

'Edie from number three, and her friends Paige and Priya. And I met

Priya's fiancé Toby. We all went to a bonfire at Wheathampstead, up at the school. We had a great time – fireworks, jacket potatoes, cider, the works.'

'So, which one is it to be – Paige or Edie?' Bill grinned. 'It's Friday night – you ought to be taking one of them out.'

'They are both just friends,' Charlie said. 'I might catch up with Edie this weekend – we were going to do some research about the...' He paused. He couldn't tell Bill any more about the ghost – his uncle would laugh. 'We'll research the history of the area.'

Bill laughed anyway. 'Whatever for?'

'These are old cottages... I just wondered who the constables were,' Charlie bluffed.

'When I was a lad, I wouldn't have wasted time with a good-looking girl researching history.' Bill tugged open a can of Coke. Charlie noticed that it wasn't the diet version Auntie Marcia allowed him.

'So, the main bedroom's nearly done.' Charlie changed the subject. 'The other bedrooms don't look too bad really.'

'They don't,' Bill agreed. 'We'll need to plaster one of the ceilings, make good any cracks in the walls and then you can decorate.'

'I would love to have a music room with my instruments, my books, a desk and a laptop – my own office,' Charlie said. 'And a spare bedroom for when my friends from London come down. They are all dead keen...'

'Hang on, Charlie.' Bill put a hand up. 'Don't you go putting down any roots. It'll be on the market next summer – even earlier if we can.'

'Right,' Charlie said sadly. 'I just thought while I was here... I'd love to get the kitchen done in time for Christmas.'

'There are seven weeks until Christmas.' Bill counted on his fingers. 'If we can throw some time at the bedrooms and get the painting and decorating done at weekends, then we could lay a kitchen floor, plaster the walls and ceiling, put up a few tiles...'

'Edie said an Aga would be nice...'

'An Aga?' Bill scoffed. 'A plain and simple, not-too-pricey electric cooker will do, one with a double oven preferably. Don't you forget – we're selling it on...'

Charlie looked disappointed. 'But can we get it done for Christmas?'

'Are you thinking of having a party?'

'That's exactly what I was thinking,' Charlie said. 'My friends from London could come down, my friends from here – I'm really getting to like Nila and Sahil Sharma and their two boys. I taught the kids again last night and it's going great. Joshit is really getting the hang of the sax and even Kavish is knuckling down.' He looked pleased with himself.

'That's a lot of people. You don't want to muck the place up.' Bill stood up, and placed a hand against his stomach. 'Oh, that hurt.'

'What hurt?' Charlie asked.

'Indigestion. I ate too much lunch...' He winked. 'I get two lunches – the one Marcia gives me and the one I buy on the way here...'

'You need to work it off, Uncle Bill,' Charlie joked. 'Come on – are we done in here? Shall we go and look at my music room?'

'Let's get stuck in,' Bill agreed.

They stood in the doorway of the second bedroom and Charlie gazed around. 'So – if I put a bed settee here for guests, and my saxophone and guitar would go against that wall, the desk would just sit nicely in front of the window so I could look out at the common...'

'You're at it again.' Bill grinned. 'Putting down roots. Our target buyer will want this as a kids' bedroom or a guest bedroom, so we'll keep it light and bright.'

'But I'll be here for a while... I need furniture.'

'Furniture?' Bill was staring at Charlie, his hands on his hips. 'I had this place down as almost empty, you sleeping on a mattress, just basically dossing down here while we renovate. You're imagining it as a bachelor pad.'

Charlie exhaled. 'Sorry. You're right. What am I thinking?'

'Don't get too attached to the place, Char. That's my advice.' Bill put a friendly hand on his shoulder. 'You're a good builder's mate – you're not afraid of hard work. Look, I was thinking...' Bill moved his ladder to the centre of the room. 'We could do this sort of job over and over. I mean – I'm sixty. I'll retire in four, five years. In that time, you and I could be onto a nice little earner. We could move on to another place, do it up, double the value. You buy yourself a little flat in St Albans, save all you can, then you and I can get a couple of properties and rent them out. Youngsters can't afford mortgages –

we could make a killing on rents, and that would pay for my retirement.'

Charlie wasn't sure. 'I was hoping we'd do up houses for young couples like Priya and Toby. They're getting married next year and they are desperate to buy.'

'The price of a mortgage, though, monthly payments, rising interest rates...' Bill chewed his lip. 'Most young couples can't afford it. Think about it, Charlie.' Bill pointed at his temple with his index finger. 'We're good at this and we can make thousands in profit if we pick the right properties. I saw one advertised in Ware, a doer-upper, three bedrooms. We could go through it in six months and double the price – triple it, the way the market is.'

Charlie nodded. He wasn't sure what he wanted to do.

Bill was staring up at the ceiling. 'Right, this is what we'll do this afternoon. We have two areas to fix. So – you know what to do here: cut back the damaged area, remove the loose material until you reach sound plaster...'

'I get it,' Charlie said. 'There's another ladder downstairs. I'll bring it up.'

Charlie sprinted downstairs to the kitchen where a stepladder had been left. Alan was in his basket and when he saw Charlie, he woofed and leaped up excitedly.

'Walkies later, mate,' Charlie said, patting the dog's head affectionately. 'Just give me a couple of hours. Uncle Bill will want to finish early. It's Friday. He and Auntie Marcia are going out for a curry.'

Alan woofed again and Charlie knelt down, kissing the wet nose.

'Where do you want to go, Al? Shall we have a nice long walk on the common?'

Alan stared towards the door, wagging his tail.

'Let's just get outside as early as we can. It'll be dark before we know it. We don't want to meet anyone on horseback.' Charlie shivered involuntarily. Alan was staring at him with round eyes, as if he knew who he meant. 'You have a rest and we'll go out for a walk soon, eh?'

Alan returned to his basket dutifully, turning round once before settling down.

Charlie moved to the kitchen window and peered out. He could see the edge of the woodland, the path that led into the thickly planted trees. He stared harder, imagining he could see a figure, a slight woman, a horse. But it was just a branch.

He heard a thump from upstairs and looked up, startled. Something had been dropped or fallen.

Charlie called, 'Uncle Bill?'

There was no reply.

He was in rapid motion, taking the stairs two at a time. Alan was at his heels, as if he knew that it was an emergency.

Bill was lying on the floor, breathing heavily. Charlie was by his side. 'Are you OK? Did you fall?' He scanned his uncle for signs of blood, twisted limbs, and found none. But Bill's face was damp with sweat.

He forced a brave smile, but it came out as a grimace. 'I came over all dizzy.' He put a hand to his heart. 'This indigestion is really bad. A pain just shot up my arm and I toppled and fell off...'

'Tell me how you feel now,' Charlie said, noticing how Bill's palm moved from his chest to his shoulder, how he was panting heavily.

'I feel funny. My jaw hurts – and my chest feels so tight I can hardly breathe...'

'Anything else?' Charlie was reaching in his jeans pocket for his phone, his fingers fumbling on the numbers.

'I feel a bit sick, to tell the truth,' Bill groaned.

Charlie moved to the doorway, where he could speak discreetly, and waited for the operator to ask which service he needed. Charlie replied, 'Ambulance please,' and proceeded to explain his uncle's symptoms and the address of the cottage.

He hurried back to Bill, who was still on the floor, wheezing.

'So, how bad is it?'

'I might be sick – I mean, properly sick. My legs ache.'

'Uncle Bill – you need to sit up.' Charlie eased him to a seating position.

Bill's eyes were wide with pain. 'It's only indigestion... I often get it.'

'Is it worse now than usual?'

Bill met Charlie's eyes and looked suddenly anxious. 'Yes – it's a lot worse.'

'Right, I've called an ambulance – it's on its way.'

Bill looked suddenly annoyed. 'I don't want any fuss – and I don't want Marcia to worry.'

'Then let's sort it all out,' Charlie said soothingly.

'I've got work to do here – I can't go to a hospital and spend all afternoon sitting about.'

'Uncle Bill.' Charlie grasped his uncle's arm firmly. 'Let's get you checked out, eh? I'd feel a lot better if we knew whether this was down to you eating too much of Marilyn's chocolate cake or not...'

Bill tried a brave smile. Then Charlie glanced through the window. An ambulance was hurtling along Ferrers Lane, slowing down outside.

'Don't move,' he murmured and hurried downstairs to open the door.

* * *

An hour later, Charlie sat in the upstairs room by himself staring at the hole in the ceiling. He'd fix it later. Bill had been taken to the cardiology department in West Hertfordshire Hospital. The paramedic he'd spoken to had reassured Charlie that his uncle would be fine, that it was likely that he was suffering from angina and that he'd be seen by a doctor, prescribed medication and given the best advice to manage his condition.

As he'd sat in the ambulance, Bill had asked Charlie to ring Marcia, who was currently at work at the care home where she was an administrator. On the phone, he'd expected her to be furious with Bill, but he could hear that she was near to tears. She'd told him she'd be on her way as soon as she'd put the phone down and once she arrived at the hospital, she'd ring Charlie with an update. She blamed herself – she had been too strict, she had made food an issue, telling him to lower his cholesterol and to eat healthy foods. Now a doctor would say the same thing, she hoped that Bill would listen.

Charlie suddenly felt tired. Perhaps half an hour in the fresh air would help, then he'd go back to work, and carry on until late in the evening. He tugged on his jacket, picked up Alan's lead and moved towards the door. It had been a long week, a hard day, and a walk on the common would blow the cobwebs away.

Alan bounded towards him and Charlie clipped on the lead, closed the door behind them and set off towards the trees. He hoped Uncle Bill would be all right, that Auntie Marcia would message him soon.

Minutes later, twigs were cracking beneath his feet as he and Alan walked through the woods. Charlie was deep in thought. He wondered what Uncle Bill's angina would mean in terms of his job. Would he need time off? Would he be advised to stop working altogether?

Today had made him realise something he hadn't really been aware of until now. He liked living at Constable's Cottages. He felt happy there, the space was welcoming, calm. The neighbours were nice. He had known all along it was just a temporary place to rest his head while he and Uncle Bill fixed it up. But now he was becoming attached to the place. For some reason he couldn't work out, number one Constable's Cottages was beginning to feel like home.

25

1659

Kate rode to Ayers End Farm the following morning. She couldn't keep away; not being with Raife made her restless, on edge, and a force she couldn't explain was tugging her towards him. Her heart thudded beneath her jacket and she smiled at the idea that she had never experienced such a sensation before in her life. Now, two things made her breathing shudder: one was the man who lived in Ayers End Farm, and the other was the sound of a coach and four horses approaching on the London road.

She arrived at the farm and noticed the animals grazing in the fields, the newly dug earth. She wondered where Raife would be – he would not be expecting her. She made her way towards the stables, inhaling the warm scent of hay. Vulcan was standing with his mother, Beleza. The mare was munching placidly, her head down, while her foal, slender on delicate legs, watched her every move. Next to the mare, Raife's stallion, Lightning, immediately recognised her, making a low nickering sound. Kate rubbed the horse's nose, smoothing the light mane, the symmetrical white blaze on his nose that gave him his name.

She felt strong arms around her waist, pulling her against him, nuzzling her ear. She closed her eyes as he murmured, 'My love – I wondered when you would come back to me.'

Kate turned round and met Raife's dark eyes. 'I rode here early and left

John the message that I had gone to London for several days... He will know something is amiss as I am travelling by horse and not by coach. But John and Beatrice will not ask questions. Besides, I wanted to see you so much.'

'My heart is warmed to hear it.' Raife smiled, his expression soft with affection. 'But what will you do while I am working in the fields?'

'I want to work with you.'

Raife touched her velvet coat. 'In these fine clothes?'

'I will wear a pair of your breeches,' she retorted.

'My Kate, in a man's garb again...' Raife murmured into her hair. 'You look beautiful whatever your apparel.'

'I will start to learn how to be a farmer right away,' Kate said determinedly. 'I will make food in the kitchen, I will tend to the horses in the stable, I will feed the animals in the fields.'

'Then come,' Raife said. 'You can make us some bread, warm some ale, cut vegetables for the pottage. The stables need to be cleaned out and the horses fed and brushed.'

'It sounds like the ideal life,' Kate said. 'I do not think it can be so difficult to be a farmer's woman.'

* * *

That evening, Kate sat on a stool, her limbs aching from a long day's work, as Raife stripped off his clothes and washed in a deep bowl of hot water. She marvelled at how the muscles in his back rippled as he dipped his head in to rinse his hair, how he rubbed his body clean. She couldn't pull her stare away.

He turned and noticed her watching him. 'You've never seen a man like this before?'

'Naked?' Kate shook her head. 'No.'

'In the summer, I bathe in the river mostly. Tomorrow, we can bathe together if you wish.'

Kate recalled how cold the water was when she had fallen from Midnight, and she imagined swimming with Raife in the icy water, splashing, laughing. 'I would like that very much.'

'And I too.'

'At The Cell, Bea lines my bathtub with sheets, collects buckets of heated water by the fireplace and fills it for me. My soap is scented with lavender and roses.'

Raife looked concerned as he gathered her in his arms. 'You look tired, my love...'

'It is hard work, cleaning stables and feeding animals. And the bread I made was the worst I have ever tasted.' Kate laughed. 'I make an unlikely farmer's woman.'

'You are the best any man might hope for, I promise you.' Raife lifted her in his arms. 'Do I not smell sweeter now?'

'You smell more delicious than anything I have known,' Kate answered honestly.

'Then let us go up to our humble chamber.'

'What will we do there?' Kate asked, her eyes twinkling with mischief.

'We will do what God intended a man and a woman to do when they love each other as we do...' Raife met her eyes. 'And then, afterwards, you may lie in my arms and we will talk into the night.'

'What will we talk of?'

'We have plans to make, you and I – how we can live together in the future, how we can be happy for all eternity.'

Kate kissed him and spoke what was in her heart. 'Now is what matters most, my love. And I pray that now will never end...'

* * *

The wooden shutters were wide open and the moon was high beyond the trees. It shed a pale ribbon of light onto the bed as Kate and Raife stared into the darkness above them, the scent of straw from the roof mingling with sweet grass from the dew outside. In the distance, a lone owl stretched its wings, hooting, a hollow, sad sound. Raife's arm wrapped around her as Kate took his large hand in her small one, leaning her head against the firm pillow of his shoulder.

'How will we fare?' Her voice was hushed in the gloom. 'My husband will come out of prison in time, and then he may sell my home and send me to live with my cousin in London. But I cannot live with him now. I cannot be as I was.'

Raife spoke gently. 'What is most important to you, in your heart?'

'You are.'

'And you to me. But what of your family name, your home? Could you leave The Cell? And what of the poor families you care for?'

Kate gave a shuddering sigh. 'I want to be with you in a place where nobody knows the name Fanshawe. I am simply Kate Ferrers, and I will gladly work alongside those who have nothing if I can live with you.'

Raife murmured, 'I wish you could be my wife...'

'I am, and will always be, in all but name.'

'But here you are known as Thomas's wife...'

'Then we will go somewhere else,' Kate said defiantly. 'We will start again, just you and I.'

'But I am a farmer. What could we do to live?'

'We could rent a piece of land, work honestly.' She squeezed his hand. 'We could have children. Our life would be our own.'

'I have little money...' Raife whispered into her hair. 'But I promise, I will find a way. I want to care for you, to provide as a man should... I will do anything.'

Kate hauled herself up on one elbow. 'I make plenty of money from stopping the coaches on the London road. If I do it for one year, just one, we could be wealthy. One robbery a month, when the twilight comes, before the moon is full. Think how rich we could be.'

Kate heard Raife sigh. 'I cannot let you do that.'

'You cannot stop me...'

'It is dangerous, my love.'

'I am not afraid...'

'I know you are full of courage,' Raife said. 'I admire that in you – your strength, your determination. But you and I both know the constables will keep watch for you now...'

'Lambert Wilmott came to my home...'

'And the life of a highwayman is not long. How many times can you steal from travellers without being caught? I will not let you face danger alone.'

'Then come with me,' Kate whispered, suddenly excited. 'What a pair of highwaymen we might make together. We would watch out for each other the whole time. We would have two pistols, not one – four eyes and ears, not two.'

Raife was staring at her. 'You and I? Highway robbers?'

'For just one year.' She brought his hand to her lips. 'By next summer, we can travel wherever we wish. We will live the life we should have together. Who knows how long Thomas may be in prison? He will suspect nothing of it. And I can give more money to the poor families with their many children...'

'I cannot stop you doing what you will, but I can come with you.' Raife's eyes gleamed. 'That way, I can protect you, we will be true partners and we will take only from those who have too much. It will not be too great a sin. But we must be very careful not to be caught.'

'We will choose a safe place to wait for the coaches as the light fades, then we will strike quickly. We will be away before anyone realises it and we will come back here, to Ayers End in the moonlight. It is close to the highway, and we can allow our horses to rest.'

Raife's brow furrowed with anxiety. 'But you will be missed at The Cell.'

'Bea knows already – she has washed my highway garb.' Kate smiled. 'She and John will be useful allies. But perhaps I will not tell them about you yet. Who knows what they might think if they suspect I have a handsome accomplice...' Kate sighed. 'What we do will be wrong – it is a sin to steal – but then the Lord said that it was easier for a camel to go through the eye of a needle than for a rich man to enter the kingdom of God.'

'What do you mean?' Raife was puzzled.

'By taking their money, we make it easier for the rich to achieve salvation.' Kate smiled.

'You are a wicked lady,' Raife said, full of admiration.

'On my life – we can do this.' Kate wrapped her arms around Raife and kissed him. 'We can do whatever we wish...'

'I believe we can,' Raife murmured. 'You and I will make for ourselves the future we truly deserve.'

26

THE PRESENT

Early on Saturday morning, Charlie lay on his bed, Alan curled at his feet gnawing noisily at a treat. Charlie was playing the saxophone, thinking of Katherine Ferrers. He felt he knew her already, slender and gallant, beautiful even in men's clothes, her dark hair tied back, wearing a tricorne hat, a kerchief across her face to disguise her delicate features. He imagined her dark eyes, determined, focused on the road ahead as she galloped along Ferrers Lane. Back then, it would have been the only route to London.

Charlie closed his eyes and played a few smooth notes. He thought of the highway woman, trying to evoke her through his music.

He blew more notes, stopping to revise and improve, and phrases became melody. It was her song, the lady of the highway. He concentrated on mood, on the sort of person she might have been, the danger she was in, the excitement. Warm sounds, the fast gallop of her horse, the charm and the courage of her character.

He played on. Melancholy, loneliness. She had been married to a man she did not choose, hadn't she? Often living alone in The Cell. He blew more notes that sounded whimsical, spontaneous – she was impulsive.

The tune changed, it became darker, foreboding. She must have known danger, fear. Then what happened to her? How did her story end? Was it a tragedy? Perhaps there was betrayal? Capture? Punishment?

He paused, playing the tune again, making each note purer, refining the sound.

He had it. It was Kate's tune. He ought to write it down, add lyrics, or record it on his phone.

There was a loud knocking on his front door. Alan leaped up, barking, excited. Charlie rushed to the window and saw Edie below, dressed warmly, Bianca on a lead. His heart skipped a beat as he hurried downstairs and opened the front door.

'Charlie – how's Bill? I didn't want to come round yesterday, but I saw an ambulance and...'

Charlie looked at Edie, a woolly hat over her wild curls, a tartan scarf, a dark jacket, and thought she personified autumn. If he hugged her, she would smell of pumpkin spice and sweet cinnamon apples, he was sure of it. He took a breath.

'He's fine now. He has angina. Auntie Marcia took him back home yesterday with a health plan and medication.'

'Oh, thank goodness he's all right.' The anxiety in her eyes seemed to clear. 'Is there anything I can do to help?'

'I'm popping round there in a bit – I have to take Uncle Bill's van to St Albans.'

'How will you get back?'

'I'll take the bus...'

'Can I come with you and then give you a lift?'

Charlie beamed. 'That would be so helpful – thank you.'

'You must have been worried about him – what happened? I saw the paramedics take him...' Edie placed a hand on Charlie's arm, then took it away.

'He fell off the ladder. He had chest pains...' Charlie patted Alan, who was sniffing Bianca's tail while she looked away, superior and indifferent. 'I thought he'd had a heart attack. He looked pale and sweaty... I was really worried, so I rang for an ambulance.'

'It's a good job you did,' Edie said. 'When are you going to see him?'

'I was going to head off in a minute.'

'I'll follow you in the car. I'll bring Bianca.'

'Great,' Charlie said.

'Did I hear you say you were going to see Bill?' Marilyn had rushed from her cottage and was standing at the hedge that separated the two properties. She held out a tin. 'I made him something. How is he? I saw the ambulance.'

'Angina…' Charlie accepted the tin. It had once contained chocolates, but it was heavy, as if a cake was inside.

'Oh no – poor Bill.' Marilyn looked shocked. 'I hate ambulances. They remind me of when my dad had a heart attack. He went away and never came back.'

'I think Uncle Bill will be fine,' Charlie reassured her. 'He's had an early warning and needs to take things easy.'

'Oh, I hope so. You don't think he'll stop working? I was going to ask him about my leaky bathroom tap,' Marilyn said.

'If water is dripping from the spout, you need to replace the washer; if it's leaking from beneath the handle, then the valve O-ring needs replacing,' Edie said and Charlie threw her a look of pure admiration. 'I could probably do it for you.'

'Oh, can you?' Marilyn looked less impressed. 'My husband used to do all that, but we're divorced. My daughter is thirty-three. She's on my side. She blames him for everything. He doesn't show any interest in her little one and Riley is nearly five.'

'That's a shame,' Charlie said, not knowing what else to say. 'But thanks for this.' He held up the tin.

'It's a chocolate sponge, made with real butter and lots of white sugar, and there's proper cream in the middle,' Marilyn said. 'I know he has a sweet tooth…'

Charlie tried his best to look thankful – Marcia would probably want to throw it in the bin, although he'd ask for a small slice first. 'We're off to Uncle Bill's now.'

'Oh?' Marilyn looked accusingly at Edie. 'Are you going too?'

'Charlie will need a lift back if he's dropping off Bill's van.'

'I see…' Marilyn folded her arms. 'I'd have been happy to drive you. I'd love to see Bill's house; I expect it's perfect.'

'Not at all. Auntie Marcia has a list of things she needs doing,' Charlie said. 'Anyway, we'd better be going.'

'And I'll come and have a look at the tap later this weekend,' Edie promised.

'Oh. Right.' Marilyn seemed disappointed. 'Well, give Bill my love and tell him I look forward to seeing him back at work soon, but obviously only when he's well enough...'

'I'll make sure he gets plenty of rest.' Charlie flourished the van keys that were in his pocket and climbed in, Alan at his heels. Edie clambered into the blue Toyota Yaris Hybrid behind him, opening the door for Bianca, clipping her in the seat belt harness, before starting the engine.

* * *

Marcia and Bill were seated in the conservatory, looking out at the patio, the landscaped garden, the paved area and the water feature. Alan and Bianca were loitering in the kitchen, gnawing treats. Marcia had made everyone lunch – a Buddha bowl of salad and chickpeas, avocado and cous- cous. Bill was staring at it as if it was his last meal from a condemned cell.

Marcia pushed her dark hair from her eyes and sighed loudly. 'You know, Charlie, I warned him time and time again. You can't keep doing that to your body, Bill – all that unhealthy food.'

Bill looked sulky. 'I can't understand it. There's not a pick of fat on me. I'm healthy.'

'Tell that to your cholesterol.' Marcia threw him a wild look.

Bill poked at a chickpea. 'I told the doctor I want to be back at work on Monday.'

'Should you be back so soon?' Charlie asked.

'No, he shouldn't,' Marcia said firmly. 'I've told him – he's staying home for a few weeks, then he's going back to have his progress checked.'

'I can't fall behind schedule,' Bill grumbled.

'I can help,' Edie offered. 'What do you have to do, Charlie? I can plaster a bit, paint...'

'Specialist jobs,' Bill protested.

'No, we'll be fine.' Charlie looked pleased. 'You just need to get well, Uncle Bill.'

'I'm on medication – I'll be all right.' Bill sniffed a piece of avocado and wrinkled his nose.

'You'll be six feet under.' Marcia glared at him and tears filled her eyes. For a moment, she seemed fragile. She reached out and patted his knee. 'You need to be sensible now...'

'Maybe I could take a couple of days off...' Bill was weakening.

'Have you got any holiday due, Auntie Marcia?' Charlie asked. 'You and Uncle Bill should go away so that he won't think about work.'

'Oh, that's a good idea – there are lots of warm places you could go in November. Then come back home and rest up for Christmas,' Edie suggested.

All the anxiety drained from Marcia's face. She leaned over and pressed Charlie's knee. 'You should hang on to this one, Charlie.' She winked at Edie. 'She's a good girl, a keeper.'

'Oh, we're not a couple...' Charlie looked from Marcia to Edie, not wanting to offend either of them.

'Then you should be.' Marcia took over, talking to Edie. 'He's one of the best, our Charlie. Even though he's my nephew, I have to say it – he's a great catch. I mean, he's good-looking, talented, hardworking – he's got the kindest nature. What's not to love?'

'Oh, no, we're not thinking about...' Edie began, as embarrassed as Charlie.

'The last girl he had...' Marcia pulled a face of disapproval. 'She was a bit flighty. I mean, she seemed very nice at first. She thought the world of our Charlie until push came to shove, but in the end, she was just plain selfish.'

'What Auntie Marcia means...' Charlie took a breath, remembering the kiss, determined not to let Edie feel uncomfortable, '...is that, like most people do at some point, I had a relationship that started off OK and then it went wrong. It was a learning experience. I'm a better person now though. I have grown and got over it.' He looked from Marcia to Bill, then to Edie. 'Edie is my neighbour, she's a mate, and we're both single and we intend to stay single. Life's easier that way.'

'I agree.' Edie beamed widely. She met Charlie's eyes and a moment passed between them. Charlie wasn't sure if it was gratitude, regret or something else.

'Ah, but...' Marcia wasn't through yet. 'I'm Honduran – family loyalty is a big thing with me. And I have a real insight into people. You should have a date, see how it goes.'

'Well, when you've done with matchmaking, Marce...' Bill put his unfinished Buddha bowl down on the floor and Alan trotted in, happily snuffling chickpeas. 'Can you get us a slice of that lovely chocolate cake with the cream filling? It's in the kitchen, in a fancy chocolates tin. I'd love a great big chunk.'

'Over my dead body.' Marcia stood up, furious. 'I have a low-fat cherry yogurt in the fridge. You can eat that – and like it.'

That afternoon, Charlie and Edie paused to stroll around the market in St Albans before going home, both dogs following on leads. Alan and Bianca were treated to a box of healthy chews each. Charlie bought himself a shirt that Edie thought was bang on-trend, and Edie bought some fresh spices and promised to invite Charlie round for a Thai green curry.

'That would be lovely. We need to do more research on the ghost...' Charlie said.

'I meant to do some checking earlier this week – I wanted to find about The Cell. Do you think we should visit?'

'That might be difficult. I was told it's privately owned...' Charlie said. 'And it's a completely different house now to the place she lived in. It's been updated and rebuilt.'

'We need to know why she is on Nomansland Common. Why doesn't she just haunt The Cell?'

'Perhaps she does,' Charlie murmured. 'Do you think she can flit from one place to the other?'

Edie looked nervous. 'I think there are other questions we need to try to answer.'

'Like, why was she a highway robber?'

'And, why did she do it alone?'

'And where was her husband all this time?' Charlie wanted to know.

'And what happened in the end?' Edie took a deep breath. 'There was such a sad feeling when we saw her standing in the woods that night.'

'I wrote her a song this morning,' Charlie remembered. 'I'm calling it "Kate's Tune". It came to me as I was just chilling out and thinking about her.'

'I'd love to hear it.' Edie looked genuinely excited.

Charlie was thoughtful for a moment. 'Do you think we'll see her again?'

Edie shook her head. 'I don't know. In a way, I hope not.'

'But she's out there, Edie. Trying to communicate. Don't you think she wants to tell us something?'

'Perhaps it will become clear the more we research. Oh...' Edie hesitated, pausing to look at a jewellery stall. She touched a bracelet of purple stones and held it up. The light bounced off the randomly shaped violet beads. 'That's pretty.'

'It's amethyst,' the calm-faced man behind the stall said.

'I might buy it...' Edie slid it onto her wrist. She looked at the price. 'Oh, that's not too bad.'

'I'll buy it for you,' Charlie offered. 'You drove me here this morning. You've been so helpful. It'll be a present.'

'Oh, you don't have to.'

'I want to.' Charlie looked at the stallholder. 'Can I pay by card?'

'Of course.' The man produced a card machine, talking rapidly about the properties of amethyst stones, something Charlie couldn't quite follow about opening doors to deep insights.

Edie smiled at the thought. She turned to Charlie. 'Now you pick one. I'll buy it for you.'

'Right...' Charlie looked confused for a moment, then he reached out and selected a bracelet of black stones that he thought looked fairly masculine. 'What about this one?'

The man behind the stall remained impassive, but said, 'That's hematite, supposed to stimulate concentration and focus.'

Charlie pulled a disbelieving face.

'We'll have that one then.' Edie's eyes shone. 'I think that equips us perfectly to find out about The Wicked Lady...'

'I was watching you choose the bracelets,' the man said quietly. He glanced from Edie to Charlie. 'I think you both have a psychic dilemma.'

'What does that mean?' Charlie frowned, glancing at the hematite bracelet on his wrist, then at Edie.

The man's voice took on a tone of authority. 'Well, I'd say that you have a connection to a sad soul who isn't at rest. You've picked out the exact stones to help you bring peace to a wandering spirit.'

Charlie turned to Edie as they walked away. She murmured, 'That was a weird coincidence, wasn't it – us picking those bracelets?'

'No – he overheard us talking about The Wicked Lady,' Charlie said skeptically. 'He's a salesman.'

'I know it's just superstition,' Edie replied. 'But it's just – the thought of the ghost waiting outside my window scares me to death.'

Charlie made a low sound of agreement. He didn't believe in psychic dilemmas, but he understood exactly how Edie felt.

27

1659

Kate felt her spirits sink as she rode back to The Cell. The past week with Raife had been glorious and it had been so hard to leave him. But now they had a plan. The next time they met, they would attempt their first robbery together. Kate asked herself how she felt about it, and three voices in her conscience answered her at once. The first response was a feeling of excitement; riding hard towards a carriage, pointing her pistol, demanding money from unsuspecting passengers gave her a sense of power she'd never known. As a child, an orphan, as Mistress Thomas Fanshawe, she had to submit to someone else's command. Now she was no longer helpless; she was strong, independent, mistress of her own life. The second emotion was one of desperation. She wanted so much to be with Raife, to live with him as his wife. It was what they both wanted. They deserved happiness.

She guided Midnight through the tall gates of The Cell and she was surprised as the third emotion hit her. Guilt – she was breaking the law. Yes, she stole from the rich and the privileged, but she recalled the looks of frozen horror on their faces as they truly feared for their lives, and it gave her a pang of remorse. She hated that she had to frighten and threaten people. And what if children were there? She always took a pistol, but that was just to show superiority. She vowed she'd never use it. How could she?

As she dismounted Midnight and left him in the stables, she wondered why fear hadn't come into it. She ought to be afraid, terrified for her life. She couldn't continue to get away with highway robbery for very long. But she and Raife had a plan; he would be by her side, and she only intended to steal from travellers until they had enough money to live their lives independently, and help a few families. All would be well. Most importantly, she couldn't wait to see him; her heart was already soaring at the thought of being in his arms.

Kate was surprised to see Beatrice waiting at the door for her. She offered her widest smile. 'Bea, I am here – I had a wonderful time in London with my cousin. My luggage will follow, I—'

'Mistress, your cousin is in the parlour, where she waits for you. John is with her, giving her tea. I heard you arrive.' Beatrice looked at her shoes, then she looked up determinedly, meeting Kate's eyes. 'Your cousin Anne is on her way back from Ware – she has been there for ten days, visiting a sick relative.'

'Oh?' Kate recovered her wits as quickly as she could. 'Thank you, Bea.'

'I have told her you had spent the week in Berkhamsted with a friend, recovering from the shock of Master Thomas's imprisonment. I explained that it had quite upset you and that you needed some time away from the home you share with your husband.'

'Thank you indeed.' Kate breathed out slowly. She could have hugged Beatrice; her heart expanded with gratitude for her loyalty and quick thinking. 'I am most grateful. I owe you and John an explanation.'

'You owe us nothing more than you give us now, mistress,' Beatrice said quietly. 'We have been here with you for eleven years. We know well how difficult things have been for you. Now, if you please...' She turned to lead the way. 'Mistress Anne will be delighted to see you.'

'I am indebted,' Kate said as the parlour door opened.

John appeared, holding a tray. 'I heard you were here, mistress. Beatrice has prepared refreshments in anticipation. I thought you might like to partake of a cup of tea.' He placed the tray on a low table and disappeared unobtrusively with Beatrice to continue his work.

'And cake,' Kate exclaimed, then she threw out her arms. 'Anne, it is wonderful to see you. How are the children? And Richard?'

'They remain well. You know how I fret about my babies, having lost so many. But Katherine remains difficult, she shows little interest in the things I wish to instruct her. Margaret is very much like me; she excels at needlework and she loves to dance. My children are my unspeakable joy, since Richard is always away.' Anne paused, then she grasped Kate's hands. 'But I forget myself. Thomas is in prison. You must be distraught. Beatrice said that you have been to Berkhamsted to stay with a friend. Pray, who do you know there?'

'Oh, an acquaintance...' Kate waved a hand, as if it was not important. 'But it is lovely to see you. You look so well, Anne.'

'I am just like you, I love to ride, to be outdoors. Of course, it becomes increasingly difficult to afford to live as we used to, as Richard exerts himself strenuously in the cause of the king, and I fear that before long we shall be facing distressing poverty. At least while Thomas is in prison, he won't be spending your money,' Anne said cryptically. 'But what of you? What will you do while he is away?'

'I will find something to occupy me...' Kate hid a smile; she knew exactly what she intended to do.

'When Richard was in prison, he wrote poetry, and now I have started to write too.' Anne adjusted her clothes elegantly and nibbled her honey cake. 'I continue to work on my book of cookery and medicaments. And I believe I have fallen upon a new recipe in my experiments. It is delicious. I call it icy cream. My little ones cannot get enough of it.'

'Wonderful.' Kate copied her cousin, taking a huge bite of cake. 'Oh, Bea's cooking is quite remarkable. I don't know where we would be without her.'

'You look rested now, Kate,' Anne remarked. 'Your cheeks are flushed, your eyes sparkle. I don't think I have ever seen you look so radiant.'

'I love the summertime – it agrees with me. Besides, the days I spent at Berkhamsted were very pleasant.'

'Oh, what did you do?' Anne asked.

'Reading, mostly, a little music, anything to take my mind from poor Thomas's plight and my fast-dwindling fortune. Do you never think, dear Anne' – Kate sighed, a deep long breath – 'we were meant for more than needlework and waiting patiently for our husbands to return?'

'I have my children, the delight of my soul.' Anne met her eyes. 'It is still not too late for you, Kate. Do you not think children would make you happy?'

'Oh, I believe they would. What could be better than to seal the pleasure of love with a beautiful baby?' Kate was surprised at her words. She put a hand to her mouth. 'But, of course, Thomas is in prison.'

'He will not be there for ever. Richard believes the king will be restored before long, then Thomas will be home and everything will be as it should be. Then...' Anne looked at her meaningfully. 'You can be a proper wife to him.'

'What will be will be,' Kate said, closing her eyes, imagining herself far away with Raife.

Anne brought a napkin to her lips. 'I believe you have a new horse? A stallion, as company for Shadow. I would very much like to see him.'

'He is called Midnight.' Kate knew that the horse would be recovering after the long journey from Nomansland Common. The road from Ayers End Lane was dusty, with many twists and turns. Midnight would be tired and need to rest, to eat and drink. She offered a smile. 'We shall go to the stables together. I believe Peter took Midnight out earlier for a morning ride – the stallion is restless if he cannot exercise first thing. But it will be nice to see him and Shadow in the stables together.'

'Then let us go, cousin.' Anne stood up, smoothing her skirt and adjusting her cap. 'It is pleasant outside and I long to hear all about your stay at Berkhamsted, and what has put such colour in your cheeks.'

'Oh, there is very little to say.' Kate took her cousin's arm and they headed towards the door. She changed the subject: Anne was clearly looking for something to tittle-tattle to her husband about later. 'Tell me all about London, about the parties in the city, and about what new gossip Master Pepys is talking about, the scoundrel. Of course...' she added with a smile, 'I may come up to London to see you soon, and I have some jewellery I wish to sell, but I hear that the roads have become particularly dangerous around Nomansland Common. Apparently, a wicked young highwayman lurks in the shadows, waiting to attack unsuspecting travellers...'

* * *

After Anne had left by coach in the afternoon, Kate decided to take a bath in warm water, rubbing her skin with lavender soap, then she returned to her room to sleep. She woke late, just as Beatrice knocked to tell her that supper was ready. She dined alone on baked ham and a salad made from purslane, primrose and parsley, dressed with oil, sugar and verjuice, a vinegar made from unripe apples. She was still hungry, so she ate the baked custard Beatrice had brought, some bread with butter, and drank a cup of wine. As she chewed hungrily, she imagined Raife alone in the farm cottage, eating vegetable pottage with bacon and rye bread, washing outside in the stream, water gleaming on his skin. She thought of him sleeping alone on the mattress beneath the straw roof, and in her imagination, she was there with him, in his arms, sharing secrets, planning a future together.

She finished the last of her wine then, as Beatrice came in to clear the dishes away, she said, 'Bea, I would like to speak to you and John in the summer parlour.'

'After I have finished up here, mistress?'

'As soon as you can, if you please.' Kate took a deep breath and stood up. 'What I have to say will not keep. Thank you for a pleasant supper, Bea. It was most delightful.'

Beatrice gave a small curtsy and Kate swept from the dining room into the parlour. She stood in the centre of the room, walking from one end of the intricate wall panelling to the other, choosing her words, deciding what to say, how to say it. Then there was a muffled knock at the door.

John came in first, standing tall, his hands in front of him, while Beatrice was a pace behind him, her head down. Kate frowned, wondering why they looked so humble, then she realised. Thomas was in prison; her funds were dwindling. John and Beatrice thought that The Cell would be sold and that they would lose their positions.

She took a breath. 'John, Bea, I am indebted to you both. I could not have two people with me who are more loyal or kind...' Kate saw Beatrice's eyes fill with tears. 'I brought you here to say thank you and to ask you to forgive me for deceiving you. I could not manage without you, nor would I ever wish to...'

Kate stopped herself. It occurred to her that when she and Raife left The Cell to start their new lives, she would have amassed enough money to give them both a huge sum, as thanks. She resolved to pay them both well.

'How can we assist you?' John murmured humbly.

'Today, I put you both in a difficult position when my cousin arrived from Ware. You had to lie to her on my behalf, and I fear that did not sit well with you. I owe you an explanation.'

'As you wish, mistress...' John coughed. 'You know we will assist you in any way we can.'

'I hope you will, but when you have heard what I must say, you may change your minds. Bea, I recall you washed my clothes...'

'I did, mistress,' Bea muttered.

'Gentlemen's clothes,' Kate said quietly. 'I have of late been short of money – Thomas has availed himself of my fast-dwindling fortune on the king's behalf, and he wished to sell my home and send me to live in London. I couldn't allow that.'

A light kindled in John's eyes and Kate suspected that he knew what she had been up to, but she needed to tell the whole story.

'I want to help the poor families too.' She paused. Beatrice still stared at her feet. 'So...' There was no easy way to say it. 'I am the gentleman highway robber of whom Constable Wilmott speaks.'

Beatrice gave a sound of surprise. 'Oh mistress... I didn't want to believe it could be true.' Her hand went to her mouth. 'How can you...?' She turned to her husband, then back to Kate. 'I implore you to reconsider, mistress. You will surely be caught and—'

'I have made my decision,' Kate said calmly. 'I am sorry if it troubles you, Bea. Naturally, I will ask nothing of you but your silence...'

'My wife and I understand the position you are in,' John said. 'I cannot say that I am comfortable with what you are doing, but I sympathise. We will help in any way we can.'

'You are too kind, John.'

Beatrice lifted her head. 'I beg you again to reconsider, mistress. What if something should happen to you?'

'There is more.' Kate took a deep breath. 'I have taken a lover.'

Beatrice turned to look at John again, who nodded slightly. 'The gentleman who brought Midnight to you as a gift? Master Ralph Chaplin?'

Kate wondered if she should tell him Raife's true name and, in an instant, she decided against it, for his own safety. 'He and I are lovers. I spend time with him when I can. I know that is not right in God's eyes, but...' Kate's voice trailed off.

'You have such a lonely marriage, mistress. John and I often say to each other,' Beatrice said. 'It is not for us to judge you.'

'But I know of no Chaplins who live around Markyate, mistress.' John appeared confused.

'Do not concern yourself,' Kate said. She imagined a time when Thomas might discover what she had done and try to find Raife, asking John questions. The less he knew the better. She hated misleading John and Beatrice – they deserved the truth. 'We meet each other when we can. I was with him when I said I had been in London. I am sorry that I deceived you.'

John said nothing.

Beatrice met her eyes. 'Do you love him, mistress?'

This time, Kate was ready to tell the truth. 'Like I never believed possible. He is a good man, a wonderful man. I am never happier than when we are together.'

'Then we will help you,' Beatrice said.

'Does he know about your... highway activities?' John asked tentatively.

'I have told him all,' Kate admitted.

'He must be worried,' Beatrice blurted.

'He is,' Kate said. 'He wishes to accompany me next time, to help me.'

'He has not asked you to desist?' John was amazed. 'But there is grave danger in what you do.'

'I know, John.' Kate took a deep breath. 'He loves me. We plan to leave together one day. We will only steal from those who have plenty, we will make sure that local families, that you and Bea, are taken care of. Then we will take enough to help us to begin again, to live as we wish, far from here.'

'Thank you for telling us,' John said. 'You know my wife and I will do all we can to help. But I have to tell you that I am afraid for your lives...'

'I take no risks – and I will never use the flintlock, even though it is in my hand.'

'Constable Wilmott is a rogue, mistress – you must be on guard. Your gentleman friend too,' John said anxiously.

'We will take the greatest care,' Kate said. 'I thank you both for your kindness and understanding. I little expected you to be so understanding.'

'You have been good to Beatrice and me,' John replied. 'In turn, we will do our best for you. We will say nothing of Master Chaplin.' A thoughtful look crossed his face. 'The less the constable and other people know about his existence, the better – especially since he plans to help you with your... business.'

'Thank you both. And he thanks you, too, I am sure of it.' Kate was delighted that John and Beatrice would help her. 'Now, if you please, I will take my leave and go to my chamber. It has been a very tiring day.'

'As you wish,' John said as he watched her walk towards the parlour door. He exchanged meaningful looks with Beatrice, his brow raised in question, her eyes shining with anxiety. Although they both disapproved, there was nothing they wouldn't do to help their bold and courageous mistress.

28

THE PRESENT

Late on Sunday afternoon, as the light was fading, Charlie and Edie surveyed their handiwork in the second bedroom. They were feeling pleased with themselves. Charlie said, 'The ceilings in both small bedrooms are good. I'll plaster over them tomorrow and let them dry out, then they'll be ready for painting. You've done a great job on the walls...'

Edie flourished a stripping knife. 'What colours are you thinking of?'

'Uncle Bill says white makes a house sell better...' He shrugged. 'If it was me, I'd have three walls in cream and one in bluish grey.'

'Then do that.'

'If I was staying, I would,' Charlie said. 'Mind you, I'd be thinking of solar panels and a big rainwater tank. I'd love to have a house like yours.'

'I recommend it. Right.' Edie folded her arms. 'Let's go to mine and cook some food. Alan can keep Bianca company while we make something to eat and we can talk about...'

'Katherine Ferrers?' Charlie lowered his voice as if the ghost could hear. His fingers went to the hematite bracelet. 'Good idea – let's see what we can find out about her.'

'Bring the saxophone too,' Edie suggested. 'I'd love to hear the tune you wrote. Can you remember it?'

'I recorded it on my phone and wrote some of it down. I just need some lyrics...'

'And a title?' Edie asked. 'You can't just call it "Kate's Tune". It deserves something more dignified.'

'You're right.' Charlie grinned. 'I'll bring a bottle of wine.'

'I have gallons of elderberry,' Edie said. 'We won't run out.'

'I'll help you cook then.' Charlie was stripping off his overalls already, standing in T-shirt and jeans. 'I'm a pretty good sous chef.'

* * *

Charlie stood in Edie's kitchen, peeling potatoes, trimming beans, admiring the oak cabinets, the warm Aga, the glowing lights. 'I'd love a kitchen like this. It's really cosy.'

Edie was pleased. 'I feel I belong here.' Bianca was sleeping in her dog basket in front of the Aga. Alan had moved into the spare one Edie had placed next to it, and both dogs were snoring. 'Don't our dogs look cute, snuggled up together?' She placed a hand over her mouth, as if to stop herself saying something else. 'They're so sweet.'

'They get on well. Ouch.' Charlie grazed his finger on the paring knife. 'That was a close shave. I have to watch the fingers – I need them for the sax.'

'So, are you going to form a band?' Edie was preparing lemongrass, ginger, chillies. 'Paige has a great voice.'

'She has.'

'We were at school together and she was in all the musicals, playing lead roles.'

'She has a jazz singer's voice, full of passion,' Charlie agreed. 'We ought to jam together some time. Do you play anything?'

'Recorder a bit, in the infants.' Edie pulled a sad face. 'I really wish I had some musical skill.'

'I'll teach you to play the saxophone,' Charlie offered gallantly.

'I don't think I'd be anywhere near as good as Joshit and Kavish.'

'They're doing well,' Charlie said. 'Kavish is learning fast, but I think Joshit will be special. He's gifted.'

'Nila's thrilled.' Edie met his eyes and looked away. 'You're really settling down here. Do you think you'll go back to London?'

'I expect so... I'd have to go where the house we'd be working on is, I guess. Especially now Uncle Bill's got angina, he needs to be thinking about retiring and he has several projects he wants me to work on before he calls it a day.'

'So you'd be a full-time builder?'

'I enjoy it,' Charlie admitted. 'Working with my hands, being creative, watching something develop that I've had a hand in designing.'

'Like music?' Edie asked.

'I suppose so, yes.'

'Not teaching?'

'I like teaching – not the last job, mind – the school wasn't right for me, but somewhere else, yes, maybe.'

'So, here's a thing.' Edie put her hands on her hips. 'Which of the three would you like to do most? Teaching, building or music? Or is there a fourth option, like you and Alan travelling the world?'

'Music, I suppose. Although the ideal thing would be to do everything I enjoy, but in different amounts. At the moment, I'm mostly a builder. In my dream life, I'd mostly play music.'

'You've decided, brilliant. Maybe you should join a band,' Edie exclaimed and Charlie knew she was teasing him. 'So – food's ready. Let's eat in here, then we can move into the other room and do some research.'

'Great, I'm starving,' Charlie admitted. 'And researching ghosts is hard work. Let's have a glass of wine and dive in.'

* * *

An hour later, Charlie and Edie were sprawled on the rug on the floor in the living room, a laptop open in front of them. The dogs had not moved from their baskets. The room was cosy and warm, the curtains drawn, the clock ticking softly.

Edie clutched a second glass of wine. 'So – what first?'

'Well, we know that she married Thomas, and the date she was born, when she died, but her story is confusing – it doesn't make sense.'

'Because there are two stories.' Edie frowned. 'In one, she's the wife of a man who took all her money, a Royalist who went to prison for his allegiance to King Charles, and Katherine died in London...'

'And the other story says she was a highway robber who dressed as a man and came to a sticky end.' Charlie was confused.

'It does say it's a myth,' Edie said.

'It says, "According to the popular legend, often told with an emphasis on several episodes of hauntings by her ghost..."' Charlie traced the words with his finger.

'So, let's see if we can find out where her ghost has been sighted,' Edie suggested.

'Good idea,' Charlie agreed. 'If she's been seen on Ferrers Lane, on the common, then we know that other people have seen her too, not just us. Perhaps we can contact them and ask them what they've experienced.'

'Right...' Edie's fingers hovered quickly over the keyboard. 'Here. "Many highwaymen were Royalist supporters who had lost their homes, estates or income and were left to make a living as best they could..." So – Katherine Ferrers would have been in good company.'

'But women highway robbers were a rarity. And most highwaymen came a bit later, the eighteenth century...' Charlie read on. '"Dick Turpin and Plunkett and Macleane operated in the mid seventeen hundreds."'

'Katherine was a trailblazer.' Edie looked impressed. 'I'm beginning to respect this woman.'

'Back to her hauntings...' Charlie looked over her shoulder as Edie twitched the mouse. '"In 1840, Markyate Cell burned down, and this was said to have been caused by the ghost of The Wicked Lady, who started the fire maliciously..."'

'"People said they felt uneasy as they tried to extinguish the blaze, that she was watching them from the woods..."' Edie read.

'I know exactly how that feels, being watched by her... it makes my spine feel like a stick of ice.' Charlie shivered.

'Me too... Here – in one of the local papers it says workmen saw the figure of a nun...' Edie sighed, confused. 'The Cell was a priory in the twelfth century.'

'And look – in 1957, a nightwatchman saw someone warming their hands by the brazier. The figure of a young man.'

'A highwayman?'

'It doesn't say so.' Charlie groaned. 'This is all superstition and hearsay.'

Edie read on. '"In the early nineteen hundreds, the occupier of Markyate Cell saw Katherine Ferrers's ghost on the stairs. She has also been reported galloping through the lanes around Nomansland."'

'We're getting closer, Edie.'

'Well, she certainly lived through the years of the English Civil War, and now we've seen her in Ferrers Lane, so perhaps we should believe the legend of her being a highway robber more than the story of her dying young in London.' Edie leaned on her elbow. 'How about we concentrate on Ferrers Lane? It carries her name – and we've seen her here.'

'So – who was the constable?' Charlie asked. 'The cottages are named after him... or her.'

Edie's fingers rattled on the keyboard. 'Constable – let's say 1659 – Katherine Ferrers would have been twenty-five then.'

'She didn't live long,' Charlie murmured.

Edie's eyes scanned the screen. 'So, "parish constables, or petty constables, performed all the main duties associated with local policing. They kept order in the inns and alehouses and kept the peace in the parishes."'

'These houses would have belonged to forerunners of policemen?' Charlie was suddenly excited. 'And she'd have been a highway robber on the common, just beyond where they lived. I wonder if they chased her down. Edie – do we have any background info on this house?'

'I'll have a look in the deeds and conveyances. There are record offices, The National Archives. Leave it with me.'

'Right. And what shall I do?' Charlie asked.

Edie grinned. 'Get another glass of wine, and let's take a break. Play me your tune about The Wicked Lady.'

'Right. I'm on it.' Charlie poured elderberry wine into their glasses and reached for his saxophone. Edie curled up on the sofa, stretching out, closing her eyes as he began to play a soulful melody.

Charlie concentrated hard, taking himself to a place where he could imagine Katherine Ferrers alone, as a child, a young bride, then an independent woman. He saw her in gowns, silks and velvets, then in a coat and breeches, a highway woman with a pistol clutched in her hand. His fingers played every emotion of the dual life she must have led. Raspy tones and soft buzzing notes were replaced with a playfulness, bubbling like a river. The smooth tune became a melancholy phrase that tugged at his own heartstrings, achingly sad.

When Charlie stopped playing, the air was filled with cold silence and he felt suddenly enveloped in melancholy. He looked over to Edie, who was curled up, her face damp with tears.

She muttered, 'That was so beautiful.'

As if in response to her words, there was a harsh banging at the door, three resounding knocks. Edie sat up, her eyes wide.

Charlie's body stiffened. 'Who's that?'

The room temperature had dropped. Charlie's heart was thudding.

Edie whispered, 'It's past ten. I've no idea...' As an afterthought, she said, 'Marilyn?'

'Didn't she say she was at her sister's today?' Charlie murmured.

Edie nodded. The silence seemed to fill every space in the room and they glanced at each other, wide-eyed.

'I'll take a look outside...' Charlie placed his saxophone back in its stand carefully, and stood up, walking on quiet feet towards the curtains. In one movement, he drew them, and swallowed his breath in a gasp.

She was there, looking straight at him through the glass. A woman's face, delicate features, widely spaced eyes, a rose mouth. Curls tumbled across her forehead. In a split second, as Charlie jerked backwards, he noticed her mournful expression. Her eyes held the pain of someone whose heart had been broken. He had never seen such sorrow before.

Then she was gone.

Charlie turned round, almost unbelieving. 'Did you see her?'

Edie nodded. She was hugging a cushion.

'I wasn't imagining it?'

'She was there...' Edie slid from the sofa, pushing the cushion away, and came over to place her hand in Charlie's. 'We need to look outside.'

Charlie stared at her. He wondered why they would do that. He felt safe indoors – he might open the door and let in... he had no idea who. Or what. He squeezed her fingers. They were icicles.

He found it hard to speak. 'All right. We need to check...'

'...if she's still there...'

Charlie took a step forward and Edie copied him. They reached the door, then Charlie lifted the latch and pushed. The door gave a muted creak and opened wide.

They blinked into darkness and shadows, at the outline of the gate, Edie's car, the shifting branches of trees beyond. The breeze breathed in their faces; beyond, the muffled murmur of moving leaves came from the woodland. High in the sky, a sliver of moon hung low among tiny diamond stars.

Then they heard it, the low echo of a horse's hooves, fading into the distance, until there was nothing remaining but the creak of heavy brushwood and the low moan of the wind.

29

1659

It was almost the end of October. Over the last few months, the talk about the highway robber had subsided. People assumed he had gone away, taken his villainy elsewhere. The days were shorter now. The earth had cooled. It was the hour where the evening light drained from the sky, and nightfall was moments away. Kate and Raife had waited patiently for long enough; now the time was right.

Two figures on horseback waited on the common, watching the empty road that led to London stretched below them. The horses nickered quietly: Midnight and Lightning knew each other well, and they seemed to know what they would need to do. They swished their manes, nervous, ready for Kate and Raife to urge them forwards.

'Our first highway robbery together,' Raife whispered. 'What will they call the two of us?'

Kate smiled. 'The dashing Ralph Chaplin – and his handsome young accomplice.'

'So I am Ralph Chaplin the highwayman now. Not the farmer Raife Chetwyn from Ayers End?'

'I hide behind the garb of a boy. You hide behind a new name. And no one must see your face when you ride – you must never be recognised. John and Bea will help us.'

'Then Chaplin I am...'

The horses' ears pricked up: the thrum of coach wheels, the clatter of hooves. Kate and Raife could not hear it yet, but they exchanged glances, tugged their kerchiefs over their noses and tilted forward in their saddles, ready to gallop. Then the coach came into sight, wheels clattering against the dirt track.

Pistols raised, Kate and Raife hammered forward at a breakneck speed. The coach driver pulled on the reins to slow the horses down. Four people clambered from the coach, all well-dressed: two men and two women, their throats adorned with jewels. Rich pickings.

Kate cocked her flintlock with a flourish. 'If you please, hand over your money to Master Chaplin. For he will show you little mercy if you do not and I will shoot without hesitation. Your jewels too, ladies and gentlemen, and be quick about it.'

'How old are you, young man?' one of the women, middle-aged and sturdy of girth, muttered. 'I'd rather *you* took my necklace from me. You have small, delicate hands in those gloves. I believe you are handsome behind that kerchief.'

'You have no business with my face, mistress, but I thank you,' Kate said kindly as she watched Raife slip a silk purse into his coat, along with a diamond bracelet.

'I have heard of you, but I do not know your name...' the woman continued. 'You are the gallant highwayman, they say, who looks as if his mother's milk were barely out of him.' She winked lewdly. 'But I have to admit, I like the cut of your jib. Next time, I will ride with a necklace fastened around the top of my thigh. I wonder then if you will remove it for me gently. It will be worth losing the piece – any piece – just to see you do it.'

'Hold your tongue,' Raife said, glancing towards Kate to make sure she was untroubled by the woman's remark. He recovered quickly, giving a little bow. 'You would not like a man as rough as I am to take it from you, mistress.'

'I care not which of you does it, in faith. I am sure you are rugged and handsome behind that kerchief, Master Chaplin.' The woman indicated a tired-looking man who might have been her husband. 'Anything is better than the cold touch of this fopdoodle, this old luggerwort who has long since absented himself from the nightly duties of a husband.'

'Hurry...' Kate looked around. 'We waste time talking...'

Raife heard the concern in her voice. 'I bid you good day, mistress. And tell the constables that Ralph Chaplin and his young friend intend no harm. We wish only to take the riches you don't need.' He pushed the jewellery into his coat, tugged his horse's reins, dug his heels into Lightning's side and they both rode away.

'Godspeed,' Kate yelled as she turned Midnight towards the open common and the shelter of the trees beyond.

'You'll both swing...' the lewd woman's husband called, but his words were lost in the thud of horses' hooves.

Kate called to Raife, 'The woman was wasting our time. Deliberately. She hoped that the constables would come quickly and catch us.'

'You are right.' Raife looked over his shoulder, listening. Lightning had heard the sound of approaching horses too. 'I can hear hooves behind us. We must move quickly – I fear we are being followed.'

Kate leaned further forward, spurring her horse onwards. 'Go as fast as you can, Midnight.' She could hear horses in pursuit now, bearing down on them, hooves crackling on twigs. A voice called for them to stop, a pistol cracked in the air.

Raife shouted, 'Head for the thickest part of the woodland, Kate, then follow the narrow path to Ayers End. Put the horse in the stables, change your clothes for the shift you left behind.'

'What will you do?'

'I will lead them the wrong way. I know these parts well. I will lose them in the forest yonder, then I will come back to you swiftly.'

'But...'

Kate had no chance to speak again. Raife turned his horse, pounding downhill. She galloped the other way, pausing only to look over her shoulder. Two constables on horseback were in pursuit of Raife; he was forging ahead, twisting into the distance. Her breath came quickly; her heart hammered. She had to get back to the safety of the farm as quickly as she could and wait for him there.

* * *

An hour had passed. Then two. Kate was waiting nervously, wearing a crisp shift, her hair brushed so that it hung in waves down her back. She had prepared two plates of bread and cheese. Now she was pacing the length of the room, pausing to stare into the leaping flames, then moving to the window, the shutters wide. Darkness was all around. There was no sound of hooves in the distance, no riders approaching.

If the constables came to Ayers End Farm, what would she say to explain her presence there? Midnight was in the stables, eating and drinking, his coat damp and hot with sweat. She had wrapped her highwayman's garb in a bundle and hidden it upstairs. She would say she had called to see Master Chetwyn – he owed her husband rent on the land – she intended to collect it, but he was not at home, so she waited.

Anxiety made her feel weak. Her heart throbbed in her throat. Outside, it was pitch dark now, as the moon slid behind a cloud. She listened – there was no one. The trees shivered in the wind. A lone owl moaned and stretched its wings. Then the night air was silent again, as if waiting too.

Upstairs, under the pillow, there were two silk purses full of guineas, a necklace of precious stones, several rings, diamond bracelets. Thomas's pistol lay next to them. If the constables found it next to the night's haul, Kate's identity would be immediately discovered. But if they came to Ayers End, then Raife would already have been captured. The thought made Kate's stomach knot with dread and panic. For a moment, she thought she might be sick.

She heard the distant thud of hooves on dry earth. How many riders were there? If there was more than one, she would run and hide in the stables. She wondered if her legs would carry her; they had suddenly become weak. She rushed to the window.

A rider approached along the lane. She'd know the shape of him anywhere. She watched him turn towards the stables. It was Raife, riding past astride Lightning. She saw the white blaze on the stallion's nose in the moonlight.

She rushed to the door. Then she was in his arms, breathing the

warmth of him, clinging to him with relief. 'You are safe...' Her face still
held tension. 'Where are the constables?'

'Lost in the forest, even now trying to find their way.' Raife smiled. 'I
gave them the counterfeit coin, as they say.' He laughed at his joke. 'The
slip.'

'Ah.' Kate breathed out. 'I feared that they would catch you. I feared—'

He kissed her to stop her words, then he said, 'We must not think of it,
Kate. We must not fear it, and it will not come to pass. But perhaps we will
lie low for a few weeks until our next escapade. They know of us and the
constables will be keeping a keen eye.'

Kate leaned against him, suddenly weary. 'Then let us rest together and
spend our time with joyful thoughts.'

'Stay with me until dawn. Tomorrow you must go back to Markyate.'

Kate's voice was husky. 'I was so afraid for you...'

'Do not speak of it again. Let us eat, drink and then we will go to our
humble bed. We will think only of ourselves and the love we share, that is
like no other.'

'My own one,' Kate murmured, pulling him against her. 'There is
nowhere else I want to be.'

* * *

Hours later, they lay on the straw mattress in each other's arms. Kate's
thoughts were tugged back to the robbery, to the frantic chase with the
constables at their heels. A frown knotted between her brows. 'My love, I
cannot help but think, what if...?'

Raife kissed her mouth, as if taking a deep draught of wine. 'What if
one of us is caught? Are those thoughts still heavy with you, Kate?'

'I am truly afraid. I do not wish to live without you...'

'And I have chosen this life, not because I wish it, but because it is a
means to be free. We must keep that as our signpost, directing us to our
future.'

'I want to believe it,' Kate began. 'My future is with you. I imagine us
older, together, blessed with many children, grandchildren.'

'You paint a pretty picture,' Raife said. Kate took in his face, soft with love, his eyes reflecting the moonlight that shone in the tallow gleam. 'But, for me, happiness is now, in your arms. I am not afraid of death.'

'Oh, I fear it – I fear anything that takes me from you.' Kate shivered.

'I have helped animals come into the world and I have seen them leave. It is what will pass for us all.' Raife gathered her in his arms again, kissing her damp brow. 'Come what will, I am happy now, and I think of nothing more. If I am caught—'

'No.' Kate struggled from him, leaning up on one elbow. 'Time is our friend; each new dawn is a blessing. We will not be caught – I will not allow it.'

'You can command time, life, death – no wonder I love you so much, Kate.' Raife smiled. 'But if you are worried, then we will commit no more robberies. We can take a chance – you may live with me here. But your husband will make it difficult. He would have us thrown out...'

'You are right – we must continue as we are.'

'We will steal from the coaches just a few more times.' Raife touched her cheek tenderly with his thumb. 'We took money and jewels tonight that will bring us riches. We must not be greedy. Just enough...'

'And it will be a long winter – the Hargreves, the Woollcotts and the Salters will need fires, clothes for their little ones, food on the table.'

'We will make sure they want for nothing. I believe next summer we will be able to leave.'

'Perhaps Thomas will be free by then. They have him in the Tower, but they cannot keep him there indefinitely. He will surely come back and try to sell the manor house.'

'While he is in the Tower, we may do as we wish, like gathering hay while the sun shines...'

'My love.' Kate lay down in his arms, taking his hand, bringing it to her lips. 'We are not doing wrong, are we? It is a terrible thing to steal – the Bible tells us – but we do it for all the right reasons, and many people have much more than they need...'

'Sleep, you are tired,' Raife murmured. 'And rest assured, while the constables look for Chaplin and his boy, no one is watching us.'

'I believe you. All will be well.' Kate closed her eyes and smiled. She exhaled, contented, and drifted into the sweetest slumber.

30

THE PRESENT

The kitchen had been completely cleared; just an open space now with so much potential. There were only two weeks until Christmas, and it was unlikely that everything would be ready, but Charlie stood, hands on hips, and couldn't help smiling. 'You've been incredible, Edie.'

Edie scrutinised her hands that held the screwdriver and the hammer. 'I quite enjoyed all that wrecking...'

They looked around. The old cooker had been taken away for recycling, the cracked Belfast sink too, and the remains of the old cabinets had been demolished and taken to the recycling waste centre in the van. The ceiling and walls had been made good and were ready for painting.

Charlie took a breath. 'So, we'll take a break – then we'll paint the ceiling.'

'Painting the walls is my job,' Edie offered. 'I'm too short for the ceiling.'

'I'll do the ceiling, then I'll start on the floor tiles.'

'I can help with those too,' Edie offered.

'Haven't you got your own work to do?' Charlie asked. 'I don't want you to fall behind.'

'I'm on the last essay of my diploma – I'm way ahead, so I'm not worried. And I might increase my hours at the pub a bit over Christmas, so everything's looking good.'

'You've been amazing while Uncle Bill has been recuperating.' Charlie stared at Edie in red overalls that were far too big, hair falling over her flushed face. 'I owe you, big time.'

Edie shrugged. 'Buy me a meal in St Albans some time.'

'I want to cook you Christmas dinner – all the trimmings,' Charlie said. 'I suppose you'll be away though...?'

'No – I'm spending Christmas Day at Constable's Cottages. I've arranged to see my mum in Markyate on Boxing Day. She's having Christmas lunch in a hotel with friends,' Edie said. 'I did invite her over, but she said she wanted a proper dinner with turkey and goose fat roasties.'

'I know – my mother would be just the same... she'll be in Spain with Sonny. She hates the cold weather. I love it though – frost and snow.' Charlie grinned.

'Walking the dogs on the common first thing when the air's crisp,' Edie added.

'And coming back with a cold nose and fingers, eating mince pies, drinking mulled wine...'

'With a tree, and lights, decorations.' Edie smiled at the thought.

'Watching the repeats on TV,' Charlie said, already feeling the warmth of an imaginary fire. 'Uncle Bill will invite me over to his place but...' Charlie folded his arms. 'Alan and I would rather stay here.'

'Bianca and I think the same. By the way.' Edie poured tea from a flask into two cups. 'I found out some more stuff about the constables.'

'Oh?' Charlie leaned against the door post. 'Go on...'

'These three cottages were police accommodation in the seventeenth century. The constable lived here in one house – the others were barns for his horses, and he'd keep an eye on Nomansland Common...'

'Watching for highwaymen?' Charlie suggested.

'And highway women,' Edie added. 'Constables were organised by JPs but they had all sorts of powers – they kept the peace in the parish, arrested people and carried out punishments, such as whipping vagabonds.'

'So someone in this cottage would have been looking out for Katherine

Ferrers?' Charlie said. 'We're living in the same place as the constable who might have arrested her.'

'Definitely – and by all accounts some of these constables took their duties too far. They weren't paid, so that left the door open for corrupt men who liked to wield power a bit too much.'

'Ambitious people, megalomaniacs?' Charlie took a breath. 'Do you think that's who was chasing Katherine across the common?'

'I can imagine it,' Edie said, closing her eyes. 'If we believe the story that she was a highway robber. The other story simply says she was a bored wife...'

'I know which I believe,' Charlie replied. 'We've seen her, Edie. That night, when I played her tune on the sax...'

'I was so scared.' Edie shuddered.

'So, should we start researching Ralph Chaplin?' Charlie asked. 'His name keeps coming up. He was her lover, apparently.'

'There was an article in a digital edition of *The Watford Observer* about how he seduced Katherine when she was young, and he enticed her into a life of crime. It was all his fault – according to the article, he was a bad man.' Edie shook her head. 'I don't believe that, though. It doesn't feel right.'

'Why?'

'You've seen her out there, Charlie. She's sad, but she's strong. She wouldn't be a highwayman's moll who did as she was told. Everything about her and Ralph is speculation.'

'There's no historical proof that her accomplice Ralph Chaplin even existed.' Charlie drained his cup of tea. 'There's no record of any Chaplins living in Markyate or the surrounding area, so we have nothing to work on.'

'Do you think they really terrorised people or was that a romanticised portrayal?' Edie asked. She tugged out her phone and handed it to Charlie. 'I saved this article from *The Hertfordshire Mercury*. Ralph and Katherine were blamed for causing mayhem, burning houses, slaughtering livestock, even killing an officer of the law. But what if it wasn't them? The crimes could be just as easily blamed on the unrest during the Civil War.'

'Maybe we'll never know,' Charlie said sadly. 'But she's out there.'

'And she's trying to tell us something, isn't she?' Edie glanced at her amethyst bracelet. 'Something about love and loss...'

'She is.' Charlie watched as Edie dragged the hop-up to the edge of the room and clambered up, paintbrush in one hand, a pot of paint in the other. 'Will you be all right?'

'I did the walls in my house.' Edie grinned. 'By myself, Charlie. With no help from anyone.'

He watched her load the brush and apply paint neatly. She was marvellous – he'd never met anyone like her before. It puzzled him. She seemed vulnerable at times, yet she was so strong, wilful, independent. In so many ways, she was just like him – sensitive, spirited.

Edie noticed him watching her and she grinned. 'What?'

'If you ever need a job...' Charlie made a joke of it. 'Uncle Bill will snap you up.'

'I might just take him up on it if the career in law comes to nothing.' Edie continued to paint. 'Where's Alan, by the way?'

'Upstairs, sleeping on my bed. He's warm up there. He'll be even warmer when Uncle Bill connects the radiators up to the new boiler. I hope he'll be able to do it before Christmas.'

'How's he getting on?' Edie asked as she worked.

'Really well. Apparently, he's a changed man.'

'Oh?'

'Auntie Marcia said he won't eat any of the stuff he used to love.' Charlie couldn't help a little laugh. 'You won't see him scoffing cake any more. Now he has ten portions of fruit and vegetables each day, oily fish, oats, beans and lentils.'

'My goodness.' Edie gave a theatrical gasp. 'He'll be going vegan next.'

'Fat chance of that, but he's bought a static cycle and put it in the bedroom,' Charlie said. 'He's even talking about getting a dog to walk to keep him fit. He wants a big dog – a Newfoundland. It would eat him out of house and home though. They grow to be about eleven stone. Auntie Marcia wants a Pomeranian.'

'Talking of dogs, I left Bianca asleep by the Aga, but I'll pop back in half an hour and she can stretch her legs,' Edie said.

'Alan and I will come – we can have a quick stroll on the common.'

'We're so lucky to live here, Charlie.' Edie paused, paintbrush in hand, and Charlie gazed at her in the paint-spattered baggy overalls.

'You've got a bit of paint...'

'It doesn't matter...'

'...On your cheek.'

'Oh... right.' Edie put her pot down and clambered from the hop-up.

'I'll do it...' Charlie felt for the crumpled piece of tissue paper in the pocket of his overalls. Edie came to stand in front of him and closed her eyes, completely trusting. He touched her cheek tenderly with the tissue, wiping the paint away. There was a pale smear left. He thought about leaving it. She looked like a beautiful goddess performing some kind of new age ceremony, her hair tumbling from its clasp, her eyes closed in meditation.

He brushed the last of the paint away and she opened her eyes. Shining, hazel, unquestioning eyes, a level stare. Charlie had never seen the green flecks before. Amber too, gold, reflecting light. For a moment, he couldn't move.

Charlie caught his breath. He said, 'There. All done.'

Edie was still watching him. 'Thanks, Charlie.'

'It's nothing.'

He wondered what to do, whether to kiss her or to pull away. A banging in the hall made him jump. Edie leaped in surprise.

Uncle Bill appeared in the doorway, grinning. 'Right, you slackers – let's get back to work.' He looked lithe, fit, fresher-faced. 'Oh, you've both done a great job. I'll have to take you on full time, Edie.'

'That's what Charlie said,' Edie joked.

Charlie was still staring at her, stunned.

He pulled himself together. 'Good to see you, Uncle Bill. You look really well.'

'I feel great. The doc says my cholesterol is much lower and I'm fit as a fiddle.' Bill put down his box of tools. 'Right, let's crack on. Floor to lay, central heating to hook up... kitchen to fit.'

'I don't think we'll be finished for Christmas,' Charlie said sadly.

'Well, that's where you're wrong.' Bill was pleased with himself. 'I've got kitchen cabinets coming tomorrow and a cooker. We'll get it done, you wait and see.' He rubbed his hands together. 'Number one Constable's Cottages will have its first Christmas in this kitchen for a long time. Well?' Bill's eyebrows shot up in anticipation. 'What are we all waiting for?'

* * *

The common stretched up towards a fading sky as Charlie and Edie walked with Alan and Bianca along the path that led back to Constable's Cottages. The dogs were off their leads, trotting ahead happily together in front. Alan had found a small piece of branch that he held in his mouth, unwilling to part with it. Bianca glanced at him once and away, as if he was completely misguided.

'It's getting dark now,' Edie said as a cold breeze blew her hair across her face.

Charlie knew she wasn't just stating the obvious; what she really meant was that, when the light had drained from the sky, they'd both be listening for the sound of hooves in the distance, peering between the trees for a shadow that watched and waited.

A thought came to him. His breath was a mist on the air. 'Why is it only Katherine's ghost that we see? Why do we never see Ralph Chaplin? Or both of them together?'

'The stuff we've read on the internet about her says she might not have been a highway woman at all – something completely different happened to her, in London. So perhaps she wants us to know that she really did steal from passing carriages.'

'Do you think she killed an officer of the law?' Charlie felt the icy wind cut through his jacket. 'Do you think they hunted her down in revenge?'

'Perhaps she and her lover were separated by them. Perhaps she's still looking for him.'

Charlie wanted to take Edie's hand, to link his fingers through hers. 'We need to find out more information. Why was she called The Wicked Lady? Do you think she was really wicked?'

'I suppose breaking the law and robbing innocent passengers was wicked – but the name adds to the romance of it,' Edie said. 'Lady doesn't refer to a title. Thomas Fanshawe wasn't knighted until 1661, so Katherine was never Lady Fanshawe. Samuel Pepys wrote something naughty about her husband in his diary. He didn't like him much.'

'I can't imagine Katherine liking him much either, if she took a lover,' Charlie remarked. 'But what we need to discover is whether she was a heroine, a rogue or a victim.'

'And who Ralph Chaplin was,' Edie added.

They were heading towards the woodland path that led to Constable's Cottages. Charlie watched Alan racing ahead, Bianca just behind.

'We'll be home before dark,' he said thankfully.

'I'm glad.' Edie's voice was filled with tension. 'Let's get back. Come in for a cup of tea.'

'That would be nice,' Charlie said as they took the path together, hurrying forward through the trees.

They didn't see the shadow that hesitated behind a thick branch of shivering leaves. The highway woman sat still as stone, tall on a dark horse, although the stiff breeze did not lift his mane or ruffle her loose curls. She leaned forward to watch Charlie and Edie pass by, her eyes narrowed. Once they were out of sight, she spurred Midnight forwards, moving slowly towards Constable's Cottages.

Her breath left no mist on the night air.

31

1659

Raife was still asleep as Kate dressed warmly in her shift, kirtle, dress and cape against the November cold. Her clothes were tighter, now. She had put on a little weight recently, although Raife hadn't noticed. Being a farmer's woman meant that she ate more bread and pottage than she was used to; her waist was becoming thicker. And being a highway robber had increased her appetite, her zest for life. There could be no mistake – she was happier, healthier. She looked forward to a slice of Beatrice's honey cake, although spiced wine seemed to agree with her less nowadays. Perhaps her tastes were changing, becoming simpler.

It would soon be December and the wind was becoming harsh, laced with ice. She kissed Raife's brow tenderly, smiling as he murmured her name, then she tucked the pistol in her belt, along with the spoils of the robbery they had staged last night, a haul of guineas and diamonds. She checked they were safely stowed beneath her robe before she padded down the steps on light feet towards the stable, hurrying from the upstairs room as the first skeins of light filtered between the shutters. Her highway-man's clothes were in a bundle beneath her arm. She needed to be on her way before anyone spotted her.

Midnight was refreshed and swift of hoof. His mane lifted in the wind. Kate's hair was loose behind her as they pounded along the lane in perfect rhythm towards Markyate, a distance of some seven miles. Kate leaned forward, her left leg over the curving pommel, keen to arrive back at The Cell as soon as possible. She'd ask Beatrice to arrange a warm bath, to get her a dish of stewed fruit with spices, bread and butter. She was hungry. A smile played on her lips as she thought of how much she longed for a hot bath now, but during the summer months she and Raife had bathed daily in the river. The water had been cold, but they had splashed and shrieked, tangling in each other's arms and swimming – he had taught her how and she had learned quickly. Afterwards, they would lie together on a woollen blanket while the sunlight dried their bodies like a warm kiss. The summer had been wonderful. The river would be cold now.

She heard the thrum of hooves beating behind her; someone was catching up. She knew it wasn't Raife; she'd have recognised Lightning from the thud of his hooves without having to turn around. At first, she wondered if it was another highway robber trying to steal from her. Her fingers moved to the pistol in her belt and her mind worked quickly. She was no more than two miles from The Cell. If the person behind her was pursuing her, she and Midnight might outrun him.

A voice called, 'Mistress Fanshawe.' Kate looked over her shoulder and felt her heart sink. Constable Wilmott was approaching fast. Because he was an officer, she ought to slow down and ask him what he wanted. She was unafraid – she knew her wits were sharp. She'd talk to him for a few minutes and be on her way.

The reins in her hands tightened and Midnight slowed to a trot. In seconds, Wilmott was beside her, smiling in an ingratiating way.

'Mistress, you are out early.'

'As you are too, constable,' Kate replied smartly.

'May I enquire where you are going?'

'I am on my way back to The Cell.'

'And where have you been?'

'Out on my horse, Constable Wilmott.' Kate gave him a scornful look. 'As you can well see.'

'As a constable, appointed by the Justice of the Peace, Master Henry Glanville, it is my duty to ensure the safety of young women out alone at an early hour. As you know, Mistress Fanshawe, there are two vagabond highwaymen on the loose and it falls to me to bring them to justice and see them hanged. And you are prey to such men, a rich beautiful woman, alone.'

'I am almost home.' Kate exhaled, losing patience. 'If you will allow me to, I shall arrive sooner and then I will be safe.'

The constable didn't move. 'You have no husband to protect you. I have heard that he will be in the Tower for a year, maybe more.' The constable slid from his horse and walked slowly in front of Midnight, patting his neck gently. 'This is a fine horse, mistress.'

'He is.' Kate wondered what the constable was implying.

'His neck is drenched with sweat.'

'We have been riding hard.'

'Where did you get him? He is new to you, is he not?'

Kate looked away, then back to meet his eyes. She felt uncomfortable: he was watching her too closely. 'I have two mounts, constable. They keep each other company and they are good company for me.' She avoided his question. 'Now, if I may be on my way, I am late for breakfast.'

The constable appeared to be inspecting Midnight. He made a low sound of disapproval. 'I think your horse has a lame leg.'

'I think he does not,' Kate replied.

'I beg you, dismount. Come and see if I am not right.'

Kate felt a moment's concern. She hoped her stallion had not injured himself on the journey. But she was sure he had no problem with his leg – she would have known.

Wilmott was standing at her foot, staring at her ankle and calf with a lewd smile. He held out a hand. 'Come, dismount. I will show you.'

Kate felt instinctively that he was wasting her time, trying to prove a point or flaunt his status. She would humour him briefly. She slid down, her bundle of clothes tied tightly to the saddle, and followed him round to the front of the horse. She examined Midnight's forelegs, then she straightened up. 'You are mistaken, Constable Wilmott. Midnight is not lame.'

'I was indeed incorrect,' the constable replied smugly. He looked pleased with himself, now he had Kate standing opposite to him. His eyes flickered over her body. 'I am concerned about you, all alone at The Cell, with no husband to care for you.'

'Please do not concern yourself at all,' Kate replied as firmly as she could. In truth, she was agitated; a warning pulse had started to quiver in her throat.

'Mistress Fanshawe, where have you been this morning?'

'I have told you.'

'Then I must ask you again... I was leaving my cottage early this morning, looking out for footpads, brigands and highwaymen, when I saw you leaving Ayers End Farm, riding along the lane...'

Kate lifted her chin. 'And?'

'And I wondered why you had been there at so early an hour.'

Kate felt her temper rise – she had been caught out. 'It is not your business to wonder, constable.'

'Farmer Chetwyn lives there by himself, does he not? He is a widower.'

'I believe it to be so.'

'And you are a woman alone, forsaken by your husband. Now I ask myself – what might you be doing there, you and he together?'

'How dare you—' Kate was furious.

'It is my duty to know these things,' Wilmott interrupted her.

'Then know – Farmer Chetwyn is a busy man who rises early to work. I went to collect rent for my husband.'

'And can you show me this rent?'

'He could not pay it.' Kate was beginning to lose patience. Her instincts alerted her to leave as quickly as she could. The way the constable was looking at her filled her with apprehension. 'Constable Wilmott, I wish to go home.'

'You need your beauty sleep, mistress... you are looking weary. I believe you have been up all night – up and down...' He licked his lips as he grasped her elbow. 'Now, if you tell me the truth, perhaps I will allow you on your way.'

Kate's heart leaped in panic. The constable was a bully; his grip tightened. She tugged away. 'I will take my leave.'

'You will not.' The constable grasped her wrist. 'Now come, pretty mistress – I just wish to sample a little of what you have freely given to Chetwyn.'

'What?' Kate's eyes were wide with disbelief.

'A kiss, perhaps a small embrace. Something more of your bounteous kindness...' He wrapped an arm around her, his free hand tugging at her skirt. 'After all, you may seem a respectable married woman, but I believe in truth you are nothing more than a common whore.'

'Let go of me,' Kate said firmly, wrenching her shoulder away.

'I suspect you are Chetwyn's paramour, and what is meat for a farmer is meat for a constable.' He tugged her against him and she smelled the rancid breath. 'A kiss or two for starters, then the main course...'

His mouth was against her neck. She pushed him away and he grasped the front of her dress. She felt the material tear. In fear and desperation, she twisted away, clawing at his face, shrieking, 'Let me go.'

There was blood on her hands, a deep scratch on his cheek. His expression was ugly with anger. 'Why, you are a vicious strumpet.' He slapped her face, pushing her backwards, and she staggered and fell in front of Midnight. Before she could clamber up, he was on top of her, tugging her skirt and petticoat, fiddling with his braces.

'Come now, mistress, you seem to like a rough man. If you close your eyes, you can imagine it is Master Chetwyn.' His lips were wet, saliva swung from his mouth. 'And if you prefer to keep them open, it is all the same to me. I will make you squeal just as he does.'

Kate felt the pain of his nails as his fingers gripped her thigh. She struggled, pushing him away. 'You will not touch me.'

Something slipped, falling from her dress, grazing the ground with a light sound. A diamond bracelet glittered against the dusty earth.

Wilmott's eyes widened. 'What is this?' He snatched it in dirty fingers. 'Where did you get this? It is worth a pretty penny...' He pushed it into his pocket, then his face shone with a new knowledge. 'Of course.' His eyes flickered to the bundle tied to the saddle. 'The boy highwayman is small, slender, as if he were a mere woman. And I suppose his clothes are wrapped inside that bundle. If I were to examine it closely, I might discover...' He gave an unpleasant laugh that made Kate's stomach twist. 'Well, Mistress Fanshawe, you are full of surprises. It looks like I may have to arrest you. But not until I have enjoyed...' He fell on her neck again, kissing her so that she could hardly breathe. Leering, he ripped her bodice, his sticky fingers pressing her flesh.

Kate's breath came fast as she heaved herself beneath him – he was a heavy weight – and her hand touched the cold steel of the pistol in her belt. She reached for it, tugging it free, and pushed it against his stomach. She eased it upwards, feeling for the trigger, squeezing it once.

The shot made her ears ring. She could smell the sharpness of gunpowder. Kate felt the constable flop on top of her, a dead weight, his eyes wide. Blood seeped from his chest onto her torn dress, into the dusty earth. She pushed him away and he fell on the dirt and did not move. She stood quickly, her body shaking, and stared at him, the hole in his chest, his breeches unbuttoned, his clothes ruffled. She adjusted her robe and rolled him over with the side of her boot, her heart thumping.

'Lie there, Constable Wilmott. You will not violate an innocent woman again.' She took a deep breath and pushed her pistol into her belt. She was surprised how calm she suddenly felt. 'Someone will find you and they will conclude that you were shot in pursuit of a criminal. Whereas, if the truth be known, you are the wrongdoer. I shall not mourn your passing.'

She stooped down, picked up the diamond bracelet and tugged her cloak around her to cover the torn material of her dress. Then she clambered onto the stallion in a swift swirl of her skirts.

'Come, Midnight, let us head for home. This rogue can stay here until someone else finds him and decides what to do with him.'

She dug her heels in lightly and Midnight galloped away, leaving the constable stretched out on his back in the dirt and his horse looking for grass to nibble.

* * *

By the time Kate arrived back at The Cell, the effect of what had happened had hit her hard. She was shivering with fear and cold. Her stomach was knotted with the horror of what she had done, and she thought she would be sick. She left Midnight in the stables and rushed into the vast hall, where John was waiting.

'I saw you arrive, mistress.' He noticed the blood on her clothes, her terrified expression. 'Are you hurt?'

'John, I have killed a man. In defence. He thought to harm me, but... I shot him before he could do so.' Her eyes swivelled, looking for Beatrice. 'I am in need of a bath... and my clothes will need to be burned. I need to sit down.'

John took her elbow, leading her into the winter parlour.

Suddenly, Beatrice was by her side. 'What is amiss?' Her voice raised in fear. 'There is blood on your robe. Has Master Chaplin tried to harm you?'

'No, he would do no such thing.' Kate was trembling. 'Constable Wilmott stopped me on the road. He guessed where I had been. He sought to accost me...'

John understood. 'He has always made a good view of you, mistress. A most unpleasant man. Few will mourn him.' He was suddenly practical. 'Where does his body lie?'

'Some two miles distant. He was shot through the chest. I felt the pistol in my hand...'

'He sought to hurt you...' Beatrice wrapped an arm around her. 'You did only what every woman would wish to do in your position.' She looked towards her husband for help, and her voice was filled with fear. 'But what is to be done now?'

'A dead man cannot speak...' John gave a light cough. 'He will lie where he is until someone finds him. They will believe he was shot by a footpad, or a highwayman perhaps.'

'You and Master Chaplin must lie low for a while.' Beatrice patted Kate's hand. 'Come, I will get a bath for you and then I will make you something to eat.'

'We will dispose of your bloodied robe, mistress,' John murmured. 'You look pale and weary, and you are shivering. Perhaps once you have broken your fast, you might sleep awhile. Then, if you wish, we may talk of this again and decide what is to be done. But I fear that more constables will keep a watch on the common now...'

'You may be right.' Kate took a deep breath, closing her eyes. She was beginning to feel unwell. 'Thank you for your kindness, Bea, John. I am forever grateful...'

'Not at all,' Beatrice said. 'We seek only to care for you. Come, mistress, I am concerned that you look unwell.'

'I am sick to my stomach, Bea,' Kate groaned. 'After everything that happened, I feel decidedly giddy and I fear I shall swoon.'

'I am here,' Beatrice said, helping Kate to her feet, propelling her towards the stairs, towards her bedroom. But before she could put a foot on the first step, Kate keeled forward, held tightly to the banister and retched loudly. She leaned forward as she was violently sick. Then she slumped to the floor and burst into tears.

32

THE PRESENT

There was only one week until Christmas and the kitchen was far from completed. Charlie had been choosing tiles and light fittings and he had even been Christmas shopping. His calendar was full – Boxing Day with Uncle Bill and Auntie Marcia, a party on New Year's Eve. He had started to feel festive.

Now, on the nineteenth, he stood in the Sharmas' living room in Markyate, Sahil and Nila smiling proudly. Kavish and Joshit, each with an alto saxophone in their hands, were giving their first concert. They had insisted on changing their school uniform for black hoodies and jeans, so that they looked identical, although Kavish was much taller and slimmer, and the more serious of the two. Joshit couldn't stop smiling.

Charlie gave a polite cough. 'Ladies and gentlemen,' he said to Sahil and Nila, 'I present to you the wonderful Sharma brothers, who will now play the tunes they have been working so hard to perfect. First, we will hear "Baby Shark", followed by "Careless Whisper" and, finally, "Dance Monkey".'

He nodded to the boys, as if sharing a secret, and they placed the mouthpieces between their lips and began to blow. Kavish made a few tentative strange sounds at first, but Joshit was note perfect, and his timing was faultless. They played the three tunes they had practised each day for weeks, one after the other, while their parents held their breath, tears gleaming in their eyes. After 'Dance Monkey', Joshit gave a small bow, followed by Kavish and then Joshit again. Nila and Sahil clapped energetically.

'And to round off,' Charlie said with a grin, 'the boys will play "Jingle Bells".'

Charlie nodded his head encouragingly, in time with the music. The Christmas tune was played flawlessly and both boys bowed again, this time in perfect synchronisation. Charlie was delighted.

'Well done – that was brilliant.'

'I can't believe how good they were.' Sahil was overwhelmed. 'How much you have learned in such a short time, Kav and Josh. And well done, Charlie.'

'They have been practising so hard, and helping each other.' Nila's face shone. 'And Josh's asthma hasn't held him back at all. In fact, his breathing has improved.'

Kavish looked really pleased with himself. 'My teacher says I can take my sax into school and perform on the last day of term. She says I can join the orchestra.' He turned to Charlie. 'You were right about girls admiring sax players. Ava Newton in my class plays the clarinet. She thinks I'm really cool, and she's well fit.'

'And I love playing the sax.' Joshit was not to be outdone. 'I've made up a little tune all of my own.'

Kavish looked unhappy. 'You didn't tell me. I'd have made one up too.'

'Charlie is staying to dinner,' Sahil murmured. 'Let's eat. Mum has made biryani tonight. I don't want it getting cold. You can play us your tune afterwards, Josh.'

Joshit looked crestfallen.

Nila picked up on her youngest's disappointment. 'Oh, the biryani can wait. Let's hear the tune first, shall we?'

Charlie's stomach rumbled but said, 'Yes, let's hear this tune, Joshit. What's it called?'

'It's my own composition,' Joshit said with a smile. 'We were doing this project at school in history and it gave me an idea, so I wrote the tune to some words of a rhyme. It's called "Treasure".'

'It sounds great. Go on, Josh,' Sahil said.

'Charlie has to introduce me first,' Joshit insisted.

Charlie noticed that Kavish was looking a bit left out, so he said, 'Kavish – why don't you be the emcee?'

'What's an emcee?' Kavish asked.

'Master of ceremonies. You have to give a really massive introduction – big it up,' Charlie explained.

Kavish stood up straight and gave an elaborate bow. Then he raised his voice. 'So, ladies and gentlemen, I am Kav the King MC and it's my pleasure to introduce my little brother, Josh, who's playing his latest hit on the alto sax. Let's hear everybody give it up for "Treasure"!'

Joshit's face was serious and serene as he blew a long note. He began to play a sad tune. His fingers moved deftly and he blew steadily, his breathing controlled – he had clearly practised hard, bringing his simple composition to a sweet, melodic end.

The audience members clapped loudly.

Sahil said, 'That was tremendous, Josh. And well introduced, Kav.'

Joshit's face shone with pride.

Nila was tearful. 'That was very moving. Well done.'

'Why is the tune called "Treasure"?' Charlie asked.

'I know, I know,' Kavish said, wide-eyed. 'It's to do with The Cell. We all study it in year seven. We have to say the rhyme.'

'What rhyme?' Charlie asked.

Kavish was still in performance mode. He recited:

> *'Near the cell, there is a well*
> *Near the well, there is a tree*
> *And under the tree the treasure be.'*

'Whatever does that mean?' Sahil asked.

'It's about The Wicked Lady,' Joshit explained slowly.

'Wicked lady?' Nila was momentarily perplexed. 'Oh, you mean the highway woman from The Cell who lived hundreds of years ago. Of course.'

'Katherine Ferrers...' Charlie muttered. 'I've heard the rhyme before. It's to do with the sycamore tree.'

'My teacher says it's a well-known Hertfordshire rhyme, so I used the beat of the words to write the tune,' Joshit explained.

'Why is there treasure there?' Charlie asked. 'Did your teacher say, Joshit?'

'It's only a myth. She didn't really exist,' Kavish said quickly. 'She was just a saddo rich woman whose husband took all her money and then she died of loneliness.'

'No, she didn't,' Joshit argued. 'She was a beautiful lady who was brave and rode her horse along the common and stole from rich people. She hid all her money and jewels beneath the sycamore tree in The Cell so no one would take them. But the tree has gone now. And so has the treasure.'

'How do you know that?' Charlie asked.

Joshit shrugged. 'I learned it in history at school.' He turned to his mother. 'I'm hungry – can we eat now?'

Kavish had lost interest. 'Yes, can we have food, Mum? I bet Charlie's hungry too.'

'I am,' Charlie admitted, but he was still thinking about the sycamore tree and the treasure buried underneath. Shane, the waiter at the pub, had said something similar about a sycamore tree. Charlie was keener than ever to find out what had become of Katherine Ferrers.

* * *

That night, Charlie's dreams were vivid. It was snowing – images and emotions of a Christmas evening swirled in his mind, the warmth of twinkling fairy lights, shop windows, the cold of twizzling snowfall against an indigo sky, the treetops covered with light icing. He was walking along Ferrers Lane, holding a woman's hand. He wasn't sure who she was, but she was wearing an amethyst bracelet and her eyes were hazel. He felt happy, a feeling of belonging, of wanting to hold her in his arms. Then he heard the sound of hoofbeats. Suddenly, he was on horseback, a black stallion, and the woman was at his side. Her hair was golden copper in the moonlight, a dusting of snow on her three-cornered hat; she was wearing men's clothes and had a pistol in her hand. A coach was approaching, rattling along the lane, pulled by four horses. The woman leaned forward and her cold fingers were icicles against his cheek. 'This will be our last time, my love,' she whispered against his ear.

Charlie didn't understand, but he was immediately anxious. 'Last time?'

'Our last robbery. Then you and I will be together for ever. Nothing can separate us now.'

Charlie wasn't sure what to do in the dream. He watched as the woman spurred her horse forward. He saw her disappear into the snow, her hair billowing behind her, dark now, no longer copper. He was suddenly too terrified to follow. He called out her name, 'Kate,' then his horse reared and he was falling.

She must have somehow caught him in her arms. She was kissing him, her body pressing against his as she clambered across him.

Charlie opened his eyes and called out in amazement. Alan was sitting on his chest, licking his face with a rough tongue. Charlie gently pushed him away. 'Your breath's terrible, Al.'

He sat up, blinking as the dog stared back quizzically from the end of the bed, his head on one side. Moonlight streamed through the window. Charlie glanced at his phone – it was past three in the morning.

He held out a hand. 'Sorry, Alan – what I said about your breath. I was dreaming...'

Alan was back over to him in a bounce, waiting to be patted.

Charlie hugged the dog. 'I had this strange dream – all about Christmas and snow and a highway woman...' he confided in Alan. 'What's going on in my head?'

Alan gave a soft snuffling sound as if he understood.

Charlie reached for his saxophone, an arm's length away on the stand, and brought it to his lips, blowing a hollow note. Alan was still staring at him.

'You get it, though, don't you, Al?' Charlie almost smiled. 'Last summer, I didn't know what to do with my life. I never thought I'd be spending this Christmas in a house I own with Uncle Bill, doing it up, and...' He frowned. 'So, Edie and Bianca are coming over for Christmas dinner. I've told her I'll cook, the whole works. Do you reckon our kitchen will be ready in time? Can we make something spectacular, you and me? All the trimmings and a pudding?'

Alan gave him a blank look that Charlie interpreted in the dim light to mean that he was probably out of his depth.

'Am I a complete numpty?' Charlie asked, laughing.

Alan barked once, in agreement.

Charlie frowned. 'Do you reckon she likes me? Edie? What if I ruin a good friendship. I like her... a lot.' Charlie sighed. 'Perhaps I need a meaningless fling, a one-night stand. Paige likes me... maybe I could...'

Alan gave a single woof.

'You're right. I'm not a one-night-stand sort of guy. I'm a commitment sort of guy. But that gets me into a mess, doesn't it?' Charlie sighed and blew another note on his saxophone. 'I can't sleep now for all the stuff that's whizzing round my head. What about we write some words to that tune I made up. "Kate's Tune"?'

Charlie blew three notes of the sorrowful opening tune. He was thoughtful.

'What rhymes with Kate? Gate? Estate? Separate?' He shook his head. 'Maybe I can try a different angle. Why doesn't everyone see her ghost? She appears to me. Is it because I understand that she's hurt and lonely? Is it because I get it? What about – "Your ghost... almost... visible on the exposed... Nomansland... I hadn't planned... to be your friend..."'

Charlie began to play the tune from the beginning, closing his eyes as he concentrated on the emotion of each note, making it as beautiful a tribute to the highway woman as he could, just as Joshit had done earlier. As he played, more words came into his head... *Friend... the end. What became of you? Treasure beneath the sycamore tree – how can you ever be free?*

He recalled her words, '*Our last time, my love,*' as she set off towards the approaching coach.

As the snow fell... she left The Cell and said farewell...

His tune became more sorrowful, and as the music drifted, more lyrics came into his head. He thought his heart might break and his face was wet with tears. This was Kate's tune, and what had happened to her must have been, like the grief in his song, impossible to bear. What was worse, he didn't know what awful end befell her.

* * *

Outside the window, among the trees below, the streaming moonlight picked out the shape of a horse and rider in the darkness. The woman was dressed in men's clothes, her hair tied back, a pistol in her belt. Her dark horse was tense, waiting for instruction, but the highway woman was statue still, listening. As the melancholy notes drifted from number one Constable's Cottages, the woman's face glistened silver, as if covered with tears.

33

1659

'Mistress, I am worried about you...'

'I am feeling a little better, Bea,' Kate said as she sat in the warm, scented bath. 'My head is beginning to clear.' Kate took a breath. 'Thank you for bringing me water to drink. The ordeal with the constable has shaken me more than I realised. He hurled me onto the floor and squeezed my flesh most roughly. My body still aches, my skin is tender from it...' She covered her chest with a stray hand. 'I am not myself. It has made me tearful and melancholy... I did not mean to kill the man. I am still shaking and filled with sorrow.'

'You are indeed not yourself, mistress.' Beatrice was staring at Kate as she lay in the bath. 'May I know? You and Master Chaplin have been together since the summer months...'

'We have.' Kate looked at Beatrice quizzically. 'But why do you ask?'

'Pardon my speech, mistress, but have you lain together?'

'Indeed, Bea...' Kate smiled, closing her eyes for a moment. 'We love each other...'

'John and I have no children, mistress – but twice I have been as you are now, and twice I have lost the treasure that I was carrying. I know the signs well.'

'What do you speak of?' Kate was puzzled.

'Forgive me if I speak plainly. I believe you are with child.'

'How can it be so? I mean...' Kate stared at her maid, as if her words were incomprehensible. Then she smiled. 'I had not thought it would take such a little time. Oh, what if you are right? I would be so happy...'

'You can be a highway robber no more,' Beatrice said, her hands on her hips. 'It would be unwise to ride your horse, to venture out and take a chance, not now.'

'But I am hardly changed. You may say that again when I grow too large to pass as a boy.' Kate laughed, her eyes shining with tears. 'Oh, what wonderful news. We will have a child. I cannot wait to tell him. It is what we wished for.'

Beatrice's hands flew to her mouth. 'But you carry a child and Thomas Fanshawe is still your husband.'

'He is...' Kate frowned. 'But he does not love me. And he is in prison. By the time he is free, I will be far away, with the man I love and our baby. That's why I need to continue my twilight activities, Bea. It will not be for much longer. One more ride, and we can leave with our child and live happily.'

'I fear for you,' Beatrice muttered. 'The constable is dead... and others will come after him now. They will look for the robber who killed him.'

'I am not afraid. I know how to be careful,' Kate said. 'Hand me a linen towel please, Bea. I need to dry myself, then I must eat and then lie down.' She stood slowly. 'Oh, do you really think I am with child? I can hardly wait to share it with him...'

Kate stepped carefully from the bath, enjoying the warmth of the linen sheet Beatrice wrapped around her. She did not notice the anxiety etched on her maid's face. She was already dreaming of being with Raife, a newly swaddled child in her arms, watching the pride that shone in his eyes.

* * *

Late that afternoon, Kate rode to Ayers End Farm, where she made a simple supper of bread, cheese and some cake Beatrice had given her. She and Raife sat in front of the blazing fire, staring into the flames, dreaming of the future, Raife placed a large hand over her belly.

'Our child. It is hard to believe, Kate, that he or she grows there. Imagine what may be. A fine young man. A strong woman, just like her mother.' Raife's voice cracked with emotion.

'And there will be many more children.' Kate's eyes shone with happiness. 'We will be far from here. We will have our own home, a farm with animals, we will grow vegetables and grain. And our children will never want for anything.'

Raife frowned. 'I have never travelled far from here. Where would we go?'

'I hear that my friend, Master Pepys from London, is travelling to the Baltic Sea to deliver letters from the government. I believe he is a Republican still.' Kate almost laughed. 'But it is cold there. Perhaps we would be wise to go south, where it is warmer.'

'South?' Raife asked.

'Italy, perhaps. I have read poetry by Italians – Dante, Petrarch – and I once saw a painting by Lodovico Carracci. He was the son of a butcher, but his paintings were so beautiful...' Kate closed her eyes. 'They say it is warm in Italy, a place of beautiful lakes and mountains. We might go there.'

'But how will we speak to people?' Raife was ever practical. 'And I have heard say that even in our own country, in the far north and the distant south, it can be difficult to understand the speech of the people who live there. Perhaps we should not stray far.'

'We will have money. We can go where we wish,' Kate said determinedly.

Raife looked anxious. 'When they find the body of Lambert Wilmott, the constables will be looking for the killer...'

'I am sorry for it,' Kate said.

'But he would have harmed you.' Raife's brow clouded. 'I would have done the same.'

Kate pushed the constable from her mind – thoughts of him filled her with regret and unease. 'I want to be with you, as your wife, and that means being far from Thomas when he comes out of prison.' She put her hand over his, on the place where the baby was growing, and her expression was suddenly fierce. 'Thomas will find out about the baby, as soon as I begin to grow big. Once my cousin Anne knows, she will tell her husband

Richard, and he in turn will pass word to Thomas – they are both for the king and thick as thieves.'

'We will be far from here by then.' Raife brought her hand to his lips. 'I have been working out how much we have in our coffer. Two more robberies, perhaps three, and we will have enough. We can give some to your loyal servants, some to the local families, and you and I will be able to leave here.'

Kate was thoughtful. 'Bea thinks the baby may come in the late spring or the early summer. It may be possible for me to lie in at The Cell. Bea will help me with the birth. Perhaps Thomas will still be in prison when my time comes.'

'Do you think it?'

'I do...' Kate said. 'Since Cromwell died, his son Richard has been Lord Protector. Some say he is weak and a poor leader. But King Charles has fled to France. Who knows if he will come back and take the throne? Thomas believes that he will, but as long as the king is in exile and Thomas in prison, we are safe together here.'

Raife wrapped a protective arm around her. 'So... we will have a child together. Do you remember when Beleza brought Vulcan into the world when I first met you? We were blessed on that day.'

'We were.' Kate snuggled closer. 'There will be three of us. Our own baby. What shall we call it?'

'You choose...' Raife's hand smoothed her hair. 'What names do you like?'

'My father was called Knighton. If it is a boy, I would like that to be his name. Raife Knighton Chetwyn.'

'And if we have a girl child?'

Kate hesitated. 'Your wife's name was Mary. Perhaps we should remember her in the naming of our child...'

'Poor Mary.' Raife stared into the firelight and Kate knew he was worrying about the birth, if Kate would meet the same end as his wife had. He had lost her and the child in an instant.

'I am strong, all will be well,' she promised. 'And we will name the child Marie if it is a girl, in her memory.'

'It is a good thought. And I pray that all will be well.' Raife touched her cheek. 'Are you afraid of the birth?'

'Not I.' Kate's face glowed in the bronze flames. 'You and I are unconquerable.'

'Do you believe it?'

'I do,' Kate said. 'We were meant to be together. Our future will be one of happiness and joy.'

'Amen to that,' Raife said as he raised his cup.

At that moment, there was a banging at the door, so loud that Kate felt her heart leap. 'Who can that be?' she asked, her eyes wide.

'It is late. No one visits at this hour...' Raife said.

'Perhaps it is to do with Lambert Wilmott... they have found his body.'

'Do you think it can be the constable?' Raife whispered, 'You must not be discovered here. Quickly – go upstairs. I will answer it.' He tugged on a hat and a scarf against the wind.

The knocking came again, a loud voice. 'Open up...'

'Go.' Raife kissed her lips briefly. 'Hide in the rooftop if you must. I will come to you when they have gone.'

Kate felt her heart jump. She hesitated. 'But what if—'

'Go,' Raife whispered, and Kate's feet were moving towards the stairs, hesitating at the top, listening.

She heard the door open, and muffled voices. 'Can I come in, farmer?'

'What do you want at this hour? I was about to take to my bed.'

'This is Edward Gale, my new constable, and I am Master Henry Glanville – do you know of me?'

'I know you not, sir...'

Kate heard the pretence of humility in Raife's voice. She held her breath.

'I am the Justice of the Peace, and I am here to tell everyone who lives on Nomansland that my constable has been appointed since the death of Lambert Wilmott.'

'Oh?' Raife sounded surprised. 'I am sorry to hear that Constable Wilmott was unwell.'

'He was not unwell. He was murdered.'

Kate closed her eyes and felt suddenly dizzy. The memories flooded back, the shot from the flintlock, the stench of gunpowder. She took a deep breath. She could not faint now. Steadily, she sank to her knees, listening harder.

'Murdered? How did that come to pass?'

'We believe Lambert was murdered in the execution of his duties, farmer. It is likely that he apprehended one of the two scurrilous highwaymen, and he was shot through the heart for his pains.'

'I am sorry to hear it.' Raife's voice drifted up to Kate as she sat, clutching her knees, shivering. 'I am sure you will find his murderer in time.'

'This is why we are calling at all houses.' Glanville's tone was suddenly hostile. 'We believe Chaplin must be known to local people – someone is hiding him. And his boy is very easily recognisable, slim, his appearance fair. Do you know of these people?'

'I do not,' Raife said, and Kate was amazed at the strength of his reply: she would have believed him instantly. 'I do know there have been itinerants, merchants and traders around Markyate over the past two months. Perhaps the robbers are known to them?'

'I know nothing of traders.' The voice was not Glanville's. It was deeper, rougher. Kate decided it must be the new constable, Edward Gale. She put a hand to her head. She felt unsteady and weak. She took another deep breath.

'You live here alone, farmer?' Glanville asked, suddenly.

'I do.'

'This farm is not your own?'

'I am a tenant. I rent it from Master Thomas Fanshawe.'

'He's in prison.' It was Gale speaking again. 'A Royalist. Locked up in the Tower.'

'Long may he stay there,' Glanville agreed.

There was a pause, then Raife said, 'If I hear anything, Master Gale, Master Glanville, I will be sure to let you know.'

'I have brought many constables from London. I intend to make my presence felt in my new job. Lambert Wilmott was feeble, an incompetent. But he is dead now and best forgotten. I am living in his cottage.' Gale's voice sounded threatening. 'My team of men will be keeping a careful watch on the common.'

'That is good to know,' Raife replied and Kate took a breath again. 'I will bid you a good night, gentlemen.'

'And to you, farmer,' Glanville said.

'Keep a watchful eye. No one is safe from these vagabonds,' Gale added.

Kate heard the door close. She waited a moment, listening for horses' hooves riding away.

Shakily, she hurried down the stairs and fell into Raife's arms.

'There is a new constable...' He spoke into her hair. 'We need to be careful, my love.'

'We do,' Kate agreed. 'Did he see your face?'

'No, I wore a hat, a scarf. And I kept my voice low. If he ever sees Ralph Chaplin, he will not connect him to me. But we ought to ride out no more, Kate.'

'We will plunder just twice more, for the sake of our child and for our future.'

'I like it not. You are with child... we will take no risks.'

'Then let us do it now. We will take them by surprise.'

'But if we wait...'

'We cannot wait. This new constable means business. He will be watchful. So, let's ride now, before he knows the lie of the land – then we will wait for the baby, and ride once more. Twice, then it is done.'

Raife's arms held her tightly. 'We must take no chances, Kate. You are precious to me as my own life, more so.'

'As you to me,' Kate replied, then she felt herself lifted into the safety of his arms as he carried her towards the stairs and up to the comfort and warmth of their straw mattress. There, they were away from the vigilant eyes and wagging tongues of the rest of the world. They were safe.

34

THE PRESENT

It was eight o'clock in the morning on a bleak Christmas Day, the sun low in the sky. But it was warm indoors as Charlie stood in the kitchen, marvelling at the new pale worktops, the pristine stainless-steel sink and the gleaming cream tiles. The white Shaker-style cupboards were newly installed, as was the smart cooker with the double oven. He and Bill had finished the job late last night on Christmas Eve, and Bill had gone home to celebrate with a glass of mulled wine and a single mince pie, courtesy of Marcia's vigilant regime. Charlie had helped himself to a cold beer from the newly stocked fridge and fallen into bed, Alan curled at his heels.

'We've got a big job ahead of us today, mate,' Charlie said to the Labrador, stretching his arms over his head, as he surveyed the bags of Brussels sprouts, potatoes, carrots, the packet of chestnuts, the ready-made puff pastry. 'Do you reckon we can do it, Al? Chestnut wellington, gravy, roasties, veg? By two, that's when Edie's coming round?'

Alan gave a smart woof. At least his dog was confident.

Charlie laughed. 'You don't have to peel all those spuds though, and I cheated a bit on the pud – I bought a vegan espresso martini chocolate mousse from the supermarket. I could pretend I made it myself, just to impress her.'

Alan eyed him steadily.

'You're right. I don't need to impress Edie. Or anyone. I'm just me. Hang on – let me put on the playlist I made...' Charlie's fingers hovered over his phone and 'Last Christmas' by Wham! burst through the speaker. Charlie selected the next song quickly – 'Fairy Tale of New York'. He didn't want to be reminded of last Christmas, of the wonderful time spent at his old flat in Peckham, just him and Luna. It had been special. But it was in the past.

He pushed his shoulders back and took a deep breath. He was ready.

'Apparently Christmas dinner is all about the timing. I think a small drink, just to get the party started. Only one, mind...' Charlie poured a small sherry into a teacup. He had no idea why. He didn't really like the stuff, but his mother always drank gallons of it at Christmas.

He picked up his phone, just to check; there were a couple of messages. Uncle Bill had sent a picture of himself and Auntie Marcia grinning, holding up a glass of champagne. They'd had it with salmon for breakfast – they were going out for Christmas lunch with friends. Sonny had sent a selfie from Spain. He was sitting by a swimming pool with a beer and a plate of kedgeree, his hair over his eyes, grinning. Charlie wondered why his mother wasn't in the picture. There had been no word from her at all.

He sat at the small wooden table, filled a bowl with potatoes, picked up a knife and started to peel the skin off. Alan settled himself at Charlie's feet, making whining noises. He wanted to go out for a walk. Charlie glanced towards the kitchen window. It was drizzling now.

* * *

An hour later, he was outside in a scarf, coat and wellingtons with Alan, squelching through the muddy woodlands on his way towards the common. The weak winter sun had emerged from the clouds, pale light on the horizon. Charlie released Alan from his lead and the Labrador bounded ahead, full of energy. Charlie wandered after him, humming to himself. It was 'Kate's Tune'. *She is there as light fades in the trees. She is a secret whispered in the breeze.* He wasn't sure about it yet. He had more work to do.

He emerged from the dripping branches of the woodland onto the common, walking uphill. There was no one around. He'd expected to see a few dog walkers, but the rain had probably kept them away. Charlie looked up at the sky. It was a strange colour, half-light, half-shadow, an ominous lead-grey shot through with bright silver, low-hanging clouds that looked like wet cotton wool. He wondered how long it would be before it rained again.

It felt eerie, when he thought about it, to be walking on the common where Katherine Ferrers had been riding her horse less than four hundred years ago. He had a clear picture of her in his imagination, loosely based on the only portrait that remained of her – dark hair, rosebud lips, widely spaced eyes. But she had been a teenager then. What was she like at twenty-five? She must have been self-assured, strong, wilful. It would take a powerful woman to dare to rob a coach. He thought again about the myth, the alternate stories. Did she die a highway woman or a rejected wife? He'd talk to Edie about it over dinner.

The thought of dinner jolted him. He ought to get back, put the oven on, throw the potatoes in with some rosemary and a splash of oil. He hoped he wouldn't make a mess of it. He'd roll out pastry, add the mixture; he'd found a recipe online, but he'd never made chestnut wellington and mushroom gravy before.

He called Alan and the Labrador trotted obediently towards him and stood still, patient. His fur was soaking. Charlie ruffled it. 'We'd better get back, Al, and warm up. We've got a dinner to make. Oh...' He remembered. 'There are no decorations. Do you think we should have got a tree? Or some twinkling lights? Mistletoe?' He gave a single laugh. 'Bad idea, I know – I don't want to look desperate.'

They headed back to number one Constable's Cottages and found Edie waiting outside, Bianca at her heels. She was wearing a short dress beneath her coat and tinsel in her hair. She carried a large paper bag which looked as if it contained gifts tied with ribbon. Charlie frowned, thinking of the single present he had bought for her, wrapped badly, lying next to his saxophone by his bed. He'd get it later – he hoped she'd like it. 'You aren't due until two and it's not twelve yet...'

'I was bored,' she said with a grin. 'I wanted to help you cook. It's more fun to do it together. Unless I'd be in the way? In which case, I could just sit down and chat while you worked.'

'Oh, I'd be glad of the help. How do you make Brussels taste nice?' Charlie asked as he opened the front door. 'I'm worried they'll come out like bullets...'

'I roast them with garlic,' Edie said. 'I'm having dinner with my mum tomorrow. She cooks them in vodka, would you believe. Mind you, my mother covers everything in alcohol when she cooks.'

'Mine would be the same, if she cooked, which she doesn't,' Charlie said brightly, closing the door behind him. 'Right – you can give me a hand with the chestnut roast. Do I just mash the chestnuts and stick them in pastry?'

'Pretty much – although they are nicer roasted with celery, garlic, herbs and other nuts...'

'Oh – I don't know if I've got all the ingredients.' Charlie hesitated and Edie held up her bag.

'I brought some extras. And I got you a present... I hope you like it.'

* * *

At five to two, the food was almost ready. Charlie stood in the kitchen wearing the black cable-knit sweater Edie had bought him. He was delighted with it, and she thought it fitted him perfectly. He had bought her a necklace of amethyst beads to match her bracelet. She'd exclaimed with delight when she'd opened it and insisted he fasten the clasp for her.

Alan and Bianca were crunching on some festive doggie treats Edie had made from Greek yogurt, strawberries and blueberries, freezing them in bone-shaped moulds. Edie lit the candles she had brought as Charlie removed the roasted potatoes from the oven, placing them in a dish next to the carrots, parsnips and Brussels sprouts, and the flaky chestnut wellington with its unevenly crimped edges. He moved back to the cooker, which had been spotless but was now splashed with spilled food which had burned on. He lifted the pan of gravy and aimed the contents at a jug. 'This smells great.'

Edie was pleased; she'd helped Charlie a little, but not taken over. 'There's too much for two here,' she said. 'But we can let Bianca and Alan have some leftovers later. They'll love it. Oh – the wine...' Edie said suddenly. 'I left the elderberry burgundy at home.'

'I have some champagne in the fridge.' Charlie was on his feet. 'Is that all right?'

'It's perfect.' Edie helped herself to crispy golden potatoes. 'Is this the first time you've made Christmas dinner, Charlie?'

He recalled last year: Luna had made turkey with all the trimmings and he'd stirred the gravy, wearing a silly Christmas hat and jumper. 'Yes...' Charlie brought the champagne to the table, popping the cork skilfully, watching the liquid splash in their glasses. He held his drink aloft. 'What shall we toast?'

'To a great Christmas,' Edie said, her glass raised, her eyes shining.

'And to the good life at Constable's Cottages,' Charlie added.

'To a brilliant new year ahead for us both,' Edie suggested.

'And to... to Katherine, our ghost.' Charlie paused. A shiver shuddered down his spine. He sat down.

'I've been researching more about her...' Edie said. 'She had a relative, Anne Fanshawe, who wrote cookery books. And she invented ice cream – what a claim to fame. She had fourteen children, but only four daughters and a son survived into adulthood.'

'That's awful, poor woman,' Charlie said, chewing.

'You know Katherine probably had a child.' Edie passed Charlie a dish piled with vegetables.

'I read that she had a baby in one of the stories. But not in the other. Not in the one where she's a highway robber. There's no mention of a baby in that.' Charlie frowned. 'That's the problem. The two stories are so different. Either she was a highway robber or she was a lonely wife whose husband took her money. But which is true?'

'I'm going to research the baby next, in case it sheds any light on Katherine's life. This is delicious, by the way.' Edie held her fork in the air.

'Thanks.' Charlie munched for a while. 'The question is, whose baby was it? Her husband was in prison.'

'Exactly. The child was born in June 1660. Thomas Fanshawe went to prison in 1659 and he was not released until 1660. The baby couldn't have been his.'

'So was it Ralph Chaplin's? The highwayman that we can't find any information about?' Charlie was puzzled. 'And what happened to the baby?'

'We can research that,' Edie said hopefully. She had eaten very little so far. 'Charlie... you don't think we'll see the ghost again, do you?'

'It's been a while since we saw her,' Charlie said. 'My theory is, she senses that we'd understand what happened to her. That's why she shows herself to us. She's trying to tell us that she's sad. Or maybe she's asking for help.'

'I'd love to know the truth,' Edie breathed. 'Her story is such a mystery. Yet I'm convinced something awful must have happened. Why is there no record of Chaplin? And what really happened to Katherine? Why is she... not able to rest?'

'Well, perhaps she'll stay away just for Christmas,' Charlie said with a grin. 'Although I bet she'd love this chestnut wellington. And the sprouts are amazing.'

'We have plenty left over if she visits,' Edie joked.

'She'd be welcome to join us...' Charlie laughed.

There was a sharp knock at the door.

Edie froze. Charlie met her eyes. 'Who's that?' he muttered.

'It's not Marilyn – she and her sister went out for Christmas dinner. She told me...' Edie looked worried. 'Could it be your Uncle Bill?'

Charlie shook his head. 'He and Auntie Marcia are having lunch with friends...'

The knock came again, this time louder and more persistent. Alan and Bianca lifted their heads, pricking up their ears. Bianca woofed loudly.

Charlie stood up, hesitating. 'I'll go...'

Edie looked as if she was about to tell him not to. She nodded. 'OK.'

Charlie shuffled towards the door and eased it open tentatively. Then he caught his breath. A tall blonde woman stood in the doorway in a pink faux-fur coat and matching hat, clutching a bag of presents. She placed it on the ground and threw her arms open. 'Charlie.'

'Mum?'

Charlie's mother grasped him tightly. She smelled of floral perfume, great wafts of it. 'My favourite son. How could I not come and visit you at Christmas?'

Charlie was puzzled. 'I didn't know you were coming.'

'Didn't I text?' She frowned, indicating the small blue estate car parked in front of Charlie's white van. 'I hired a car yesterday for a week. This is just a flying visit. I'm off to see my friend Lucille in Brighton later on. She's on her own again, poor love. Dumped, two days before Christmas. I got your address from our Bill. Sonny's got a girlfriend in Spain – Mira – and they're having Christmas with her parents. I didn't want to be a gooseberry, did I? Besides, I had to come and look at your new place, give it the once-over. Oh...' She inhaled deeply. 'I can smell roast potatoes. Are you having Christmas dinner? Is there any spare? I'm starving...'

Charlie's mum pushed past him and followed the smell of cooking to the kitchen. She paused when she saw Edie sitting at the table, and her frown became a smile. 'Hello. Charlie didn't tell me he'd got a new squeeze. Pleased to meet you. I didn't like Luna much, to be honest. She could be a bit stand-offish. But I'm pleased to meet you... I'm Jayne Wolfe, Charlie's mum. I can't stay long – I've got a friend to cheer up. I'll have to be off by half four. Have you got another plate? I can help myself to food... I hope you've got plenty of pudding, Charlie. Breakfast was ages ago. And I hope you haven't guzzled all of that champagne... I could murder a small glass.'

35

1659

It was the day after Christmas. Kate and Raife sat high on their horses, waiting silently in the trees. A raw, biting wind rustled the leaves, but they were listening only for the sound of approaching hooves. The afternoon was cold; the sun had already started to fade. Raife glanced towards Kate and she knew that he was looking at her clothes, at the heavy cape that kept her warm, the hat almost covered her eyes, and how the waist of her breeches fitted her snugly now. She no longer looked like a slim boy.

'I wish you had not come,' he said softly. 'I wanted you to stay at the farm where you would be safe.'

'My place is by your side,' Kate replied. 'I can still ride as fast as you. I have promised this will be my last robbery before our baby comes.'

'And afterwards, you must not think of doing it again. I will go alone, for one last time,' Raife said.

'Perhaps,' Kate muttered, then she leaned forward. 'Listen. I can hear the London coach. It is not far away.'

Midnight made a muffled snort and Lightning replied with the same sound.

Raife reached for Kate's hand. 'Please – allow me to speak to the passengers. Let me do the work. Stay in the background where you will be safer.'

'If you wish it,' Kate said. She raised an eyebrow. 'I will follow your lead, Master Chaplin.' She couldn't deny the surge of excitement, the blood pumping faster through her veins. Then she saw the coach come into sight.

It rattled along the road. Beyond, Kate could see the constable's cottage, where Edward Gale now lived. She knew he would be on the lookout. But they had been quiet for a while. She hoped he'd think they'd moved on.

Raife shouted to the horse and Lightning galloped forward. Kate was just behind him, Midnight leaping across the common surefootedly. The coach slowed down and Raife gave the familiar order. 'Stand. Deliver your purse.'

Three gentlemen and a lady emerged. The oldest man held out a large velvet purse and Raife whisked it into his coat. He repeated the action for the other two men, bowing his head towards the woman. 'Your fine jewellery, if you please...'

One of the men spoke up, a quiver in his voice. 'Are you Ralph Chaplin, the notorious highwayman, with your boy?'

'I am,' Raife said courteously. 'And I thank you kindly for your donation. And this' – he took a handful of jewellery from the woman's shaking fingers and handed it to Kate – 'will be very useful. I thank you.'

Kate pointed her pistol. Her voice was clear behind the kerchief. 'Mistress, you have not been entirely honest with us. I can see a diamond bracelet on your wrist beneath your cape, and a heavy ring on your finger. We'll take those from you. Then you can travel lighter. I hope it will bring you ease.'

The woman scowled and handed over the last two valuable pieces.

Kate nodded gallantly. 'I thank you, mistress. Now be on your journey. I wish you Godspeed.'

They watched as the passengers shuffled into the carriage.

Raife waved a pistol. 'Now get you on your way.'

The horses turned and Midnight bolted towards the safety of the trees, followed by Lightning.

Raife called, 'Let us head towards home and count our treasure.'

Kate's voice trilled on the wind. 'We are almost there, Master Chaplin. And it will soon be the new year, the one that will allow us to be together every day of our lives.'

* * *

The new year came – 1660. Kate travelled to London in a carriage to meet her cousin Anne and they dressed in their finest clothes to attend a party at a rich merchant's house in Lincoln's Inn Fields. Kate noticed that many of the men wore ribbons and lace on their long coats. She had chosen a pale dress of silk brocade and satin petticoats, with a laced bodice that fitted her snugly. The pink silk jacket edged in white fur was intended to disguise her thicker waistline. Anne wore a long-waisted robe with an off-the-shoulder neckline and short, full, cartridge-pleated sleeves, the bodice lacing through eyelets at the back. Her gaze lingered on Kate's dress and she murmured, 'You are looking well, cousin.'

'You mean I am getting plump.' Kate's laughter trilled. 'Bea's custards and cakes have been my constant companions. I fear Thomas will not recognise me when he comes out of prison, I will be so rounded. But it is fashionable for a woman to be well made, is it not?'

'I believe you look healthier than ever.' Anne seemed satisfied with Kate's explanation. 'But Richard seems to think that Thomas may not be in prison for many more months. There is rumour afoot that King Charles will be asked to return to the throne by the summer.'

'By summer?' Kate tried her best to disguise her alarm. She forced a smile. 'Oh, that is good news. When, pray, will this happen exactly? May, June, later? I hope poor Thomas will not languish in the Tower for too long...'

'I have no idea. I seldom listen to talk of politics. I just behave as a good wife should and follow my husband wherever he follows the king. I recall when he was in prison years ago, very like Thomas, he left me in Oxford in delicate health, with scarcely a penny and a dying firstborn.' Anne looked around her. 'Now Richard is in Flanders with the king and he writes that they will soon return to England. I wish for it more than I can say, Kate.'

'You must long to see him,' Kate said quickly. She wondered if Anne, who had given birth to so many children, recognised that she too was with child. Of course, she would know the truth when the child was born – the news would reach her in London – but Kate and Raife would be far away by then. She was quick to change the subject. 'Oh look – there is my dear friend, Master Pepys,' Kate trilled. 'Do excuse me, cousin. I need to ask him all about the latest gossip.'

Anne smiled benignly as Kate lifted her skirts and hurried towards Samuel, who was staring at her just as Anne had.

'Mistress Fanshawe – I thought your husband was in prison. Yet you appear to have been tumbled...'

'Not I.' Kate's eyes flashed. 'I am a woman who lives alone now, and my only solace is sweetmeats and cakes.' She dipped a little curtsy. 'But tell me, Master Pepys, what is the news of the king? Is it true that he will return to England soon?'

'It is, I believe. But I remain bored at home, with just my writing for company, and of course my wife, and my servant Jane, who is always very accommodating to my whims. My wife dressed the remains of a turkey last night and in the doing of it she burned her hand. Thus, I am plagued by a complaining wife. It serves me best to dine here. And yesterday I received a dozen bottles of sack, which cost me an entire shilling for my pains. I need good cheer tonight – my mood has been somewhat melancholy. Keeping a diary is my only consolation.'

'But what of the king?' Kate encouraged him. 'Will he return soon?'

'You ask me because of your husband who remains languishing in the Tower? Ah, Kate, I fear I shall become a Royalist again very soon.' Samuel drank the last of the wine in his cup. 'The young Cromwell is not like his father. He is weak and useless. There is talk that later this year I shall be sent with a party to bring the king back to England. He is living in exile in Holland, but he is needed here...'

'So, what of Thomas?' Kate asked as eagerly as she could.

'If I were you, I'd expect him to be released in the summer months. He may be back to Markyate by June or July. And do you know, I believe the first thing he will do will be to sell the place. As I always say, Thomas Fanshawe is a witty but rascally fellow, without a penny in his purse. I recall talking to him a few years ago, when he was asking what lofty positions there might be in the Navy for him. He is always on the lookout for a favour or a position and, indeed, I believe our new king will give him one. I don't suppose prison has changed him for the better.'

Kate was not listening. She gave a sigh of relief. If Thomas came home in June, the baby would be born and she and Raife would be far away. There was one robbery more to stage, then they would be rich enough. Her mind flashed to the jewellery in her velvet purse. 'Samuel – there is one more thing I must ask of you.'

'Name it, Kate,' Samuel said, pinching the flesh of her cheek. 'I am your humble servant.'

'You once arranged for me to meet Master Garvey, who lives in Bread Street Hill. I would very much like to meet him again. Is he still there?'

'He is. Do you have more family heirlooms to sell?' Pepys asked under his breath.

'I do – jewellery that belonged to my mother. In anticipation of Thomas's swift return, I believe I must get the best price I can.'

'Leave it with me to set up a meeting,' Pepys murmured. 'Master Garvey often asks of you. The last time you visited him, he was most pleased to purchase the pearls you offered him.'

'Then I will have to put up my prices.' Kate raised an eyebrow. 'These are hard times for all of us, Master Pepys.'

* * *

It was four and a half hours until the new year. Charlie was excited, as he sat with Alan in the kitchen, feeding the dog kibble in a bowl.

'I'm going out, Al. Edie's working in the pub all night, but she said to bring the sax. There will be live music at The Sycamore Tree. I can't wait to play with some musicians...' He ruffled the dog's head. 'Will you be OK here, mate? I'll be back just after midnight. I won't hang around for all the "Auld Lang Syne" stuff. We'll go for a long walk tomorrow morning. Imagine – a new year. I reckon by May we'll be done, and we can sell the place. Then I suppose we'll start on another project...' He pulled a face. 'I'll be moving on goodness knows where...'

Charlie decided he wouldn't think too much about the future. The brand-new year could take care of itself. Tonight, he simply wanted to play some jazz in the pub. He scurried upstairs and changed quickly into a clean T-shirt and jeans and the jumper Edie had bought him for Christmas. He glanced in the mirror. He looked every bit the jazz musician about town. He shrugged on a jacket and scarf, leaving Alan one more treat and some music to listen to on the smart speaker, then stepped outside into the cold winter air. He turned left, hurrying down Ferrers Lane, one hand in his pockets, the other clutching his saxophone case. His breath was mist on the air. He increased his pace, looking around him. The branches whispered in the woodlands, as if a voice was calling his name.

'Charlie…'

It was his imagination, surely. He saw the colourful lights in the distance, The Sycamore Tree, all ready for a New Year's party, and he felt his spirits lift. This year was going to be a good one. He was sure of it.

36

The Sycamore Tree bar was crammed full of people, music bouncing from the restaurant where all the chairs had been cleared and a stage set up. A DJ was currently playing pop songs and dozens of people were dancing. Charlie walked up to a tiny space at the bar where Edie was busy serving customers alongside Shane and Jerry.

Edie gave a welcoming grin and handed him a pint of Neck Oil. 'Have you brought your sax?' she asked, and Charlie nodded, about to answer as another customer grabbed her attention with an order of drinks.

He felt an arm around his waist and a voice murmured, 'It's heaving in here – come and dance.'

Charlie twisted round to see Paige wearing a velvet dress covered in sequins, satin and feathers. He muttered, 'You look glamorous.'

'Thanks, Charlie.' Paige was thrilled. 'I want to look stunning – I'm singing later.'

'Oh?' Charlie was interested. 'Karaoke?'

'On your bike.' Paige laughed. 'Tom Barker's here tonight, with his guitar. I offered to join him for a few songs.'

'I don't know him.'

'I'll introduce you then,' Paige said excitedly. 'He's a maths teacher at the school in Markyate, but he's a folk singer too.'

'Folk? Does he do jazz?' Charlie lifted his sax. 'I'm looking for a chance to play.'

'Come and say hello. He's with Danny White, who plays double bass. They'll be in the corner – Tom hates dancing. They'll love it that you brought the sax.' Paige grabbed his hand and dragged him to a table in the corner where two men and a woman were drinking pints of beer. Paige wrapped an arm around Charlie. 'Guys, this is Charlie, who I told you about. He's a brilliant sax player. And...' Paige reached for a glass of wine that was going spare. 'This is Tom, and Danny, and Livvy.'

'I play piano.' Livvy shook her smooth dark hair. 'I'm classically trained, but they've got me on keyboards tonight.' She leaned towards Danny. 'The things I do for love...'

'I'm Tom.' Tom was fair-haired, bearded. He extended a hand. 'Pleased to meet you.'

'Danny. Likewise.' Danny reached for his pint. He was shorter, thicker set. 'Are you going to join us tonight?'

'If you want me to,' Charlie said with a grin. 'What sort of stuff do you do? Folk, I know, but...'

'I'll play anything. Take a seat,' Tom said and Paige sat next to Charlie, moving closer. 'I was just going to do "Meet on the Ledge" with Paige singing... but everyone else offered to join us on stage as a one-off. It's going to be great. Of course, it's just for fun. Jerry asked if we'd all be up for it. Do you know "Meet on the Ledge"?'

'Yes – I can put some sax in that easily,' Charlie offered.

'Won't you need to rehearse?' Danny asked.

'I can improvise,' Charlie said eagerly.

'Then let's do "Baker Street" and what about some stuff by The Gypsy Queens? Do you know their music?'

'I love them,' Charlie enthused.

'Then can we do "L'Americano" and "Aicha" and "Volare"...'

'Yes, to all of those,' Charlie said, as if it was simple.

'And "Scarborough Fair"? You promised we could duet on that,' Paige said.

'I wrote a playlist and we were just going to go through it. It'd be great if you could join us – if you feel confident,' Tom said, opening a document on his phone.

'Are you sure you don't need to practise?' Danny looked dubious.

'Charlie's professional.' Paige pushed an arm through his. 'He writes his own songs – he's done one about The Wicked Lady, the highway woman... I haven't heard it, but Edie told me it's brilliant.'

'Is Edie your girlfriend?' Livvy asked.

Paige tugged Charlie's arm harder. 'No, they're just neighbours, friends – she works behind the bar...' she explained. 'Shall we dance, Charlie? Livvy and Danny can look after your sax.'

'Well...' Charlie wasn't sure, but Paige wasn't taking no for an answer. She hauled him to his feet.

'I love this song – it's "Enchanted" by Taylor Swift.'

Charlie made a face – it wasn't his kind of music – but he allowed himself to be dragged onto the dance floor. Paige laid her head against his chest and wrapped her arms around his neck. He glanced towards the bar, where Edie was still busy, sharing a joke with Shane. He wondered how he could tell Paige kindly that he wasn't looking for a girlfriend. Briefly he asked himself why he wasn't attracted to her. He was sure he was over Luna. But he wouldn't think about it for now – he was looking forward to playing music. Hs mind buzzed with all the songs, the saxophone notes. The first set couldn't come quickly enough.

After half an hour, all the dancers disappeared to the bar while the musicians set up on the stage. Charlie borrowed a microphone for his saxophone and watched while Tom, Livvy and Danny checked sound levels and played a few notes. Paige rushed to the toilet to adjust her make-up and was back, ready, a mic in her hand, checking the playlist. Charlie noticed Edie watching him from the bar. She put a thumb up and he grinned back.

They launched into the first song, Tom introducing the band as The Auld Lanxieties, which Charlie found hilarious. Then Paige was singing 'L'Americano' and 'Volare' in her strong, confident voice. Charlie was impressed at how slick the other musicians were. It was incredibly easy to play alongside them. Tom introduced each song, a good witty, spokesman, and he was a very competent guitarist with a lovely, soulful voice. Danny was a showman. He'd found a trilby hat and sunglasses from somewhere and was wiggling dramatically as he played double bass. Livvy impressed him the most; quietly professional, she took everything in her stride on the keyboard, not ostentatious but absolutely note perfect. Charlie played each song from the playlist as well as he could. He felt pleased with his performance and he was enjoying himself.

The audience crowded close to the stage, clapping, dancing, waving hands as Paige launched into 'I'd Rather Go Blind', wrapping an arm around Charlie as if she was singing the love song just for him. He noticed some of the men in the audience giving her admiring glances; she was a magnetic personality. Charlie felt a glowing sense of pride: it was coming back to him, the joy of playing in a band, the rapport with the other musicians, the audience's applause and the thrilling adrenaline rush that accompanied it. He realised that he was smiling; he hadn't a care in the world. He just wanted to play all night.

At the end of the set, Paige clung to his arm, but it seemed that everyone in the bar wanted to congratulate him. Jerry shook his hand, gave him a free pint of Neck Oil and told him there could be the chance of more gigs in The Sycamore Tree in the new year. Charlie said with a grin that he'd love to be part of a band that played weekly.

Danny was impressed with Charlie's skills and admitted he shouldn't have been at all worried, and did Charlie want to form a serious jazz band? Livvy explained that she was looking for an outlet: she and Danny had a three-year-old, and she longed to play more music.

Tom was keen to play more folk gigs with Paige – he liked writing his own material, but he wouldn't rule out playing guitar in a jazz band. Charlie couldn't believe how easily it was all happening; by the time he'd finished his pint, he'd agreed to go into Markyate twice a week to rehearse at Livvy and Danny's house. For the first time in ages, his new year was filled with the possibilities of making music and playing live gigs. He turned to find Edie, to tell her how excited he was, but she was busier than ever.

It was time for the second set and he was back on stage, Paige singing 'The Love Of My Man' and 'My Baby Just Cares For Me'. He had to admit, she was talented, a sparkling performer. He enjoyed playing the second set even more than the first. On several occasions in the middle of a song, Tom waved at Charlie and breathed into the mic, 'Take over, Mr Sax Man,' and Charlie improvised a few solos. He loved that most of all. At the end, the audience clamoured for more, so The Auld Lanxieties played 'L'Americano' again, with everyone in the bar singing along. Charlie spotted Priya and her fiancé Toby dancing in the throng. Priya waved to him and rolled her eyes as if to say that the music was out of this world. He winked back, grateful to have support.

Jerry rang a bell. It was ten minutes to midnight. Charlie glanced across to where Edie was pulling pints and she blew him a kiss. He blew one back, wondering if she'd join the throng for 'Auld Lang Syne'.

Paige was next to him, tugging his sleeve, manoeuvring him towards the hall, where groups of people were assembling, couples already smooching. She threw her arms around him, kissing his lips. 'Happy New Year, Charlie.' He could taste alcohol and the scent of her perfume was overwhelming. She was about to kiss him again.

'Happy New Year, Paige...' He planted a gentle kiss on her forehead that was meant to be platonic. 'It's going to be a good one. I'm so excited about playing in a band with you. It will be brilliant.'

'It will be dreamy,' she purred.

'But I have to say – I'm not... I'm not looking for a relationship.' He spoke quickly: he thought she needed to know, before she kissed him again.

'Oh? But...'

'You're a great person. But I'm not the man for you...' Charlie knew he was talking in clichés. 'There are so many other men admiring you tonight... I mean, you could—'

'Is it Edie? Do you have feelings for her?' Paige asked bluntly. 'I did wonder about you two...'

Charlie shook his head. 'I don't know – I haven't thought about it.' He took a breath. 'Look, I'd better grab my sax and go. Alan's at home. I ought to get back. He doesn't like it if I stay out too late.'

It was a weak excuse and Charlie could see in Paige's expression that she thought so too.

He kept trying. 'But Happy New Year, Paige. I'll see you for our rehearsal at Danny and Livvy's. I can't wait.' In the spirit of the occasion, he planted another placatory kiss on her brow, turned and rushed towards the stage, grabbing his saxophone case, scurrying past the bar, through throngs of customers, waving frantically to Edie, then out into the fresh air.

He took off down Ferrers Lane at a fast pace. He'd be home in ten minutes at this rate and he had no intention of looking towards the woodlands on the way. His head was too full of crashing thoughts to think about the ghost tonight.

He wanted to play music, of course. That was what he wanted to do, so much, and it had filled him with a new sense of self-worth, of accomplishment. He had liked Danny, Livvy and Tom. He was making friends.

But a strange feeling was wriggling at the back of his head. When Paige had asked if he had feelings for Edie, Charlie didn't say no. He couldn't.

So what exactly was going on in his heart? What did he feel for Edie? Was she a friend or more than a friend? He honestly had to admit, he wasn't sure.

Or perhaps he was. Perhaps he'd known for some time now. Perhaps this new year was the right time to do something about it...

37

1660

The months had flown past. It was early June, a warm day. Kate was lying on a woollen rug in the grounds of The Cell. Raife was beside her, his hand on the rounded dome of her belly, which was now drum-tight. 'I can feel our baby in there, legs moving so fast as if on horseback. He or she will be a fine rider.' He smiled. 'As soon as the child is born and you can travel, the three of us will be far from here.'

'I'm sure the baby will come today or tomorrow. I have been plagued with pains in my back for days now. Oh, the time cannot come quickly enough.' Kate placed her hand on top of Raife's, linking their fingers. 'Then we can move away, as a family. I long to travel south with you, far beyond London. And on to the west country. No one will know us there.'

'I believe there is good farming to be had in Wiltshire,' Raife said. 'Small enclosed fields, just right for cattle and sheep, and the land is good, like it is here – marsh, meadow, heath, down. We'll buy ourselves a small farm and we will live well, the three of us.'

'Life will be simple and we will be happy. There, no one will have heard of Thomas Fanshawe and he will never see me again. When he comes out of prison, I will be long gone. Then in Wiltshire I will call myself Mistress Chetwyn,' Kate exclaimed.

A moment of sadness crossed Raife's face. 'I wish that you could be my wife in the eyes of God.'

'It matters not to me,' Kate insisted. 'God knows you and I love each other. That is the important thing, not standing together in a church. When I married Thomas at thirteen, it was not a real marriage of hearts and minds, as ours is. I am turned six and twenty now, and if I could push back time, I would have married you and not him on that day, but it was not to be.' She turned gentle eyes on Raife.

Raife looked anxious again. 'I pray God that it will be an easy birth.' He brought her hand to his lips tenderly, and Kate knew he was remembering Mary.

'I am not afraid,' Kate said, and she meant it. 'You and I have good fortune on our side. But I hope this little one will not take much longer to come, for I am anxious to leave as soon as possible. The king has returned – he has entered London and there is talk of him being crowned next year. I should have been at The Strand to see his arrival, but I told Anne I was feeling unwell. Thomas will be released from the Tower before long.'

'We can be away before he comes back.'

'John and Bea have been wonderful,' Kate said. 'They know you come here, that you visit my room at night using the secret passage, yet they say nothing. Bea leaves extra food and John insists that Peter cares for Midnight but says nothing to anyone.'

Raife frowned. 'Has the constable been here?'

'Edward Gale has visited several times. John tells him that I have become frail from worry because Thomas is in prison. I do not wish him to see that I am with child.'

'And Gale suspects nothing?' Raife asked.

'Nothing at all. He visits to say that he believes he has frightened the highwaymen away, that news of his name has reached Ralph Chaplin, who is too terrified to ride again for fear of the consequences.' She gave a muffled laugh. 'It suits us for him to think so.'

'It does...' Raife said quietly. 'Tonight, the London coach will pass at sundown and I intend to make the final robbery, in readiness for our departure, my love.'

'You shouldn't go alone.' Thoughts of Raife attempting the robbery worried Kate more than she could say, but she could not go with him now. 'I will think of you constantly...'

'It will be done quickly. We can give more money to John and Beatrice...'

'And to the local families who have worked so hard for so little recompense. Then we will leave...' Kate met Raife's gaze. 'Perhaps by the end of the week we may be away. But I am afraid – how I wish I could be by your side when you stop the final coach.'

'Not this time.' Raife grinned, his hand on her belly. 'You have other work you must do first.'

'Indeed I do.' Kate forced a smile, but as her hands moved on top of his, she gasped.

Raife paused, anxious. 'What is it, my love?'

At first, Kate couldn't speak. Then she muttered, 'A pain so strong it took my breath. Much greater than the pains I have been having. Now it...' She closed her eyes, trying to block the force of it. 'It comes again. Raife, I think it is time. I must go to my room and prepare.'

'Of course...' Raife helped her to her feet. 'Do you believe our child will come today?'

Kate nodded.

'Then let us get you to your chamber and we will call upon Beatrice.' Raife's arm was around her waist. 'Shall I carry you?'

'I may walk yet...' Kate said, her breath shallow. 'Just hold onto me and I will take small steps.' Her eyes were wide. 'I did not think the pains would be so great. I hope Bea will be able to help me. I have told you, she knows a woman of good character in Markyate, who is greatly trusted, who will come to assist me and will baptise the baby as soon as it is born. Bea fills me full of courage.'

They walked slowly towards the house. Raife said, 'Kate, I will not ride tonight. I will stay at The Cell with you.'

'You wish to stay?' Kate turned to him. 'What can you do?'

'I will be close by when the baby comes. I want to be there if you need me.'

'I will not need you.' Kate smiled. 'Birthing is women's work. No men are allowed near.'

'But we were both there when the baby was made and I want to be by your side now.'

Kate almost laughed. 'Although I love you, I do not wish you to be with me when I bring forth our child. Go and stop the London coach. Take Midnight. Bring back some jewels and as soon as we can, we will leave for Wiltshire.' She leaned towards him, kissing his lips. 'It is good that you ride on Nomansland Common this evening. It will keep your mind on our future.'

'It will.'

Kate's fingers tangled in his hair. 'I am in safe hands. I have Bea, and the goodly wife who will attend, and God will take care of me. Trust them...'

They had almost reached the front door. Raife called, 'Beatrice, help here, if you please...'

Beatrice hurried out, wrapping her arms around Kate, turning her back on Raife. 'Oh, my mistress, is the baby coming?'

John was just behind her. 'I will send Peter for Mistress Margaret Carew and tell her to hurry.'

'Margaret Carew will be paid well for her services. She will not breathe a word to anyone of this child. And she will take the best of care of you both. Come, mistress, let us take you to your chamber.' As Kate doubled over in pain, Beatrice turned to Raife, who was watching, wide-eyed. 'Why are you still here, Master Chaplin? Your work has been done long since. Come back tomorrow and you may be a happy father made.'

'Raife...' Kate reached out and took his hand, squeezing his fingers. 'It is as she says. Come back tomorrow...'

'I will go, but I think only of you.' Raife brought her fingers to his lips. 'You are in my heart at all times.'

'That may well be,' Beatrice interrupted him. 'But a baby will not wait for any man. Go. And be sure you pray for my mistress. For she will need God's kindness.'

Beatrice supported Kate as she moved slowly towards the stairs. Neither of them looked back.

Raife stood alone in the hall and exhaled. His horse was in the stables and it would be a long ride back to Ayers End Farm. His brow furrowed; his mind filled with anxious thoughts. It would be a long wait.

38

THE PRESENT

It was late January. Charlie had been busy for the last three weeks: his life had been a whirlwind. Bill had been asked to work on leaking windows in a large house in Hemel Hempstead and Charlie went with him. Entire gutters had needed replacing and it had taken four days out of their schedule. He made up for lost time at weekends, working on the downstairs rooms, repairing the ceilings, plastering walls, ripping out the old fireplace. His evenings had been busy too, now he was in a band. It had been non-stop.

He and Bill had discovered an old bread oven at the back of the fireplace in the living room, that Bill was sure dated back to the seventeenth century. Charlie wondered if the constable who lived in the cottage, or his wife, made bread there. It had certainly been a huge hearth, used for heating and cooking. It would be nice to talk to Edie about what he had been doing. He'd left it too long.

Charlie was now on his way to number three, Alan trotting at his side, holding two bottles of wine. It was almost six o'clock in the evening and the sky was already dark. He wanted to apologise for not having seen her for a while. They had caught up occasionally first thing in the morning to walk the dogs, just as it was light; once, he'd popped round for coffee and she'd been in the middle of an essay.

He knocked and heard the familiar sound of Bianca barking. Warm lights glowed inside.

Edie came to the door in a dressing gown, pink pyjamas and fluffy slippers. Charlie thought she looked unbelievably cute. She grinned. 'Hello, stranger.'

'Hello...' He held out the wine. 'I'm sorry. It's been mayhem at work and I haven't had a minute...'

Edie made a face as if it didn't matter and indicated the dressing gown. 'I just had a shower,' she said by way of explanation. 'I'm cooking something. It's just a traybake – veggies, tofu, some tahini sauce. Have you eaten?'

'No – oh, that sounds great.' Charlie could smell the succulent aroma of roasting food.

'Come in. Stay for dinner.' Edie led the way. 'Tell me what you've been doing that's made you so busy. I've hardly seen you since the New Year do at The Sycamore Tree. I told you the band were wonderful though. People are still talking about it.'

'I've been rehearsing on Mondays and Wednesdays with the guys in Markyate. Paige is singing and we've really perfected some old jazz classics. Then on Thursdays I give Joshit and Kavish lessons. Doing up the house is full-on, especially now Uncle Bill is giving me all the heavy lifting jobs, and Alan...' Charlie patted his dog. 'Well, Alan keeps me awake at night. He likes to hear me practise the sax before we go to sleep...'

Edie pressed his arm affectionately. 'You mean you're rehearsing every night?'

They had reached the kitchen. Charlie stood in the warmth of the room, approaching the Aga, where Bianca nestled in a fluffy bed. Alan collapsed on top of her, in an attempt to share the warmth and the space. Bianca bared her teeth, unwilling to move over, but Alan flopped down, oblivious, and snuggled against her white fur.

Charlie stretched out his hands, feeling the heat. 'Oh, I love this room – it's so cosy.'

'Is it still cold in number one?'

'Not in the rooms with radiators on. The new boiler is good. I bought

Alan a bigger, warmer bed and he has extra blankets, but he still tries to get in with me at night.'

'How are the renovations coming on?' Edie asked.

Charlie looked pleased with himself. 'On schedule. The living room's half done. The dining room will need a lot of work...'

'I can help sometime, if you like. I've nearly finished my last essay,' Edie said. She opened the oven door and pulled out a tray of roasted vegetables.

Charlie found himself mesmerised by the burnished colours of cauliflower, sweet potatoes, peppers, squash, parsnip, broccoli. His stomach rumbled. He'd been too busy to cook, living off beans on toast, soup and overcooked cauliflower cheese. But Edie's food smelled so good.

Edie offered him a smile. 'Come on. Let's eat. And you can open one of those bottles. It's been too long, Charlie. We deserve some downtime – and we need to catch up on our research. We've been neglecting The Wicked Lady...'

* * *

Their plates were empty apart from smears of sauce. Half a bottle of wine had been drunk, glasses almost empty, as Edie and Charlie were hunched on the sofa, their shoulders touching, a laptop between them. Alan and Bianca were chewing on a piece of roasted parsnip each, lying on a rug.

Edie frowned. 'We still can't find much about what happened to Ralph Chaplin. Perhaps he's fictitious?'

'It says in *The Dark Haunted* blog that there seems to be no historical proof that Ralph ever existed.' Charlie scratched his head. 'Perhaps we should rule him out?'

'There's so much conflicting evidence,' Edie agreed. 'It says here in the *Heritage Daily* there is no record of Katherine ever having lived in Markyate Cell, as it was leased to tenants after her father's death. So what about the secret passage she was said to use?'

'And it says here that Katherine was a wicked robber who burned houses and slaughtered livestock. She even killed a constable.' Charlie was baffled. 'Was she really an evil woman? She's a refined lady one minute and a hooligan the next.'

'Maybe we should look again at the National Archives...'

'Perhaps the baby is the key...' Charlie said. 'We know it was supposed to have been born in June 1660. And we've already established that it wasn't Fanshawe's child because he was in prison. So perhaps Ralph Chaplin did exist? The child had to have a father.'

'So – this baby...' Edie wondered. 'Let's find out what happened to him or her. It says here that Thomas Fanshawe did not marry again until 1665. He had four children by his second wife, Sarah, who was the daughter of Sir John Evelyn and widow of Sir John Wray. So, if he had four children with Sarah – what about Katherine's child? There's no record of it. We don't know the name, or if it was a boy or a girl...'

'Or if he or she even survived,' Charlie said sadly. 'We need to dig deeper. National Archives it is.'

Edie's eyes shone. 'Definitely – the baby may tell us about what happened to Katherine and Ralph.'

'Come on, little baby...' Charlie's fingers pressed keys. 'Let's work out what your link was with Katherine.'

Alan jerked his head, his ears pricking up. Bianca watched him carefully, slumped down on the rug. The Labrador stood up, his body tense, and he barked, turning towards the door, barking again as if something had disturbed him.

'Alan? What is it, mate?' Charlie asked.

Bianca was on her feet, the half parsnip discarded, watching Alan, who scampered into the hall, his paws scratching at the front door. He began to bark again.

'What's the matter, Al?' Charlie called. He glanced at Edie. 'Perhaps someone's outside?'

'It's probably Marilyn.' Edie suggested.

They were both standing in the hall now, perplexed. Alan leaped up at the door, barking again, a loud anxious sound. Behind them, Bianca began to bark too. Both dogs yapped in a cacophony of noise, then Bianca began to growl.

'Oh, I expect he needs to go to the loo.' Charlie stepped forward. 'I'll take him outside. Hang on, Al – it's all right.'

Charlie opened the door a little and at once Alan bolted. In the light from the hall, Charlie saw him scurry across the road, hurtling towards the woodlands.

'Alan. Alan, no. Come back. Come back here, there's a good boy.' He turned an anxious face to Edie. 'He's never done this before. Alan's usually so obedient.'

'We'd better go after him,' Edie said.

Charlie indicated her pyjamas, the dressing gown and slippers. 'You stay here.'

'No, I'll come with you...' Edie pushed her feet into the wellingtons by the door, reaching for a warm coat and a hat. 'I'll grab a torch. And Bianca's lead. The two of us will find Alan in no time.'

Charlie breathed a sigh of relief as he put on his coat and shoes, and reached for Alan's lead. 'Thanks, Edie.'

They stepped out into the cold, walking towards the woodlands. Edie shone a beam of light from her torch onto the road in front of them. It melted away into the darkness beyond the shadows of trees. Charlie was tempted to grasp Edie's warm hand and hold it tightly. Instead, he called, 'Alan? Al? Where are you, mate? Come back, there's a good boy.'

There was no response. Only silence and the rustling of the trees.

'Alan?' Edie murmured. Bianca walked at her side, tugging on the lead, growling. Edie shook her head. 'Bianca's not keen to go in the woods. You don't think there are adders in here? Perhaps something has scared the dogs...' Her eyes were round in the half-light. 'You don't think it's a burglar?'

Charlie kept his voice cheery. 'No, I expect Alan's just having a moment. Something we couldn't hear or see, that he wanted to chase. An owl...' He realised how foolish his words sounded. 'Alan – come back here, boy.' As an afterthought, he called, 'Edie has treats...'

The trees hushed him as he tramped towards the edge of the woodlands.

'Alan?' Charlie could hear the edge to his voice: he was nervous now. 'He'll come back any minute with a rabbit or something...' Charlie, said, hoping that Alan would leap from the darkness soon.

Edie linked her arm through his and snuggled close for warmth.

They edged forward, and Charlie called again, 'Alan?'

There was no sound. The wind had whipped up and was cold against Charlie's face. He blinked in the almost darkness, trying to discern a shape, hoping to hear the bounding of a dog, the crunch of twigs underfoot. They walked on, past a tall oak that stretched thick branches towards the dark sky. Edie snuggled closer.

'Al,' Charlie called, his voice tense.

'He'll be back soon, I'm sure,' Edie whispered. Bianca pulled back on the lead, stopping dead. 'Charlie, she doesn't want to go into the woods.'

'Go back home if you want,' Charlie said gently. 'I have to find Alan...'

He felt Edie tug on the lead and Bianca took a few tentative steps. Edie shone the torch ahead, illuminating grey tree bark, gnarled fingers of twigs, shivering leaves. Their feet squelched in mud.

Edie's grip on his arm tightened and she whispered, 'Where is he, Charlie?'

Charlie took the torch and directed the beam into the shadows. He shook his head. 'He's probably just sniffing at an animal scent, or having a pee somewhere,' he said confidently. The torch beam lit up shifting shadows in the distance. The wind whimpered among the leaves. Charlie called again, 'Come on, Al.'

They were in the thick of the woods. There was ice in the wind, and Charlie shivered. The torchlight shone on muddy ground, on sturdy trees, tangles of weeds. He saw Alan – and froze.

The beam of light revealed the dog sitting absolutely still, looking up at something, growling. Charlie could hear the noise: it was low, unearthly, an unrecognisable sound. As he raised the beam, he saw the pale grey outline of a horse and rider. She was mounted high. Charlie could see the hat, the breeches. He could hear the flap of her coat-tail.

The beam rose to her face and Charlie held his breath as he peered in the dim light. Katherine Ferrers was staring ahead, her face like marble, forlorn, carved in sadness. The torch made her eyes glisten like ice. Her cheeks were wet. She was crying silent tears.

The torchlight faded to nothing and they were standing alone in the cold darkness.

39

1660

Kate cried out again as the light faded from the bedroom. It was late evening, and a few tallow candles had been lit in sconces on the wall. She had been labouring for hours on the birthing stool and she was exhausted.

Margaret Carew, a middle-aged woman who had eight children of her own and had delivered many more, was unperturbed and businesslike. She said kindly, 'The baby is very close now, Mistress Fanshawe. You are almost delivered of it. You will need to make one more effort after this, perhaps.' She turned to Beatrice. 'All is well. Bring the hot water, the linen and the sharp knife as I will need to cut the navel string.' Then she was by Kate's side, whispering in her ear, 'Come, mistress, let's give your husband the heir he wishes for so much... I have heard in Markyate how much he desires a child.' Her eyes searched Kate's face, full of sympathy. 'And that is all anyone needs to know.'

Kate clenched her teeth and groaned. She was tempted to say that Raife was the baby's father, that she loved him, a simple good-hearted farmer, and not Thomas Fanshawe, with his meanness and his airs and graces. But at that moment she wanted only to push the baby out. Her body took over and she gave a low sound as she felt something move deep within her.

Margaret Carew said, 'Once more, mistress, and the birthing is done.'

Kate closed her eyes and made an enormous effort. Then she was falling backwards on the stool, where Beatrice held her fast and whispered into her ear, 'It is all well now, mistress.'

Kate shook herself, opening her eyes wide. In the shadows, Margaret Carew had turned away. She was holding a bundle in her arms. Kate could hear water splashing, but there was no sound of a baby's cries. She called out weakly, 'How fares my child? Does he live?'

Margaret did not reply. She remained with her back turned, working quietly. Kate's heart thudded and she wished with all her heart that Raife was by her side. It was their child; she couldn't bear to lose him or her. All their plans had been made for three of them: a farm, a good life together, more children, happiness every day in the warmth of his smile.

She called again, 'Mistress Carew, for pity's sake, I must know.'

Margaret approached, holding out a bundle, swaddled and clean. She handed the baby to Kate, who caught her breath as she saw Raife's gentle eyes and his smile in her child's face. Margaret said, 'You have a daughter. She is strong and healthy.'

'She will be a companion for you,' Beatrice whispered. 'All women want a daughter to be their best friend in the world. She will share the secrets of your heart for the rest of your days.'

'She is the very image of her father. I cannot wait for him to meet her.' Kate felt tears of joy brimming in her eyes. 'I thank God for such a gift. May my daughter have a long and happy life.' She glanced at Margaret. 'Can you baptise her, as is the way with newborns?'

'What will you call her?'

'She is to be named Marie.' Kate held her daughter close, feeling the velvet of her skin against her own. She lifted a round fist, soft as pudding, and kissed it. 'She is more precious than my own life. I am truly blessed.'

'I pray she will live well and long.' Beatrice was at Kate's shoulder, her tears falling freely. 'She is beautiful to behold. I always wished I had such a child. She looks like her father – she has his dark, kind eyes.'

'But she does not have his sturdy frame – she is slight, like me,' Kate said, her face shining in candlelight.

'She is strong and hale. And when she cries, we will know how powerful her lungs are.' Margaret smiled. 'You might put her to the breast soon, mistress. And I will prepare something for you to eat. We will help you into bed. You will be tired.'

As Margaret moved away to prepare a plate of food, Kate whispered, 'But I will not sleep until Raife comes.' She reached for Beatrice's hand. 'I long for him to see our child. He will be so happy. I believe he wanted a daughter first. Next time, we will have a son.'

Beatrice wrapped a blanket around her mistress's shoulders. 'You grow cold. It is time for you to rest.'

'Shh.' Kate lifted a finger. 'Listen – I hear footsteps on the stairs. Someone approaches.'

There was a loud knock on the door and John's tentative voice could be heard. 'Master Chaplin is here, mistress. I am not sure I can keep him outside for much longer.'

The door burst wide and Raife rushed towards Kate, kneeling at her feet. 'I rode here swiftly. I was followed at first, but I managed to lose them in the woodlands.' He took in the fact that Margaret Carew was still in the room and his expression changed: he would say no more of the robbery. His eyes were on Kate's face. 'You have brought the child into the world...' His eyes fastened on her and then on the baby, his fingers tracing her face gently. He kept his voice low. 'Kate, I have helped mares with foals, but I never thought to be a father myself after what happened to Mary. It fills me with more joy than I can express.'

'Our baby is called Marie. She looks so much like you.' Kate's lips were against his ear, her voice thick with pride.

Raife looked for Margaret, whose back was still turned. Briefly, he wrapped his arms around Kate. 'I thought of you all the time while I...' He paused, then he lowered his voice. 'We are rich now, my love. We can leave this place, and all will be as we planned.' He took the ruby cabochon ring from his finger and placed it on the fourth of her left hand. The scarlet stone reflected warm light in his eyes. 'You must wear this now. You will be my wife in every way. We will be together always.'

'I can hardly wait.' Kate closed her eyes, relief and happiness on her face. She rested her head against his shoulder. 'Rubies symbolise love, devotion, courage and happiness. My life is complete.'

Raife took her hand, bringing it to his lips, kissing her ring finger. 'I am the happiest man alive.'

'I have you and Marie. What more can I wish for than the wonderful things I possess in this moment? I have never been more joyful,' Kate said with a sigh.

John was standing in the doorway as it banged wide and he shouted a warning, a strangled sound in his throat.

'Mistress – I could not keep them out. They must have followed Master Chaplin here from Nomansland. They forced open the door and would not stop. The constables are here...'

40

THE PRESENT

The following week, Charlie and Bill were plastering walls in the downstairs living room. Bill held his hammer in the air, his mouth open wide in surprise as Charlie said, 'Alan saw her, standing there, just as I can see you. Honestly.'

Alan woofed in agreement from the corner, where he was curled up in his bed.

'You're having a laugh...' Bill shook his head.

'Honestly. Edie and I both saw her in the woods, in the torchlight. Before Edie's torch ran out of battery.'

'Then what? Weren't you terrified?'

'We just stared. She seemed to have faded away. I put Alan on his lead and we hurried back to Edie's in pitch darkness. Al was tired out, bless him. He and Bianca both fell asleep in the dog bed as soon as we got back. And Edie and I had a cup of tea...'

'Just like that?' Bill was amazed. 'You saw a ghost, then you went home and had a cuppa?'

'No, not just like that. We were both terrified. We just sat there with our mugs, shaking, talking about what we'd seen.'

'I asked Marilyn next door if she'd heard anything about a ghost when I popped in to replace the broken tile on her kitchen floor yesterday. She just laughed. She's lived here longer than you and Edie and she's never seen anything. I was careful what I said, mind. I didn't want to worry her.'

'Why do you think Edie and I see the ghost and Marilyn doesn't?'

'You have vivid imaginations?' Bill shrugged. 'I don't know.'

'Edie thinks it's because we are empathic...' He glanced at the bracelet on his wrist. 'And that we've both – you know – had broken hearts, and so has the ghost. I think it's more to do with the fact that people think she's a myth and she wants us to know the true story of what happened to her. There's a story that she died in London giving birth, but it doesn't make sense. The other story is that she was a highway woman, and the ghost might be telling us that it's true...'

'A rich woman as a highway robber who gave her name to Ferrers Lane?' Bill's laugh wasn't entirely confident. 'The Wicked Lady?' Bill gave a chuckle. 'She sounds a right barrel of laughs. I'll have to tell Marce about her. I'm not sure I want to see her though. And don't say anything to anyone else about her, Charlie. We're putting this place on the market in the spring. We don't want to scare punters off by telling them that the woods outside are haunted by a woman on a horse with a pistol.'

Alan barked once and Charlie gave him a calming look. 'It's all right, Al. She's gone now.' He turned to Bill. 'Edie and I have been thinking that the clue to what happened to Katherine Ferrers might be to do with her baby. The details of the child's birth are a bit weird. The birth wasn't recorded and her husband was in prison, so he couldn't have been the father.'

'Perhaps she was having a bit of hanky-panky with the highwayman bloke, Ralph whatever.'

'Who doesn't seem to exist.'

'It stands to reason he'd have kept a low profile, Char. He wouldn't have advertised the fact that he was a highwayman and her secret lover...'

'Edie and I just need to find out now what happened to all three of them.'

'Edie and I again...' Bill teased. 'I said to Marce, it's about time you two got together. You need a girlfriend.'

'I don't know. Maybe.' Charlie smiled. 'But I have asked Edie out, sort of. Next Friday night there's a Valentine's evening at The Sycamore Tree and Edie's not working. So we're going to go. Just for a meal...'

'A romantic meal,' Bill suggested, wiggling his eyebrows. 'You should book a table quickly.'

'I have booked one. Priya and Toby are coming too.'

'Four people? For a Valentine's meal?'

'I thought it would take the pressure off. If things go well, I might...'

'Make your move?'

'I like her, Uncle Bill. A lot.'

Alan leaped up from his bed, turned round, settled down again and lifted a toy in his mouth. He shook it and it whistled.

'Alan likes her too,' Charlie added. 'And he likes Bianca.'

'It sounds like a marriage made in heaven,' Bill teased, then his face was serious. 'That reminds me, my marriage won't be good for anything if I don't sort out a nice Valentine's evening for Marce and buy her some flowers.'

Charlie was quiet, thinking. He didn't want to plan ahead in too much detail. But he imagined him and Edie enjoying a pleasant meal with Priya and Toby, then they'd go back to number three for coffee – it was warmer there than in number one, which wasn't a romantic setting at all yet – and he'd tell Edie what was in his heart. It could be the right moment for them both, especially if Edie had feelings for him too.

And he was sure that she did.

* * *

The next week passed quickly in the usual flurry of work on the house, band rehearsals, a good lesson with the Sharma boys and a couple of brief walks with Edie and the dogs. They shared a coffee and their latest research on Katherine Ferrers. What happened to her child was still a mystery. Edie resolved to delve further into the child's background, but there was little information to be found.

The fourteenth arrived and Charlie called for Edie. He was surprised that he didn't feel at all nervous, although when Edie appeared at the door in a short sparkly dress, his heart missed a beat. He handed her a single red rose and offered his most charming smile. 'Are you ready?'

'I am.' Edie's eyes twinkled. 'There's one thing though, Charlie.'

'Anything,' he said honestly.

'Can we not mention Katherine Ferrers? I don't want to think about her tonight. Especially since we're leaving the dogs at home for a couple of hours.'

'No more ghosts,' Charlie promised and held out his arm gallantly. Edie grasped his elbow and they set off in a brisk walk towards the pub.

It was a cold night, the air was damp, and the trees rustled shivering leaves in the woodlands as they crossed Ferrers Lane towards The Sycamore Tree.

'So, Priya's sending out invitations – their wedding's in September and they still have nowhere to live.' Edie was in a chirpy mood as she chattered, her breath a mist on the air. 'She and Toby are getting married in Marky-ate. She wants to keep the wedding simple, but I think Toby has lots of family and the list of guests is growing.' She winked. 'You and I are invited.'

Charlie wondered if their invitations would be separate or as a couple. It was early days... He recalled the last wedding he had been to, in London, where he had stood alone and drunk beer all night, feeling sorry for himself. Times had changed. He reminded himself to text Ben and Rachael soon. 'Does Priya need a band for her wedding? We could play...'

'You'll need a name first,' Edie said. 'You can't call yourselves the Auld Lanxieties again.'

'We're still arguing over names.' Charlie smiled. 'Danny wants to call us The Cobras, Livvy likes The Monarchs, Tom desperately wants us to be The Ultimate Wildcats and Paige has set her heart on Graceful Storm.'

'Hmm.' Edie thought about them all. 'And what do you think?'

'I thought Ghost Riders... or Sycamore Highway...'

'Oh...' Edie's eyes widened. 'Katherine really has become a big part of our lives, hasn't she...?'

'We'll leave her behind tonight.' Charlie took her hand in his. 'Are you looking forward to tonight?'

'I am, of course, but...' Edie's eyes shone. 'It might be nice if it was just the two of us.'

'Maybe next year,' Charlie said and Edie stared at him in surprise. Charlie realised that he'd offered commitment, of sorts, and that it was the perfect opportunity to brush his lips against hers, but the moment had passed. They had reached the pub and Charlie held the door open for Edie to walk through.

Priya and Toby were already seated at the table, Priya in a long dress and Toby, lean, in round glasses and a smart jacket. Charlie was unsure if he had dressed up enough in a clean T-shirt, peacoat and black jeans. But as they settled in their seats and Shane brought a bottle of wine, his thoughts were only for Edie.

They shared a baked camembert for starters and Edie was excited to try the potato and mushroom wellington served with hen-of-the-woods mushrooms. Charlie readily ordered the same. Priya asked for the spiced squash tartlet and Toby ordered steak and chips.

Charlie raised his glass. 'A toast – to us all.'

'To friendship...' Edie began.

'And romance,' Priya added.

'And to happiness... and prosperity,' Toby added. 'I have just had a promotion at work.'

'We're looking to buy a flat somewhere. It's good news all round,' Priya said.

'And my essay has been sent off. I'm virtually done with my GDL course. I can start looking for jobs,' Edie added.

Charlie wondered what news he could bring to the table. 'We've almost finished one of the downstairs rooms in the cottage. The fireplace looks lovely now. We just have the dining room to do and the hall. The cottage will go on the market in the spring.'

'What will you do next, Charlie?' Priya scrutinised his expression. 'Will you leave and go on to another venture?'

'I think so. Uncle Bill is already looking for the next doer-upper. He saw a place in St Albans last week, but he said it was overpriced. He's looking at another house not far away, an old farm cottage,' Charlie said. 'He's dead keen to get stuck into another project.'

'I wouldn't like to spend my time like that, though,' Toby admitted. 'It's living rough, all the time. The place must be freezing cold in the winter.'

'It was, but it's cosier now with the heating on,' Charlie said with a grin. 'I bought Alan a thermal dog bed and I have two duvets. I used to be able to see my breath when I lay in bed.'

'I bet it's nicer at Edie's though,' Priya said meaningfully.

'It is,' Charlie agreed, then he realised that she was making mischief, dropping a hint. He smiled at Edie in complicity and she winked back.

'I'd miss you if you went to live somewhere else, Charlie,' Edie said quietly. 'I've got used to having you as a neighbour.'

'I'd miss it too.' Charlie picked up his wine glass. 'And now I'm in a band, I'd love to stay on. Tom says there may be a job coming up soon, teaching music at his school, but I'm not sure if I want to go back to that.' He took a swig and noticed the disappointment in Edie's face. She didn't want him to leave. He tried again. 'I'll work something out. There are loads of reasons why I want to stay and only one reason to move away...'

Shane arrived to take away the empty plates and Charlie was glad of the change of conversation. He hoped he hadn't said the wrong thing and made Edie feel unimportant. In all honesty, the opposite was true. He was dreading leaving once the cottage was finished.

Priya and Toby ordered puddings. Edie said something about not being particularly hungry, but perhaps she and Charlie could share one. He murmured, 'Of course – let's do that. You choose.'

Someone who had just walked into the bar caught his eye. Charlie watched the woman who was standing in the doorway. She was wearing a light green coat and knee boots, pushing back long hair that shone like silk. Charlie couldn't help staring.

'Shall we have the carrot cake?' Edie asked, studying the menu.

'Yes, if you like.' Charlie was still looking at the woman. She had his full attention. She lifted a hand, waving small fingers in his direction, a greeting. He stood up. 'Can you excuse me for a minute? There's somebody I... I need to talk to.'

He grabbed his coat – he wasn't sure why – and hurried towards the doorway. The woman stepped back into the bar so they were out of sight.

Charlie looked into the intense blue eyes and caught his breath.

'Luna...' He could hardly believe it. 'Luna – what are you doing here?'

'I had to see you, Charlie...' Luna murmured. Her eyes suddenly filled with tears. 'I had to...'

I had to see you, Charlie…' Lottie murmured. Her eyes suddenly filled
with tears. 'I had to

41

1660

Constable Edward Gale strode into the upstairs room, his pistol raised. In the low light, his face marked with smallpox, he looked furious. Behind him, several other constables stood in a row, clutching pistols. Gale shouted, 'Ralph Chaplin, you are a notorious highway robber, but you have been caught. You will come with us, where you will be questioned and sentenced for your crimes.'

Raife didn't move. His eyes were fixed on Kate's as he knelt by her bedside. He whispered, 'Trust me, Kate. I will go with them. But I will find a way back to you, I promise.' Slowly, he stood, turning to the constable, his voice muffled. He pushed his hat down low and raised his neckerchief over his nose, determined not to be recognised. 'This woman has just given birth. You are to conduct this business outside. I will come with you.'

Gale stared around the room, taking in Kate and the baby. He frowned. 'Why are you here, Chaplin?'

'I rode away from you and your men when you gave chase.' Raife's voice was full of dignity. 'I'm a traveller – I pass this way often. I came here because I heard a rich woman resides here alone. I thought to rob her of her jewels.' He bowed gallantly to Kate. 'I am sorry, mistress, I did not mean any harm. I wish you and your child every blessing.'

His eyes held hers again and Kate wanted to cry out, to tell the truth, but there was something in his expression that prevented her. Marie snuggled in her arms, asleep, her rosebud lips pursed in a smile, and Kate held her breath.

Gale waved his flintlock. 'Is this true? Did this man come here to steal from you?'

Kate could not speak.

For a few moments there was silence, then John muttered, 'It is true. I know the scoundrel. I have seen him around these parts. He is as he says – an itinerant trader. But I believe he meant no harm to my mistress.'

Gale nodded towards Raife and three officers stepped forward, gripping his arms.

Raife pushed them aside. 'I will come with you. But I forbid you to show violence in front of this lady.'

'And what of your accomplice?' Gale approached Raife, his face tense and angry. 'The young highwayman who rides alongside you?'

'My brother died several months ago of a fever – may his soul rest in peace,' Raife said simply.

'May he rot in hell, where you will go too, scoundrel,' Edward Gale began, but John coughed meaningfully.

'Officer, please would you take this gentleman from my lady's room? Your business here is done, and you are out of place here.'

Gale bowed slightly to Kate. 'My apologies, mistress, if I have caused distress.'

Kate found her voice. 'In truth, Master Gale, you astonish me with your rudeness. I almost feel sorry for the gentleman you have arrested.' She took a breath to steady her nerves. 'It is true – this highway robber shows more manners and courtesy than you have. Perhaps I will sell what jewels I have and offer you money for the poor man's release.'

Gale gave Kate a searching look. 'You might do much, mistress. Now I will take the scoundrel away, along with all the money he has stolen. I bid you a good day.' He nodded towards his officers, who grasped Raife's arms and tugged him from the room.

Raife stared over his shoulder, his last gaze upon Kate. The door closed.

Beatrice was by Kate's side. 'John had to say what he did, mistress. He thought to save you and Marie from the constables. He meant no harm...'

'Please – take her...' Kate lifted Marie, handing her to Beatrice. 'I must get up...'

'You will do no such thing,' Margaret Carew said sternly. 'You must rest, mistress. You know it.'

'But how can I rest? How will I sleep knowing the man I love has been taken away?' Kate looked around for support. 'I must help him. I have to find out where he will be held, then I must free him. They will take him to the gallows, and I know I can prevent it. They have to keep him for three days, to interrogate him. That is usual. You heard what the constable said. I can give him money, bribe him and Raife will go free.'

'You must rest first,' Beatrice soothed. 'When you are strong, we can discuss what to do.'

'No. I must act as soon as possible,' Kate insisted. 'They believe the young highwayman to be dead. They will not look for him. So I will ride again. There is a goods coach on the London road, late tomorrow night, coming back from the city. I will be there, to take whatever I can. Then I will go to the constable and pay for Raife's release. Edward Gale is greedy – you could see it – he will not refuse me. Then we will go away as planned.'

'You must not think of it yet,' Beatrice pleaded. 'You will not be strong enough.'

'I will be well enough tomorrow.' Kate's eyes flashed. 'Do not speak of this again, I beg you, Bea. I will need your help more than ever, and yours too, John. And Mistress Carew – I will pay you well for your silence...'

Margaret turned her face away as if in agreement.

Beatrice clutched Marie in her arms. 'But think of this little one, mistress. If anything should happen to you...'

'I think of nothing else but my child,' Kate said wildly. 'She will need a father and I need a husband.' She took a breath, falling back on the pillow. 'Tonight, I will rest and tomorrow, I will steal enough to pay for his release – he cannot stay where he is for long. I cannot imagine what they will do to him. I beg this, one time – please give me your loyalty, your help.'

'Mistress, we will do what we can,' John said.

'But you must rest now. You have just given birth,' Beatrice said. 'I pray all may be well.'

'Amen to that,' Margaret added. 'I will go downstairs, Beatrice, and accept your offer of food and drink, and recompense for my pains. I will stay here until dawn breaks then I will take my leave.' She turned to Kate. 'I swear I shall never speak of what I have seen this night, mistress. You have my word on it.'

'Thank you,' Kate said, closing her eyes. 'And when you pray, please mention the name of the man I love. For he has grave need of our prayers. Now I must rest and become stronger. Tomorrow I will ride for the final time.'

* * *

Kate sat on top of the hill, looking down over Nomansland Common. Her breath came fast and hard, leaving mist on the air. Midnight was still beneath her, watchful, tense. The moon was high, round as a gold coin. The sky was studded with tiny stars. Kate shivered, and her body ached from the arduous ride which had left her feeling dizzy and gripped with pain. Each time Midnight had stumbled on a stone, Kate thought she might faint. In truth, she still felt weak from Marie's birth. Cold and fear made her bones feel brittle. The London coach would not be long. She cocked her pistol, ready. As soon as she heard the clang of wheels against the dust track, she would make her move.

She thought of Raife in prison somewhere, and she tried desperately to send her love to him, wherever he was. He would be comforted by thoughts that she would soon set him free.

Earlier tonight, she had suckled baby Marie and left her in Beatrice's arms. Quickly, she had tugged on her highwayman's garb, the boots, hat and neckerchief, and set off on a fast and painful gallop towards Nomansland. It was her last robbery and, truly, she was glad to make an end of it. All she wanted now was peace, to hold Marie and to feel the comfort of Raife's arms.

She felt the horse move abruptly beneath her. There it was, the clatter of hooves and wheels, the shuddering sound of a lonely wagon. Kate was ready.

She lifted her pistol and hurtled forward, Midnight thundering downhill. Her face was frozen in a new desperation. She called out, 'Stop. Deliver what you have or I will shoot.'

The coach driver seized the reins and came to a halt. The horses stood obediently.

'Give me all the money you have,' Kate ordered. She forced herself to sit upright. The pain that clutched her abdomen was intense, but she was desperate. She wiped perspiration from her brow.

'Sir – I am alone on this journey. I have no passengers, just goods to deliver. I carry supplies for an inn at Gustard Wood, near Wheathampstead. I will give you my purse willingly, but it is not much.' The driver had a crafty face, a hat tugged low over his brow.

'Get down from your seat. Open the coach – I wish to see inside,' Kate commanded.

The man did as he was told, opening the door.

Kate peered in. She could see bottles, ornaments and piles of fancy clothing, a chest. She frowned. 'What goods do you have in there?'

'Whisky, gin, cloth. Nothing of much value to you.'

'Give me your money. Any jewels you have.' Kate's head swam. She felt suddenly apprehensive, a sense of dread. Her instinct screamed at her to turn Midnight around, to ride away.

The man held out a thin purse. 'I have but a few shillings. There is nothing here for you, young man.' His eyes didn't move from her face. 'I know who you are. You're the young accomplice of Ralph Chaplin, he who was arrested yesterday.'

'He will be freed...' Kate retorted without thinking. 'I will set him free.'

'And where will you go to do that? Hell itself?' The man gave a mocking laugh.

'Why do you say that?' Kate's heart lurched with fear and foreboding.

'Ralph Chaplin will rob the highways no more. He is dead.'

'You are lying.' Kate felt tears spring to her eyes. 'The constables keep robbers for three days, to interrogate them.'

'This one was quickly pronounced guilty. He was hanged on Finchley

Common this very afternoon. Constable Gale wanted him dispatched in case he tried to escape. I saw it myself. I was there with the many people who came to watch. A good hanging it was, too – one of the best collar days I've seen. Some people even brought food and drink. I saw them put the rope around Chaplin's neck with my own eyes.'

'Be silent,' Kate ordered. Her clothes were damp with perspiration and she felt unsteady. 'I will not listen.'

'He made a good end of it, Chaplin.' The man ignored her, his face filled with pleasure. 'They tied his hands in front of him so that he could pray, and brought him to the gallows on a horse-drawn cart, sitting on top of his own coffin.'

'Say no more.' Kate pointed the pistol and her hand shook.

'The crowd cheered for him as if he was a hero because he was so proud, so well turned out.' The man laughed again. 'You should have seen Chaplin. A fine figure, dignified. His last words were for his wife and child, how much he loved them, asking God to protect them. Everyone enjoyed that one. But then the hangman did his work and Chaplin's neck was quickly broken. The people went mad – they rushed the stage to try to get a souvenir from the body.'

'Be quiet...' Kate's finger tightened on the trigger. Her body was trembling, racked with pain. 'I am warning you – say nothing more of it.'

The coachman was enjoying himself. 'The hangmen flogged the body and cut off pieces of Chaplin's clothing to hand out. They even sold bits of the rope that broke his neck...'

Kate clenched her teeth, shivering, her heart thumping. 'No more...'

'Oh, you should have seen it – a good time was had by all, except for Chaplin, who deserved everything he got. By all accounts, he was a bad 'un...'

A shot cracked. There was a spark, the instant stench of gunpowder. Kate wasn't sure if she'd meant to do it or if she had lost control. Midnight jolted in shock as she fired directly at the coachman. He fell back in slow motion, his face surprised as she watched a rose of blood spread across his stomach. Kate caught her breath. She was trembling. She could hardly believe what she had done.

Something moved inside the coach, beneath the folds of cloth. Two figures wriggled out, pointing pistols. Kate realised too late that the passengers had been hiding. She tugged Midnight's reins quickly, digging in her heels, and the horse galloped away uphill. She heard the cry of voices behind her and the loud sound of a pistol being fired, then a second, like the boom of a cannon. The impact shuddered throughout her body as Kate slumped forward onto Midnight's neck. She had been hit. Her eyes blurred and her breath emptied from her lungs all at once. For a moment, the earth whirled beneath her, yet still she clung to the reins as Midnight galloped on towards Markyate.

She was barely conscious as Midnight thundered through the gates of The Cell. Her body was numb; her shoulder felt as if it had been crushed. The horse slowed down, then busy hands were helping her from the horse. She heard Beatrice's cry, then John's calm voice.

'Is the mistress still alive?'

'She has been hit. She is bleeding.'

'What will we do, John?'

'Bring her to her chamber, through the secret passageway. Tend to her wounds, stay the bleeding. I will arrange for a coach to take her to London, and quickly. Richard Fanshawe and his wife have much influence. They will take care of her and provide the best of surgeons. I fear we may not have much time.'

Kate closed her eyes and there was nothing more but the dull throb of her body and the soft scratching of voices above her head.

42

THE PRESENT

'How did you know where to find me?' Charlie asked.

'I knocked on your door and your neighbour came out. She told me you'd gone to The Sycamore Tree. Your Uncle Bill told her you were going out for the evening with friends...' Luna was suddenly awkward. 'Am I interrupting?'

'Well,' Charlie replied and was immediately furious with himself for hesitating. He wished he'd said yes, he was on a date with Edie. He should have told the truth straight away.

Luna looked down at her boots. 'Can we talk? Can we go somewhere?'

'I'm having a meal...' Charlie shuffled uncomfortably. 'How did you get here?'

'I've got a car,' Luna said. 'My job's finished in Cornwall. I drove straight here – there's stuff I need to say.'

Charlie glanced back towards the table. Edie was looking round for him. He was not sure whether to go back and explain. But he didn't know what to say. He couldn't tell Edie his ex had turned up on Valentine's night and wanted to talk to him. He owed Luna a few minutes of his time, surely? His loyalty was pulled two ways.

'It won't take long. I want to explain... to tell you about why I left.' Luna's expression was desperate. 'Please, Charlie?'

'Can we talk some other time?'

'It's important – five minutes, that's all.'

'What about tomorrow?'

'I'll be gone tomorrow. Out of your life. Please.'

He sighed. 'All right.' He'd talk to Luna, find out what she wanted. He stood in the doorway as Luna reached for his hand. At this moment, his mind was a jumble of thoughts and emotions. His heart was racing.

'We can't talk here...' Luna said. 'What about going to your cottage? It's not far.'

'As long as we're really quick.' Charlie promised himself he'd stay briefly, then text Edie and run back to the pub.

Luna said little to him on the way to the cottage, and Charlie wasn't sure how to start a conversation. The rain was falling lightly now. Charlie opened the door to number one, ushered Luna inside and murmured, 'It's a bit cold in here – the heating is off. And downstairs is a mess. I'm doing it up.' He glanced round at the pots of plaster, the hop-up, ladders. Luna didn't seem to notice. She was looking at him, her hair damp, her face illuminated, happy.

Luna met his eyes and wrapped her arms around his neck. 'I've come home, Charlie.'

He felt her lips against his, a familiar softness, and he waited for his body to respond. Instead, he felt cold and miserable. 'Luna...'

'I made a mistake. I should have stayed with you in London. But I had to find that out for myself. I spoke to Jules. She and Kofi are still in Peckham. She had your address. Jules said you came to a Halloween party and spent the night dancing. She said you were getting a band together.'

'That's what I've done...'

Luna stood back, still clinging to his arm. 'You look so well. The old Charlie. My Charlie...' Luna took a breath. 'The choreography job didn't work out.'

'I'm sorry.'

'Is there a warmer room?' Luna suddenly seemed to feel the cold. 'Somewhere we can have a coffee perhaps? Or we could open some wine...'

'I need to get back,' Charlie said. 'Maybe we can talk in the kitchen?'

He led her to the next room, flicking on the light. Alan looked up from his basket and bounded over to Luna, licking her hands.

'Oh, I've missed you so much, Alan.' Luna knelt down and hugged him. 'Look, Charlie – he's missed me too.' She stood up, walking over to Charlie, who was leaning against the sink, in need of support. 'I've missed you most of all...' Her lips were against his neck.

Charlie closed his eyes briefly, to refocus. Then he eased her away from him. 'What happened in Cornwall?'

'It was good at first. The job was great. And the theatre is wonderful – in winter, they put up beautiful lights for visitors at The Minack and it's so atmospheric. But it was too cold to perform and we moved the show to the theatre in Truro. I had a bit of a fling with one of the dancers. But we weren't right for each other. He spent most of the time in a bad mood and it really affected me.'

Charlie had seen the photos of Luna and the new man on Facebook. He'd known.

'But it made me realise – he wasn't you. It was you all the time that I needed. You're kind and sweet and you care about me.'

'You broke my heart, Luna.' Charlie's voice was a whisper. 'It took me ages to get my old self back.'

'But here you are...' She took his hands, smiling. 'And here I am.' She swayed, in a little dance. 'And it's perfect. We can get back together on Valentine's night.' She snuggled close to him, her lips against his ear. 'Do you want to show me upstairs? I bet your room is lovely and warm...'

'No.' Charlie heard the determination in his voice. 'No, it wouldn't work.'

Luna stepped back. 'But we love each other...'

'Once.' Charlie felt sad. 'Once we loved each other. Then you left.'

'But you can forgive me...?' Luna was wheedling, making cute expressions. 'We can be good again, you and I.'

'I don't think so.' Charlie shook his head. 'We should both move on.'

'Move on?' Luna put a hand to her face as if she'd been slapped. 'But I've driven all this way...' She wrapped both arms around Charlie's neck. 'Let's sleep on it. See how you feel tomorrow? I'm sure I can change your mind.'

'You won't,' Charlie said. He wanted to get back to Edie. Right now, he needed more than anything to make Luna realise it was over between them. 'Look, Luna – you should message Jules, drive to Peckham. You can be there by half ten. Stay there, with her and Kofi. Then – I don't know – your life's your own. But we have no future, not now...'

'No future?' Luna repeated. There were tears on her face. 'But you're my rock. You've always been there for me.'

'Not now. I need to get back to the pub – I've already been too long...'

'Is there someone else?' Luna asked.

'Yes.' Charlie met her eyes. 'There is. Someone I care for. Someone who cares for me. And she's waiting.'

Luna took a step back, her face miserable. 'I've been stupid. I left you, and you've moved on.'

'Don't...' Charlie said quietly. 'You and I were good once. Let's keep it like that, a sweet memory. But you have a new path to find, Luna. Discover what you want to do and follow it with your heart.' Determinedly, he met her eyes. His feelings for Luna were purely ones of concern.

She nodded slowly.

Charlie took in her expression and remembered how much he had loved her. But Edie filled his thoughts now. He needed to go back to The Sycamore Tree. 'You should go.'

'Right.' She took a deep breath. 'A girl knows when she's no longer wanted.'

'It's not like that,' Charlie murmured. 'It's just the right thing to do. You know it is.'

'I tried...' Luna sighed. She stood up straight, pushed her hair from her eyes. 'Right. Yes. I'll message Jules and Kofi. They'll let me stay until I sort myself out. I'm sorry things worked out this way. I'm sorry for hurting you... for hurting myself.'

Charlie moved towards her. 'I'll walk you to your car.'

'Thanks,' Luna said, and Charlie led the way to the door, Alan at his heels.

Luna ignored him as she approached her car. She slid in the driver's seat, started the engine and drove away.

Charlie knew he wouldn't see her again. He paused for a second, then he was running full pelt down Ferrers Lane towards The Sycamore Tree in the pouring rain, Alan at his side. The lights were glowing in the distance, and Charlie hoped Edie would still be there, waiting for him. His heart thudded as he ran through the haze, mud squelching beneath his feet. What if she had left already? She must have seen him with Luna. What would she think?

He hurried through the door into the bar, his coat wet, his trainers full of water, hair dripping in his eyes. Alan's fur was soaked. They blundered through the crowds of drinkers into the restaurant, which was now almost empty. Priya and Toby were holding hands, talking to Edie, who looked up as Charlie approached. Three empty coffee cups sat on the table.

Edie looked bewildered as Charlie sat down opposite her and Alan snuggled beneath the chair at his feet. Charlie took Edie's hand and said, 'I'm sorry I left. I'm back now.'

Edie tried to smile. 'Where have you been? I saw you talking to some-one... I just assumed...'

'Luna – it was Luna, my ex. She came to see me. She wanted us to get back together.' Charlie was gabbling.

'So you went off with her?' Edie said, a small indentation between her brows.

Charlie met the hazel eyes. He could see all her emotions there, the hurt, sadness, anxiety. At that moment, his heart expanded and he realised he loved her more than he could find words to say. He squeezed her hand quickly. 'I needed to tell her that it was over. Luna and me – we're done. She drove here from Cornwall, gave up her job. She wanted to get back with me – because it was Valentine's Day...'

'I see...' Edie was still unsure.

'No, you don't, Edie. I told her I don't love her any more.'

'Oh?'

'I love you.'

'You do?' Edie took a breath.

'So much...' Charlie breathed.

Toby stood up. 'Right, Priya – this is our cue to go. It looks like these lovebirds have plenty to talk about.'

'We do... yes... thanks,' Charlie agreed.

'I'll text you, Edie,' Priya said as Toby took her hand and dragged her towards the bar, murmuring, 'I'll pay for our half of the bill on the way out...'

Charlie didn't watch them go. He was too busy staring at Edie, holding her hand in his as if it was precious. 'It's been you for a long time, Edie. No one else. Only you.'

Edie took another breath. 'I wasn't sure, Charlie. I hoped...'

'I didn't want to get it wrong. You'd been hurt before. So have I. But the truth is...' He grinned, brimming with excitement. 'Over the last few months, you've got under my skin and stayed there. I mean – it's like you're part of me now. We are two halves of the same coin. Two peas in a pod. A matching set. Two hearts, one mind... Am I talking in clichés?' Charlie burst out laughing, then his face was serious again. 'I love you. I know I do. It didn't take Luna to make me realise it. I knew already. I was going to tell you tonight, before all this happened. I planned it out...'

Edie launched herself across the table, throwing her arms around his neck, kissing his lips. Charlie tugged her to him. The table was in the way, but he kissed her back for all he was worth.

When he opened his eyes, Shane was hovering nearby, about to speak.

'Will there be anything else?'

Charlie spluttered a laugh. 'Oh, I hope so. Years and years of it.' He made his face straight and said, 'Yes. Two brandies, please, Shane. That's if you want to linger here a little longer, Edie.'

Alan woofed from beneath the table, turning round once and settling himself down comfortably by Charlie's feet.

'A brandy would be lovely, Charlie.' Edie's eyes glowed. 'And when we've finished, we can walk home and... you and Alan can come back to number three. We have a lot we need to talk about...'

Kate opened her eyes and felt immediately confused. She didn't know where she was. She blinked hard and waited for her vision to clear. She was in a dim room, a yellow glow in the corner from a tallow light. Her body ached; her head throbbed. She tried to speak, but no words would come. Her lips were dry, her throat was swollen, and there was a constant noise behind her eyes. Someone was at her side, pouring water, holding a cup to her lips.

'Drink, mistress.' It was Beatrice's voice. 'Quench your thirst.'

'Where is Marie?' Kate's first thought was for her child. 'Can I see her?'

'She is in a crib next to you.' Beatrice took Kate's hand gently. 'Here – you can feel the softness of her skin. She is not far away.'

Kate was still confused as she allowed Beatrice to guide her hand towards the crib. A small fist curled around her finger and she felt a moment of hope. 'I long to hold her, but I am not strong...'

'She is smiling, mistress.' Beatrice was looking at her through tears.

'She has the same sweet smile that her father had,' Kate said. 'Tell me, how does she seem?'

'Beautiful,' Beatrice said, her voice cracking. 'Like you. Like Master Chaplin. She will be the best child, a strong young woman. She has your strength, I'm sure of it. Your determination. And her father's dark eyes, full of love.'

'Perhaps I will never see her grow...' Kate said weakly. 'I am not at home – this is not my chamber.'

A kind voice from the other side of her bed murmured, 'You were brought to London. You are in the home of a friend of Sir Richard Fanshawe, your cousin Anne's husband.' It was John, who stood tall, giving his familiar small cough. 'A doctor has been to tend to your wounds, mistress. You were shot by a pistol. You have lost a lot of blood.'

'My cousin Anne knows I am here?' Kate asked weakly.

'I believe she has been told that you have been brought to this place to bring forth a child.'

'Will I live?' Kate asked weakly.

She noticed John and Beatrice exchange anxious glances.

John mumbled, 'If God allows it.'

'Listen – I beg you...' Kate reached out a hand and grasped Beatrice's small one. 'If I should die, Bea – please take Marie. Bring her up as your own.' A breath shuddered deep in her lungs. 'Raife has gone. I heard that he was hanged at the gallows in Finchley. I fear the end for us both now...' She gulped back tears, determined to be strong, but the emotion engulfed her and she began to sob. 'I could not save him. I cannot save myself. All that remains is my child.'

'Rest, mistress – all may be well yet. If you recover, we can begin again back at The Cell...' Beatrice sat down heavily on a chair with velvet cushions next to the bed. She was doing her best to calm her mistress. 'It cannot be such a bad life, being the wife of an important man. And your husband has been loyal to the king. He will be well recompensed for all he has done. You and Marie may thrive.'

'My husband? What do you mean?' Kate remembered the ruby cabochon on her finger. She touched it, making sure it was still there, then she groaned. 'There will only be one man I will call husband, and that will never be Thomas Fanshawe.'

John said patiently, 'Times and circumstances have changed, mistress. The master has been released from prison. King Charles is to be crowned again. The only way now is for you to try to become well, to resume your old duties at Markyate...'

'And beg him to take little Marie as his own child,' Beatrice added. 'It is the best thing to do.'

'I will never allow it.' Kate struggled to sit up, but the pain made her weak. For a moment, consciousness left her. She focused her vision. 'John. Tell me honestly what the doctor said of my wounds. May I be well again?'

John hesitated and Kate knew the truth. Her chances were slim. John took her hand. 'We all pray for your recovery, mistress.'

Kate took a deep breath, suddenly resigned. 'I thank you both for all you have done. John – in my room, back at The Cell, beside my bed, there is a deep wooden chest of clothes. At the bottom of it, there are jewels and much money. We took it when we stole from the coaches. It is for you and the local poor families. I want you to take it all.'

'John?' Beatrice looked at her husband.

'Mistress, Beatrice and I have spoken of this. We will not take money that has been stolen. We could not bring ourselves...'

'But I don't want Thomas to have it,' Kate moaned. The pain that racked her body was worsening. Her vision was dim now. She said in a muffled voice, 'If you will not take it, then throw it down the well. The one near the sycamore tree. Thomas will not find it there.'

'Your money should go to Marie,' Beatrice muttered.

'I will make sure she gets it somehow,' John said.

'That is for the best,' Kate murmured. 'Can you leave a map or some means to her finding it?'

'I will see to it,' John soothed. 'I will leave word for her.'

'We could write a letter, keep it until she comes of age.' Beatrice's eyes filled with tears. 'And we could make up a nursery rhyme to tell her as a child. Just imagine, John. *Near the cell, there is a well...*'

John's face was filled with sorrow. 'I promise the money will not go to Thomas. It will be done in your name.'

Beatrice murmured, 'Rest now, mistress. Perhaps the doctor will come back soon and give you more medicine.'

'I thank him for his pains,' Kate said, her eyelids heavy. 'Where is he now?'

'He is outside, talking to your husband.'

'Thomas?' Kate shook her head again to clear her thoughts. 'Thomas is here?'

'As I said, your husband has been released from the Tower, and is in London. He and Sir Richard have been meeting with the king,' John muttered. 'It is a good thing that we brought you to this place. Your husband came quickly when he heard where you were. And Richard Fanshawe has much influence now. He paid the doctor for his troubles and arranged for you to stay here.'

Kate closed her eyes. The Fanshawes had organised her care; Thomas was outside, allowing the servants to tend her. It was too much to bear. Her final thought before she fell asleep was that she never wanted to see Thomas again. She decided that she'd be better dead than to resume her old life at Markyate. But thoughts of Marie and what might happen to the child kept her heart beating.

* * *

Hours later, Kate woke again, still groggy. Two shadows seemed to hover in the corner. She moaned, 'Bea... are you there? I need water...'

'It is I, Thomas.' An unemotional voice came back to her. 'You have been asleep for a long time. Richard has been most generous, arranging for your care. He has only agreed to it because you are my wife. I must be honest with you. The doctor has told me that it is unlikely you will recover from your wounds, Katherine.' He took a step forward and Kate noticed he was leaner, older. The time in prison had not been kind to him. He spoke quietly, as if he wanted no one else to hear. 'I cannot imagine what you were thinking of while I was in the Tower. I have heard of your activities – stealing from coaches like a common highway robber. And there is the problem of the child...'

'Marie...' Kate breathed heavily. 'Bea will take her. And raise her as her own.'

'I think it best that she does,' Thomas said. 'You have disappointed me, Katherine. My reputation is greatly tarnished by what you have done. Fortunately, I have friends who will do their utmost to enable me to recover from your misdemeanours. What has happened must never be spoken of.'

Kate closed her eyes. She reached out a hand. 'Please, promise me you will take care of Marie...'

'The highwayman's child?' Thomas's voice was clipped. 'She lies beside you, but she looks nothing like you.'

'Marie is all that remains of Raife and me...'

'I will make sure she is cared for,' Thomas promised. 'I wish her no ill.'

Kate felt that she was sinking into the softness of the pillows beneath her head. She could not see Thomas now. He was a shadow, blurred and fading. Her eyelids were heavy and she was slipping away.

The image of Raife came before her. She saw him as she had the first time they met. He reached out a hand to her and his eyes glowed like burning coal; his dark hair tumbled in waves over his eyes and again he reminded her of a painting she had once seen of Vulcan, the Roman black-smith god of fire and volcanoes. His voice was gentle: 'Come to me, my love.'

Kate reached out a hand. 'I am here.' She was entwined in his arms, his lips against hers, and she murmured, 'I am yours again.'

She opened her eyes. Raife was gone and Thomas stood in his place. Another figure shuffled forward, next to him. She saw a man with a face marked from smallpox, hunched, waiting.

Kate groaned weakly. There was no fight left in her. She breathed out, exhausted, beaten.

No breath followed.

Thomas stepped forward and spoke to the man at his shoulder. 'It is over, Edward. She has gone from this world.'

The constable moved from the shadows to the bed, his eyes on Kate. 'She has died of her wounds. But nothing further will be said of it. We will say that she died giving birth to the child. As many women do. No one will speak of her wild actions on Nomansland Common.'

'It is well,' Thomas said. 'In time, I will wed again. Richard knows nothing of what she has done. The king has assured me that I will become a Knight of the Bath. My family name and my reputation will remain intact. I thank you for your services, Edward, and for making sure that I knew all that had passed between my wife and the highwayman.'

'I thank you for your payment.' Edward gave a small bow. 'Now all that remains is to take care of the child.'

'I have promised Katherine that she will be safe, and I am a man of my word. Katherine and I were never close, but we eventually came to an understanding. Her daughter will go to a good home where she will thrive. I wish to hear no word of her again,' Thomas said. 'I will go to see Anne and Richard and explain what has come to pass with poor Katherine, that in my absence she was misguided and took a lover, that she has died birthing his child. And will you speak to the servants, Edward? I believe Beatrice is keen to raise the child. It is good that she and John will give her a home. I am happy to pay John well for his charity.'

'Leave it with me, master,' Edward said, glancing at Katherine's body as she lay on the bed, and then at Marie, who was wide awake at her side, staring around the room. 'Consider it done.'

'It is well,' Thomas said. 'I thank you again and bid you good day, constable.'

'A good day it is for us all,' Edward said as he watched Thomas leave the room. He turned to Kate, who lay lifeless, the bed soaked in her blood. 'Well, mistress, it has come to pass – you have reaped what you have sown.' Edward's face was cruel in the half-light. 'Your highwayman is hanged; you have died of your wounds. Now all that remains is for me to deal with this child, who should never have been born. Master Fanshawe is a goodly man and he would not have the courage to do what I now will do. He thinks his faithful servants will adopt the baby, and he can forget her forever. But there are other ways of dealing with a problem, better ways...' He turned to Marie, who was smiling up at him with trusting eyes, her little fists in the air. He reached to the chair for a velvet cushion, moving on silent feet towards the baby's crib. 'The child should never have entered the world in the first place. It matters little...'

* * *

Charlie was sprawled on the sofa in number three Constable's Cottages, his arm around Edie. His hair was dry now, and his damp coat was hanging up in the hall. Alan was sprawled at his feet, dozing. Bianca was asleep in her bed. Edie was still researching, her laptop on her knee. There were cups of cold coffee at their feet.

Charlie glanced at the clock. It was past midnight. 'Valentine's Day is over now...' He tugged Edie next to him, kissing her brow. 'I wonder where we'll be this time next year.'

'Where do you want to be?' Edie asked contentedly.

'With you, of course. Every year.' Charlie grinned. 'So, how's the research going?'

'Not good...' Edie said. 'So, it says here that stories persist of ghostly sightings of a woman at Markyate Cell, and of a figure on a black horse galloping across Nomansland Common in the darkness.'

'We know that – we've seen her,' Charlie said. 'But what about her child?'

'There's nothing much, really. Just that Katherine's baby was called Marie, her birth was not recorded, and her burial entry was inserted quite a long time after her death. Look – "Marie, the daughter of Sir Thomas Fanshawe." Sir? He wasn't knighted until much later...' Edie pressed a key. 'Wiki Tree says, "Marie Fanshawe daughter of Sir Thomas Fanshawe, was born in 1660"... and the newspaper article here says, "The child in question was not buried in the same location as Katherine, who was interred at St Mary's Church in Ware, on 13 June 1660." So we still have no idea what happened to Marie. Did she die as Katherine was giving birth or a few months later? It's a mystery.'

'But we're pretty sure Marie was Ralph Chaplin's child with Katherine? There's nothing more in the research linking them to each other though. It's as if they've been forgotten, or their history has been deliberately erased.' Charlie scratched his head. 'Whatever happened, it was a tragedy.' He tugged Edie into his arms. 'It's just the story of a resourceful woman who got married too young...'

'To a man she didn't love...' Edie added. 'Who squandered her money... Poor Katherine.'

'Will we ever know the truth?'

'I don't think we will.' Edie kissed Charlie again. 'But we do know she was unhappy. After all the things that we've experienced here, seeing her ghost... we can understand that what happened may have broken her spirit.'

'Perhaps we need to learn from her life,' Charlie murmured. 'The important thing is that we're happy and we stay happy. And we'll treasure what we have, always.'

'We will,' Edie said, her eyes closing. She wrapped her arms around Charlie and snuggled closer. Charlie whispered something in her ear, something sweet, inhaling her perfume, breathing in happiness, feeling warm and loved.

EPILOGUE

A year had passed. Two dogs lay in two baskets in the kitchen at number three Constable's Cottages, munching happily on homemade peanut butter dog treats. Edie busied herself, boiling water on the Aga, slicing vegetables, stirring sauce. She was making linguine with avocado, tomato and lime, and roasted cauliflower steaks for four. There was a tiramisu chilling in the fridge.

She glanced at the clock as she heard the door click. It was half past five. Charlie was home bang on time. He hurried into the kitchen, in jeans that were spattered with plaster, and a dirty coat. Edie rushed into his arms. 'How's Ayers End Cottage coming along?'

'We're making good progress.' Charlie grinned. 'I hate working Saturdays, but Uncle Bill and I need to be finished by April, for when I start my new job.' He kissed her nose. 'How does it feel to be living with a music teacher?'

'I'm so glad you got the job at Kavish and Joshit's school. You'll love it there.'

'I think I will.' Charlie inhaled. 'Oh, the food smells good. What time are Priya and Toby coming round?'

'At seven. You have time for a bath.' Edie smiled. 'It's not as if they are driving. It's nice having them as neighbours. They love living at number one.'

'And how was your day?' Charlie asked, sweeping Edie into his arms.

'I went into St Albans with the dogs, did some shopping. It's been a long week...' Edie stretched her arms. 'I've been really busy.'

'Working from home, accompanied by two adorable dogs?' Charlie teased.

'My new job in social housing has its advantages,' Edie countered. 'You know, I love it – I wouldn't change a thing.'

'It beats working on a Saturday. But Uncle Bill thinks when we sell Ayers End Cottage, he'll be able to retire. The old farm cottage will be nice when it's finished. It has such a homely feel to it. And, of course, I'll have my new music job to keep me out of mischief.'

'Plus weekly gigs at The Sycamore Tree, and other bookings. We'll be in clover.' Edie smiled.

Charlie hugged Edie closer. 'My brother's visiting over Easter with Mira, Mum's got herself a sensible boyfriend at last. It was great to meet up with them last week. Uncle Bill's got a clean bill of health and he and Auntie Marcia are off to Italy to look at properties out there. It's working out so well.'

'And we haven't seen The Wicked Lady for a long time,' Edie almost whispered.

'She's left us now,' Charlie said. 'It's just you and me...'

'And today it's Valentine's Day,' Edie murmured, her lips against Charlie's neck. 'It's a whole year since we got together, now you've moved in, and here we are.'

'Here we are. So... to mark the occasion, I've got something for you...'

Edie looked up into his eyes. 'You gave me a single red rose last year. I remember.'

'Well, this is the same colour as a rose,' Charlie said. He fumbled in his pocket and held out a piece of tissue paper. 'I can't wrap things for toffee but...' He handed it to Edie. 'Go on. Open it. I hope you like it...' He watched as Edie unwrapped the paper, a tentative smile playing on his lips. 'I remember you telling me once you weren't a typical diamond ring sort of girl...'

Edie gasped as she held out a ruby cabochon ring. 'Is that what I think it is?'

'If you'll say yes, then it is,' Charlie said playfully. He flopped down on one knee and took a breath. 'Edie Berry, will you—'

'Of course I will.' Edie tugged him to his feet and she was in his arms, kissing him.

Charlie couldn't stop grinning as he slipped the ring onto her finger. 'And I wrote you a song, on the sax. The band are going to play it next week. It's called "Edie's Tune".'

'My own song, played by Graceful Storm...'

Charlie rolled his eyes. 'I still don't like the name, but Paige got her way...'

Edie was still staring at the ring, the red stone reflecting light in her eyes. 'Oh, Charlie, it's beautiful. Wherever did you get the idea of a ruby ring? It's perfect.'

'It just popped into my head when we were doing the upstairs room at Ayers End Cottage.' Charlie shrugged. 'So, when Priya and Toby get here, we'll tell them the good news. Do we have any champagne?'

'Two bottles in the fridge,' Edie said.

'You think of everything...' Charlie smiled, kissing her again.

Alan raised his head, stared around, and noticed that Bianca had fallen asleep in a fluffy white heap of paws, half of her peanut butter treat uneaten. He sloped across to her bed and picked it up in his mouth, taking it back to his own space, gnawing it noisily without a care.

* * *

Outside, it was raining heavily. Hazy lights gleamed from the windows of the three constable's cottages. Ferrers Lane was desolate and quiet; heavy clouds hung low and a moon had risen, thin as paper amid tiny stars. The trees rustled, rain pattering against leaves; the woodlands were cloaked in eerie silence. An owl hooted, a wood pigeon lifted itself into the air on slow wings, then the stillness stretched again.

Something moved from the shadows. The only sounds were the single flap of a coat and the low snort of a horse. No hoof prints remained in the mud as Midnight took several steps forward.

The Wicked Lady tugged the reins and watched, as if waiting for her moment. She adjusted the neckerchief across her face and leaned forward, whispering to her horse, ready to move. Darkness had fallen. It was time for her to ride the highways.

She would never be at rest.

AUTHOR'S NOTE

The powerful story of Katherine Ferrers grabbed me immediately because of the injustice of her short life. I was disturbed by the fact that she married before she was fourteen years old. Thomas Fanshawe was sixteen; he was matched to her for her money. It was entirely a mercenary marriage, since the Fanshawes contributed heavily to the Royalist cause and needed him to marry someone with a fortune.

I was also captivated by Katherine's other story: the young woman who became a highway robber in the seventeenth century, before famous men such as James Macleane and Dick Turpin made a name for themselves. I looked at Katherine Ferrers' picture at the age of fourteen, the only one of her apparently, which now sits at the Valence House Museum. She has a sweet face; there's an innocence to her features, but there is something determined in the set of her mouth, something idealistic in her wide eyes. I believed at once that she could have been The Wicked Lady of the myth.

And there was another intriguing aspect: the two parallel stories about her life didn't match. The first is the tale of a rich heiress whose husband took control of her finances and disposed of her inherited assets; in the second, she is a highway robber attempting to recoup her fast-dwindling fortune.

There is the interesting question of Marie Fanshawe, whoever she was, whose birth was never recorded, and whose burial entry was inserted sometime after her death at a few months of age. Was she Katherine's child? And if so, who was the father, since Thomas was in prison? What really did happen to her?

Ralph Chaplin is a mystery too. Was he a farmer, a highway robber, a bad influence on Katherine, or was he simply the man she fell in love with? Did he exist at all? There is little evidence that he did.

I had so many ideas to play with in this story, both factual and hypothetical. So I was thrilled to write the tale of Katherine, The Wicked Lady. The popular myth is that she was shot during a highway robbery on Nomansland Common on the edge of Wheathampstead, and died of her wounds while rushing to the safety of the secret staircase at Markyate Cell. But there is also the belief that she was a lonely, deserted wife who died young, giving birth.

Writing this story is an author's dream, given the wealth of material and the amount of legend attached to it. It's so much fun, weaving myth and researching fact. And, of course, I enjoyed bringing in some of the literary giants of the time, such as Samuel Pepys, John Milton, Andrew Marvell and John Donne.

There have been so many sightings of Katherine's ghost, not just in Ferrers Lane, on the edge of Nomansland Common in Hertfordshire, but also in Markyate, near The Cell, which still stands, although it has been greatly refurbished. Fact and legend combine so well.

Katherine's ghost is the important link between what may have happened in her tragic life and the unfolding romance between Charlie Wolfe and Edie Berry in the present. I hope you have enjoyed reading this story as much as I have enjoyed researching and writing it.

Much thanks go to the many wonderful people I met in St Albans, Markyate and Wheathampstead while I was researching Kate's story. Special thanks to Julie at the B&B, who furnished me with a lot of books and photos, and to Professor Simon Sandall from Winchester University, who was a valuable source of information about the historical background of Royalists and Parliamentarians.

Alan on Nomansland Common

Ferrers Lane, Nomansland Common

The sign for the common

View of The Cell

Katherine Ferrers, via Wikimedia Commons

ACKNOWLEDGEMENTS

Thanks to Kiran Kataria and Sarah Ritherdon, whose professionalism and kindness I value each day.

Thanks to the supportive family of Boldwood Books; to designers, editors, technicians, voice actors. You are all magicians.

Thanks to Rachel Gilbey, and wonderful bloggers and fellow writers. The support you give is beyond words.

Thanks to Jan, Rog, Jan M, Helen, Pat, Ken, Trish, Lexy, Rachel, John, Shaz, Gracie, Mya, Frank, Erika, Rich, Susie, Ian, Chrissie, Kathy N, Julie, Martin, Steve, Rose, Steve's mum, Nik R, Pete O', Martin, Cath, Chris A, Chris's mum, Dawn, Slawka, Katie H, Tom, Emily, Tom's mum, Fiona J and Jonno.

So much thanks to Peter, Avril and the Solitary Writers, my writing buddies.

Also, my neighbours and the local community, especially Jenny, Claire, Paul and Sophie.

Much thanks to the talented Ivor Abiks at Deep Studios, and the wonderful Steve Ford for his incredible insight and creativity with building and renovating.

Thanks and love go to Ellen, Hugh, Jo, Janice, Lou, Norman, Angela, Robin, Edward, Zach, Daniel, Catalina.

So much love to my mum and dad, Irene and Tosh.

Love always to our Tony and Kim, to Liam, Maddie, Kayak, and to my soulmate, Big G.

Warmest thanks to you, my readers, wherever you are. You make this journey special.

ABOUT THE AUTHOR

Elena Collins is the pen name of Judy Leigh. Judy Leigh is the bestselling author of *Five French Hens*, *A Grand Old Time* and *The Age of Misadventure* and the doyenne of the 'it's never too late' genre of women's fiction. She has lived all over the UK from Liverpool to Cornwall, but currently resides in Somerset.

Sign up to Elena Collins' mailing list for news, competitions and updates on future books.

Visit Elena's website: https://judyleigh.com

Follow Elena on social media here:

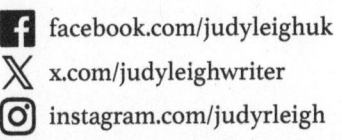

facebook.com/judyleighuk

x.com/judyleighwriter

instagram.com/judyrleigh

ALSO BY ELENA COLLINS

Letters from
the past

Discover page-turning
historical novels from
your favourite authors
and be transported
back in time

*Join our book club
Facebook group*

https://bit.ly/SixpenceGroup

*Sign up to our
newsletter*

https://bit.ly/LettersFrom
PastNews

Boldwood

Boldwood Books is an award-winning fiction publishing company seeking out the best stories from around the world.

Find out more at www.boldwoodbooks.com

Join our reader community for brilliant books, competitions and offers!

Follow us
@BoldwoodBooks
@TheBoldBookClub

Sign up to our weekly deals newsletter

https://bit.ly/BoldwoodBNewsletter

Milton Keynes UK
Ingram Content Group UK Ltd.
UKHW041829170724
445671UK00002B/8

9 781802 800357